Hallways in the Night

A Legal Thriller

R.C. O'Leary

This book is a work of fiction. Characters, names, incidents, and events are either the product of the author's imagination or fictionalized as part of the story. Any resemblance to actual persons, living or dead, business establishments, professional organizations, or locale is entirely coincidental.

The Library of Congress Cataloging-in-Publication Data
O'Leary, R.C., 1969-
Hallways in the Night: a novel/R.C. O'Leary.
p. cm.
1. Police—Fiction 2. Legal Trial—Fiction 3. Sports—Fiction
4. Attorneys—Fiction
LCCN: 2014901643

Published in the United States of America
ISBN
(print) 9780985838287
(ebook) 9780985838294

First Edition

3 1969 02252 0919

REVIEWS

"An edge of the seat legal battle that will keep you turning the pages until the very end.....A totally unputdownable book." ***Bookstory***

"Hard to put down....a very readable, fast-paced book with good character development and some surprising plot twists." **Bob D'Angelo, Tampa Tribune**

"A tightly-wound story of suspense and intrigue that will keep even seasoned mystery and legal thriller readers guessing to the end." **Diane Donovan, eBook Reviewer, Midwest Book Review**

"**5 of 5 stars.** Outstanding story that should be read by all fans of legal thrillers." **Lance Smith, the "SportsBookGuy."**

1

SOBER, REMO Centrella would have never tried to make the exit. He was almost past it and driving at over ninety miles an hour. On this night, however, baseball's home run king wasn't sober. He was half-drunk and at the tail-end of an eight-week steroid cycle that made him feel invincible. Instead of waiting for the next exit, he cut his wheel hard to the right.

His eyes were locked on the exit ramp, and he didn't see the 18-wheeler riding in the slow lane. But the woman in his passenger seat did. She saw the truck and realized Remo was about to drive them into the side of it.

"Look out," she said.

Remo turned his head in time to see that the truck was about to block their path to the ramp. Even drunk, he realized they were too close to try and slow down. Braking would just guarantee they drove into the truck, at a point of impact that would likely decapitate them. So instead of hitting the brakes, Remo jammed the horn and drove his gas pedal to the floor.

The driver of the truck, a good ol' boy from Panama City, Florida named Chuck Spencer, heard the sound of a horn and squealing of tires to his left. He turned and saw a red Porsche heading at him with a blonde woman in the passenger seat, who was screaming out in terror.

Chuck slammed on his brakes, and his truck began to jackknife. He knew the smart thing to do would be to re-accelerate to try and pull his trailer back in line. But he couldn't bring himself to do it because he knew it would mean a deadly crash for the passengers in the car. He kept his foot on the brakes and tried to steer his way out of trouble.

As Chuck fought to keep control his truck, Remo swerved his car to the left and cut across its nose.

"Sonuvabitch," Chuck said as he watched the Porsche dart up the ramp to safety. He pulled his foot off the brake and pressed down hard on the gas. The burst of acceleration jerked the trailer back into alignment.

The jackknife was averted. Chuck had regained control of his truck, but now he was struggling to breathe. Afraid he might be having another heart attack, he downshifted and drove off the next exit. He came to a stop at the top of the ramp and pulled out the pack of cigarettes that was tucked into the front pocket of his t-shirt. He grabbed a cigarette, lit it, and took a hungry inhale.

As the smoke settled into his lungs, Chuck's hands stopped shaking and the tightness in his chest went away. A fresh batch of nicotine began to flow through his system, and his feelings of panic began to dissipate.

"False alarm," he said as he finished the cigarette. He stubbed it out and calmly lit a second one.

As Chuck smoked a fresh Winston, he looked to his right and saw the golden dome of the Georgia capitol building. It was shining brightly in the night sky. Ahead in the distance, he saw the upper level of Wilson Field, silhouetted in light from the interstate. Through his side mirror, he could see the slow stream of highway traffic as it continued to roll through the night, oblivious to the fact a deadly crash had barely been avoided.

Chuck thought about calling the cops, but decided it wasn't worth the hassle. He didn't want to waste a couple hours of time answering questions about a driver who would probably never be caught. And he didn't feel like dealing with a cop who might run his license and find out he had been popped for a DUI three years earlier.

"Screw it," Chuck said and flicked his cigarette out the window. Better to keep his mouth shut and continue making progress towards home.

He looked at his watch and decided he would drive south on I-75 for another hour or two, before checking into one of the economy motels that littered almost every exit between Atlanta and the Florida state line.

It was 3:04 a.m. when he put his truck back in gear and rumbled back onto the interstate. Three miles away, Remo Centrella blew through a stop sign before turning left onto Haywood Avenue.

Haywood Avenue was a quiet street in the roughest part of Atlanta, a section of the city that the Atlanta Police Department designated as Zone 3. It was a mile and a half south of downtown and two blocks west of Wilson Field.

The homes on Haywood were row houses. They had been built without garages, a generation before Atlanta's working class could afford cars. In a better location, yuppies would have bought the houses, fixed them up, and called them townhomes. But no amount of renovations could change the fact that the homes on the west side of Haywood Avenue were adjacent to the busiest stretch of highway in the Southeastern United States.

Both sides of Haywood were lined with parked cars. In the haze of the streetlamps, they looked as worn down as the people who owned them. A couple of the cars were probably stolen, but most were bought from "eazy credit" lots that sold the scraps rejected by the brand name dealers.

Halfway up the street, Dave Mackno, a veteran Atlanta Detective, sat inside a late model Chrysler Sebring. He was near the end of a five-hour stakeout and counting down the minutes until he could go home.

Dave had spent most of his career working in Zone 3, but rarely spent much time on Haywood. From a policing perspective, the street was largely irrelevant. There were no retail shops on it and no foot traffic during the day. On most days, the closest commercial activity came from the hookers and dealers who plied their trades on the other side of the highway.

The only time Haywood Avenue came to life was during baseball season, when it filled up with car and foot traffic on the way to Wilson Field for a game. At 3 a.m. on a summer night, the street was dead.

Dave looked at his watch. *3:05.* Twenty five minutes until he could punch out and get a reprieve from the summer heat. He had been trying to kill time by listening to some Springsteen tapes, but the batteries in his Walkman were almost dead, which made it sound like even the Boss was beginning to wilt in the summer heat.

Dave looked across the street to the house he was watching. Its lights had been off for over two hours. "He's not going anywhere tonight," Dave said as he reached into his backseat and grabbed a can of Bud Light from his cooler.

Dave had originally planned to wait until he was officially off the clock to have a beer, but they had been calling his name for almost an hour. He cracked open the can and drank down a third of it. The beer felt smooth and electric. He placed the aluminum can against his forehead and closed his eyes. As the beer worked its magic, everything began to feel, as the brothers in Zone 3 liked to say, *copasetic.*

Dave tilted his head back against the seat and stared out at the top half of Wilson Field, as it hovered quietly above the neighborhood.

"The Keith," as it was known, was home to the Atlanta Barons, one of baseball's most valuable franchises. They had won three World Series titles in the previous decade and were the pride of the South. Their rise, from a mediocre, second division ball club to baseball's winningest team, had paralleled the region's, as it evolved from the Deep South to the New South.

As Dave looked at the Keith, he recalled some of the games he attended, including a Game 6 of the World Series when Remo Centrella hit a walk-off home run against New York to give the Barons their first World

Championship. That game was considered one of the greatest in baseball history, and attending it had been one of the highlights of Dave's life. He had never experienced anything else close to the joyous pandemonium of 55,000 fans going crazy after Remo drove a 1-2 pitch from New York's Stacy Williams over the centerfield fence to win the Series. It was an unforgettable moment from a cold October night that felt far removed from a sticky night in August when the temperature was stuck in the middle 90s.

Dave grabbed a handful of ice from his cooler and dropped it down the front of his shirt. The ice felt good as it slid down his chest, but it was no match for the heat wave that blanketed the city. The local forecasters were predicting it would break the record set in 1980, but Dave had his doubts. He didn't think there was any way Atlanta would ever get as hot as it had that summer. That's because 1980 wasn't just a summer of record heat, it was also the second summer of the Atlanta child killings.

In all the years Dave had been a cop, the summer of 1980 had been the toughest. The child killings, which had become a national story, had inflicted huge damage to the city's psyche. Everybody was on edge. Atlanta had begun to turn on itself, and a visceral sense of evil seemed to permeate the air.

As Dave thought back to that summer, he remembered a similarly hot night when he almost killed a black teenager.

By August of 1980, Atlanta felt cursed. June and July had been brutal as the killer had begun to pick up his pace. Five children had been taken and killed in less than 60 days. It was an average of one kid every twelve days: a fucking nightmare.

No one knew why the killer had entered what one FBI profiler described as an "almost manic stage," but every time a call came through his radio, Dave expected to hear another body had been found.

The killer targeted black kids exclusively, and the African American community was convinced he would have already been caught if the victims had been white.

Even worse for the cops working in Zone 3, a rumor had taken hold in the projects that the killer was a white cop using his badge to lure kids into his car.

The relationship between the predominantly white cops and the overwhelmingly black residents of Zone 3 was never good, but as the killings remained unsolved, it deteriorated to the point where regular policing had become almost impossible.

With the city near its boiling point, Dave's supervisor, an old school cop named Tommy Platt, was nervous. The Mayor of Atlanta wanted the police to increase their presence inside the projects, but Platt told the officers working for him to ignore the directive. He was convinced one dumb move by a cop, especially a white one, could trigger the kind of riots that made Watts look quaint.

"Be as visible as possible," Platt told his guys, "but don't get too close. Make sure you're not the one who ignites the fuse."

At just before dusk on the first Saturday in August, Dave and his partner, Bobby Morello, were following orders and patrolling their zone. But instead of patrolling too close to the projects and inciting trouble, Bobby convinced Dave they should head over to Haywood Avenue before the Barons game, just in case the killer happened to be wearing a sundress.

Dave and Bobby were cruising Haywood, profiling potential suspects, when a *BOLO* call came across the radio to be on the lookout for a black male, who had attempted to rape a white woman in the parking lot of the Buckhead mall. The dispatcher said the woman had fought off her assailant, who escaped on a Yamaha motorcycle. Reports indicated the suspect was heading south from Buckhead towards Zone 6 and possibly down into 3.

Dave and Bobby turned off Haywood and started to drive a wider vector in search of the suspect. They were nine blocks east of Haywood when Dave turned his car onto Spruce. As soon as he made the turn, he saw a motorcycle speeding towards them.

As the rider got closer, Dave got a clear look at him. He

looked nothing like Dave expected. When the dispatcher said a black male attempted to rape a white woman, he had pictured an older, hard looking dude, not a skinny kid with glasses.

The kid panicked when he saw the police car drive around the corner. He squeezed his brakes too hard and dumped the bike on its side. He should have let go, but instead, he hung on as the motorcycle slid sideways down the street for twenty feet before grinding to a stop between the front tires of the car. A wave of dread passed through Dave as he realized the kid, who wasn't wearing a helmet, might be dead.

He and Bobby jumped out of the car. When they did, the kid popped up and started to run towards a vacant lot that backed up to the rear entrance of Father Paneck Village, the toughest housing project in Atlanta.

Straight up, it would have been no contest. The kid would have left Dave and Bobby in the dust, within the first three hundred yards. But the kid's leg was torn up and he was limping badly.

Dave was sprinting hard after him. He might have caught him, except he was getting winded from his pack-a-day habit and had to slow down. Bobby was trailing behind, running like the second-string catcher he had been in high school.

Dave watched the kid, who was silhouetted against the setting sun, run across an empty basketball court into the center building.

Father Paneck Village consisted of five mid-rise towers built in a horseshoe pattern. They had been configured in a way that was intended to create a close-knit, supportive community, but things had not turned out as planned. Shortly after opening, Paneck's central courtyard, which had been optimistically labeled the "village green," began to take on the dynamics of a prison yard.

Dave had never understood how LBJ's best and brightest could think it was compassionate to bring the poorest people in the South to Atlanta and stack them on top of each other in industrial-looking cinder block buildings. The idea might have sounded good over a hash pipe at Berkeley, but it had been a disaster from the first day FPV opened.

By 1980, Father Paneck Village was as tough as any public housing complex in the United States. Even calling it a village sounded like a cruel joke. That's because kids didn't grow up in FPV, as much as they survived it. It was such a dangerous place that even the killer had stayed away.

As Dave pulled up from his run to try and catch his breath, he saw half a dozen men had stopped what they were doing to stare at him. Even before the "child killer is a cop" rumor took hold, nobody in FPV appreciated seeing a white cop chasing after a black kid.

"Where you at Bobby?" Dave said to himself, hoping the residents couldn't possibly think the killer was actually two cops working together. It took Bobby almost a minute to catch up. When he did, they started walking in lockstep. Both of them were sweating profusely in their dark blue summer shirts as they nodded in acknowledgment to the men watching them.

Dave knew they were in over their heads. The last time he had gone into Father Paneck was to execute an arrest warrant for a gang leader, who was wanted on a murder charge. On that occasion, he was one of a dozen cops, all of whom were dressed out in riot gear. This time, he and Bobby were by themselves and doing exactly what Platt had warned them against.

When they reached building number 4, they went inside. It was silent. Dave pointed to a trail of lightly splattered blood that led to a stairwell. Bobby nodded. They drew their guns and headed up three flights of stairs to a dimly lit corridor. The trail of blood stopped halfway down the hall.

The kid was holed up inside what had been designed to be a public laundry room. The window to the door was missing, and whatever washers or dryers had been there were now long gone.

"Police," Dave said, but the kid didn't answer.

His back was against the cinder block wall on the same side as the doorway. "We found you, Kid. Now come out and make sure we see your hands."

"Don't do anything stupid," Bobby said.

"You ran me over."

"You ran into my car," Dave said.

"Come on out and let's go talk to your mama," Bobby said. "We can get this straightened out."

"Y'all gonna beat me up. I'm not stupid. I know what's up."

Dave looked across the hall at Bobby who was inching forward, ready to pounce. But Dave wasn't ready for Bobby to make a move. He put his thumb up and jerked it back to let Bobby know to ease up.

"We don't want a problem here, Kid" Dave said. He was breathing easier, but the heat inside the building was oppressive. "We just want to find out what's going on. Don't make this worse than it is."

After a few seconds, the kid said, "Okay, I'll come out."

"Good," Dave said, and wiped his mouth with the back of his wrist. "Drop to your knees and crawl out slowly. Keep your hands out front where we can see them."

Dave saw a hand break the plane of the doorway. A second one was followed by the kid's head and shoulders. Before he got halfway across the threshold, Bobby dropped a knee onto his back.

"On the floor!" he said, as the kid let out a painful cry.

Dave stepped forward and pulled Bobby off him.

"Relax!" he said and pushed Bobby towards the wall.

He turned the kid over and saw his lip was bleeding.

"Get up," Dave said, and picked the kid up with one arm. He saw the kid's jeans were sliced down the left side. There was blood drying underneath his knee, and black tar marks from the road were seared into the denim. "What unit do you live in?"

"What?" the kid said, looking surprised.

"*Where do you live?*" Dave said, and tightened his grip on the kid's collar. "This building or one of the others?"

"I don't live in the projects. I'm from Dunwoody."

"Bullshit," Bobby said. "*I* live in Dunwoody. There's no coloreds up there."

Dave moved closer to the kid. "Tell us the truth."

9

"I am," the kid said. "I do live in Dunwoody. My father's an orthodontist."

"Yeah, sure," Bobby said. "And I'm George Jefferson."

"Why would a kid from Dunwoody run into Father Paneck?" Dave said.

"I know some dudes who live here. They told me that cops are afraid to come into Paneck. I figured if I ran in here, y'all wouldn't come after me."

"You didn't think we could trace the bike you dumped?" Bobby said.

"I didn't care. I just wanted to get away until I could call my father and make sure my rights were protected."

"What rights?" Bobby said.

"My Constitutional rights, man. I know what white cops do to black men. I knew—"

"You're not a man," Bobby said. "You're just a kid."

"If I could get home, my father could get a lawyer to defend me."

"Too late for that," Dave said. "Now, move. We can call your father from the station."

Dave escorted the kid by the arm, and read him his rights as they walked down the stairs. As soon as Dave was done Mirandizing him, Bobby said, "Why'd you try to rape that white lady at the mall?"

"What?" the kid said, and looked at Dave pleadingly. "I didn't try to rape anyone. She dropped her wallet when she walked out of Sears. I picked it up and was trying to give it back to her, but she started freaking out. *Like I was going to steal her purse or something.*"

"Hmm, I wonder why would she think that?" Bobby said.

"I walked up to her and I was like 'Yoa, Lady, relax, I'm not trying to steal your purse.' That's when she started going nuts. Yelling out 'Rape, rape, I'm gonna be raped.'"

The kid shook his head in disbelief.

"She totally freaked out, man. I tried to calm her down, but then she swung at me."

The kid pointed to his left ear, where Dave saw a fresh cut, the size of a quarter.

"See that," he said. "That's from her key chain."

"That's called self-defense," Bobby said. "You're lucky it wasn't my sister, she would have maced your ass."

"Why did you take off from the mall?" Dave asked.

"Because I saw two huge dudes running after me, and one of them had a crowbar." The kid turned to look directly at Dave. "They weren't cops, were they? They had no legal right to hold me, so I was like, 'Yoa, I'm out of here.' I hopped on my bike, and that's when I saw a security guard come running out the doors yelling 'freeze,' like he thought he was on TV or something.

"I was like *damn*, all these people going crazy just because some lady freaked out. Part of me thought about staying there and trying to explain what happened, but I knew there was no way they were going to believe me over a white lady driving a Cadillac. *So I took off.* That's when I heard all the sirens. Next thing I know, there's like six cop cars lit up and coming after me from every direction. Crazy."

"Why didn't you go back up to Dunwoody?" Dave said.

"I couldn't make the left onto Peachtree. There were two cop cars coming at me from that direction, so I was forced to turn right. That's when I decided to just out-run them in the City. I was planning to go into Piedmont Park when I remembered one of my boys said cops don't go into Paneck at night. I figured if I could get down here, I could hide out for a little while and then head back home when it got dark."

"How much time have you spent in FPV?" Bobby said.

"It's my first time."

"It could've been your last," Bobby said. "The Village Boys don't like strangers that come running onto their turf."

As they reached the bottom of the stairs, Dave gave Bobby a look that said he thought the kid's story sounded plausible.

But Bobby shook his head, "no way."

They opened the door, took a few steps outside and stopped. The half dozen men they had seen on the way into the building had grown to a couple of dozen people who didn't seem to appreciate their crime fighting efforts.

"Where you trying to take that kid?" a tall, older man asked.

"You can't come in here and start taking our kids away, muthafuckas."

"I knew it was a cop."

The crowd was standing about ten feet back from Dave and Bobby. It seemed to be slowly recoiling, as if on the verge of springing forward any second. Dave knew it wouldn't take much, especially within the current environment, to incite them to violence.

"Let the boy go. He ain't done nothing to you."

"Yeah, Crackers, let him go," the tall man said.

Dave gave a sideways glance to Bobby to see if he had any good ideas. He didn't.

The crowd formed a semicircle that didn't leave any openings to pass through. For a brief moment, Dave thought about drawing his weapon, but decided it would likely act as a trigger for mob violence, and that he and Bobby would end up at the bottom of a pile.

Dave took a step back and felt for the door handle. When he did, he heard the lock click. He turned and saw three teenagers inside staring blankly back at him.

"Shit," he said to himself and moved his hand to his walkie-talkie. His finger was on the red emergency button that would signal "officer down" if he pressed it. The problem was, Dave knew it would take at least ten minutes for the dispatcher or anybody else to figure out their location. Looking at the growing crowd, he didn't think he had that much time.

2

"THIS KID'S a suspect in the child killings," Dave announced, in the voice he used for crowd control. "We need to take him in for questioning."

His statement got the crowd's attention.

"That him?" the older man said.

"Never seen him around here before," a woman wearing a blue bandanna said. "He's wearing glasses, like in the picture."

"Hold up," the kid protested. "I'm not the—"

"Keep your mouth shut if you want to get out of here in one piece," Bobby said in the kid's ear. "Keep talking and we'll leave you here to explain things for yourself."

The crowd was momentarily distracted, and Dave sensed an opening. He pushed the kid forward, and the crowd gave way. Somebody in the crowd smacked the kid in the side of the head.

"Don't look back," Bobby said, once they were on the other side of the crowd. "Put a nickel in it, but don't run. Hear me, Cuz?"

The kid nodded, and the three of them kept walking at a brisk pace until they got back to the police car.

"Stay here," Dave said.

He went to his radio and called the dispatcher.

"Dispatch, this is Officer 3933. What's the status on the female victim from the Buckhead mall? Is she available to make an I.D?"

"Negatory, 3933," the dispatcher said. "She left the scene. She didn't want to press charges."

"Repeat?"

"The victim had a dinner engagement," the dispatcher said, sounding bored.

"Copy," Dave said and hung his walkie-talkie back up. He shook his head. "Unbelievable."

He stared out at the kid who looked a lot more scared than tough. "That kid ain't a rapist," he said to himself.

Dave walked around to the front of his police car and pulled the bike out from underneath the Crown Vic. The muffler on the Yamaha was dented, and the yellow paint was scratched, but the bike was intact. Dave started it up and revved the engine. The motor sounded good and the tires looked fine. He rolled it to the back of the car and signaled Bobby to come closer.

"I'm gonna cut him loose," he said.

"You're what?"

"The victim doesn't want to press charges."

"So what?" Bobby said. "We don't need her. We got him for fleeing the scene of a crime and resisting arrest. That's more than enough to pinch him."

Dave looked and saw the kid was trying his best to look stoic.

"I ran the kid over, Bobby. I almost killed him."

"He fled."

"You blame him?" Dave said. "And what are you talking about resisting arrest? He came crawling out when we found him. You almost broke his nose."

"I was just subduing him after he tried to evade us," Bobby said, his voice raised loud enough that the kid could hear him. "You know as well as I do that this little nigger's pulled some other bullshit. Let's at least take him in and run his name. He probably already has a record."

Dave walked over to the kid, grabbed him, and pushed him into the back seat of the police car. He pointed at him and said, "Do not move," before he shut the door.

"What the fuck was that?" Dave said, turning back to Bobby. "What are you doing calling this kid that? He's not a hardened criminal. This kid can barely shave."

"That doesn't mean anything."

"How many kids you know from the hood wearing an alligator shirt? Or call us 'Officers?' This kid ain't a thug, Bobby. He might not live in Dunwoody, but he's not from FPV."

Bobby was shaking his head.

"This is a bunch of bullshit, Dave, and you know it. I'm not out here busting my ass in the heat so you can play Father Flanagan. Some punk leads me on a chase, he's getting clipped."

"He's a kid."

"Who tried to rape a white woman."

"I doubt it."

"Why?"

"The lady already left the scene. You think she would do that if she really thought this kid wanted to rape her?"

"He ran from the police," Bobby said. "He put our lives in danger."

"He got scared and panicked. I would've done the same thing if I was him."

Bobby spit on the ground in disgust. "You probably would have," he said.

"Okay, Dave. I'm not going to fight you on this because I'm not in the mood to fill out paperwork, but you know as well as I do we'll be arresting this kid in the future. After he does actually rape somebody."

"I don't think so," Dave said and started to walk to the back of the car.

"You're just postponing the inevitable."

"Maybe. But if you're wrong, he gets a second chance to avoid a record."

"He gets a second chance to do it again," Bobby said, as he turned away from Dave and lit a cigarette.

Dave opened the back door of the car. "Get out," he said.

"You're not arresting me?" the kid said.

"Not today, my man."

"What about the lady at the mall?"

"What about her? I thought you said you were just

trying to give her back her purse?"

"I was."

"Then you're good. Get back on your bike and head home to Dunwoody, or wherever you live."

"I do live in Dunwoody."

"I don't care where you live. Just get the hell out of here before I change my mind."

The kid's expression shifted from fear to relief as he scrambled back onto his bike.

"I'd stay out of Paneck if I were you," Dave said.

"Yes, sir."

"And one more thing," Dave said, as he tapped a Marlboro out of its pack and put it in his mouth. "This is a one time pass. Next time we meet, you don't get a second chance."

Dave flipped open his lighter and lit his cigarette. The kid nodded his head and took off up Spruce. Dave watched as the bike fishtailed for a few feet before the kid straightened it out and rode out of sight.

"*Father Mackno*," Bobby said. "You're getting way too soft on these guys. You know as well as I do, he was just shucking and jiving us."

Dave took a drag off his cigarette as he looked up the street.

"I think he was actually telling the truth. He seemed like a decent kid."

"He just knows how to talk to Whitey," Bobby said. "These little nig-nogs know exactly what they're doing."

"You know what?" Dave said as he took an inhale off his cigarette, "if I'm wrong, he'll eventually get sucked into the system. But if I'm right, we did the right thing."

"Don't say we, Bro. That was all you. If it was up to me, he'd be going to jail. Zero tolerance. That's the only thing that's going to keep this city from turning into Zimbabwe."

"I think running him over was punishment enough," Dave said, and flicked his butt to the ground. "Hop back in the car, Jim Crow. First round's on me tonight, okay?"

"That makes no fucking sense," Bobby said.

"What?"

"Calling me Jim Crow."

"What are you talking about?"

"That's what they used to call the brothers, not the white folks. If you want a little education, it's actually a lyric from a black minstrel song."

Dave nodded his head as if impressed.

"Two history classes at Georgia State and now you're Alex Haley, huh?" Dave said and climbed back into the driver's seat. "Must be nice to be such a genius."

"It can be very frustrating at times," Bobby said and winked.

Dave let out a small laugh, signaling that their disagreement was already in the past.

Dave knew Bobby had not been happy about his decision to give the kid a break back then, but he was pretty sure Bobby would have a different perspective if the same thing happened again.

Dave put the empty can of Bud Light back in the cooler and opened a second one when he heard the sound of a high-pitched engine coming up from behind. He looked in his rearview mirror and saw a set of round headlights driving towards him.

Dave could tell the car was speeding based upon its closing rate alone. But before he could turn around and get a better view, the Porsche sped by so close that the inside of the Sebring shook. Dave figured it had to be going at least 80 miles an hour on a street zoned for 25.

He would have been tempted to chase the driver down if he had been in his own car, but he knew there was no point of even thinking about it while in his wife's Sebring. It had the speed of a heavily pregnant frog.

"It's your lucky day," Dave said as he watched the car drive up the hill.

The Porsche was just about to disappear over the ridge when it surprised Dave by turning right onto Bruce Webster Drive. That didn't make any sense. Webster dead-ended at the main gate to Wilson Field, which meant the Porsche would have to turn around.

Dave glanced at the house he was staking out. Every light in the place was off. There had been no movement since 1 a.m., and Dave was pretty sure nobody was going anywhere until at least the next morning.

"Hasta mañana, Esteban," Dave said, and saluted, as he pulled out of his parking place.

He felt a rush of excitement for the first time in three nights. He floored the car, but the Sebring had trouble picking up speed. "Come on," he said, and hit the steering wheel with the heel of his hand to try and give the car a little bit of giddy up. He wanted to get onto Webster before the driver of the Porsche had the chance to turn around and get back out to Haywood. He would have a lot more leverage if he could make the approach from behind.

No cop liked making stops in the middle of the night, but Dave wasn't nervous as he made the turn. In his experience, truly bad guys didn't drive Porsche 911 Carreras. He figured that whoever was driving the car was more likely to be strapped with gold bracelets than guns.

When Dave made the turn, he saw the Porsche parked at the far end of the street. He instinctively reached for the glove box to take out his magnetic "bubble" light before remembering he wasn't in his Caprice Classic.

Dave drove closer and saw the passenger door of the car was open. A blonde woman was struggling to get out. The driver had a hold of her by the wrist.

Dave honked his horn, and the driver released her hand. The woman, who appeared to be in her mid to late 20s, turned to look back at Dave. When she did, he saw the glint of a fresh shiner underneath her left eye.

Dave felt himself get angry, the way he always did whenever he knew that a woman had been hit. It was an anger he had carried inside of himself ever since he had seen a man hit his mother.

Dave was eight years old when it happened. It was early spring, late on a Friday night, during one of the times his father wasn't living at home. One of the times when his mother used to tell him that "Daddy went out to look for a job."

Dave had been asleep when a loud voice woke him up.

He sneaked up the hall, into the kitchen, and crawled underneath the table, where he could get a clear look into the family room.

The man was very tall and thin. He had short black hair and was wearing a stained white t-shirt.

"Come on Darrell, just leave," his mother said. "My little boy's asleep."

"I ain't leaving," he said.

His mother put her hands on his chest to push him towards the door, and the man responded with a hard slap across her face. It knocked Dave's mother down.

"I said I ain't leaving."

Dave stayed stone still when he saw his mother get hit. Part of him wanted to run out and rescue her, but he was too scared. He prayed the man didn't see him as he walked through the kitchen, close enough that Dave could smell the oil on the man's work boots. The man went into his parents' bedroom and started to yell out for Dave's mother.

"Colleen! Colleen! Col-leen!" the man yelled, as Dave's mother lay on the floor.

He then got louder and angrier.

"Colleen!" he yelled out. *"Col-leen! COL-LEEN!*

His drunken voice filled up the entirety of their small house.

Dave watched his mother sit halfway up. She squinted her eyes closed for several seconds, before standing up and walking past Dave towards her bedroom, leaving a heavy trail of cigarette smoke and perfume in her wake.

Dave didn't move from under the table for almost an hour, until he saw the man leave and his mother go back into her room and shut off the light. When he was convinced his mother was asleep, he snuck quietly back to his room, soaked in feelings of guilt and shame.

The next morning at breakfast, Dave saw his mother had tried to cover up the bruise on her cheek with make-up. He didn't say a word, *he was too afraid of her,* and she acted like her usual distant self.

As Dave grew older, he wondered why his mother, a strikingly beautiful woman, seemed to resent him. He had always been a good kid. His father always seemed proud of him, but his mother never did. He never got the feeling that she felt lucky or blessed to be his mother.

It was only when Dave was older, after his father died, that he found out the reason. While helping his mother pack up some of his father's possessions to donate to the Salvation Army, he came across a copy of their wedding certificate. The date said February 11, 1956. *Five months before Dave was born, and a year later than his parents claimed to have been married.* It was a revelation that answered a lot of questions.

Dave never mentioned the wedding certificate to his mother, just like he never mentioned hiding under his kitchen table to her or anybody else, including his wife. But seeing his mother get hit had a major impact on his personality. It was a big part of the reason Dave ended up becoming an MP in the Army, instead of going to college after being offered a baseball scholarship from Appalachian State.

That change of plans happened because Dave assaulted a kid named Ben Cartwright one night while working the concession stand at Crowley's Drive-In.

Dave didn't know Cartwright, who was a couple of years older than he was, and a student at Mercer State. But he knew the girl with him, Stephanie McClure. She was a couple of years behind Dave in high school, and they had been in typing class together. Stephanie was a quiet girl, who seemed embarrassed about being poor. She and Dave had exchanged a few smiles. He thought she was pretty. The kind of girl he might have asked out, if he wasn't going steady.

Dave smiled in recognition when she approached in line. Stephanie smiled back and made the mistake of blushing, which made Cartwright, who was clearly drunk, upset. He smirked at Dave and started grabbing on her. He pinched her ass hard and winked at him.

"Hey, buddy," Dave said. "Why don't you sober up and stop pawing on her, huh?"

Ben turned to Stephanie. "This boy a friend of yours?" he said.

"No," she said and looked down at the ground.

"Then why'd you smile at him? Why are you smiling at some high school boy who's supposed to be serving me popcorn, huh?"

"I don't know. I'm sorry," Stephanie said, while staring down at the ground.

"Well, don't do it again, ya hear?" he said, while pushing his index finger into her cheek and forcing her head to turn.

Stephanie looked like she was about to cry.

"Sober up, Buddy," Dave said. "You okay, Stephanie?"

Ben turned quickly and stared at Dave.

"Why don't you mind your own business and do your job?" he said.

They stared each other down for several seconds until Cartwright slowly turned his large bucket of popcorn upside down. He then dropped the empty container onto the ground.

"Uh-oh," he said. "I guess somebody better get to work."

Cartwright laughed and pulled Stephanie by the wrist. "Let's go back to my car. Popcorn boy needs to clean up my mess."

Dave came out from behind the concession stand, stepped towards Cartwright, and hit him with a right cross that sent two of his teeth flying into the spilled popcorn. Cartwright's upper body wobbled, and he fell backwards to the ground. He looked like he had been knocked out for a couple of seconds.

Dave knew he was in serious trouble as soon as he hit him. His boss, Mr. Crowley, had seen the whole thing and called the police. Dave was a new employee and Crowley didn't have any loyalty towards him. It was Crowley's first summer leasing the concession stand from the town, and the last thing he could afford was one of his employees assaulting a customer.

Twenty minutes after Dave knocked Cartwright to the ground, two cops showed up and placed him under arrest.

"So, let me make sure I understand exactly what

happened," the Judge said to Dave, on the day he was arraigned. "A drunk kid dropped his popcorn, grabbed his girlfriend by the hand and you broke his jaw. That sound about correct?"

"Yes, sir," Dave admitted, with his father and lawyer standing beside him in court.

"Well then you, your daddy, and your attorney need to decide if you want to enlist in the United States Army or go to trial on these charges, Son. Y'all got one week to let my law clerk know your decision."

It was an easy choice and one month later, Dave's father drove him to Fort McClellan, near Anniston, Alabama, where Dave started training to become a Military Police officer.

Almost thirty years later, he was still ashamed of the fact he never called the baseball coach at Appalachian State to tell him he wouldn't be showing up at school because he hadn't been able to control his anger. The same exact anger he now felt after seeing the blonde woman's black eye.

The woman looked scared as she looked back and forth between Dave and the inside of the car. It looked like she was trying to hear what the driver was saying.

Once Dave could see she was no longer actively struggling, he turned on his high beams. When he did, he saw the silhouette of a man's head inside the Porsche.

The guy was big. He practically filled up the inside of the car and was making quick, jerky movements. He looked like he might be coked up or on meth. With one sudden reach, he pulled the woman back inside the car and shut the door. Both of them were now sitting still, as if the matter were resolved. As if Dave should simply move along.

Dave inched his car forward into the bumper of the Porsche. He had a feeling that a guy who hit women probably wouldn't appreciate his expensive car being hit.

It was then he saw the license plate: BIG STK44. Dave's breathing got a notch tighter when he read it. *Remo Centrella.*

Even though the Porsche was parked outside the gates

to Wilson Field, it hadn't crossed Dave's mind that one of the Barons might be driving. Before seeing the plate, he assumed he was probably dealing with a rich prick from the suburbs who had roughed up his girlfriend. But now, after seeing the tag, he knew who it was.

Remo Centrella was no longer the best player in professional baseball, but he was still the game's biggest star. A four time league MVP, he was the major reason three World Series banners flew above the Keith.

Off the field, Remo was a commercial icon who banked millions of dollars a year in endorsements. A mixed race superstar, he had come along at an inflection point for race relations in America, when a person of color could become Madison Avenue's favorite pitchman.

A father of three, Remo was married to a former star R&B singer named Tiffany Hill. And even though Dave didn't read the tabloids, he had seen enough pictures of Remo and Tiffany together to know that the blonde woman in the silver cocktail dress was not her.

Dave got out of the Sebring, un-locked the safety on his holster, and approached Remo. He held his badge out in front of him, elbow high in his left hand.

"Get out of the car!" Dave said, pointing hard at Remo. "Now!"

Remo watched Dave, who looked like a shorter, less handsome version of Tom Selleck, approach his car. "This is not fucking happening," he said and gunned his engines as a warning for Dave to retreat.

"Take a fucking hike, Bro," Remo said to his mirror. "Don't be stupid."

Dave flinched slightly at the roar the engines made, but kept walking forward toward the vehicle. He was trying to make eye contact with Remo.

"Get out of the car!" he said.

"Yeah, okay, Starsky. Here I come," Remo said.

He turned and looked at Dave. "Fuck you!"

"Fuck me? No, sorry, pal, fuck you," Dave said to himself.

"Get out of the car," he ordered.

Remo turned his head and stared straight ahead. Dave

stepped up to the Porsche and put the barrel of his gun against the window.

"Exit your vehicle," he yelled, but Remo didn't move.

Dave knew his options were limited. There was no way he, or any cop, was going to shoot anyone for failing to get out of his or her car. But that normally didn't matter because ninety nine percent of the time people followed orders.

Dave banged the heel of his hand hard against the window. "I said get out of the car."

Remo didn't react. He kept staring forward.

"Get—" Dave began, when his words were drowned out by the night-shattering sounds of Guns N' Roses' *Welcome to the Jungle.*

Remo had the loudest Street Blaster that Dave had ever heard, and the music was so loud it hurt his ears. He had to take a step back to re-center himself as Axl Rose's voice screeched through the night.

Remo turned to Dave, pointed to himself, and nodded his head.

"Fuck you, Remo," Dave said to himself. "Let's see how much shit you talk after you sober up."

He re-holstered his gun and started back to his car in order to call for backup. He took a step backward, his eyes still locked on the Porsche, when the music stopped and Remo drove into the fence.

3

——

THE FENCE didn't break because of its steel crossbar, but the Porsche put a big dent into it before Remo shifted into reverse and executed a 180-degree turn. The car was now facing Dave and blinding him with its headlights. He drew his gun and assumed a shooter's stance.

Dave couldn't see past the high beams to Remo, but he knew Remo could see him. "Turn off the car," he yelled over the noise of the engine.

Remo hit the gas and the Porsche accelerated towards Dave. He dove to his right and shot at the car as it swerved to his left. His first shot hit the front left tire. A second one ricocheted off the ground, as the front quarter panel of the car started to scrape against the pavement.

Remo tried to keep driving for about twenty feet, but the tire stripped away from its mount. Orange sparks started to shoot off the axel as it spun against the pavement.

Dave jumped up. He saw the woman was once again trying to get away from Remo. She was trying to pull free, but he had her by the dress.

The woman was a lot smaller than Remo, but she was a runner, who had strong legs. It was her leverage and desperation against his strength. Remo's wrist was flush against the door jamb as she used her body weight to try and get some separation. She planted her right foot on the ground and used her left foot to "mule kick" the door into Remo's right wrist. The door hit the bone hard and fractured it. Remo yelled out in pain as the woman sprung loose and ran off into the night.

Dave watched her flee, as Remo climbed out of his car. He looked even bigger than Dave expected.

"Yoa," Remo yelled, in a voice that was deep and hoarse. "Get back here, Girl."

"On the ground!"

Remo clasped his right wrist, and grimaced in pain. "Fucking bitch."

Remo was wearing olive green suit pants and a white tank top that showed off massive arms and shoulders. His upper left arm was nearly covered with the dark blue ink of his "Big Stick" tattoo. As Dave looked at him, he realized the whispers were true: Remo Centrella had definitely been juicing. He was huge and bore little resemblance to the wiry kid Dave had once met, long ago, at a Hooters up in Marietta.

Sizing him up, Dave saw a feral aspect to Remo's eyes that surprised him. He assumed the woman must have seen it, too, because the area around Wilson Field was not the kind of place twenty-something women ran into by themselves. She must have been very afraid.

All of Dave's senses were now on high alert.

"On the ground," he said. "Now!"

Remo's attention snapped from the girl back onto Dave. He had a look of pure contempt on his face, and Dave had no doubt Remo would have attacked him if a gun wasn't aimed directly at his chest.

They were standing close together, but Dave knew there was enough distance between them that he could click off a couple of rounds before Remo could get to him.

"What?" Remo said, disgustedly.

"Go to the ground, Remo. Now!"

Remo looked at Dave, and his expression seemed to change. It was a little less angry, as if, even under the circumstances, he appreciated the fact Dave knew his name. Remo took his eyes off Dave and looked back across the roof of his car.

"Get back here, Girl," he yelled. But there was no answer.

"Stupid bitch," Remo said. He looked up Webster in disappointment before he turned back to Dave. "What's your name, Brother?"

Dave was shocked at the arrogance. "I said to get on the ground."

"Alright, alright," Remo said. His words were slurred. He put up a hand in front of his shoulder. "You know who I am, now put the fucking gun away....Yoa, let me call my agent. He'll fix this shit. He'll get the car towed, and I'll make sure you get paid."

"You tried to run me over, now get the fuck on the ground."

"I wasn't trying to run you over, Bro. I was just trying to get you to back the fuck up."

Remo let out a small laugh.

"Get on the fucking ground, Centrella," Dave said. He could feel the adrenaline pulsing through him.

Remo was looking directly at Dave. He could see the toughness in Dave's eyes, but ignored the warning signs.

Remo was beyond rich and lived in a world where everybody deferred to him. But he had grown up poor, in a working class neighborhood on Staten Island, where he had developed a street instinct that was now telling him Dave was a lot tougher than he looked. The problem was that Remo's instincts were being drowned out by a dangerous mixture of alcohol, ego, and steroids.

"On the ground."

Remo had been insulated from reality for so long he had forgotten bad things could happen to him, and that the ability to hit more home runs than anybody else on the planet did not actually mean that the fundamental rules of life didn't apply.

He reached into his pocket and pulled out his wallet. "How much you want, Bro?" he said. "What's this going to cost me?"

Dave tensed, but didn't flinch. He knew from a visual search that Remo wasn't carrying a gun.

"I said to get on the ground. Now!"

"Don't worry, Bro, Remo's going to take care of you. I'm gonna hook you up now, so you can roll out. But don't worry. Gimme your name and I'll make sure Shane spiffs you real nice. He'll get you some tickets and money. I'll tell him to throw in an autographed jersey. You can sell it on eBay, Bro."

Remo looked at his Porsche and shook his head. "Shit. I'ma have to get a fucking tow," he said as he began to pull some bills out of his wallet.

Dave swiped hard at Remo's hand and hit the part of his wrist that had been broken. Remo's hand opened in pain, and he dropped his wallet.

"What the fuck?" Remo said, and looked disappointed, as cash and credit cards slid loose across the pavement.

Dave had sprung forward and retreated back in one quick move. He was quicker than he looked, and Remo hadn't seen it coming.

"Keep your fucking money to yourself, and get your ass on the ground," Dave said.

Remo looked down at the ground and shook his head.

"You for real?" he said.

Remo's eyes narrowed in confusion for a couple of seconds, and then he got a slight smirk on his face. His heavy head swiveled back and forth as he stared in confusion at Dave.

"You're so fucked," he said after several seconds. "You know that, Bro? You really think you're going to pull this shit with Remo?"

Remo turned his head to his right and spit.

"This is my fucking city," he said. "I own it."

"On the ground, Remo. Now."

Remo turned his head, spit again, and then looked back at Dave.

"Stupid bastard," he said.

"On the ground."

"You got me, okay?" Remo said, raising his voice. "You fucking got me. I was fooling around with a woman I shouldn't have been, and you caught me. Don't make this into an international fucking incident where you end up losing your job, because that's what will happen, Bro.

"Think about who you're dealing with. I got people that fix shit for me and you don't. That ain't bragging, Bro, that's a fact. You don't even know."

"You hit that woman, now get on the ground."

"That woman? Is she what you're so mad about?"

Remo looked up and to his right for a couple of seconds, as if trying to process what he just heard.

"She came at me first, Bro," Remo said. "But I ain't worried. She'll keep her mouth shut."

"On the ground."

"Stop fucking saying that, dude. You're like a broken record."

"You're under arrest."

"Yeah, right." Remo shook his head. "You got no fucking clue, Bro. You know that?"

"On the ground."

It was the middle of the night, but Remo Centrella looked around as if the world was watching. He tilted his chin up and started bobbing his head in defiance. He was staring up into the sky, trying to deny what was happening. He closed his eyes, like he was struggling to think. It was an amateur mistake in a situation where there was no room for unforced errors.

"You got a fucking choice here, dude," Remo said as he clenched his fist and raised his voice. "What the fuck do you—"

Dave sprung up underneath the inside of Remo's left arm. He hooked his right arm up to the back of Remo's shoulder and clawed his fingers into the side of his neck.

"Shit," Dave thought to himself. Remo's neck felt like a tree trunk. Because Dave was spotting Remo so much size, he knew he better get him on the ground if he wanted to keep the upper hand.

Dave shifted his balance onto his left leg. He leg-whipped Remo with his right leg, knocking him off-balance and taking him to the ground. Dave stabbed his right knee into Remo's ribs.

He grabbed Remo's right wrist and twisted it backwards. The move forced Remo onto his stomach, and

Dave shifted his knee onto Remo's back. He put his left hand onto the side of Remo's head and used his full body weight to press down hard. Remo spun reflexively, but Dave moved his knee up towards Remo's neck and pinned it against the ground.

"Give it up," Dave said, his voice muffled by his heavy breathing.

With Remo pinned, Dave pulled out his handcuffs and cracked one of the bracelets onto Remo's right wrist, *the one that was fractured.* Remo swore out in pain.

Dave thought the cuff was locked on, but Remo's wrist was too big. The bracelet caught, but it didn't fully lock.

Shifting his body weight, Dave jump-switched knees on Remo's back. He had Remo's right arm, *the one he thought was cuffed*, pinned behind his back and was using his knee to drive the metal ring deep into Remo's wrist. Dave knew the technique caused excruciating pain. He was now using his weight and knees to keep Remo trapped on the ground, which kept his two hands free to try and grab Remo's flailing left arm.

Dave had the advantage of leverage and experience. He knew all he had to do was get Remo's second hand cuffed. At that point, the fight would be over. Nobody could fight back once they were in handcuffs.

But Remo wasn't giving up. The steroids in his system were super-charging his adrenaline. Instead of realizing he was simply being arrested and that Dave would disengage once he submitted, Remo was fighting back like he was in a battle for life or death. He let out another loud grunt, and the skin on his face turned clay red. His eyes looked like they were trying to force their way out of their sockets.

Dave was trying to get Remo's left arm cuffed, but he couldn't lean forward enough because he had to use his knee to keep Remo's right arm pinned against his back.

"Gimme that arm," Dave said.

He inched forward, but misjudged the distance, and got hit in the face by the back of Remo's hand. Remo's World Series ring tore open Dave's upper lip. He tasted metal as the ring slammed into his mouth, and he felt one of his teeth rip away from his top gum. Blood began to fill his mouth and drip down his chin.

Remo's arm came back towards Dave, and this time he grabbed it. He clamped onto Remo's wrist with both hands and started to pull it back over Remo's shoulder. But Remo was shifting his weight onto his side making it harder for Dave to pull.

Dave was stunned by Remo's strength. He was using his full body weight to bend Remo's arm backwards, but it was just barely starting to give. Dave knew he would have the leverage he needed if he could just pull it back a couple of more inches. He almost had the arm cuffed when blood from his mouth landed on Remo's cheek and began to trickle into his mouth.

Remo started pumping his legs back and forth furiously on the ground to try and get some traction. His suit pants ripped as his legs pumped like pistons against the pavement. Remo was able to rotate his hips sideways, which was enough to make Dave lose his balance. He planted his knee on the ground to try and get some stability.

With Dave off-balance, Remo pulled his left arm free and brought it underneath his chest. He braced his forearm against the pavement and used it to lever himself off the ground.

As Remo rose to one knee, Dave lost control of Remo's other arm. He was still on Remo's back and began hitting him in the head, but his punches had no effect.

Remo started to spin around. He was reaching back, yelling, and trying to grab the back of Dave's head with his hands.

Dave knew he was in trouble and switched into defensive mode. He tried to get a chokehold on Remo, but Remo pinched his chin down to his chest. Remo bent forward and tried to flip Dave off him, but Dave held on. Remo grabbed Dave's arms and tried to pry them apart, but Dave pulled his hands loose and fell off Remo's back.

Remo was now free and turned around to see where Dave had landed.

Dave wanted to run, but he was trapped between

Remo and the fence. Remo's slacks were torn down the front, and blood was running down his legs from his knees. He looked directly at Dave, but didn't speak. He growled and looked down at the handcuff on his right wrist.

Remo spit and yanked it hard. The cuff broke off, and he let out a triumphant yell at what he thought was his display of strength. He was now within ten feet of Dave.

Dave reached for his gun, but it was gone. It had flown out of its holster when Remo had tried to flip him forward.

Remo exploded towards Dave, who sidestepped to his right. Remo missed, but he was able to grab a handful of shirt. Dave tried to back away, but Remo held onto him by the collar. Dave's polo proved stronger than expected, and Remo reeled him in close enough to throw another punch down at his head. Dave lifted his left arm and blocked most of it, but the hit still connected with enough force to get his head ringing. Remo followed up with an off-balance punch that landed above Dave's right ear. It stung, but didn't do any damage.

Remo saw Dave's gun on the ground and made a move towards it. Dave lunged underneath him and had a clear shot straight into Remo's groin. Dave coiled his arm back to release an upper cut. He unleashed it right as Remo stunned him with a roundhouse kick to his head. The kick hit Dave with full force and sent him stumbling backwards. Remo followed up with a fast two-kick combination to Dave's head and midsection that he delivered with a karate style yell.

Dave fell into the broken part of the fence. Remo crouched halfway over him. His knees were bent and his hands were in attack position. He was exultant as he hissed into Dave's face. Remo had seen Dave making a move towards his groin and had been too quick for him.

"I got a black belt in jujutsu, motherfucker!"

Remo wiped his mouth with the back of his wrist.

"Nobody fucks with Remo Centrella," he yelled. "Nobody!....You feeling me, Bro? You feeling Remo?"

Remo picked his right knee up in the air and pulled his

hands down across it like he was breaking a bamboo stick in half. He then let out an open-jawed scream as he slowly dragged an imaginary knife across his throat.

4

——

ON EARLY Thursday morning, the East Coast of the United States woke up to news of a shooting outside Wilson Field. Details were not known, but the Atlanta news desks were reporting that based upon the large number of police vehicles at the scene, it was a serious situation. Initial reports indicated there was at least one fatality.

The headline of a shooting at the Keith was added to the cable networks' morning queue, but it was still just getting a brief mention until the 7:25 local hit. That's when a production assistant for WBC in Atlanta reported to her counterpart in New York City that she was hearing a rumor Remo Centrella may have been involved.

Just the possibility that baseball's reigning home run king might be involved in a shooting moved the story to the top of the list, and the headline was immediately added to the station's ticker. When WBC came back on air at 7:30, the story had been elevated to "Breaking News" status.

Behind the scenes, show runners at the networks demanded their staffs get more information on what happened, but it was tough. Police scanners, normally one of the best sources of information, were not carrying much traffic about the shooting, other than requesting more assets to report to the scene.

At 7:45 AM, the Atlanta Inquirer, Atlanta's flagship newspaper, uploaded a headline on its website which read:

Remo Centrella victim of attempted Car Jacking at Wilson Field. Attacker dead. Centrella transported to Grady Memorial Hospital with life threatening injuries. More information to follow.

Because it was from the Inquirer, the headline was taken as fact and picked up by wire services across the country. The reaction on TV was serious and fast paced. Regular segments were cut, and scheduled guests were told they would have to be re-booked. A shooting involving one of the biggest names in sports was going to get bumper-to-bumper coverage.

In Atlanta, the local media split up between Grady Memorial Hospital and the stadium, while GSN, the 24 hour Sports Network based in Syracuse, was using the temporary quell in the story to discuss Remo's career. Left unspoken, but not un-thought, was what impact the shooting would have on the playoff races. Nobody would be stupid enough to say it on the air, but everyone who followed baseball knew it would be good for St. Louis if Remo ended up being out for the season.

It wasn't until 8:10 a.m. that the Inquirer learned the facts. When they did, they immediately put up a correction on their homepage:

CORRECTION: Remo Centrella Killed. <u>This story is a Correction</u>: Remo Centrella not in surgery. Never sent to Grady. Dead at scene. Shot by off-duty police officer. Police shooter in surgery with life threatening injuries.

In New York City, the Mississippi born morning anchor for SUN News stopped talking to the reporter doing a live shot from Atlanta, and instead turned to address a producer standing behind the camera.

"Are you sure Allison?" he asked. "Are you absolutely

sure?"

People watching the morning show only heard one side of the conversation, but Allison must have been sure, and the news must have been bad, because everyone saw the look on the anchor's face grow dark, as he sucked in a long breath and announced, "Ladies and gentlemen, SUN news has just been informed that baseball star Remo Centrella is not, in fact, under going surgery at a hospital in Atlanta."

He paused out of necessity.

"Ladies and gentleman, it is my sad duty to report that baseball's home run king, Atlanta Barons' star, Remo Centrella, has been killed. Gunned down outside Wilson Field, in the early morning hours, apparently by an Atlanta police officer."

A "church bell" sound effect rang as the anchor finished his statement, and a huge "Breaking News" banner came hurtling across the screen, followed by the headline:

DEATH of an ATHLETE: Remo Centrella Shot Dead.

A second year cop named Pete Windham was drinking coffee at a Waffle House when the first call about a possible carjacking at Wilson Field had come through. He had hustled to his car and was the first officer to arrive.

He parked his car, stepped out, and took in the scene. Dave's dark green Sebring was parked with its hazard lights on. Remo's candy-apple Porsche was parked off at an angle, its driver side door open and front-left tire blown out. The front corner of the Porsche was crumpled where it had been dragged across the ground.

Pete saw a wallet with several hundred-dollar bills and credit cards spread out nearby. Looking at the scene, he had no doubt it was a carjacking turned deadly.

As Pete walked toward the cars, he could see a stocky-looking man lying fifteen feet past the Porsche, up against the fence. He looked dead. Next to the Porsche, he saw a pair of black Gucci loafers and tan ankles sticking out past the front bumper. He walked past the edge of the Porsche to get a look at who was wearing the shoes. They were big, so Pete had expected to see a big guy on the ground. He just never expected to see his favorite athlete splayed out dead on the concrete.

Remo's suit pants were shredded, and a sweat stained muscle t-shirt was still tucked into his pants. The gold Rolex on Remo's left wrist glimmered in the night. Remo's neck was turned and his head was resting on its side against the concrete. His thick black hair was matted down, and his face glistened under a glaze of 5 o'clock shadow.

As Pete stepped closer, he saw a thin maroon pool of coagulating blood under Remo's head. Coffee came up into his throat when he saw where Remo was shot.

Pete crouched down like a catcher to try and stabilize himself. As he made the sign of the Cross, he saw the gun that killed Remo on the ground next to Dave. He knew not to touch it before the CSI arrived.

"Where the hell is everybody?" he said.

After an almost five minute wait, Pete heard sirens approaching in the distance and his breathing eased. He turned and started back to his squad car when he caught a glint of movement from Dave's watch. He processed it instinctively and ran back to help him.

Pete got down on his knees and grabbed Dave's wrist. He felt a faint pulse. Without moving him, Pete used his thumb to push up Dave's eyebrow and pry open his eyelid. Dave's eyes didn't engage his, but they moved involuntarily in response to his eyes being forced opened.

"Can you hear me, Bro? Bro, wake up," Pete said. "Come on, Buddy, you hear the sirens? That's help. Stay with me."

As Pete was talking to Dave, two ambulances pulled up, one after the next. Pete waved his left arm to signal the driver while his right arm gently held Dave's hand.

"Priority here," he yelled. "This guy's alive."

Four EMTs jumped out of the ambulances.

"What happened?" the first EMT asked, as she shined her silver mini flashlight into Dave's pupils.

"Car jacking. Remo Centrella's dead."

"No shit?" she said.

The techs ignored Remo. It was a pure triage situation, and under the rules of engagement, dead men got lowest priority. Even if they had been a World Series' MVP.

The EMT put her hands on Dave's side to prepare to pick him up, but pulled them back reflexively. "This guy must have been run over," she said.

"He probably was," Pete said.

"Let's hope he makes it to Grady. We'll see if they can perform some of their magic."

One of the other EMTs put his hands under Dave's back.

"No. Keep him curled up," the lead EMT instructed. "Who knows what might rip open if we unfold him."

As the EMTs worked the scene, two more police cars arrived. Pete went over and briefed them on what he had seen. They saw Dave being loaded into the back of the ambulance and peered ahead to take a quick look at Atlanta's most famous athlete.

Once Dave's gurney was loaded in the ambulance, the siren lights were turned on and they sped away. The ambulance reached the emergency entrance at Grady Memorial Hospital shortly after 5:15 a.m. The paramedics had radioed ahead and a full trauma team was posted at the door waiting to receive him. Because his wallet had slid under Remo's Porsche during the confrontation, no one knew his name and he was checked in as a John Doe.

By 6 AM, a phalanx of first shift cops and investigative personnel had arrived at Wilson Field, where Remo lay covered under two crisp white sheets. As part of their crime scene investigation, one of the cops pulled Darlene's registration information and showed it to his supervisor.

Mackno wasn't a common name, but nobody at the scene made the connection to Dave because everybody was thinking Remo had been shot by a carjacker. It wasn't until one of the cops on the scene, a third-year guy named Jerry Huffman was looking underneath the cars that he found Dave's badge. He brought it to his Sergeant, Jimmy Coyle.

"You think it was Mack?" Coyle said.

"He was shot with a revolver, not a semi-automatic," Huffman said

Coyle looked puzzled. "Why the hell would Mack shoot Remo Centrella?"

"I don't know," Huffman said, before lowering his voice, "but Cowan found a six-pack of beer and a cooler in the car. Two were empty."

Coyle shook his head. "Alright, you know the drill."

Jimmy Coyle walked over to the Sebring. He nodded at the two police officers standing next to it and opened the back door. Coyle leaned in, gathered up the beer cans, and removed the cooler from the car. He then walked back to his vehicle, put the cooler in his trunk, and went back to surveying the crime scene as if nothing had happened. Nobody reacted to what he had done.

Coyle's arms were crossed as he looked around at the other cops on the scene. After about a minute, he called over to a cop who was about twenty feet away.

"Reardon, you know Dave Mackno pretty good, don't you?" Coyle said.

"I do."

"I want you and DeSantis go to Grady and get me a positive I.D. In the meantime, I'm going to send Umphress up to notify his wife."

"Aye, Sarge," Huffman said.

At shortly before 9 a.m., Atlanta's Police Chief, Ronnie Berzanski, walked into the front entrance of Grady Memorial Hospital and called the assembled press together for a statement. Camera clicks filled the air as he began to address the press.

"Good morning," he said, looking shaken up. "I'm here to announce that preliminary reports indicate Remo Centrella was killed by an Atlanta Police officer, who was on duty in an official capacity, in what appears to have been an act of self-defense."

Flashes were going off like strobe lights, and audible sounds of surprise filled the air.

"We won't be releasing the name of the officer until his family has been notified. Obviously, as with any killing involving a police officer, this department, in conjunction with our Internal Affairs unit, will conduct a full and complete investigation into the shooting."

Berzanski paused for a moment to maintain his composure.

"This is obviously a tragic day for the City of Atlanta. I'm fully aware what Remo Centrella means to this community. *What he means to this State.* I know a lot of you will have questions, and I can assure you that each and every one of them will be answered in due time. For now though, I ask the people of Atlanta for their patience and to pray for the full recovery of our downed colleague. He's a veteran of our police department who has committed his life to protecting the people of this city. I thank you very much."

The assembled reporters began shouting questions at Berzanski.

"No questions at this time," he said.

Berzanski put his hat on, lowered his head, and walked out a side door.

Within minutes of the briefing, Dave's name had been leaked to the media. It took about five seconds of soul searching before one of the national news channels announced it on the air.

The decision was probably unavoidable. The networks were in the middle of a "sweeps week," which meant the stakes were too high to risk getting scooped by a rival. And besides, the producers told themselves, it wasn't like Dave was dead. He was merely in surgery.

It didn't take long before an old headshot of Dave, taken in his dress uniform, became the stock photo shown on almost every channel. Contrasted against the picture of Dave, was a seemingly endless loop of Remo Centrella photographs and videos.

The exact scenario that Ronnie Berzanski wanted to avoid, ending up happening. Five minutes before Officer

Umphress rang the doorbell at her house, Darlene Mackno learned from Good Morning America that Dave was undergoing surgery in an attempt to save his life. She nearly passed out when she heard the news. It would be another three hours before a surgeon walked into the chapel at Grady and told her that Dave had survived.

A day after the shooting, Dave's condition improved enough that his doctors announced he had been upgraded from critical to stable.

"Great, more bad news," Atlanta Barons owner, Ray Manning, said when he saw the headline cross. The senior executives with him laughed nervously, even though they didn't think he was joking.

A day earlier, as Remo's body was found outside Wilson Field, Ray had been in Europe with his two oldest children. Halfway through an annual summer trip, they had spent the day hiking in the mountains near Lake Geneva, Switzerland.

It had been a perfect summer day. They were returning back to the Montreux Palace when the concierge met them at the entrance and whispered to Ray, "We've just received some very troubling news from America, sir. One of your players, Remo Centrella, has been hospitalized after being shot."

Ray was stunned by the news, and he and his kids headed upstairs to their suite. He couldn't understand how Remo could have been shot near the stadium. Ray knew the area around Wilson Field was rough, but none of his players had ever had a problem.

"Who the hell would want to shoot Remo?" he asked.

He was in the process of placing a call to his attorney in Atlanta when he heard CNN's International anchor announce, in her crystal clear English accent, "In breaking news from the United States, American baseball star Remo Centrella has been killed overnight by an Atlanta police officer."

"Killed?"

Ray dropped the phone back into its cradle and sat

down. He couldn't speak and simply signaled for his son to bring him a drink.

A headshot of Remo in his Barons' uniform was displayed on the television screen above the CNN anchor's shoulder. Ray drank down a large glass of bourbon as he stared at the screen in disbelief. His hands began to tremble as memories from his nearly 20-year relationship with Remo began to flood his mind.

On the field, Ray and Remo had won three World Series titles together. Off the field, they had become close friends. *Sport* Magazine said they had the closest owner-player relationship in professional sports. Close enough that Remo had served as the Best Man in Ray's third wedding. And close enough that for almost a decade, they spent a week together in the offseason fishing the Southern Caribbean on Ray's yacht, *Diamond Money*.

Ray was struggling to process information that felt impossible to believe. *Remo couldn't be dead.*

He didn't know what to say or do, other than he knew he had to find a way to get back home. His Gulfstream V was parked in Atlanta and wasn't scheduled to return to Switzerland for another week. He had his daughter call the concierge, who arranged for Ray to be flown back to the States on a private jet owned by a Geneva based commodities trader.

Ray didn't get back to Atlanta until almost 2 a.m. He was hung-over and exhausted, but when his alarm went off at 7 a.m. he woke up. Even with jet lag and the emotional trauma of Remo's death, he forced himself to do 30 minutes of cardio on his treadmill before taking a hot shower and heading into his office at the Keith.

Ray had already begun drinking by the time he convened his front office staff to a 10 a.m. meeting to try and figure out a strategy for dealing with Remo's death. Nobody in the Barons' front office was surprised to see Ray knocking back drinks at such an early hour. He had always been a heavy hitter. The fact was, the ability to consume vast quantities of alcohol was practically a job requirement for working in the Barons' front office. If you weren't a drinker, you didn't last. You took a job with a different team, one whose owner hadn't learned to drink on Bourbon Street.

Ray Manning was a 53-year-old Louisiana native who inherited the Barons, along with the Donergy Oil Exploration company, from his father, Chet, who died from a massive stroke at the age of 58. Six foot three, with a square face and fashionably long reddish brown hair, Ray was just 34 years old when he took control of the team.

Chet had picked up the Barons as part of a larger financial transaction and was never willing to spend any money on the team. "They're a good tax write-off," was the way he had once described the team.

But Ray loved baseball and was determined to turn the perennial cellar dwellers into winners. He made his intentions clear during his first press conference when he announced he planned to be a hands-on owner who would do whatever it took to bring a World Series title to Atlanta.

Ray's first major decision was to overrule the team's long-time General Manager and select Remo with the 9th pick in the draft.

Ray had taken a trip north to Southern Connecticut State University in New Haven, where he watched Remo play in a double header against La Salle. Remo went 4-for-7, including two home runs, and Ray came away convinced he had the potential to become a big-time power hitter.

But his GM, a baseball lifer named Jay Perla disagreed. He said Remo was too much of a risk, and that the Barons were going to draft a left-handed pitcher from Arizona State instead.

"Centrella's too slow and he's got the mentality of an ox when he's at the plate," Perla lectured Ray. "He's a middle second, possibly even third round pick at best. If he's around at that point, I'll consider drafting him."

But Ray overruled Perla, reminding him he was now the one signing the checks.

"I know my father might have given you complete control, Jay, but he no longer owns the team. *I do.* So, if you want to keep working for the Barons, you'll be working for me.

"The days of you acting like this is your team are now over," he said. "We're drafting Centrella. End of discussion."

Perla resigned in protest, insulting Ray through the press in the process.

"There's a reason Chet never trusted the kid with any responsibility," Perla said in an interview with Baseball Digest's P.J. Foley. "He knew his son didn't have what it takes to manage a complex organization. He thought Ray was at least twenty years away from being mature enough to handle the responsibility.

"Chet must have told me a hundred times that he wanted me to continue to run the team if anything ever happened to him. The kid knows it, too. Unfortunately, Ray's the type of kid who doesn't have enough respect to honor his father's wishes. He didn't respect his father when he was alive, and he doesn't respect him now that he's dead.

"He's a know-it-all who is just going to do whatever the hell he wants. That's just who he is. It used to drive Chet crazy. You can mark my words—this kid will turn the Barons into a train wreck."

But Perla had been dead wrong. The pick of Remo turned out to be one of the best decisions the Barons ever made. And it ended up being the first of many picks that gave Ray a reputation for being one of the best talent evaluators in baseball. If anything, Ray's guidance of the Barons proved that Chet Manning had been a terrible judge of his son's abilities.

Remo was the foundation upon which the Barons' dynasty was built, and he was the major reason they went from being a punch line for Chris Berman to the most dominant team in baseball for over a decade. During that run, Remo became baseball's biggest star, and the team became more valuable than Ray's father ever imagined.

That explained why, even though the Barons' P.R. department had issued the requisite press release stating that the team's prayers were with Dave and his family,

Ray was continuing to lament that it was Remo, and not Dave, who was dead.

Ray Manning might not have been happy that Dave's condition was upgraded, but Remo's fans were. Not because they were overly concerned about an Atlanta cop they had never met, but because it meant they could now openly mourn Remo without being emotionally conflicted about the fact he might have killed a cop.

Within a couple of hours of the report that Dave was going to make it, a small number of Remo's fans began to make a pilgrimage down to the Keith. Two of the first were a father and son carrying flowers. A reporter doing a live shot for Channel 5 was there when they arrived. The son was a photogenic kid who looked to be about six or seven years old. He had one hand in his father's and the other in his baseball glove.

The son was crying as his dad led him towards Wilson Field's "Ring of Honor." With the cameras rolling, the father instructed his son to place the flowers in front of the mural of Remo. A picture of the kid ended up on the front page of the Inquirer.

Soon after the kid set down the first bouquet of cellophane-wrapped flowers, other fans began to follow his lead. Within 24 hours, hundreds of Remo's fans gathered to hold a vigil and build a makeshift memorial out of flowers, hand-written signs, and Barons' memorabilia.

On Sunday afternoon, three days after the shooting, and five hours before the Barons were scheduled to play their first game since Remo's death, thirty thousand fans piled into a painfully hot Wilson Field for a memorial service. Remo's huge white coffin was displayed on an altar at home plate, while Monsignor Federici presided over a funeral mass.

Highlights from Remo's career were played on the stadium's Jumbotron, while Ray delivered a eulogy that was carried live by GSN and the local networks in Atlanta.

When the ceremony ended, and Remo's coffin was

loaded into a hearse, a small flock of news helicopters took to the air and followed its slow procession to Oakland cemetery, where Remo was buried in a private ceremony.

Remo's death marked the end of an era and the beginning of some serious problems for Ray Manning.

5

TWO WEEKS after the shooting, Dave met with a couple of detectives from Internal Affairs, who were in charge of the investigation. His upper body was still in a cast, but his meds had been lowered to a level at which he was alert and could think coherently. Bobby, who had been alternating shifts at the hospital with Darlene, was allowed to sit in on the interview, as a professional courtesy.

Everything about the process was standard operating procedure. Any time a cop discharged his weapon while on duty, an investigation was automatically triggered. And any time a cop actually shot someone, he or she was immediately put on suspension until a full review was completed.

Dave had been through the routine once before, back when he was a younger cop and killed a 20-year-old kid who was in the process of strangling his girlfriend.

Dave had been a police officer for a little less than three years when he shot the kid on a cold night in the middle of December. At the time, he was taking night classes at Georgia State in pursuit of his Bachelor's Degree. He had just returned to his car after a final and was planning to head up to Pop Young's Tavern for some beer and chili, when he heard over his walkie-talkie that there was a possible stabbing in progress at 1949 Kingsley Avenue.

Kingsley was less than a dozen blocks away from

Georgia State's campus, so instead of turning left to meet up with some buddies, Dave turned right and headed south. When he pulled up to the row house, he saw the front door was swung open, despite the temperature being in the low 30s. He jumped out of his car and ran up the steps. Once inside, he saw a wild-eyed kid who had a pregnant girl in a neck lock.

The living room of the cramped house had been tossed. A TV was knocked backwards on the floor, and the bottom end of a marble statuette was sticking out of its broken screen.

The girl, who looked close to full term, had gone limp and was dangling like a puppet. Her eyes were open, but when Dave tried to make eye contact, she didn't acknowledge him.

Dave stepped forward with his gun drawn and badge displayed. The kid pulled a switchblade and pressed it against the girl's pregnant stomach.

"Get outta here or I'll cut this bitch," he said.

The girl's black skin was starting to turn grey, and her legs were bent backwards.

"It's cool," Dave said, trying to stay calm. "I don't want a problem. We cool."

The inside of the living room was cold, but Dave was sweating through his flannel shirt. The kid looked depraved. He was wearing tight, acid washed jeans and a blue nylon jacket with a faux fur collar. His pupils were the size of pin pricks.

"She stole my money," he sniffed. "Took two hundred dollars off me while I was asleep."

The kid was pushing the blade into the girl's stomach without even realizing it.

Dave listened to see if he could catch the sound of a siren, but the night was silent. He looked at the girl and thought she might have stopped breathing.

"Okay, I got you," he said. "It's between y'all."

Dave made a show of putting his gun back into his holster and putting his hands up to show they were empty. "Y'all work this out," he said and started to walk backwards.

The kid sniffed his nose again and gave Dave a couple of jerky nods of his head. He took his eyes off Dave and re-focused them on the girl.

"Where's my money?" he said and raised the knife up underneath the girl's chin.

Dave squeezed off three quick shots, *pop, pop, pop,* towards the right side of the kid's head. The first shot landed in the drywall behind the kid's shoulder, but the second and third shots hit their target. The kid dropped dead, and the girl fell to the floor. Dave ran to her and started performing mouth-to-mouth resuscitation until another cop and an ambulance showed up. When the EMTs arrived, they strapped an oxygen mask on the girl, transferred her to a gurney, and rushed her to Grady. Forty minutes later, she delivered a healthy baby boy by Caesarian Section. Doctors later told Dave and his Sergeant that both the mother and the baby would have likely died if Dave had not started performing CPR when he did.

The next night, the guys on Dave's beat took him out to Pop's to celebrate. Bobby said the department should have thrown Dave a parade for saving a baby and his mother, but the problem was two white cops had killed two unarmed black teens in the previous six months. Because of the political fallout from those shootings, there was no way APD was going to celebrate the death of anybody black at the hands of a white police officer.

Dave didn't care. He didn't think he had done anything different than any other cop would have done.

The Internal Affairs investigation into the shooting of a junkie strangling his pregnant girlfriend was nothing more than a rubber-stamped formality. *It might have been the least controversial shooting in APD history*, but Dave knew the investigation into his shooting of Remo Centrella was going to be a lot more scrutinized.

When the two investigators from Internal Affairs arrived, Dave walked them through the events of the confrontation with Remo. He told them about seeing a fresh welt on the woman's eye and explained he didn't call for backup right away because he had not expected to be attacked.

"It was Remo Centrella," he said. "I was a fan just like everybody else."

He described how the confrontation escalated. "I was heading back to my car to make the call when Centrella tried to run me down. I dove out of the way and shot out his tire. It was a purely defensive measure to avoid getting run over."

Everything about Dave's account jibed with what the investigators expected to hear, and at the end of the interview they confided that a pack of steroid vials and five hypodermic needles were found in a gym bag in the trunk of Remo's Porsche. Official results would take a few weeks to confirm, but initial indications were that Remo's blood samples had tested positive for both Trenbolone, a steroid designed to increase the muscle quality of cattle, and Testosterone Decanoate, a drug known throughout major league locker rooms as "Mexican Beans."

"He was apparently double-stacking the drugs during his cycle," the lead investigator, a woman with a thick southern accent, told Dave. "We think his personal trainer was the one supplying him. We're pursuing that angle aggressively."

"That's good," Dave thought, knowing a lot of Remo's fans would want to make sure somebody was held accountable for his death.

At the end of the interview, the investigators brought in a sketch artist to draw a picture of the woman who had run from the car. Dave gave them as much detail as he could, but the sketch ended up looking like half the women out in Buckhead on a Thursday night.

Three days after the interview with Dave, the police department called a press conference where they unveiled the sketch and announced an arrest warrant had been issued in the name of "Jane Doe." Now officially a fugitive, she was wanted for multiple charges, including obstruction of justice, fleeing the scene of a crime, and accessory to the battery and attempted murder of a police officer.

When the press conference was over, the police spokeswoman pulled a reporter from the Inquirer aside and leaked the information on Remo's initial blood sample. The leak was a scoop for the paper's Metro Desk, and the story was still hot enough to command front-page real estate in the paper's Sunday edition.

The two thousand-word piece quoted Dr. Stuart Seewald, an endocrinologist from Georgia Tech, who declared, "an eight week steroid cycle could absolutely effectuate a person's mind chemistry to the point where normal anger was transformed into uncontrollable rage."

The story also quoted an un-named veteran pitcher on the team who said he had noticed Remo's increased bulk and shrunken testicles back in Spring Training. The same pitcher said there was no way that Barons' manager, Nick Katzenbach, could not have known Remo was taking steroids.

"Katzie had to know what was going on. Remo was swinging the bat like he was 27 years old again," the pitcher said. "Not to mention the fact his head got so big they had to get him a custom-made batting helmet. Everybody in the clubhouse knew what was going on, especially when they started letting his personal trainer have full access to the facilities down in St. Pete."

The information about Remo's use of steroids was another black mark on baseball and more proof the steroid era was in full swing. The national media jumped on the reports and demanded to know when professional baseball was going to clean up its act. Without betraying even a trace of irony, many of the same sportswriters who had praised Remo's resurgence at the plate wrote articles condemning his use of PEDs.

P.J. Foley, the self-appointed Dean of American baseball writers, wrote a scathing article in Baseball Digest, in which he declared the use of steroids tainted Remo's career. He wrote, "It makes complete the pall of suspicion that has descended over this game I still yearn to love."

Foley said the record books should put an asterisk by

each of the Barons' World Series titles, and that Remo Centrella would never get his vote for the Hall of Fame.

Ray was livid when he read Foley's article. He had expected the baseball community to rally around Remo after his death, not bring out the long knives. Especially Foley, to whom the Barons had given a ton of preferential access over the years in a tacit exchange for stories that flattered Ray and the organization.

"It's hard to stomach getting lectured by a guy who's got half the hookers in Philly on speed dial," Ray said to his wife after reading Foley's piece.

He was feeling increasingly under siege since Remo died. In addition to having to work through the emotional pain from Remo's death, which was worse than he expected, Ray also had to contend with the financial fallout from it.

From a purely dollars and cents perspective, Remo's death could not have come at a worst possible time. Ray was more dependent than ever on cash flow from his baseball operations because his oil company was in the middle of a project in Alberta, Canada that was hemorrhaging huge amounts of cash. To make things even worse, the Barons' life insurance company was claiming they did not have to pay out on the 45 million dollar policy the team held on Remo.

Less than two weeks after Remo had been killed, a certified letter arrived at the Barons' offices from their insurance carrier, All-Life Insurance. The letter was a formal denial of Ray's claim to collect on the policy the team had taken out the same day Remo signed a three-year contract extension.

The letter from All-Life was signed by its General Counsel and stated it was denying the claim based upon the insurance policy's "felony clause."

Ray had never heard of a felony clause, but his attorney, Johnny Wiemer, explained it was a standard rider on every life insurance policy.

"Think of it this way, Ray. Guy robs a bank and the security guard guns him down in the process. His widow can't collect on his life insurance. Because of the felony clause, the act of robbing the bank, *a felony,* nullifies it.'"

"But Remo wasn't committing a felony. He was a victim of excessive force. I've been saying that since day one."

"Emotionally, I agree with you Ray, but from a legal perspective, it's an uphill battle," Wiemer said.

"This is a bunch of bullshit," Ray said as he studied the letter, which included a quote, highlighted in yellow, that Ronnie Berzanski had given to WBC. Berzanski's quote stated, "Detective David Mackno was forced to shoot Remo Centrella in self-defense. If he had not shot Mr. Centrella when he did, Detective Mackno would almost certainly be dead."

"Why the hell is Ronnie Berzanski shooting off his mouth before Internal Affairs finishes their investigation?"

"I don't know, Ray" Wiemer said.

"Somebody needs to tell him to shut his yap."

Ray shook his head in disgust.

"Bottom line it for me, Johnny, they're just trying to force a settlement, right?"

"I called and asked that same question, Ray. I spoke with their G.C. up in Stamford and asked if she had a number in mind."

"What did she say?"

"She told me she could probably get us four million dollars if we signed a full waiver and release."

"Does she think we're stupid? We've been a customer of All-Life since Chet owned the team. They're crazier than hell if they think they can screw me out of money. I'll drag their ass down here to Atlanta and stick them in front of a jury stocked with Baron fans."

"I already have a call into Artie Nierengarten about a lawsuit."

"What did he say?"

Wiemer inhaled before saying, "He wasn't too encouraging. Artie said that based on the police reports, All-Life's got the facts on their side. He said we could tie them up in litigation for a few years if we want, but at the end of the day, we'll probably lose and end up having to pay their attorneys' fees.

"Which," Wiemer added, "All-Life will run into the millions. He's advising against litigation."

"Tell Artie I appreciate the advice, but remind him that will be my call to make. If he doesn't have the cojones, I'll find somebody else who does. Call Ellie Corcoran," Ray said, and picked up a cigarette from a tin on his desk. "She won't be afraid of them."

Ray lit the cigarette as he leaned back in his chair and put his feet on his desk.

"Okay, worst case scenario, Johnny," Ray said as he exhaled. "Let's assume they don't pay. How do we void the contract?"

"Void the contract, Ray?"

"Yeah. Remo left his family plenty of money. Tiffany had millions before she even met him. She sure as hell doesn't need 45 million more from me."

Wiemer looked directly at Ray.

"We can't void the contract, Ray. *It's fully guaranteed.* Shane Straka insisted on it. According to the terms, we need to pay the remaining amount in a lump sum to Tiffany within 180 days of Remo's untimely death."

"Lump sum?"

"There's an acceleration clause."

"All you fucking lawyers," Ray said. "Do they actually teach you this shit in law school?"

Wiemer didn't answer.

"I don't have 45 million dollars," Ray said, after a minute of silence. "I got no cash. Alberta is eating me alive, and Cohen, Wolfe is threatening to call my loan if I miss another installment."

Ray rubbed his forehead.

"The fucking squids, moving in for the kill now they know I'm bleeding." Ray stubbed out his cigarette and picked up a printout off his desk. "Look at this. We're 2-9 since Remo died, and attendance hit another fucking low last night. We're down sixty five percent from July. I was already bleeding red ink from Canada, and now I'm losing money on my cash cow."

Ray shook his head as he studied the spreadsheet.

"I got another ten million due to Cohen, Wolfe in a week, and I'm not going to be able to make it. I'm completely illiquid. All my equity is either tied up in the club or buried in the ground in Canada. That means I'm looking at a default. You're looking at the brokest billionaire in the United States."

Ray stood up and walked slowly towards the large window of his office that looked down onto the field.

"There's no way I can come up with 10 million for the Wolfe and 45 million for Tiffany Hill. I'd have to shut down Alberta, which would end up bankrupting me."

"What about an equity raise against the team?" Wiemer said. He knew Ray wouldn't want to hear it, but he felt bound, as a fiduciary, to bring up all the options he could think of.

"Tapped out. I already borrowed a hundred million against my share last year for phase two of Alberta. The rest of it's either cross-collateralized or in trusts I can't borrow against. I got one too many divorces on my resume. The only way I can get access to any more equity is if Monica agrees to re-structure Chandler's share, or if I sell a controlling stake in the team to a non-affiliated third party. Neither one of those scenarios is an option. Monica still isn't speaking to me, and I'll never sell a controlling interest in the team."

Ray stared down at the field for several minutes.

"Alright, here's the plan," he said, after several minutes. "Don't acknowledge the letter until I speak to Cutter directly. I'll convince him to honor the policy. We can get Dale Agee involved if we have to. I'll have him threaten to drop All-Life as a sponsor if they don't follow through on their commitments."

"Okay, I'll sit tight until further instructions," Wiemer said and stood up to leave.

As Johnny Wiemer walked out of Ray Manning's office, he thought about how Ray's call to the Commissioner of baseball might go. It had only been a few months since Ray told the *Sporting News* he thought Dale Agee was the least competent executive in all of professional sports.

The pull quote, which GSN had highlighted throughout a full 24-hour news cycle, was when Ray said the Commissioner had done such a lousy job negotiating the last collective bargaining agreement, that he doubted if Agee "could convince the Pope to go to church on Sundays."

6

TWO WEEKS after his meeting with Johnny Wiemer, Ray Manning was sitting next to his second ex-wife, Monica, in the principal's office at Notre Dame High School. Three days earlier, the Assistant Dean of students had found two grams of marijuana in Ray's 15-year-old son, Chandler's, locker during a routine police dog sweep.

The drugs put Notre Dame's administration in an awkward position of trying to determine whether or not it should expel the son of its wealthiest benefactor, three weeks into his sophomore year.

Notre Dame's principal, a Monsignor in the diocese named Archie Dwyer, was taking advantage of his captive audience to lecture them on one of his favorite subjects: how the modern day church must navigate the delicate line between discipline that *forms* the soul and discipline that *wounds* the soul.

As the Monsignor droned on, Ray was trying to figure out how much of the lecture was sincere and how much of it was designed to maximize the check Ray would have to write to keep Chandler in school.

It wasn't the first time Ray needed to buy his way out of a problem with Notre Dame. Ten years earlier, Emily cost him five grand in the fall of her senior year, when she and two of her girlfriends showed up drunk at a Sadie Hawkins dance.

Ray was afraid it would jeopardize her early admission to Princeton, but fortunately, Notre Dame's Principal at the time, a soft spoken old-timer from Italy named Father Senatore, liked Emily. He chalked it up as a minor indiscretion.

"I've no doubt a private confession will more than suffice, Raymond," Senatore had counseled. "And I'm sure that a one time offering of penance will be more than enough to see that nothing permanent makes it onto Emily's transcript."

Ray got the message. He wrote the Alumni fund a check and the problem disappeared. Emily's senior year got back on track, and Princeton was never the wiser.

But this time, the stakes were higher. Chandler was only a sophomore, and it was Mary Jane, not Peppermint Schnapps. Even worse, Father Senatore had retired home to Italy and been replaced by Dwyer, a humorless battle axe from Massachusetts who loved nothing more than delivering pedantic lectures in his foggiest Boston brogue.

When the Monsignor's lecture finally came to an end, he excused himself to summon the school's drug and alcohol counselor to the meeting.

"Since when does Notre Dame need a full time drug and alcohol counselor?" Ray said.

But Monica ignored him. He wasn't surprised. He knew she was still angry about finding him in their hot tub with his now third wife, Tina.

Ray was too worn down by recent events to worry about Monica's feelings. He was actually grateful to have a few minutes of time to stare blankly at a wall, while he waited for Dwyer and the drug counselor to return. He was studying an old black and white poster of St. Peter's Square that was taped to the Monsignor's wall when his cellphone rang.

"Sonuvabitch," Ray said, when he looked down and saw the incoming number had an international area code of 044. England.

"Perfect fucking timing."

Ray knew it was the return call from William Cutter, the CEO of All-Life General Insurance agency, who he had been trying to reach for almost two weeks.

Monica gave Ray the glare he had seen a hundred

times during their marriage, when he was about to do something she didn't appreciate.

"You better not even think about answering that phone," she said, breaking her silence.

It buzzed again.

"I gotta take it," Ray said, trying for a little sympathy. "I've been trying to reach this guy for a week. It's about Remo."

"Whatever. Take the call. It will be good for Monsignor to see what I'm up against."

Ray stood up. He rolled his eyes and said in a loud whisper, "Make sure you also mention to him how tough it is to deal with the twenty five grand a month I send you in alimony. I'm sure that should be good for some sympathy points from his eminence."

"I earned every penny of it," she said. "Married to you."

Ray smirked at Monica and answered his phone.

"Sir William Cutter's office calling from London for Raymond Manning," a prim voice said. "Is this Mr. Manning?"

"The one and only."

"Please hold, sir."

"*Mr. Manning,*" a smooth and enthusiastic British accent said, a moment later. "William Cutter here. Very sorry to take a bit to get back to you. Schedule's been a bit crazy, I'm afraid. Stuck on the Continent almost all of last week. I'm sure you know how that goes."

"No worries, Sir William," Ray said. "You're a busy man, I understand that. I'm just glad to get a chance to speak with you, especially, as y'all *are* the official insurance provider of professional baseball."

"Please, please, call me William," Cutter said. "And let me add on behalf of our associates at All-Life, we are absolutely delighted to pay your league twenty million dollars a year for the privilege."

Because of the accent, Ray couldn't tell if Cutter was being sincere or mocking him.

He and Cutter had once met in London. They had run into each other over drinks at the bar in the Grosvenor House, and Ray had come away with the distinct impression Cutter took him for a wealthy rube who walked around with Georgia clay stuck to his shoes.

"I assume you know why I've been trying to reach you, William. Seems like we got a little miscommunication taking place between our two companies. *Couple of attorneys who might not understand the special relationship your company has with professional baseball.* I hate to tell tales out of school, William, but I'm afraid your lawyers haven't left me any choice.

"Seems y'all have a lady working for you calls herself Doreen English. Sent me a very unfriendly letter the other day. Said she was going to deny the life insurance policy that we took out on the home run king."

"Remo Centrella," Cutter said.

"That's right. Now, I don't know what Mrs. English's agenda is, William, but I'm afraid that in her over-zealousness she might could create some serious problems for you. Not to mention the kind of bad PR y'all would have to deal with if the press somehow got ahold of her letter."

William Cutter looked around at his colleagues in the large conference room and wondered if anyone else thought Ray's southern accent was as laughably ridiculous as he did. *Law-yahs, matt cood, sumpin, y'all.* Even after thirty years of doing business with Americans, Cutter never failed to marvel at the use of the word 'y'all' by supposedly educated people. How such a word had been accepted into the American lexicon was beyond his ability to comprehend. He couldn't believe anyone would show such disrespect for the English language.

Cutter was standing at the head of a large conference table on the 37th floor of the All-Life building in "the City," the U.K's version of Wall Street. He had a phone against his ear, while a small team of All-Life senior executives was huddled around a speakerphone.

In Atlanta, Ray began to walk out of the Monsignor's cramped office, but turned back around when he saw the Monsignor and a college-aged girl talking to Chandler. He walked back into the office and faced the wall, so that his back was to Monica.

"Actually, Mr. Manning, her last name is Hengesch and the letter was not a mistake. It went out under her signature per official protocols, but she did, of course, pass it through my office before posting it to you. The letter has my full endorsement."

"You approved the letter?"

"Of course," Cutter said, cheerfully.

"The denial of my claim?"

"Denial's not the actual term, Mr. Manning. The technically precise thing to say is that based upon the unfortunate circumstances surrounding Mr. Centrella's death, All-Life has processed your claim in full accordance with the terms of the policy. In an instance such as this one, cash compensation would never be permitted to be remitted."

Cutter winked at his Treasury officer.

"May I be candid for a moment here, Sir William, would ya mind?" Ray said, continuing to turn up his Southern accent for Cutter.

"Not at all."

"With all due respect Sir William, *pardon my French so to speak,* but that sounds like a load of horseshit to me. The *unfortunate circumstances surrounding Remo Centrella's death*? No disrespect intended, but I've been around long enough to know when someone's trying to run a hustle on me."

"Oh, it's not a hustle, Mr. Manning. Far from it. It's merely a succinct summation of the legal reality that we both must face."

"You're actually claiming you don't have to pay me my money?"

"Of course, Mr. Manning," Cutter said, with the slightest of chuckles. "I'm afraid Lloyd's would never permit us to engage in such a willful breaking of contractual terms. We're running a global business here at All-Life. To do that successfully, we have to respect all of our stakeholders. We can't just simply pretend that certain clauses don't exist when they pose an inconvenience, now can we? That wouldn't be equitable to our other stakeholders."

"What about keeping your word?"

"I'm sorry, I don't follow your logic."

"You don't follow my logic? Let me try to explain it to you in simpler terms, then. I took out a life insurance policy on Remo Centrella back in the spring. One of your reps, a guy by the name of Elliot Emmett, sold it to me. I paid the premiums, and now, unfortunately, Remo's dead. When that happens, since I got a life policy on him, you need to pay me my money. You can follow that logic, William, can't you?"

"I understand your concern, Mr. Manning. I truly do. The problem we're facing is Mr. Centrella died while in the process of committing a felony."

"Says who?"

"Says everyone. Come on, now."

"Not me, William. I don't say that, and I'm the customer. I'm the one who paid the premiums, and I can personally guarantee you, Remo Centrella never committed a felony in his life. We got a cop down here who used excessive force and forced Remo to act in self-defense. The only reason the SOBs at APD want to say it's a felony is because they want to avoid responsibility."

"Actually, Mr. Manning, certainly not trying to be disagreeable, but Mr. Centrella was technically in the process of committing multiple felonies when he was killed."

From across the room in London, All-Life's General Counsel gave Cutter a "thumbs up" sign.

"And because of that—"

"Did you even listen to a word I just said, William?"

"We're simply unable to pay off any type of a claim. Now, we are, of course truly sorry, and I can assure you that we certainly understand—"

"Stop right there. I don't need your understanding, William. I need you to pay my claim. I'm not asking for any kind of special treatment here. I just want you to honor your word."

Cutter didn't answer.

"Hullo?" Ray said. "You still there, William?"

"I'm still here, Mr. Manning. One moment please."

Cutter looked down at a note that had been slipped in front of him.

"I'm afraid, Mr. Manning, that because of the criminal actions of Mr. Centrella, we're unable to pay your claim."

"Criminal actions? Are you seriously going to try to screw me out of my money."

"Mr. Manning, I—"

"I'm not finished," Ray said. "I realize you probably think were just a bunch of hicks down here in Georgia who you can roll while hiding behind small print, but let me explain something to you, Mr. Cutter, that's not the way we do things in America. In America, we honor our contracts. If that somehow offends your European sensibilities, I'm truly sorry. But you need to be fully aware, I got a team of real aggressive lawyers who are chomping at the bit to get you in front of a Georgia jury. And let me tell you something else, that jury ain't gonna give a rat's ass that the Queen of England tapped you on the shoulder with a sword and now wants the rest of us to go around calling you "sir."

"Really, Mr. Manning? Is that what you honestly believe is going to happen? That you're going to bully my company into paying you thirty million pounds to which you are not entitled."

"It's not a threat, Cutter. I don't make threats. I make promises."

"Then I'm sorry to tell you, Mr. Manning, but you, dear sir, are grossly misinformed," Cutter said, his tone much harder than at any previous point in the conversation. "Let me explain *sumpin* to you, my friend. *Contracts go two ways.* You signed a policy that had a felony clause in it. It's a standard clause in every life insurance policy we write. *Zero exceptions.* Industry standard. That's what you agreed to when you signed it, and that, dear sir, is the policy you own."

Sir William lowered his voice to where it was almost a whisper in order to make sure he would have Ray's complete attention. "If that's too complicated for y'all to understand, maybe your lawyers can explain it to you," he said.

"I know what it—"

"The clause is both binding and controlling, despite what you may fancy or threaten. And because of that, I regret to inform you, Mr. Manning, your claim is nugatory."

"Nugatory?" Ray said. He wasn't exactly sure what the word meant, except he knew it was Cutter's condescending way of telling him to go to pound sand.

"You know something, Cutter? Fuck you."

Ray's face was now flushed a crimson red. He raised his voice. "Screw you and the high horse you came riding in on you condescending British motherfu—"

Ray felt a hard pull on the sleeve of his blazer. He turned around and saw Chandler looking up at him with an expression that was a combination of shock and embarrassment. The Monsignor was standing behind Chandler with his mouth half-open.

"Aww, shit," Ray said and hung up his phone.

In London, Cutter looked around the conference room.

"Just what in the bloody hell was that?"

"I told you he was a loose cannon," All-Life's Treasurer, Dennis Gardner, said.

"If he thinks we're going to pay him even one pound after he speaks to me like that, the man is a certifiable loon. As a matter of fact, I don't want any of his policies renewed. I've never heard anything like that in my entire life. Are we agreed, Dennis?"

"Absolutely, sir," Gardner said. "Remo Centrella did this to him, not us. All we're doing is following the contract."

"Where do we stand with our friend, Mr. Agee? He's always struck me as a reasonable chap."

"No problem there. I phoned him last week to give him a courtesy brief about what was taking place with the Barons. I asked if it was going to cause us any difficulty with the league. He assured me it would not. He understands we have a business to run. From what I gather, Mr. Manning's brash ways haven't exactly endeared him to the commissioner."

"Good," Cutter said. "Make sure we invite him to my

box at Wimbledon next year."

Gardner made a note on his legal pad.

The mood in All-Life's 37th floor boardroom was one of relief, bordering on elation. Coming up with their plan on how to deal with the Barons' claim had been stressful.

It was almost cocktail hour in London, and Cutter ordered a trolley of drinks brought in. He poured himself a tall Johnnie Walker Black on ice and proposed a toast.

"To the felony clause," he said, with an impish smile.

His toast solicited a chorus of muffled "hear, hears."

"Un-bloody believable, these Americans, what they think of themselves," Cutter said, with a whiskey-tinged laugh, as he poured himself a second drink. "They all seem to think they're John Wayne. As if they're entitled to get their way simply by persisting about it."

Inside Monsignor Dwyer's small office, Ray Manning's embarrassment and anger were still obvious to everyone as he sat stone-faced in his small chair. He listened as the school's twenty something guidance counselor told him that Chandler was basically a complete screw-up, and that it was mainly due to the divorce that everyone in the room knew had been caused by Ray.

"And that's why we've agreed to let Chandler remain a student at Notre Dame, Mr. and Mrs. Manning," the counselor said, in a tone Ray thought was usually reserved for people with double digit IQs.

Ray was tempted to remind her she was speaking to a billionaire, but didn't want to increase the amount of the check he would need to write. He sat in silence and listened to her lecture, while praying there was an uncomfortable section of Hell for the anti-tobacco mob who had somehow managed to turn Georgia into a "clean indoor air state."

Ray would have been willing to stroke a ten thousand dollar check on the spot for the chance to smoke one of the Marlboro Lights that were taunting him from inside the pocket of his suit jacket.

"But we will ask a contribution from you Mr.

Manning," she said.

"You don't beat around the bush, do you, Honey?" Ray thought to himself, happy, at least, that the request for a donation meant the lecture was almost over.

"You will be required to attend bi-weekly counseling sessions with Chandler, the Monsignor and myself, until we can all feel confident he's back on the right track."

The counselor smiled at Chandler, who didn't have a reaction.

"Every young man Chandler's age needs the chance to spend time with their father," the Monsignor intoned, as if Ray were some sort of derelict parent who neglected his kids. As if Dwyer could understand what is was like dealing with a surly fifteen-year-old son, while trying to juggle the dynamics of an angry ex-wife, a demanding new wife, and a business on the verge of entering a financial death spiral.

Ray glanced sideways and saw an unmistakable smirk of satisfaction on Monica's face. He refused to give her the satisfaction.

"Sounds good to me, Father," Ray said and stood up. He knew if he didn't get a cigarette fast, he would try and put his fist through the wall. "Whatever we need to do to get Chandler back on track, the answer is yes. You can count on my one hundred and ten percent support."

He walked over and gave Chandler an awkward hug before leaving the Monsignor's office. He was no more than twenty feet down the hall, an unlit cigarette in his mouth, when the Monsignor caught up and asked if they might have a private word.

"Outside," Ray said, and lit his cigarette.

7

IT WAS early afternoon when Ray reached his Wilson Field office. When he arrived, he noticed a kid in an expensive suit sitting in the reception area and reading a back issue of *Sports Illustrated*. He asked his secretary to follow him into his office.

"Who's the kid, Connie? Do I know his father or something?"

"No, sir. He works for Cohen, Wolfe. He's been waiting here since 9 AM."

"He's been here all morning?"

"Yes, sir. Mr. Gaffney called and insisted he be allowed to wait."

Ray looked angry. "Okay, send him in," he said.

Connie went back out to the waiting area, but the kid was gone. Her phone rang and she picked it up. It was Malcolm Gaffney, head of Investment Banking at Cohen, Wolfe.

"Hello, Connie," Malcolm said. "Geoffrey just told me that Ray has finally shown up to the office. That explains a lot."

"I'm afraid he just stepped into a meeting, Mr. Gaffney."

"Then get him out. My call should be the most important thing in his life."

"One moment please, sir," Connie said. She put Gaffney on hold and informed Ray who was on the phone.

"Okay, I'll take it," Ray said. He made Gaffney wait almost three minutes while he fixed a drink and tried to channel some positive energy.

"Hey Malcolm, how you doing, Buddy?" Ray said when he picked up the phone.

"You're becoming a very hard man to reach, Ray. I don't appreciate having to send a kid, who I'm paying a hundred grand a year, to sit in your office just to get you on the phone. That's the kind of thing that makes me want to be unpleasant."

Ray knew he was finally speaking to the true Malcolm Gaffney, a heartless prick with zero compassion for anybody or anything that didn't make him money.

At one time, back when Cohen, Wolfe was jockeying with three other banks to lend money to Ray, Gaffney had spoken to Ray as if he would have donated a kidney to him. But that was a lifetime ago. Now that Ray had missed a payment on his loan, their relationship had been reset on very different terms. Now Ray was the one having to try and make Gaffney happy.

"I apologize, Malc. It's been crazy down here. You can imagine."

"I'm not interested in excuses, Ray. I'm interested in finding out when we're going to get our money."

"I know. I hear ya."

"It was supposed to be here ten days ago and we still don't have it. So now *I* look like a schmuck every time Lloyd Molendyke calls to ask about our loan to Donergy. I truly don't appreciate being treated like this by a man I consider to be such a close, personal friend."

"I hear you," Ray said, "and I'm in the process of getting the funds, Malcolm. You know I am. It's just that Monica's been out of the country for the past two weeks. Some fucking cruise she took with her mother. I don't know what they're up to. She's supposed to be back in a week or two, and then she'll sign the release to free up the equity. She's already agreed to it, but she's breaking my balls in the process just because she can. You got ex-wives, Malcolm, you know how they get."

"I don't depend on my ex-wives for money," Gaffney said. "They depend on me."

"It's a one time hiccup. Tell Lloyd I'm getting you the money."

"I hope so for your sake, Ray, because my work-out team is frothing at the mouth at the chance to foreclose on Alberta. They've been studying your geological reports around the clock. Nobody around here has the slightest clue of how you've managed to turn such a promising project into such a world-class clusterfuck."

"Wow," Ray thought to himself, "not even a pretext of deference anymore."

"It's almost on-line, Malcolm," Ray said. "We're so close to production, I can almost taste the oil."

"So can we, Ray."

"Gangsters," Ray said to himself. Monica had been right. He should have stuck with Merrill Lynch.

"Don't wait too long, Ray," Gaffney said. "The Wolfe doesn't like it when clients miss payments. It makes her angry, and it makes my investment committee want to get aggressive. There's only so much I can do to protect you when that happens. If the committee decides to label you in breach, every last dime you owe us will get called. From what others in your unfortunate predicament have told me, that's an experience that feels even worse than death."

"I understand, Malcolm. Just buy me a little bit of time. I'll get you your money. I swear to God."

"I need to run, Ray. I'm late for a massage," Gaffney said and hung up.

It was a Thursday night in early October when Maurice Bass, Atlanta's District Attorney, drove up to a large house in Buckhead that was considered modest compared to its neighbors on Valley Drive. The driveway was gated, and Maurice had to give his name through the intercom before it opened.

He drove his silver Audi up the long driveway until he got to the front of the house and saw Georgia Governor,

Frank Durkin, waiting for him on the top step. He was standing between the white columns that framed the front of his house.

"Moe-reese, how you doin', Buddy?" Durkin said. He gave Maurice a warm handshake and a slap on the back. "Any trouble finding us?"

"No," Maurice said. "No problem at all."

"Good, good," Durkin said. He was smiling broadly.

Maurice didn't return Durkin's smile. It was the first time he and the Governor had met since Durkin publicly insulted him, and Bass wanted to make sure that Durkin knew it hadn't been forgotten.

It wasn't a major insult. Frank Durkin had just given what he considered to be an honest answer when asked by a reporter what he thought about Maurice's decision to run for Atlanta District Attorney against the incumbent, Claxton King.

"Maurice Bass isn't qualified to be the District Attorney," Durkin said. "Claxton's done a great job for the people of Atlanta for almost twenty years. The last thing the city needs is a guy whose only experience has been chasing ambulances and organizing marches."

Maurice had not appreciated Durkin weighing in on the race, even though his comment paled in comparison to the things Claxton King said about him. One of which was, "there's no way the city too busy to hate would ever elect a race baiter."

That charge, *race baiting,* had been the most frequent attack against Maurice Bass during his career, and it became the central theme of King's re-election campaign. But Maurice fought back hard against the charge. He labeled the accusation a "slur borne of laziness," and said it "smacked of a collectively racist mindset by those in Atlanta's political elite.

"Standing up and saying African Americans in Atlanta are treated as second class citizens by the city's justice system isn't race baiting," Bass said, during his debate with King, "it's a statistical fact. And the fact is, during Claxton King's reign, blacks in Atlanta have not been afforded the equal protection that the United States'

Constitution is supposed to guarantee."

Bass also lectured the Atlanta media to stop referring to him as a "black civil rights attorney," when discussing his campaign, unless they were going to refer to Claxton King as "Atlanta's white district attorney."

"We've become a majority black city in Atlanta, *Black Mecca as it's called,* so if anybody needs to be identified by his race it's Claxton King, not me."

Bass had run a campaign that completely confounded King, who had not faced a primary challenger in four cycles. He had no clue the level of support Bass had in the African American community. Because of that, he didn't take him seriously until it was too late. King was genuinely stunned when he lost the primary by almost four thousand votes.

But Bass wasn't surprised. He knew he could win, and more importantly, he knew he had the brains needed for the job. A fact that even his critics in City Hall were beginning to concede.

Frank Durkin was still smiling at Maurice, as if he couldn't have been happier to see anybody. "You're looking good, Maurice," he said. "I see success agrees with you...that's for damn sure."

Maurice let out a smile despite his best efforts. It was such an over-the-top compliment that would have sounded completely patronizing coming from anybody else. But somehow it sounded mostly sincere when Durkin said it.

Nobody in Georgia politics was better known than Frank Durkin, the "Big Dog," and nobody in the South was better at retail politics. Originally from the Savannah area, Durkin had a charisma his supporters loved, and his opponents either despised or envied. He had used his brains and guile, along with a marriage to the right girl, to rise from middle class beginnings to the Governor's mansion.

Originally elected to the Georgia Statehouse, Frank Durkin had never lost an election. After four years in the State House, he served three terms as a Congressman in D.C., before returning to Georgia and running for

Governor. He won the race in a landslide, against a weak opponent who had run a campaign better suited for Alabama or Mississippi.

It was now accepted wisdom that Durkin's next step would be national politics. His closest advisors, both inside Georgia and the Beltway, were already beginning to whisper he had what it took to make a serious run for the White House.

"I appreciate you meeting me here, Maurice," Durkin said. "It's nice to have a chance to get out of the "People's House" once in awhile and spend a little time in my own."

"You have a beautiful home," Bass said, as he followed him inside.

"Say hello to Maurice Bass, Sonny," Durkin said to a tall man, with a light brown crew cut, who was sitting in an armchair in Durkin's living room.

"How you doing?" the man said, barely looking up from his paper.

"Evening," Maurice said. He knew who Sonny Komanski was. A former "special operator" in the Army, who was rumored to have been an instructor at one of the CIA's no longer secret schools down at Fort Benning.

Part consigliere, part fixer, Komanski was in charge of Bass' personal security detail. More importantly, he was the guy that connected people in Georgia went to when they needed some unofficial help from the Governor.

"And this, of course, is the First Lady," Frank said, as Sheila Durkin appeared from around the corner. She was wearing a long blue dress with low heels and a double string of large pearls. "Resplendent" was the word that came to Bass' mind as he looked at her.

"It's a pleasure to meet you, Mrs. Durkin," Maurice said. He shook her hand, while thinking Frank had to know most people thought Sheila, who towered over her husband by at least four inches, was beginning to look more like his mother than his wife.

Sheila Durkin's matronly look was in contrast to her husband who, although now exhibiting a lot more salt than pepper in his hair, still exuded a Kennedyesque youthfulness that was equal parts scoundrel and country innocent. With his pompadour hairstyle sprayed firmly into place, Maurice thought Frank Durkin looked like he could be James Brown's white twin.

"I don't know about you, but I could use a drink," Durkin said, and led Maurice into a large room decorated like a men's club. It had a billiards' table in the center and two flat screen televisions mounted on one of the walls. There was a brown leather sofa and four leather chairs facing the televisions. Durkin walked to the bar that was built into the back wall and removed two cigars from a humidor.

"I have it on good authority that you're a man who likes Cohibas," Durkin said. He had a big smile on his face while he handed a cigar to Maurice. "I picked these up last month while on my economic fact finding mission to the Dominican Republic."

Durkin lit his cigar.

"They were a personal gift to me from the President of the D.R.," he said.

Maurice saw that the label read "Habana." It was a genuine Cuban.

"Thank you," Maurice said. He put the cigar in his mouth, and Durkin lit it with a silver torch lighter.

"Wow," Maurice thought to himself. The Cohiba was as smooth as butter. It was unlike any cigar Bass had ever smoked and nothing like the counterfeit ones he had bought off the docks in Mexico, while on a cruise.

"That's yours," Durkin said, and pointed to a yellow box that said Monte Cristo in red letters. It was still wrapped in cellophane. "Not Cohibas, but a little something to thank you for your time this evening."

"That's very generous," Bass said, deciding he should probably forgive Durkin for something he said during the heat of a campaign.

Durkin pondered his cigar for several moments before turning back towards Maurice.

"I've been watching you, Maurice," Durkin said, in his folksy drawl. "And you, my friend, have what it takes."

"Thank you," Maurice said, his cigar held gently in his mouth.

Durkin exhaled a puff from his cigar and let the smoke waft through the air.

"I don't say that lightly. You've got real talent, as my good friend Claxton King was sorry to find out. Not many people could do that, Maurice, take on a popular incumbent and win. That took a special combination of talent and balls. Most politicians I know have one or the other. You appear to have both."

Maurice gave Durkin a humble nod of acknowledgment. The truth was, he agreed with the statement.

"With the right friends and a little bit of a push, you could be looking at some very exciting things on your horizon."

Maurice took another draw on his cigar and tried his best to look nonchalant. But it was obvious, based on the long wind-up, Durkin was going to be asking for something big.

"Tell me, Maurice, how are things progressing with the investigation into the Remo Centrella shooting? I understand from the Mayor that the folks from Internal Affairs are close to wrapping it up."

"They are. They're supposed to have their report to me by the 15th."

"What do you think it will say?" Durkin said. With the cigar in his mouth, his speech sounded clipped.

"I think it'll exonerate Detective Mackno. It will say he killed Remo Centrella in self-defense."

"What do *you* think, Maurice?"

"Ah," Maurice thought to himself, *"there it is."*

"I'm not really sure. I need to read the report."

It was a lie. Bass knew exactly what he thought, but he wasn't about to lay his cards on the table until he knew the stakes he was playing for.

"Let me ask you, Maurice...clarify something for me, if you would. What would happen, *hypothetically*, if you didn't agree with the report's recommendation? What if the report made one recommendation, but you were of a different opinion? As the District Attorney, you would have the authority to overrule it, would you not?"

Bass paused to contemplate the question, which he was sure Claxton King had already answered for Durkin.

"Legally, yes. The report's instructive, but not binding. Under the city's charter, the district attorney has final authority on whether or not to file charges in a criminal matter."

Durkin paused a moment to smoke some more of his cigar

"That puts you in a very unique position, Maurice. It gives you a lot of power. More than you might realize."

"I think of it more as a responsibility," Maurice said, as he picked up Durkin's lighter and touched up his Cohiba.

"Of course," Durkin said, with a slight smile. "That's exactly how I view my position in public office. *As a servant of the public.*" He put a cautionary finger in the air. "But, that doesn't mean you should forget about your own career, Maurice."

Bass took a puff from his cigar. "I won't," he said.

"I hope not. As a matter of fact, Ray Manning was at the mansion the other day, and he and I were talking about your future."

"Ray Manning?"

"Ray's a good friend of mine," Frank said. "One of my closest advisors."

"And biggest fundraiser," Bass thought to himself.

"He was one of the first guys with money who ever backed me. Sheila's father, Phillip, had done some legal work for him and made the introduction.

"I was just starting off, running for State Rep and Phil took us to lunch. Ray and I hit it off, and he went all out to help me get the win. *Even knocked on some doors with me, believe it or not.*"

Maurice had a hard time picturing Ray Manning going door-to-door in Atlanta.

"He's been a good friend of mine ever since. He's one of the main reasons I won my first election. Sheila's father had the connections, but Ray had what I needed even more: money."

Durkin smiled as he held the cigar between his teeth.

"I never forget a friend, Maurice, and I never forget a

favor."

Bass nodded.

"Ray is still in a lot of shock about what happened to Remo," Durkin said. "It's causing him a lot of heartache. It's also costing him a lot of money. Enough that he felt compelled to ask me for my help."

"And that's why you wanted to meet with me?"

Durkin took a puff of his cigar, arched his head and exhaled. "Yes. After spending some time discussing the situation with Ray, he's convinced me that Mr. Mackno needs to be held accountable for shooting Remo Centrella. What I need to do, Maurice, is convince you of the same thing."

Maurice didn't answer. He shifted in his seat and leaned a bit forward, as he now understood the purpose of their meeting.

"Have you ever thought about a career in Washington, Maurice?"

"No," Bass said, even though he knew Durkin would know he wasn't being honest.

"How did you enjoy your time at Howard?"

"It was great."

Bass wondered if he was supposed to be either flattered, or impressed, that Durkin knew some of the basics of his biography.

"D.C's a hell of a city," Ray said, with a clear sparkle in his eye. "Just as many perks as New York City, but with time to enjoy them. Nowadays, it's becoming just as easy to get rich in D.C. as it is on Wall Street."

Durkin tapped his ash into the ashtray.

"I'm not sure if I could think of a better place to raise a couple of young daughters. D.C.'s got great culture, and Northern Virginia has some of the best private schools in America."

Maurice nodded noncommittally. *Howard Law, two daughters.* Durkin had been prepped. The Governor shifted in his chair and leaned in towards Bass.

"Tell me, Maurice, how closely do you follow politics?"

"A little bit," Bass said, while holding his cigar between his thumb and fingers. "I'm like everybody else, I like to keep up with what's going on."

"Then I'm sure you know Buddy McCray is up for re-election next year."

"I do."

"But I bet you didn't know he wasn't going to run for re-election? That's something only a very select group of people know."

Durkin took a puff from his cigar and gave Maurice a slightly mischievous smile.

"So select, I'm not sure even Buddy knows it yet."

Maurice gave Durkin a puzzled looked. "Buddy Mac" was a three term Senator from Georgia who was the second most popular politician in the state.

"Buddy's a good man," Durkin said. "He's been a good friend of mine and he's served this state well for a long time. But he's got some personal issues that might make his re-election a challenge. That means the time is right for somebody else to take his seat."

Durkin leaned in even closer.

"I'm going to confide something to you, Maurice, that I don't want to leave this room," he said in a conspiratorial tone. "We're gonna put Brian Pike into Buddy's seat. He's done a good job in the House, and he'll be even more helpful in the Senate."

Durkin made an open gesture with his hand that was holding the cigar.

"That means his seat in 4 is going to be open. We're going to need somebody to fill it. That somebody could be you."

"Me?"

"You'd be perfect for it. You're an articulate, well-educated black man with a law degree. You're an up and comer, and you've already proven you know how to win."

Bass considered telling Durkin that calling a black man articulate was an insult, but decided against it based upon the overall arc of the conversation.

Durkin paused to make sure Bass understood he was completely serious.

"Brian and I would watch out for you. I'd use my influence with the national party to make sure you got a good committee assignment. Make sure you got your fair share of the D.C. bacon. And with the way the demographics are trending, 4 would be one of the safest seats in the House."

Durkin took another puff from his cigar. "If we put you in there, Maurice, you'll be guaranteed re-election for as long as you want."

Bass didn't say anything. Now it was his turn to use his cigar to stall for some time.

"It's the opportunity of a lifetime, Maurice. I've got twenty people that would kill for the chance to run for the seat, but I'm prepared to offer it to you."

"In exchange for holding Detective Mackno accountable," Maurice said.

"No. In exchange for helping me help Ray Manning."

Maurice felt as if he might lose his breath. What Frank Durkin was offering was so big, and so unexpected, he had to work to look unimpressed. Like any ambitious politician, Maurice had allowed himself to dream about running for Congress one day, and now the Big Dog was offering him his dream on a virtual silver platter. With only one string attached.

It was a big string, but the truth was Maurice was already planning to bring an indictment against Dave. It would be a controversial decision. He had no illusions about that. But Maurice had already convinced himself the public good required him to make an example of Dave in order to ensure every cop in the city understood there would be serious consequences for killing an unarmed citizen.

"There's a new Sheriff in town," was the message Bass planned to send with an indictment.

Maurice also knew the trial would be the career opportunity of a lifetime. It didn't take Dominick Dunne to realize the kind of media coverage that the trial would generate. It might be one of the most watched trials in history, *definitely one of the biggest television events of the year,* and because the State of Georgia allowed cameras in its courtrooms, any lawyer involved would get the kind of publicity that would last a lifetime.

At a minimum, Bass figured he could score a seven-figure book deal if Dave didn't plead out and the case went to trial. And because Bass was the one who would be offering the plea, he could make sure it was an offer that Dave would never accept.

He let out a long breath. "I'm sure I don't need to tell you, Governor, you're asking me for a lot."

"I'm offering you a lot."

"It's not something I can make a decision on right away. I'll need some time to think about it. We're talking about a decision that will have major ramifications."

"I would expect nothing less."

Bass spent almost a minute focused on his Cohiba.

"Hypothetically, say I agree to do it, you do understand there's no way to guarantee a guilty verdict."

"All I need is an indictment, Maurice."

Both men smoked in silence for several minutes.

"No disrespect intended," Bass said, "but what kind of assurances do I have that you'll do what you say?"

"You've got the ultimate assurance, Maurice. My word. You can ask anybody in Georgia politics, *any friend or any enemy*, Frank Durkin never breaks his word."

"I don't have the money to fund a campaign."

Durkin smiled.

"That will be the easy part. Ray Manning is prepared to give you his full financial support. When my donors find out you're running in an uncontested primary, they'll be lining up double-file to write you checks. All you'll have to do is show up, smile, and cash them."

Durkin paused.

"This is a lay-up, Maurice."

"How can you make sure it's uncontested?" Bass asked.

"You let me worry about that," Durkin said, and stood up. "You just decide whether or not you want to be a Congressman."

Frank handed Maurice the box of Monte Cristos and put his hand gently on his back as he guided him to the door.

Durkin stopped when they got to the foyer that led to

his living room.

"One more thing, Maurice. If you decide not to help me, there are no hard feelings. You don't owe me anything, and you have every right to say no to my request."

Bass nodded.

"If you decide not to do it, this conversation never took place. But if you ever need a favor, my door is always open. You just let Sonny know what you need, and I'll see what I can do to help."

"Thank you," Maurice said.

The governor walked Maurice back through the living room. Sonny was still there reading the paper, but there was no sign of Sheila Durkin. When they got to Maurice's car, he and Durkin shook hands. Maurice was about to get into his Audi when he stopped and called back to Frank, who was walking back up his front stairs. The Governor turned around.

"How do you know I won't decide to bring an indictment against you for attempting to bribe a public official?" Maurice said.

Frank laughed.

"I've been playing this game my entire life, Maurice. If I didn't know how to read people, I'd have ended up selling real estate in Savannah. Nobody in the state of Georgia would have ever heard the name Frank Durkin."

Bass smiled. He waved good-bye and climbed into his car for the drive home.

8

———

AT FIVE ten and a half, *six feet if anyone asked,* Maurice Bass wasn't a big man. He had a medium, un-athletic build, and looked more like a law professor than an alpha male. But that had never bothered him. With a law degree to back him up, Maurice considered himself one of the toughest brothers in Atlanta. *A guy who knew how to make an impact.*

Bass' toughness had been on display the year before he ran for the DA's office, when he represented the families of two young girls killed by stray bullets while walking home from school. It was a case that solidified his position of prominence within the African American community because he had been absolutely relentless in his pursuit of justice for the girls' families.

Even though all the evidence pointed to the girls being random victims of a turf dispute between a couple of rival drug gangs, *one Mexican and one homegrown,* Bass initiated a lawsuit against the city. He claimed the city of Atlanta had violated the girls' civil rights by failing to provide the same level of protection to them that was provided to white children walking home from school in Buckhead.

As part of his prosecution of the cause, Bass organized marches and protests throughout Atlanta to demand equal justice under the law. He was on the street almost everyday, pushing his case and forcing the issue.

One day he was picketing City Hall, the next he was leading a candlelight vigil with five hundred people at the scene of the shooting. Another time, he brought two busloads of inner city residents to picket outside an elementary school in Buckhead in order to make the point that the kids at the upscale school weren't any more important than the little girls who had been killed while walking home from Walton elementary.

Through a constant drumbeat of protests, interviews, and activism, he was able to start an almost citywide movement. Within a month of the shootings, the protests grew from mostly black residents in the girls' neighborhood to a wide-ranging coalition that even included some of the white parents from Buckhead, whose kids' school had been the target of his protest.

Bass' advocacy on behalf of the girls' families ultimately forced the city to take responsibility. The Mayor agreed to set up a taskforce on equality and to increase funding for after school programs in the inner city. He also got City Council to authorize a five million dollar settlement and a public apology from the city to the girls' families.

It was a settlement Claxton King publicly opposed, calling the lawsuit "extortion," and a "brazen money grab."

Publicly, King stated it would set a dangerous precedent for the City to admit culpability in the girls' death. Privately, he told City Council members Bass was "exploiting the death of the girls, and the grief of their families, for his own financial gain. The man doesn't have an honorable bone in his body."

It was that statement, which Maurice learned about from a source who had been in the closed-door session, that had been the deciding factor in his decision to run for District Attorney. It was that statement which sent Claxton King into private practice.

As Maurice drove south on the I-285 perimeter, he was trying to figure out what the downside risk would be if he accepted Durkin's offer. Obviously, the biggest risk if he got caught wouldn't be that he would get disbarred, it would be that he would be go to prison.

There was also the risk Durkin might not make good on his promise. But Bass' gut told him Durkin wouldn't break his word and that it would be tough, perhaps even impossible, for anyone to prove there was a *quid pro quo* for the Congressional seat.

"Especially since I've already told two people in my office that we were going to indict Mackno," Bass reminded himself.

Technically, the Barons' season ended on the first Sunday in October when they played their last game of the season against Boston on a wet, raw day at the Keith. But from a practical standpoint, the season, and for that matter an entire era, ended the night Remo died.

The last game of the season was meaningless; win or lose, the Barons would finish with the worst record in baseball. Their collapse had been stunning. On the night Remo was shot, the Barons had beaten New York to move within a game of first place. They had been on a tear in July and August, having won 21 of their previous 27 games, and Remo was leading the league in home runs for the first time in five years. After a season in which they had missed the playoffs, Atlanta was once again being discussed as serious World Series contenders.

But after Remo was killed, the team lost 46 of their last 57 games, and was mathematically eliminated from post-season contention by the second week of September. It was the worst statistical reversal in over fifty years, but it barely registered even a footnote in the national media. *Even the stat junkies who grew up playing Strat-O-Matic didn't seem to care that the Barons were making history.* They, like everybody else in the world of sports, were trying to forget what happened in Atlanta.

Attendance at the Keith plummeted after the shooting, falling beneath the lows set during the 1970s oil embargo. Nobody, who had the choice, wanted to go to a game and be reminded Remo was dead every time they looked in left field and saw a skinny kid from Venezuela who was hitting .206.

Less than three thousand fans showed up for the final home game. It was the lowest paid attendance for a regular season game at any major league ballpark in almost twenty years. When Remo's replacement struck out to end the season, the smattering of fans still at the Keith rose up through the light rain and gave the team a standing ovation. They were grateful that the nightmare of a season was finally over.

Ray Manning was one of the people who had stayed away for the last game. As it ended, he was parked in McDonough, twenty miles south of the city, getting ready to meet Sonny Komanski.

Ray was smoking a Marlboro Light and drinking a cup of coffee in the Dunkin' Donuts parking lot as he listened to his team's announcers sign off for the final time of the year. He had just lit a fresh cigarette when he saw a blue Ford Explorer drive into the self-serve car wash across the way. Ray flipped his cigarette out the window and drove into one of the open bays. He got out of his Lexus and walked to the back of the next stall, where Sonny Komanski was applying a high-pressure rinse to the front end of his SUV.

Sonny was wearing a pair of navy blue Dickies and a stone gray t-shirt. He and Ray were the only two people at the car wash on a drizzly day.

"How you doing, Ray?" Sonny said, as he lowered the spray gun to his side.

"I'm alright," Ray said and handed him the briefcase.

Sonny took it from him and put it into the backseat of his Explorer. "I'll see this gets where it needs to go."

"Thanks," Ray said. He shook Sonny's hand, walked back to his car, and headed home to pick up his wife for Sunday dinner at their club.

A month and a half later, on the second Sunday night in November, Maurice Bass was sitting in his home office on the third floor of one of the larger homes in Southwest Atlanta. It was a home he purchased five years earlier, with money he won representing an Auburn student who had been beaten by a group of cops during Freaknik. The three million dollar verdict against the city was one of Maurice's first big paydays and one of the reasons Freaknik was no longer an annual event in Atlanta.

Bass had an Amstel Light in one hand, and a cordless phone in the other as he leaned back in his La-Z-Boy. His daughters were tucked in for the night, and his wife, Lisa, was in their second floor bedroom, fully engrossed in a Grisham thriller.

Bass had a computer monitor next to him. He was alternating between hitting the refresh button on the Inquirer's website and surfing the channels on his large screen television.

He looked at his watch again. It was now 8:25 p.m. Over thirty minutes had passed since he hung up with the third of three phone calls he placed after dinner.

"What's the hold up?" Bass said to his television. "Let's get this show on the road."

He took another pull from his Amstel, and flipped back to Channel 5, when he finally saw it. Fox News Channel's national desk cut into one of their Sunday night cartoons with a "Breaking News" hit.

"We interrupt this program with breaking news from Georgia," the anchor, who had cheekbones that looked carved out of marble, said. "Fox News has just confirmed that Atlanta's District Attorney has obtained a sealed indictment against Police Detective David Mackno in connection with the killing of Remo Centrella.

"According to Fox News sources, a grand jury was convened late on Friday afternoon and returned the indictment against Mackno. The indictment, which sources say charges Detective Mackno with manslaughter, will be unsealed during a press conference tomorrow afternoon. It supersedes a report from Atlanta's Internal Affairs division that exonerated Mr. Mackno for his actions on the night Remo Centrella was killed."

A large chyron appeared in the lower third of the screen announcing what the anchor was reporting.

"Fox News will continue to bring you updates on this breaking story as we get them. But for now, the news is that the police officer who killed Remo Centrella is facing an indictment for manslaughter."

As soon as news of the pending indictment hit the wires, every cable news producer in the country began to give thanks that the drought they had been facing since Labor Day was over.

It had been a dismal couple of months for the cable news industry. Unfortunately for those who made their living from crises, both real and manufactured, the world had been mired in a period of relative calm and tranquility. It was a non-election year, and America wasn't involved in any wars. Congress was out of session, no white kids were missing, and nobody in Hollywood was acting as if they were in need of a 5150 involuntary hold. There hadn't even been a decently destructive weather event worth talking about. That left the 24-hour news channels reduced to trying to sensationalize some seriously mundane stuff, like car chases in Los Angeles and labor unrest in Europe.

Remo's death had been the biggest story of the year, but it had appeared to run its course. Until now. Hopes for a criminal trial were confirmed when WBC moved the story forward with some specific details on the indictment. Their legal reporter, Katie Danielle, had been one of the beneficiaries of an off the record conversation with Bass, and she was explaining to WBC's viewers what was likely to unfold.

"Because the District Attorney chose to go with a *direct indictment*," Danielle said, "there was no requirement for him to issue any advance warning to the defendant or his legal counsel. That means Maurice Bass simply went in front of the grand jury and presented his evidence to it. There was no opportunity for Mr. Mackno's attorney to present any testimony or evidence that could be exculpatory in nature.

"As one of my law professors once analogized, going in front of a Grand Jury is like playing football on a field without the defense," Danielle said. "It's why prosecutors love them. Grand juries give them an enormous amount of power, as well as an enormous amount of discretion.

"A little bit of history: federal grand juries were actually incorporated into the Fifth Amendment of the Constitution in order to be an investigative arm of the Government. But over time, the grand jury process evolved, *some might argue regressed*, into what is, in many cases, nothing more than a rubber stamp for prosecutors. That's why many states have abolished grand juries in favor of preliminary hearings.

"But that's probably a discussion for another time," Danielle said in response to an irritated Long Island accent coming through her earpiece.

"Drop the law school lecture and stay focused on the indictment," the voice in her ear said.

"Because tonight the big story is that the District Attorney of Atlanta has decided to indict the cop who killed Remo Centrella."

Dave's home phone rang while Katie Danielle was in the middle of her analysis. It was a reporter from the Daily News asking Dave for a comment on the impending indictment.

"I don't know what you're talking about," Dave said. He had been reading an Elmore Leonard Western.

"Then you better turn on your television, Detective. Your life's about to get a lot more interesting."

Dave called Darlene into the room. She turned on their TV as Dave picked up the phone and called his attorney, Mike Sullivan. Dave was stunned to hear he had been indicted because, less than a month earlier, Sullivan assured him Bass had no plans to bring any charges.

Dave had seen a couple of news reports suggesting Bass was thinking about over-ruling the Internal Affairs report, but Sullivan told him not to worry.

"I've personally been told by Maurice Bass that he has no plans to indict you," Sullivan said. "I ran into him last week down at the courthouse, and he told me, off the record, he agrees with the Internal Affairs report. He knows you acted in self-defense."

Dave was reassured by what Sullivan told him; the

problem was Sully had lied. He hadn't had any communication with Maurice Bass in over a month.

The call to Sully's cellphone went straight to voicemail. Without even thinking about it, Dave called down to Hurley's Tavern, the preferred watering hole for cops at an age where they preferred whiskey over women.

A bartender picked up the phone and called him to the line. Before Sully even finished his first sentence, Dave realized he was too far into his cups to be useful.

"Hold on a second, Davey," Sully slurred into the phone. "Let just see what's going on here."

Dave heard him put his hand over the phone and tell somebody to "turn on CNN."

"Never mind," Dave said. "Sleep it off, and call me first thing in the morning."

"What—?" Sullivan said, but Dave had already hung up the phone, while admitting to himself what he had known for a while: Mike Sullivan had become a ham and egger.

"Fucking tragic," Dave said.

He remembered Sullivan from when he first started representing cops. Back then, he had a razor sharp mind, news anchor looks, and an athletic kind of charisma that made people gravitate to him. Dave had pegged him for a guy destined to run for political office.

But life had a different agenda planned. The grind of being a lawyer, a couple of messy divorces, and twenty years of heavy drinking had exacted the requisite price on Sullivan, who had become a bloated remainder of his younger self. As the Police Union's designated attorney, he was now more like a drunk priest living off the kindness of his parish, instead of the clear-eyed power broker he should have become.

"I'm going to have to get a different lawyer," Dave said to Darlene. "Sully's too much of a lush for something this big."

Darlene nodded in agreement. "We need to get you the best defense attorney in Atlanta. I don't care if we need to mortgage the house to pay for it."

"We might have to," Dave said. "The union won't pay if I don't use one of their designated guys. I can only imagine what the best lawyers charge."

"It's only money," Darlene said. She gave Dave's hand a squeeze on his way to their refrigerator where he pulled out two fresh Coors Lights. He gave one of the brown bottles to her and sat back down to watch television.

Even though Dave was the central focus of the news, he was going to have to watch TV, just like anyone else, to find out what was about to happen to his life.

"This is surreal," Darlene said as they watched the coverage. "After all you've done for this city? This is how they pay us back?"

Dave took a large drink from his beer and began channel-surfing to try and figure out what exactly the indictment was going to mean.

At shortly after 9 p.m., he clicked over to GSN, where he saw their lead baseball reporter, Tony Annunziatta, on the air. He had called into the network from his home in Colorado with an update on the indictment. Like Katie Danielle an hour earlier, Annunziatta had been the beneficiary of an off-the-record conversation with Bass.

Tony Annunziata had built his television career by being GSN's "man of the people." A former major league player who never hit better than .258, Tony had grown up on Staten Island and retained the accent, even while trading his New York roots for custom-built homes in Palm Beach and Vail. His blue-collar persona had been extremely lucrative for him, even though it was a bit of a con. Now universally known at Tony, *Antonin* Annunziatta's father, Mario, had been one of the first big-time bond traders on Wall Street. Nino, as he was then called, had grown up pampered in the most exclusive section of Staten Island. The same borough, but a world away from where Remo had grown up the son of a single mother, who had been knocked up by the assistant manager of Luigi's pizzeria.

Mario Annunziatta had wanted his son to go to Columbia or Wharton and get a respectable job in Finance. But Nino's first love was baseball, and he had been born with the ability to hit a curveball. He was drafted out of high school by the Angels, and moved west where he started calling himself Tony, when he found out California girls liked blue-collar jocks.

Annunziatta's voluble style had been a perfect fit for GSN, as the channel grew from a small industrial park near the Syracuse University campus into the most lucrative channel on the cable spectrum. Now, thirty-four years after leaving Staten Island, Tony was almost as rich as he would have been if he'd followed in his father's footsteps at the House of Morgan.

Tony had always played up his Staten Island roots and become Remo's go-to *paisan* in the media. In the days after the shooting, as the extent of Dave's injuries became clear, his had been one of the only voices in the media defending Remo, even after his bosses at GSN warned him to be careful with his tone. *Don't forget Tony, we've got a cop involved here.*

But Tony, like Ray Manning, refused to believe Remo could be to blame. He had been on GSN's air the afternoon of Remo's death, when Dave's prognosis was still uncertain. The pain on his face had been obvious as he made a plea for everyone to take a step back and put Remo's life into context.

"I've been with this man as he walked the halls of St. Jude's," Annunziatta said, with tears rolling down his cheeks. "I know this man's heart. I know the amount of time and money Remo spent helping disadvantaged youth in his community. Ask the parents of the kids Remo helped, ask the guardians of the kids who got to join a youth sports team because of him....ask them what was in this man's heart."

Annunziatta's voice choked as he raised it to speak over the other analysts, who were trying to make less emotional points about the shooting.

"You guys can say whatever you want about Remo," Annunziatta said, "but don't *evah* tell me he wasn't a good man. Don't *evah* try and tell me he wasn't a great man, because he was. And that's the story that needs to be reported. You don't take one moment in a man's life, and use it to try and tear down his entire legacy."

"But he almost killed a cop, Tony," one of the other

talking heads, a jaded newspaper guy from Chicago said.

"You don't know that. You weren't there, Dino, you're just speculating."

"I'm speculating based upon facts," Dino said, and Annunziatta simply waved his hand in disgust.

More than one media critic blasted Tony for his lack of objectivity, but he didn't care. He loved Remo too much to even pretend to be objective. Which meant that now, three months later, he was holding court on live television like a man who had been vindicated of a crime.

It was vintage Tony, as he breathlessly detailed what he had confirmed from his sources *–his sauces–*that there was no way the killing could be justified as self-defense.

Tony proclaimed Remo was "unequivocally, *without a doubt,* a victim of criminal negligence. This is a flat-out case of excessive force and manslaughter, my friend. Plain and simple. Mark the tape."

"Got it," GSN's lead host said, finding a point at which he could jump in and bring Tony's commentary to an end. "Tony Annunziatta, thank you."

"Hey, my pleasure guys," Annunziatta said and hung up. The headshot of him talking on a phone was taken off the screen.

Dave had never been fan of Annunziatta, but it was still unpleasant to listen to a guy state with so much emotion and conviction just how certain he was of his guilt. He wondered how many other people shared Tony's opinion, while admitting that he didn't really want to know the answer.

After Annunziatta signed off the air, Dave began to cycle back through the news channels looking for any new information. It quickly became clear there were no new details to report. As the night wore on, the analyses were devolving into redundant mashups of what had already been reported.

At midnight, GSN signed off from live coverage and made the switch to a strong man competition from Sweden. With most of the other channels switching to infomercials, Dave's life was on pause until the morning.

He went to bed even though he knew there was no way he would be able to sleep.

9

———

ON MONDAY morning, Maurice Bass' office unsealed the indictment and issued an arrest warrant for Dave. It also announced Bass would hold a press conference at one o'clock to discuss the indictment and his decision to overrule the recommendation of the Internal Affairs Unit.

GSN, which was leading off each hour of SportsReport with a live shot from outside the Keith, put a countdown bug in the lower corner of its screen that showed how much time was left until the press conference was scheduled to begin.

At a few minutes after one p.m., Maurice Bass walked into the main ballroom at the Marriott Marquis. The room was packed with journalists, reporters, and cameramen. Dozens of cameras flashed and clicked as he stepped to the raised podium.

Maurice felt fully alive as he stepped in front of the media, while wearing a bespoke, blue pinstripe suit he had picked up the previous summer, from Savile Row, while in London at a legal conference.

"Good afternoon," he began. "Earlier today, my office unsealed an indictment against Atlanta detective David Mackno for the unlawful killing of Remo Centrella. The indictment charges Mr. Mackno with manslaughter. The decision to bring it is not one that I made lightly. I fully understand there are times when it is both justified and appropriate for a police officer to use deadly force to defend himself or other people.

"At the same time," Maurice said and raised his index finger in caution, "nobody in Atlanta is above the law. As District Attorney, I have the utmost amount of respect for the professionals who staff the department's Internal Affairs division, and I want to commend them for the thorough job they did with their investigation. At the end of the process, however, I have reached a different conclusion.

"I do not believe the facts, as now known, justify the killing of Remo Centrella under the doctrine of self-defense. Quite the contrary. I believe the facts of the case demonstrate Detective Mackno's actions created an incendiary set of circumstances which would have been avoided if he had not acted in such a negligent manner, *with such apparent disregard for established police protocols.*

"Ultimately, however, this issue will not be resolved by myself or a report from Internal Affairs. It will be decided in a court of law, by a jury of Mr. Mackno's peers.

"For too many years, the scales of justice in Atlanta have been tipped in favor of the powerful at the expense of average citizens. I made no secret of my belief that my predecessor had been too lenient, *too often*, with those who have the honor to wear the badge. The cumulative, negative effect of such a policy has been to create a culture in which accountability was severely eroded. That culture must change.

"If we fail to hold our police officers accountable when their actions merit it, that failure doesn't strengthen our police department, it weakens it. It may sound counter-intuitive, but the fact is, by holding Detective Mackno accountable, we honor all the police officers who act lawfully.

"Let me be clear: on my watch, every citizen in Atlanta can rest assured they will get equal treatment and equal protection under the law. That's the duty I owe all the people of Atlanta, and that is the reason I have no choice but to bring this indictment.

"Because this is now an active case within our judicial system, I will not be able to answer any specific questions about the case. I will, however, be happy to answer some questions on the process I employed to reach my decision."

Maurice picked up the plastic bottle of water that was underneath the lectern, took a long sip, and then began to answer questions.

"Complete double-talk," Dave said to his television, as he watched Bass, whom he considered to be a glorified ambulance chaser, wrap himself up in the Constitution. He couldn't believe a guy like him had been given the power to ruin his life.

Dave looked at his watch and shook his head. "Where are you, Sully?" he said.

Mike was almost 45 minutes late. He and Dave had spoken earlier in the morning, and the plan was for Sully to pick Dave up at 12:30 so they could complete the booking process, while the media was still focused on Bass' press conference.

When Sully did finally show up, he looked like a guy trying to keep his life together with duct tape. His gray suit had a soft shine and was pinched in the back. His shoes, which looked like they had probably been expensive, were scuffed and their heels were worn down.

As they walked outside, Dave thought Sully looked more like a drunk headed to court on a DUI charge than he did an attorney representing the most high profile defendant in the city.

Sully apologized for being late. He said there was an accident on Highway 400, and that he left his cellphone in his girlfriend's car. Dave decided there was no point in calling him on it because he was going to cut him loose before the afternoon was over.

"Let's just get this over with," Dave said.

The two of them got into Sully's car and headed up the cul-de-sac.

Dave's street was quiet. The neighborhood kids were in school, and their parents were at work. At the top of the street, Dave saw two cruisers with their blue lights flashing silently, while parked in front of a couple of wooden sawhorses. Beyond the barricades, Dave saw a dozen news trucks lined up on the side of the road. A group of reporters was huddled together in front of the ABC news van, watching a live feed of Bass' press conference.

An older, heavyset cop with a mustache pulled the barricade back so they could get onto North Benson.

"Bobby Knot must have sent a couple of his guys out here," Dave remarked as he looked down the street.

Before they could make the turn, the small pack of reporters sensed Dave was in the car and began to run towards it.

Dave pointed in Sullivan's direction. "Hook a left," he said, "we can go the back way."

As Sully turned left, Dave looked in the side view mirror and saw the reporters break into a sprint, microphones extended, as if he might yell something to them.

"You believe this shit?" he said.

They gave up after about twenty-five yards.

"The friggin media's going crazy," Sully said. "My voicemail was already full of messages by 9 a.m."

"Don't talk to them," Dave said.

"Don't worry, Dave, I won't."

They wound their way through some side streets before getting onto 400 South. They reached the small police station in Vinings at two o'clock, and the booking process went quickly. It was handled by a female officer who looked about half Dave's age. She took his prints, picture, and personal information. When they were done, Dave posted bail through a veteran bondsman he had known since early in his career.

"Do I still get my annual Christmas whiskey?" Dave said, after the bondsman put up the money.

"As long as you and Darlene don't skip town to Mexico."

When the booking was over, Dave and Mike left out a side door. None of the media had been tipped off in advance, but by 4 p.m., AP reported Dave had turned himself in. It wasn't much longer before his mug shot began to show up on the news channels and internet sites.

At shortly before five o'clock, they were back in Alpharetta and pulled into Dave's driveway. Sully was again apologizing for taking Bass at his word when Dave cut him off and said they needed to talk.

"Mike," he said, "I want to sincerely thank you for everything you've done since the shooting. It's been appreciated. *It really has.* You're a good guy. But I've decided I'm going to hire a new attorney to defend me against this thing."

Sully looked crestfallen. He had already told the boys at Hurley's that he would be representing Dave. It was going to be the break he needed to get his life back on track. A shot at redemption, in which he would have the chance to square up a lifetime of bad decisions.

Sully had even sworn to himself he would quit drinking during the trial. The problem was Dave had figured out the case had come a decade past his ability to handle it.

"Who are you planning to hire?" Sullivan said. "Who's got more experience defending cops than me?"

He sounded even more desperate than Dave expected.

"I don't know," Dave said. He had a couple of people in mind, but he didn't want to get drawn into a debate. They both knew the honest answer was "anybody but you."

For a moment, Sully looked like he might try to muster up the energy needed to protest, but couldn't do it.

"I need to get home," he said, looking like a guy in desperate need of his first drink of the day.

"I understand," Dave said, knowing he sounded just as patronizing as he felt.

He watched the Lincoln Continental bottom out as it backed out the driveway. As Dave watched Mike Sullivan drive away, he wondered how long his front hubcap had been missing.

On Friday afternoon, Dave and Darlene stepped off an elevator on the top floor of the Wachovia building in downtown Atlanta. They were there to meet with Whitney Taylor, a senior litigator at Krouse & Koltis LLP, the third largest, and second oldest, law firm in Atlanta.

Dave had called two days earlier to request the meeting. He told Whitney he planned to interview potential defense attorneys and that he remembered his work during the Ziggy Wolfson trial.

Whitney told Dave he would be pleased to meet with him, and that he appreciated the chance to be considered. He had followed the media's coverage of the shooting. He knew the basics of Dave's biography, but hadn't realized their paths had previously crossed. After hanging up with Dave, he called down to K&K's law library and asked the staff to send up everything they could find on the shooting, as well as the archived files from the Wolfson case.

"Thank you, Ziggy, wherever you are, you crazy sonuvabitch," Whitney said as he stepped onto the elevator and headed downstairs to pick up his afternoon coffee from the Starbucks kiosk in the lobby.

"Whiggy" Ziggy Wolfson was a second-generation jeweler in Atlanta who had been charged with running over his business partner, Mel, while Mel was walking through a parking garage at the Buckhead Mall. The alleged motive was that Ziggy found out Mel had embezzled a half a million dollars from their store and ran him over in anger.

Dave and Bobby had been the cops who arrested Ziggy, in what looked to be an open and shut case. Security cameras had captured Ziggy's Mercedes, with its "ZGSTR" license plate, running over Mel.

But unlike a normal criminal, Ziggy had not fled the scene after running over his business partner. Instead, he parked his car in front of the mall and went inside the Tavern at Phipps, an upscale pick-up joint that was packed on Friday nights.

Thanks to security cameras, and the fact Mel's wife, Mera, knew Ziggy's Friday night routine, Dave and Bobby were able to locate him less than two hours after Mel was hit. When they arrived at the Tavern, Ziggy, dressed in a dark blue suit and wearing blue tinted eyeglasses, was chatting up a redhead and didn't seem surprised to see a couple of cops walking towards him.

"That was fast," he said, with a laugh.

As Bobby cuffed him, Ziggy flipped his business card to the woman and told her to give him a call sometime.

"I'll take you someplace where they don't just let a couple of cops come walking in off the street," he called out as they led him away.

As the arresting officer, Dave was scheduled to testify at trial about the details of the arrest, including the fact Ziggy seemed to be expecting it. On the morning of his scheduled appearance, he met with the prosecutor who told him the case was a slam-dunk.

"He's a fucking fruitcake," she said. "The jury will hate him, especially after the victim testifies. He's looking at ten to twelve, but he's too arrogant to take a plea. He's got a high-priced lawyer who seems convinced he can get him acquitted."

Mel was still injured when the trial began and had to be rolled into court by Mera. Halfway through the prosecution's direct examination of Mel, the Judge called a sidebar conference with the lawyers. When he did, Ziggy turned around, signaled for Mera, and whispered something to her. In response, she jumped over the courtroom's divider, onto his back, and tried to choke him.

Ziggy managed to stand up and spin around, but he couldn't shake her off him, until a bailiff whacked her in the butt with his blackjack.

Mera yelped in pain, and Ziggy shook her into the front row of the jury box. She tried to scramble back up, but two of the jurors held her down until the bailiff could get her in handcuffs. The Judge held her in contempt and banished her from the courtroom for the rest of the proceedings.

She was sitting in a jail cell when Whitney began his cross examination of Mel. He tried to get Mel to admit he and Mera were so desperate after being caught for embezzlement that they decided to try and frame Ziggy for a crime.

"It was part of a plan to extort Mr. Wolfson," Whitney claimed.

Through Whitney's cross-examination, he proved Mel had access to Ziggy's car keys and that he could have made a copy of them at almost any time. He also got Mel to admit he knew Ziggy went to Phipp's Tavern every Friday night.

Whitney's theory was that it was Mera, not Ziggy, who was behind the wheel when it ran over Mel. He argued it was supposed to have been just a gentle brush, but that she was used to driving a mini-van and ended up hitting her husband a lot harder than planned.

Dave thought it was an interesting, but completely implausible theory. He didn't think there was any way the jury would buy it, until he saw Whitney use Mera's attack of Ziggy to make his case for him.

Whitney claimed that if Mera was crazy enough to physically attack Ziggy in open court, she was crazy enough to try and frame him for hitting her husband with a car.

The key moment of the case came when the bailiff brought Mera back into the courtroom in shackles. Whitney argued that because she had attacked his client, she should be physically restrained during her testimony. His motion was heard outside the presence of the jury and the prosecutor was livid. She claimed that restraining Mera would be too prejudicial, a *farce*, in her words, and that Whitney knew it. She said he was trying to turn the trial into a circus with Mera as the clown in the center ring.

But Whitney was unfazed. Instead of getting defensive, he remained completely calm and simply stated Mera had already proven herself a threat. He argued that his client had the right to feel safe in court.

The judge knew he was being played, but he also knew he didn't have a choice: Mera's attack was in the record. He begrudgingly granted Whitney's motion, and Mera was brought into court looking like a prisoner, with her hands and feet in restraints.

Whitney kept her sitting in shackles for almost an hour as he slow-walked her through his list of questions. The longer Mera was displayed in shackles, the more wild-eyed she became. By the time she was escorted back off the witness box, Dave knew Ziggy would be acquitted.

Dave thought Whitney's work during the trial was as good as he had ever seen. It was the reason he and Darlene were sitting across from him in an office that offered the most spectacular view of Atlanta that Dave had ever seen.

Whitney Taylor had aged since Dave had seen him last, but he had done so in a way Dave thought made him seem even more honest and credible. Whitney was very tall, *Dave figured he had to be at least six foot six,* but he moved with an economy of motion that made him seem elegant. He still had a full head of hair, but it had turned from black to silver.

"No disrespect to Mr. Sullivan," Whitney said, "but I find it stunning he didn't know Maurice Bass would over-rule Internal Affairs. The surprise to me would have been if he hadn't brought an indictment."

"You weren't surprised?" Dave said.

"No, because I've known Maurice Bass, and lawyers like him, for a long time. This is the type of case a guy like him lives for.

"Think about his background before he became DA, and then think about the kind of media attention this trial will generate. He probably started hyperventilating when he heard Centrella had been killed."

"That's what I thought," Dave said, "but Mike kept telling me not to worry."

"I don't know what to tell you, Detective, other than you were very smart not to trust your freedom to an attorney chosen by your union. There are very few attorneys in the state who can handle Maurice Bass."

"You actually think he's a good lawyer?" Dave said.

"He's one of the best. I'm not sure if he's ever lost a case in which he was the lead counsel."

"I thought he was just a loudmouth," Dave said.

"That's what Claxton King thought, and now he's cutting TV commercials for Palmer & Marks."

"But you can handle him," Darlene said. "Right?"

"I can," Whitney said. "But full disclosure, I went up against him once before and lost."

"When was that?" Dave said.

"A long time ago, Mr. Mackno, and it only happened because I was overconfident. It was back when I was a mid-level partner at the firm and Bass was a solo practitioner. He was less than a year out of law school and working out of the back of his father-in-law's store. I mistakenly assumed he was a lightweight who would fold under the pressure of going against a big firm. I was wrong. He wasn't intimidated. He actually seemed energized by the opportunity to go head to head against me. He prepared for trial as well as anybody I ever went up against.

"He caught me sleeping," Whitney said, "and won a verdict against my client for a quarter million dollars. *Back when a quarter million dollars was still a lot of money.* It was an expensive lesson, and it almost got me fired from the firm. If I hadn't already been a partner, I'm pretty sure they would have asked me to leave. But I survived the storm and made a vow I would never underestimate another lawyer again."

Whitney looked at Dave and Darlene. "I never have," he said.

"I appreciate your candor," Dave said.

"What other attorneys are you talking to?" Whitney asked.

"I got a meeting lined up with Barry Reed on Monday."

Whitney smiled.

"Good choice," he said. "I like Barry. He's an excellent attorney, especially if you want to cop a plea. Based on his experience as a prosecutor, he'll be able to cut you the best possible deal.

"But," Whitney said, and raised his index finger to emphasize his point, "if you plan on going to trial, Reed's not your guy."

"Why's that?" Dave said.

"Don't misunderstand me, Detective, Barry Reed is very good at what he does. It's just that when it comes to arguing a case in front of a jury, I'm the best in the Southeastern United States. If you're going on trial for a capital offense in the state of Georgia, I'm the only guy you want representing you."

Dave wasn't sure how to interpret Whitney's matter of fact declaration of his own greatness, except to think a healthy ego might be a good quality for the lawyer he chose.

"I'm not taking a plea," Dave said. "I was forced to shoot Centrella in self-defense, and I need the world to know that. The only chance I have to try and get my life back is to go to trial and win."

"Then we're on the same page, Detective, because that's exactly what I was thinking when you walked in the door."

Whitney leaned in towards Dave and Darlene.

"Let me be perfectly clear, Mr. and Mrs. Mackno, I can't guarantee a result. Juries do unexpected things everyday. But here's the truth: if I didn't think I could get you an acquittal, I would recommend you hire Reed and negotiate a plea. That would be the smart play.

"Living through any trial is an extremely unpleasant process, but with the amount of media attention this trial will get, the pressure on the two of you will be even worse than you expect. As District Attorney, Bass has a lot of resources at his disposal, and he is going to do everything in his power to try and ruin your reputation. It wouldn't be worth living through the pain if you didn't have a very strong chance at acquittal."

Both Dave and Darlene nodded.

"The good news is, based on everything I've seen and read about the shooting, as well as everything you've told me today, there's no doubt in my mind you acted in self-defense. More importantly, there's no doubt in my mind about my ability to convince a jury of that. Maurice Bass is good, but at the end of the day, his case is weak. It's your word against his theory."

Whitney looked directly at Dave.

"You're a veteran cop who was nearly killed by Remo Centrella. That's a story any jury will be able to understand, and that's the story we're going to tell."

For one of the few times since the indictment, Dave could feel the pressure in his chest loosen. A sense of optimism entered his mind as he listened to him speak. There was something very reassuring when Whitney stated his belief in his innocence.

When Dave looked over at Darlene, he saw her eyes were moist.

"I have one non-negotiable requirement," Dave said. "I take the stand."

"I can't make that promise to you, Mr. Mackno. There are too many variables. Too many things could happen between now and that point in time.

"Odds are, I'll put you on to testify, but you need to understand something up-front, once the trial begins, it's my show. You may be the defendant, but I'm the star."

The comment was arrogant, but it had the effect of convincing Dave that Whitney Taylor would be fully invested in getting an acquittal.

"That's how the rules and the system work," Whitney said. "You'll always retain ultimate authority on the objectives of the case. You make the final call on the big questions. You will be the one who determines how you plead, and it will always be your decision on what to do with any plea deals offered."

Dave nodded his head as he listened.

"But when it comes to trial strategy and tactics, that's my call. So, hypothetically, if I end up deciding not to put you on the stand, you'll have to live with my decision."

"But you think you'll put him on?"

"That will be my plan, Mrs. Mackno, but I can't guarantee it. I could always, for some strategic reason, change my mind."

Darlene looked at Dave. "You need to be sure about

this, Honey," she said.

Dave stared out the window for several seconds. He wanted to take the stand, but he wanted an acquittal even more.

"I am," he said and shook Whitney's hand. "You're the one."

Two weeks after the media reported Dave had chosen Whitney Taylor to defend him, Mark Clemens, an amateur bodybuilder from Huntsville, Alabama, was waiting for Whitney in K&K's 53rd floor conference room.

"Sorry to keep you waiting, Mr. Clemens," Whitney said. "I trust someone has offered you something to drink."

"They have, thank you," Clemens said and stood up to shake Whitney's hand. "Call me Mark."

"I appreciate you contacting us, Mark. I know this is a difficult time," Whitney said as he tried his best to ignore how strange Clemens looked. Even though it was early December, Clemens was tan to the point of almost being sunburned. As Whitney looked at the way Clemens' large forehead and small nose contrasted, he got an image in his head of a Mr. Potato Head doll.

"I had to call after what I've been seeing," Clemens said, in a voice that was raspy. "All these stories about Remo, talking about him like he was a saint who spent all his time helping out crippled kids at St. Jude." Clemens shook his head in contempt. "Remo wasn't that guy, Mr. Taylor. He treated most people like crap."

"Tell me about your relationship with Remo, Mark," Whitney said, donning his best kindly uncle persona.

Clemens' entire aura reeked of a desperately macho guy who felt disrespected, and Whitney was confident he would respond positively to a little deference and encouragement.

"I met him last year while I was doing some personal training at the Concourse. He saw some of the work I was doing with a couple of the Falcons and asked me about it."

Whitney nodded.

"He wanted to know about some of the techniques I was doing. He could tell I'm the kind of guy who knows how to get results, you know. We ended up going to the bar for protein shakes, and he asked me what I did to get my physique. Remo was embarrassed about his loss of power and was looking for a way to get it back. He said at least twelve of the balls he hit in the previous season would have been home runs if he had the strength he used to."

Clemens seemed to get excited as he talked about his relationship with Remo.

"I started training him, and after a few weeks Remo asked me my opinion about steroids. I'll be honest with you, Mr. Taylor," Clemens said, with a self-conscious smile on his face, "I told Remo I love steroids. That ripping weight while on juice is better than sex."

"So Remo initially approached you about steroids?" Whitney said.

"Probably fifty-fifty. I probably hinted around to the point where he asked, you know, was it possible to get a boost without getting caught? I told him there were things you could do to mask them and ways to time a cycle in order to beat the test."

"So you started helping him with a steroid program?" Whitney said, trying to sound as non-judgmental as possible.

"I did. I'm not a saint, Mr. Taylor, but I'm not the low-life the media says I am. I'm not some jock sniffer who went around trying to hang out with stars. I'm a former Mr. Northern Alabama. I've competed against some of the biggest guys in the South and won titles. I got the medals on my living room wall to prove it if you don't believe me."

"I believe you, Mark," Whitney said.

"I also ran a successful business training athletes long before I ever even met Remo," Clemens said. "I had a great reputation in this city until the media started coming after me."

Clemens shook his head in anger.

"Did you see that article in the Inquirer with the picture of me walking out of the Gold's in Carrollton? 'Centrella's drug dealer,' it said. I should get you to sue them for slander."

It was technically libel, but Whitney didn't see the point of correcting Clemens. He would never be a client of K&K.

"Is that why you're here, Mark?" he said. "To try and regain your reputation?"

"It's one of the reasons, but not the main one. The main reason I'm here is I got a nine-year-old kid, who's been getting dogged on at school everyday. He came home crying last week and asked me if I was a drug dealer."

Clemens paused and looked out the window for several seconds.

"Can you believe that?" he said. "Little friggin fourth graders picking on my kid? They're lucky I didn't discuss the issue with their fathers."

Clemens twisted his thick neck.

"My kid means everything to me, Mr. Taylor. He's the best thing I've ever done. He's the *only* decent thing his whore of a mother's done." Clemens let out a quick breath of disgust. "Hogan's nothing like her, I'll guarantee you that."

"Wow," Whitney thought to himself. He had never heard any man talk about the mother of his child with such vitriol.

"Hogan's a good name," Whitney said, trying to turn the conversation back positive. "It's strong. I like it."

"Thank you," Clemens said. "I named him after Hulk Hogan. He was my idol growing up. Not for what he did in the ring. *I obviously know most of wrestling is fake.* But for what he stands for—Pro-American, good nutritional choices, following your dreams. You know, basically just trying to be your best. I wanted to set the bar high for my son so he would have something to shoot for."

Whitney gave Clemens the kindliest smile he could muster. "That's very inspiring," he said.

"Whatever happens to me, I want Hogan to know I tried to do the right thing."

"I can tell you're a very dedicated father, Mark."

Clemens looked humbled for the first time during the conversation.

"I try," he said. "After all the embarrassment I caused him, I'd like him to be proud of me for something."

"I'm sure he will be, Mark. Tell me what you know about Remo Centrella so you can tell Hogan that you helped to keep an innocent man out of jail."

"I know two things, Mr. Taylor. First, I know from personal experience that steroids made Remo Centrella violent."

Clemens pulled a photograph out of his wind jacket.

"Take a look at this," he said. It was a picture of Clemens with a bruised nose and swollen upper lip. "Remo did that to me one Saturday afternoon in Chicago when a needle broke off in his ass."

Whitney arched his eyebrows. "How did that happen?"

"The Barons were playing Chicago, and Remo flew me up to meet him. It was late June, and he had just taken his second test of the season, so we figured it would be safe to start him on a new cycle.

"It was the afternoon before a night game, and I went to his room at the Drake to inject him with a vial of "Mexican" that I brought up from Atlanta. When I did the insertion, the needle either hit a nerve or a bruised part of his muscle, *I don't know which,* but it stung him bad, and he spun around too fast. I was still holding onto the syringe, and the needle broke off."

Clemens shook his head.

"Remo started bleeding bad. I had to run downstairs and get pliers from one of their maintenance guys. When I got back to the room, I poured a couple of those little vodka bottles on it to sterilize it and pulled it out.

"You would think Remo would have been happy I was smart enough to get the needle unstuck from his ass, right? But, no. He wasn't. He slapped me in the face and asked me if I was a retard. I'm not a retard, Mr. Taylor."

"What did you do when he hit you?"

"I didn't hit him back, if that's what you're asking," Clemens said. "But I did tell him to go eff himself. *That I quit.* I left his room, but before going back to my hotel, I bought one of those throwaway camera at a Walgreen's on Michigan Avenue. I figured I could use it against him in case he tried to Jew me out of the money he owed me."

"Did you tell anybody about it when it happened?" Whitney said.

"Just my girl. She picked me up at the airport and saw my face."

"She can confirm this?"

"If I can find her. I haven't seen her around the gym in a couple of months. I heard she moved to Florida with the father of one of her brats."

"Why didn't you file a police report against, Remo?"

It was clear from Clemens' expression that he thought the question was a stupid one.

"I had three thousand dollars worth of juice in my gym bag, Mr. Taylor. What was I going to do, call the cops? I already have one arrest on my record. Besides, like I said, I needed to get Remo to pay me back for the steroids I already bought."

"Did you consider suing him for assault?"

"I got four hundred dollars in my savings account. Is that enough to sue somebody like him?"

"Probably not," Whitney said, while refusing to get annoyed by Clemens' tone.

"But listen, don't get too sidetracked by what Remo did to me in Chicago. That's what they call small potatoes. I know something a lot bigger than that. I know who was in the car with Remo. I know who he was banging, and I know why she's in hiding."

"You do?"

"Yeah, I do," Clemens said, with a look of absolute pride on his face. "It was Tina Manning, Mr. Taylor. Ray Manning's wife."

10

——

"REMO TOLD me he started nailing her during Spring Training. He was bragging, like he always did. Said he turned her into a little nympho."

Whitney was stunned on two levels. Firstly, that Remo had an affair with Ray Manning's wife, and secondly, that he had shared intimate details with a guy like Clemens. Whitney would think twice before telling Clemens what was on his grocery list.

"This is very important information, Mark," he said. "Tell Hogan that I said he should be very proud of his father."

"I will," Clemens said. "I appreciate it."

Whitney asked Clemens some more questions, and he was happy to share everything he knew about Tina and Remo. There weren't a lot of details, but that didn't matter. Just the information about her being in the car might help ensure Dave's acquittal.

After their meeting wrapped up, Whitney called one of K&K's senior associates, Gina Kantor, into his office and told her to close the door. He had a big smile on his face.

"We've got a chance to shut down this case before it even gets to trial, Gina," Whitney said and began to recount what Clemens had told him.

It was almost a week later when one of Krouse & Koltis' private investigators, a retired FBI agent named Victor Bolch, called to tell Whitney that Tina Manning was in a location where he would be able to approach her.

"She just went into the Capital Cities club for a work-out," Bolch said. "She's driving a forest green Range Rover. I'll keep a watch until you get here."

"On my way," Whitney said and hustled down to his car. He had been a member of Cap Cities when his sons were growing up and knew the back roads that would get him there the quickest.

When he arrived in the parking lot, Bolch pointed to the Rover and drove off. Whitney pulled his BMW into a space three rows behind it.

He had never considered trying to set up a formal meeting with Tina Manning because he wanted their first contact to be a complete surprise. The last thing Whitney wanted was for her to lawyer up before he had a chance to ask her some questions.

His pulse quickened when she finally walked out the front doors of the club. She was wearing a baseball hat pulled down low over her face. Most of her blonde hair was hidden underneath the cap, but even bundled up, Whitney could see she was a very attractive woman. She had a look that Whitney had always appreciated, sexy but wholesome. He got out of his car and walked towards her.

"Mrs. Manning," Whitney said, when he got within speaking distance. He was wearing an expensive camel hair overcoat with black leather gloves over a dark suit. He knew he looked wealthy enough that she would stop and talk to him. "May I speak to you for a moment?"

She stopped walking.

"May I help you?" she said.

"My name is Whitney Taylor, Mrs. Manning. I represent Detective Mackno, the police officer who shot Remo Centrella. I was hoping you might give me a moment of your time."

"I know who you are," she said, looking a bit pale. "But I'm afraid I can't help you."

She put her head down and resumed walking to her car.

"This is a very serious matter, Mrs. Manning," Whitney said. "I know you were the woman in the car with Remo

Centrella, and soon the world will know it, too."

Tina stopped and turned back around to look at him. She looked a little bit stunned, like a fighter who had been punched after the bell.

"I'd like to help you if I can," Whitney said.

Tina looked at the ground and shook her head a few times before looking back up.

"I can't talk to you Mr. Taylor. I need to go."

"If you think you can ignore the situation and it will go away, that's not going to happen," Whitney said, making sure to keep enough space between them that she would not feel threatened. "I've met with Mark Clemens, Mrs. Manning. He told me about your relationship with Mr. Centrella."

A look of disgust flashed through Tina's eyes. She shook her head in disbelief. Whitney thought he might have heard her say "fuck."

"I've actually come here out of respect for your privacy. I could have already gone to the police or the press with this information, but I didn't. Where I come from, that kind of courtesy entitles me to at least a few minutes of your time."

"I'm afraid you're too late, Mr. Taylor."

"How's that?"

"They already know."

"Who already knows?"

"The District Attorney. Mr. Bass."

"Maurice Bass knows about this?"

"My attorney said I'm not supposed to talk about it. I need to go."

Whitney stepped closer to Tina.

"This is an extremely serious situation, Mrs. Manning. What you're telling me could have very serious consequences for everyone involved. You and I really need to talk."

"I'm sorry," she said and took a step to the side to try and move by him. "I can't."

Whitney let her pass and she got into her car.

A rush of thoughts swirled in his head as he watched her drive off, including the fact he was going to get

Maurice Bass formally sanctioned, and possibly even disbarred, for failing to disclose that he knew Tina Manning was a material witness.

Failing to disclose a material witness was such a bright-line violation of the rules of criminal procedure, that Whitney didn't think any lawyer who wanted to keep his license would even think about it. He was stunned Maurice had been that brazen.

Whitney also wondered if the police department was involved in a cover-up. The "Jane Doe" warrant had been in place for over three months. Whitney had assumed the cops would give Ray Manning's wife special treatment after an arrest, but he was shocked to think they might not have arrested her. His thoughts were still in overdrive when he returned to his office.

"How'd the ambush go?" Gina asked.

"Not good. I was the one who got blindsided."

"What do you mean?"

"Bring me the number for Maurice Bass' office, we need to call him."

Gina walked out of the room and returned sixty seconds later with a number that she dialed into the speakerphone's keypad.

"District Attorney's office," a proficient voice said when she picked up.

"Whitney Taylor calling for Maurice Bass."

"Mr. Bass is unavailable at the moment," the voice said, so quickly that Whitney knew it was the default response to any caller trying to reach Bass through the main switchboard.

"I'm the attorney representing the Atlanta police officer going to trial for the shooting of Remo Centrella," he said. "I need to speak to Mr. Bass without delay. Somebody needs to go and tell him I'm on the line."

"One moment please, sir," the operator said, and several minutes later Maurice picked up.

"Whitney, how's it going?" he said.

"This isn't a social call, Maurice. I'm calling to give you the chance to convince me why I shouldn't file sanctions against you."

"Sanctions? You'll have to be more specific than that, Whitney," Maurice said. "I have no idea what you're talking about."

"The only reason I'm calling you in advance of filing is out of respect for the fact we've known each other a long time. I've always had a good opinion of you, Maurice, which is why I can't believe you would think you could get away with a stunt like this."

"Hold up a second, Whitney—"

"You're on speakerphone, Maurice. My colleague, Gina Kantor, is sitting next to me. She'll be taking notes on everything we say to ensure we have an official record of this conversation."

"You're coming on awful strong here, Whitney. I'd expect a little more comity from you, to be candid."

"I'll be filing a formal complaint against you with the court this afternoon, Maurice, in which I'm going to request that you be formally sanctioned. In addition, my firm will also be filing a formal complaint with the Georgia Bar Association for professional misconduct. You have crossed the line into behavior unbecoming a licensed attorney."

"Those are some pretty serious accusations, Whitney, and I have absolutely no idea what you're talking about. You going to give me some details, or am I supposed to just divine what the hell you're talking about?"

"I'm talking about failure to disclose a material witness," Whitney said, his drawl now replaced with a sharp edge. "That's a clear violation of Title 17, Section 17."

"What material witness?" Bass said.

"Tina Manning."

"Her?" Bass said. "This conversation is about Tina Manning? You really stepped into it this time, Whitney."

"Don't be a wiseguy, Maurice. You're not in private practice anymore. You're the top law enforcement officer in Atlanta, involved in the highest profile case this city has seen in my lifetime. You don't disclose you've located the most material witness to my case? Did you seriously think you would be able to conceal that from me?"

"You're jumping to a lot of conclusions," Bass said.

"This is one of the dumbest, and definitely the most egregious, violations of the discovery process I've ever seen. Are you *trying* to get disbarred, Maurice?"

"You're out of line, Whitney. You have no basis for what you're saying."

"Well see what the Georgia Bar Association has to say about it."

"Whitney," Maurice said, speaking louder, but more slowly, "I haven't disclosed Tina Manning as a witness to you because I just found out about her yesterday afternoon. Before you start throwing around baseless charges about sanctions and me getting disbarred, you might want to slow down a little bit and gather some facts."

"You know what, Maurice?" Whitney said. "You're being glib. You're not being forthcoming. Mrs. Manning admitted to me you knew about her and Centrella."

"That's because I do, Whitney" Bass said. "*I just told you that I did*. As a matter of fact, without tipping my hand too much, she's coming to my office tomorrow to play Queen for a Day."

Whitney felt like he had been punched in the gut.

"She is?"

"Yes, Linda Slotnick is representing her," Bass said. "She contacted my office yesterday and told me Mrs. Manning wanted to turn herself in on the warrant. Obviously, we'll be disclosing her as a witness to you. I'm shocked you would even think otherwise."

Whitney's face was red. He realized how stupid he sounded. Gina was trying to conceal her embarrassment for him by looking down at the file folder.

"What about the warrant for her arrest?" Whitney said.

"I can't divulge specifics, Whitney, but suffice it to say it's in process. You know as well as I do, we need to make sure every 'T' is crossed before we make an arrest of somebody so high profile."

Whitney didn't say anything.

"I'll have my office expedite a fully updated witness list for you by tomorrow morning, if that will make you happy. You got anything else you want to get off your chest? I'm late for court."

"No," Whitney said.

"Then I guess I'll see you at Detective Mackno's deposition on January the 9th· Oh, by the way, in case we don't speak....Merry Christmas."

"Go to Hell, Bass."

"Yeah, you too, Maurice," Whitney said.

Bass disconnected the call.

With a small gesture of his hand, Whitney signaled to Gina he wanted to be left alone. He couldn't remember the last time he felt so stupid.

As Whitney stared out the window, he realized he had just lost a battle he considered won. All the prideful exhilaration he had been feeling since Mark Clemens' visit to the office, *"this case may never even make it to trial, Gina,"* was now replaced with feelings of embarrassment.

Looking across the city, Whitney wondered if he had made a mistake out of arrogance or if it was something deeper. If now, approaching 60 years old, he had finally lost the proverbial step. Normally, Whitney would respond to such negative thoughts by reminding himself he was born with enough horsepower that he could lose several steps and still be the smartest guy in the room. But after the conversation with Bass, he wasn't sure if that was still true.

"Litigation is a young man's game. Older lawyers need to be honest with themselves and get out before they become an embarrassment to the firm."

Those words sounded a lot harsher now than they had twenty years earlier when Whitney said them to K&K's management committee. At the time, he was trying to convince the firm to cull some of its senior partners through an institution of a mandatory retirement age. Now Whitney wondered if the words applied to him.

Maurice Bass had picked his pocket, and he had never even seen it coming.

"Sonuvabitch," Whitney said, and banged the arm of his chair with his fist.

It was three days earlier, around dinnertime, when Jamie Alexander, the Assistant District Attorney tasked with pre-trial investigation, walked into Maurice Bass' office and closed the door behind him.

From a tenure standpoint, Alexander was the most junior ADA in Atlanta. But that didn't mean much, in terms of access, because he and Maurice were close friends. They went back over ten years, when Bass hired him directly out of Florida A&M law. Alexander had been the first attorney Bass hired after he was sworn in as DA.

"You're not going to believe this, Moe," Alexander said. "I just got off the phone with Las Vegas PD, and I think we got a match for the prints."

Bass looked surprised as he took a bite of the General Tso's chicken he had ordered in for dinner. "I thought the prints were too smudged?" he said and wiped his mouth with his napkin.

"They are," Alexander said. "We could never get them into court. But there were enough markers in them that the Feds generated a list of possible matches."

"What do you got?"

"Take a look," Alexander said and handed Bass a nine-page fax that bore the FBI's insignia.

It was a list of approximately 500 names of which Alexander said there was between a twenty five to thirty five percent chance that the fingerprints could be a match.

"Quantico originally wanted to send me a list of over 2000 names, but I told them to cut it down to snowflakes between the ages of 22 and 34."

Maurice was scanning through the names on the first page.

"Page 3, halfway down," Alexander said.

Maurice flipped to the third page where he saw a name circled in red. The name was "Christine Valentine," and it had her place of birth listed as Darien, Ohio. In the final right-hand column of the page, under a heading titled

"May Also be Known As," he saw the names "Christine Valescu" and "Christine Manning" listed.

"You gotta be kidding me," Bass said.

"According to Vegas, Mrs. Manning was married to a card dealer who also dealt a little blow on the side. They busted them for possession with intent to distribute."

"Ray Manning's wife was arrested for dealing cocaine?"

"They cut her loose when she agreed to testify against the husband," Alexander said. "The bad news for her is that Vegas PD uploaded her prints into the FBI's database after she was clipped."

"What happened to the husband?"

"He plead out and is doing a stretch of seven to ten out in Reno. She got a drive-thru divorce and moved to Atlanta, while he settled in into his new digs."

Alexander looked down at a notepad.

"She enrolled in Delta's training program, but never went to work for them. Instead, she went to work with LuxJets where nine months later she became...drumroll please, Ray Manning's personal flight attendant."

"Why am I not more shocked?" Bass said.

"Because this babe has got a rack on her that should be hanging in the Louvre?" Alexander said. He handed Maurice a photograph of Tina Manning. "Look at that body. Playboy should devote two separate months to her."

Bass arched his eyebrows towards Alexander. "You really need to reconsider that test I told you about."

Alexander laughed. "Ain't nothing out of balance here, Moe. I can't help it if the Good Lord blessed me with a world-class libido. Everybody has a gift. Weren't you the guy who told me that?"

Maurice shook his head.

"Lisa's always asking me why a good-looking guy like you isn't married," he said. "I haven't had the heart to tell her the truth."

"It wouldn't be fair to the female race to choose just one woman for the honor," Alexander said with a smile. "It's more of a burden than you might think."

"I can imagine," Bass said.

"You think Manning knows his wife was having an affair with Centrella?" Alexander said.

"No way," Bass said. "Who else in the office knows about the prints?"

"Nobody. I just found out about them myself."

"What about the Feds?"

"It's a computerized print-out. I doubt anybody even took the time to look through the list before faxing it to us."

"How about Vegas?"

"I told them I was calling because of a recent break-in."

"I've taught you well," Bass said.

"You and I are the only ones who have seen both sides of the coin, Boss man."

"Good," Bass said and put the printout into his briefcase. "We need to keep this quarantined for the time being. If APD gets wind of this, Ronnie Berzanski will hold a press conference on Ray Manning's front lawn."

"You're not going to tell them?"

"Not yet. Not until I have a chance to meet with her myself and tell her we matched her prints."

Bass smiled as he reached into his bottom drawer and picked out the box of Monte Cristos that Frank Durkin had given him. He opened the lid and handed a cigar to Alexander.

"I thought this was a no smoking building," Alexander said.

"Prosecutorial discretion," Bass said, as he lit a cigar for himself and flipped the lighter to Alexander. Bass had a huge smile on his face.

"Congratulations, Jamie," he said. "You just found the state of Georgia its star witness."

11

────

IT WAS a little before 11 a.m. the next day when Maurice Bass walked into Goldberg's, a locally famous delicatessen in Vinings. The morning rush was over, and there were less than a half a dozen customers in the cafe. Tina Manning pumped herself a cup of coffee and was heading down the counter to pick up a bagel with lox, when Maurice stepped in her path.

"Excuse me," she said, without fully looking at him.

"Mrs. Manning?" Bass said, feigning surprise and giving Tina a smile that had once been reserved for prospective clients.

Bass could see from the fear in her eyes that she knew exactly who he was. But Tina regained her composure quickly, gave him a terse smile, and turned her gaze back towards the floor.

Bass didn't move out of the way.

"May I speak with you for a minute?" he said, in a hushed voice. "It's about Mr. Centrella."

Tina looked surprised.

"There's an empty booth in the back," Bass said and nodded his head towards the rear corner of the restaurant. He started walking and she followed him. Maurice took off his trench coat, folded it in half, and set it next to him on the booth. Tina sat against the wall. Her eyes were darting around the restaurant.

"Relax, Mrs. Manning," Bass said. "This is Atlanta. Nobody's paying any attention to us."

She nodded. The only customer near them was a tall, older man who was eating a roast beef sandwich, while engrossed in a copy of the New York Post.

"I'm here to help you," Bass said.

Her hands had a slight tremble. "You are?"

"Yes. I know you were in the car with Remo Centrella, Mrs. Manning. That means, at some point in the very near future, you're going to be arrested."

Tina looked like she might get sick.

"But you can relax, for now. It's not going to happen today."

"I was never in a car with Remo Centrella," she said.

"We got your prints, Mrs. Manning, and we just matched them to the ones you gave to the cops in Vegas."

A look of "a-ha" flashed through her eyes. "Frickin' Kenny," she said. "Do the police know?"

"I haven't given the information to them yet, but I'll obviously have to."

Tina stayed silent for several seconds as Bass pulled two napkins from the dispenser and handed them to her. She wiped her tears away.

"What happens now?"

"Depends on you."

"What do you mean?"

"There's two ways this can play out, Mrs. Manning," Bass said, as he prepared to play his bluff. "The first is I can let the police department know we've matched your prints to the ones taken from the Porsche. If that happens, an arrest warrant will be issued, and the cops will come to your house.

"Because you fled from the scene and never turned yourself in, they won't give you any advance warning. A team of cops will show up unannounced, and they'll take you out in your nightgown and handcuffs.

"And oh, by the way," Maurice said, "they'll tip off the press in advance, which means there will be a picture of your frog walk on the front page of every paper in the country."

"You can't be serious."

"I am," Bass said. "Dead serious. Which is why I strongly recommend you choose option number two."

"What's that?"

"Option two is where your lawyer arranges an opportunity for you to turn yourself in discreetly. Under that scenario, you come in unannounced. You still get arrested, but you get processed and bonded out before anybody knows you've been there. You avoid being dragged out of your house in your nightgown, and your arrest doesn't turn into a public spectacle.

"But," Bass said and held up his index finger, "to do it that way you're going to need a lawyer who knows how to cut a deal. Do you have an attorney, Mrs. Manning?"

Tina shook her head. "Not my own," she said. "My husband does, but I don't have one."

"You should probably think about how you're going to tell your husband about this," Bass said. "I wouldn't recommend you do it at your house. You should probably call and ask him to meet you somewhere public for lunch. This is not the kind of thing you announce casually over coffee."

"My husband's not in the country at the moment."

"Where is he?"

"He's in Canada," she said.

"Does he have *any* clue about this?"

"No," she said, while she looked down at the table. "Ray has no idea. He would never suspect, especially not with Remo."

"What happens when he finds out?

"He'll cut me off," she said. "I'm his third wife. I'll be lucky to get out with my jewelry and a little bit of cash. Maybe he'll be nice and let me keep my car."

"I'm sorry to hear that," Bass said. "I know you're in an extremely difficult situation, which makes me even more determined to try and find a way to help you stay out of prison."

Tina brought her hand up towards her mouth. "I can't go to prison," she said.

They were the magic words Bass wanted to hear.

"Then you better find a lawyer who knows how to cut a deal," he said. "Somebody who can keep you out."

Tina Manning looked numb as Maurice took a piece of paper from his shirt pocket and put it on the table. It had a 770 phone number written above the name "Linda Slotnick."

"Linda Slotnick's a good lawyer," Bass said. "She's a former public defender, who opened her own shop in Decatur. Linda's tough and knows what she's doing. She's the lawyer I would go to if I knew I was about to be arrested."

Tina was studying the piece of paper.

"I suggest you call her," Bass said. "Like right after you and I finish up. Tell her you were in the car with Centrella, and that you want to turn yourself in."

"And if I do that, then what happens?"

"For starters, you retain some control of the situation. As for the rest, a lot of what happens will depend upon what happened the night Remo was killed."

"I'm not sure I understand," she said.

"I'm the District Attorney, Mrs. Manning. I've made the decision to over-rule the Internal Affairs department and bring a manslaughter indictment against a cop. I'm fighting an uphill battle, here. But, as the prosecutor in this case, I have a lot of discretion about what other charges I can bring *or not bring.*

"I have no way of knowing what exactly happened between Mr. Mackno and Mr. Centrella," Bass continued, "only you and he do. But I'm sure you can imagine I'm going to be a lot more lenient with a witness whose testimony helps me convict this defendant than I will be with a witness who offers testimony that makes my job harder."

Tina nodded as Bass picked up his coat.

"I have the power to grant immunity when it makes sense. But it's entirely dependent upon my negotiations with your attorney and how comfortable she can get me with regard to your potential testimony."

Maurice paused to look at Tina. "Do you understand what I'm trying to tell you?" he said.

123

"I do," she said.

Bass stood up.

"Good. I need to go now, Mrs. Manning, but I hope our meeting has been of some help to you. I hope you realize some of your options are better than others."

Tina nodded her head.

Maurice put on his trench coat and pointed towards the outside of the restaurant.

"A major storm is brewing, Mrs. Manning. I wouldn't waste a lot of time if I were you. At some point in the next 72 hours, *at most*, your husband and the rest of the world are going to find out you were the woman in the car with Remo Centrella."

Maurice began to button his coat.

"You don't want to find yourself alone in that storm when it hits because it's going to be like nothing you have ever seen."

Tina Manning was biting her lower lip. She looked even more scared than Maurice had hoped.

At 10 a.m. the next day, Tina Manning met with Linda Slotnick. She told her about the meeting with Maurice, and Linda immediately understood the opportunity he was offering. But as soon as Tina began to tell her what happened on the night of the shooting, Linda cut her off. As her newly retained defense attorney, she didn't want to hear Tina's version of events until Tina had a chance to listen to her hypothetical version of what might have happened.

With Remo dead, Linda understood the trial was going to be a literal situation of "he said, she said." That meant they would have a lot of leeway in developing testimony that would earn Tina immunity from prosecution.

And that, *immunity*, was the only thing that mattered to Slotnick. Now that Tina Manning had retained her services, Linda had only one goal: keep her out of jail. That was the outcome Tina Manning needed, and that was the outcome Linda was going to deliver.

The fact her advocacy on behalf of Tina might lead to

Dave's conviction had zero impact on her. The criminal justice system, as Linda had been taught from day one at Boston University law school, was set up to be an adversarial one. Her job, as a defense attorney, was not to pursue justice or find out the truth; that was for a judge and jury. Her job, the one to which she had sworn an oath, was to be a zealous advocate for her client's interests. That was the *sine qua non* of being a modern day defense attorney. It was the core ethic in which Linda believed, and it was the reason she spent almost two hours hypothesizing and discussing various scenarios with Tina.

At no point in the process did Linda instruct Tina to lie. She didn't have to. All she had to do was lay out a menu of hypothetical possibilities, *a cafeteria style offering of potential testimony,* from which Tina could choose.

It wasn't rocket science, and by noon she had become comfortable enough with Tina's potential testimony to make the call to Maurice. She excused herself from the boardroom and went into her office.

"Ms. Slotnick," Bass said, when he came to the phone. "Good to hear from you. Just an FYI, I have you on speakerphone because I've got Jamie Alexander sitting next to me. I believe you two know each other."

Maurice winked at Jamie.

"We do," Linda said, as the three of them silently remembered the minor brouhaha that occurred a few years earlier at the Bar Association's Holiday party, when Linda's co-worker, and now husband, thought Jamie was dancing a little too closely with her.

"How you doing, Jamie?" Linda said.

"Good, Linda. How's Merrick?"

"He's very good," Linda said.

Bass smiled.

"Send him my best," Alexander said.

"I'm sure he'll appreciate it."

"Jamie's assigned to this case, Linda, so, obviously, anything you want to say to me you can say to him."

"Understood."

"What's going on?"

"I'm calling to inform you I'm now representing Tina Manning. I understand that as part of your investigation process you met with her yesterday."

"That's correct."

"From this point forward, all contact will need to go through me."

"Of course."

"After meeting with Mrs. Manning this morning and discussing her situation, I'd like to set up a time to bring her in to play 'Queen for a Day,'" Linda said, using the colloquial name for a proffer session, in which a witness seeking leniency from a prosecutor agrees to come forward and disclose their potential testimony.

Proffer sessions are a straightforward mechanism that enable prosecutors to get an advance peek at potential evidence a suspect or witness can provide prior to agreeing to a plea deal. The two major stipulations of a proffer session are that the witness offering evidence receives immunity for anything disclosed during the session, and that none of what is proffered, unless otherwise already known to the prosecutor, can be used after the session unless discovered by independent means.

"I'm a buyer," Maurice said. "What's your goal here?"

"Immunity."

"That's a steep hurdle, Linda. Your client is facing a boatload of possible charges."

"She has the potential to be of significant help to your case, Maurice. With Mr. Centrella dead, you might not want to go into court without an eyewitness to back you up."

"Are you saying your client's testimony will help me get a conviction?"

"Is that the type of cooperation for which you might be willing to offer immunity?"

"I'm focused on the big picture, Linda. My goal is to bring this defendant to justice. If your client's testimony can help me do that, I can try my best to keep her out of prison."

"Not good enough, Maurice. She either gets full blown immunity, or I advise her to plead the 5th. Then you're back to square one, except you'll be crying in your Wheaties over what you could have had."

"The optics won't look good," Bass said.

"Ours is not a perfect world, Maurice, but I'm sure you'll be able to live with any bad optics once you hear what she has to say."

"You think it's worth immunity?" Bass said and winked, again, at Alexander.

"I have no doubt it is, but I understand why you might, which is why I'm offering to have the session."

There were several seconds of silence until Bass broke it.

"Okay, I'm in, but it has to be in conjunction with an arrest."

"Can't do it, Maurice."

"You've got no choice, Linda. This isn't an either or situation. Tina Manning is going to be arrested. You already know that. The only thing to be resolved is whether she's going to turn herself in as part of the proffer process or whether APD is going to pick her up on the warrant. There is no third option."

"Alright," Linda said. "It is what it is. You can book her at the end of the session, but I want her bond to be reasonable. Ray Manning might be rich, but she isn't. She gets a monthly check from him and that's about it."

"Understood."

"And I don't want any media to know what's taking place until it's over. I need your word on that, Maurice."

"You have it. Nothing gets to the press until after she makes bond."

"I'll need a couple days to get everything prepped," Linda said. "Does Friday afternoon work for you?"

"It does."

"Good. I'll have her lie low until then."

"One thing, Linda," Maurice said, "you do acknowledge there is no way I can prevent the media from finding out about the arrest once it happens? All I can do is give you a little bit of lead time between when she's booked and when the press picks it up."

"That's all I expect."

"Then we'll get a formal proffer agreement faxed out to you by tomorrow. Just make sure Mrs. Manning understands I can use it to impeach her in the event she has a change of heart at trial."

"I'm very confident you'll have her full cooperation."

"That will be the best course of action for everybody involved," Bass said.

"I know," Linda said.

After Linda finished up her call with Bass, she called Tina into her office and advised her they should call Ray.

"In the long run, it will be a lot better if he hears it from us," she said.

Tina was initially reluctant, but eventually accepted that Linda was right.

Ray Manning was 120 miles northwest of Edmonton, Alberta in an early morning meeting with his foreman, a geologist, and two engineers when his cellphone rang. His week in Canada had been a hard slog, as he and his team had been working around the clock to try and figure out why the project was still not producing any oil. Ray looked at his caller ID. He didn't recognize the number, but saw it was from the 404 area code.

"Excuse me," he said and answered the phone.

"Mr. Manning, my name is Linda Slotnick. Your wife has retained me as her legal counsel."

"Hold on a second, Honey," Ray said. He put the phone by his side and asked the men in the room to step outside. He sat down on one of the chairs in the construction trailer. "One more time. My wife's legal counsel? What's going on? Is Tina okay?"

"Yes, Mr. Manning, your wife is fine. She's asked me to contact you regarding an extremely sensitive matter."

"I've never been good at doubletalk, Honey. Where is my wife?"

"She's sitting next to me."

"Then just go ahead and put her on the phone, if you

don't mind."

"I can't do that until—"

"I don't want to speak with you until I speak to her."

"I'm afraid I can't do that, Mr. Manning. I'll be happy to permit you to speak with your wife once you and I—"

"You'll be happy to *permit* me to speak with my wife? What is this, some kind of a joke?"

He hung up on Linda and dialed Tina's cellphone.

Linda answered.

"Mr. Manning, please, sir," she said, "I'll let you speak with your wife, but first you and I need to talk."

"What the hell is going on here? I'm in middle of the biggest project in the history of Donergy oil, and you and Tina are playing games."

"I don't play games, Mr. Manning."

"What's your name again?"

"It's Linda Slotnick. I'm the founder and managing partner of the Slotnick Law Group."

"Never heard of you, Sweetheart. Now please, put Tina on the phone before I decide to get some real lawyers involved. I promise you that you won't like that."

"I can't do that, Mr. Manning. I'm calling because your wife didn't want you to hear about this in the media."

"Hear about what?"

Linda looked over at Tina who looked like she had begun to cry.

"Let me preface by saying, obviously, this is something your wife would have preferred to be communicated to you in person, but unfortunately, due to the current set of extenuating circumstances, we don't have that luxury."

"Just cut to the chase, Honey."

"I'm sorry to have to inform you, Mr. Manning, your wife was the woman in the car with Remo Centrella on the night he was killed."

"Tina was in the car with Remo?....*Bull-shit.*"

"Now that your wife has retained me as her legal counsel."

"Wrong. She's represented by Johnny Wiemer. You don't represent anybody. Now stop the bullshit and put her on the fucking phone."

"Hold one second," Linda said, and put her phone on mute. "You want to talk to him? You don't have to. He's very upset."

Tina nodded 'yes,' and Linda handed her the phone.

"Ray," Tina said, her voice was breaking and barely audible.

"Is it true?"

"I'm so sorry," she said.

"You fucking tramp."

He stood up in the trailer, dumped over the aluminum desk, and let out a yell loud enough to be heard by the men outside. When he was done, he collapsed back into the seat and sat still for almost five minutes before he placed a call to Johnny Wiemer.

"Send some of the security guys over to my house with instructions that my bitch of a wife is not allowed on my property. If she tries to get in, don't let her."

"Okay," Wiemer said. He had lived through previous crises involving Ray's personal life and knew how to roll with the punches.

"I'm on my way back to Atlanta. Call Craig Bourgeois and give him my cell number. Tell him I want the three of us to meet at my house tomorrow afternoon."

"Will do," Wiemer said.

Ray hung up and called his pilot.

"I need to go home. Pick me up at the site and we'll drive straight to the airport."

"Okay, I'll pick up Nicole and we'll be on the way over."

"No," Ray said. "She's not flying back with us. Tell her my secretary will arrange a one way ticket home to Orlando."

Ray hung up the phone and shook his head.

"I'm done with flight attendants," he said.

At a little after six o'clock on Friday night, Maurice got ready to leave his office for the weekend. The proffer session had ended mid-afternoon, and Tina Manning had been booked and released on bond. Things had gone better than he hoped. Linda Slotnick was a pro and had done a stellar job of preparing her client. She had done such a good job that Maurice was feeling increasingly confident about his chance to get a conviction.

With the *quid pro quo* firmly in place, Bass felt almost giddy as he packed up the files he needed for the weekend. He dialed his home phone and Lisa picked up.

"I'm leaving the office now, Honey," he said.

"You better hurry up, Big Boy. The girls are at my parents, and I'm wearing something that I bought for you from Victoria's Secret."

"God is good," Bass said. "Make yourself one of those chocolate martinis you like to drink."

"The ones that get me really drunk?"

"Exactly. I'm on my way."

He stepped outside his building and was hustling north towards the municipal employees' lot when a black Town Car pulled up beside him. The backdoor opened, and Sonny Komanski leaned across the seat.

"Hop in, Maurice," Komanski said with a smile. "The governor wants to speak with you."

"You gotta be kidding me," Bass said to himself. "How often do I get Lisa drunk with the kids out of the house?"

He looked down at his watch.

"I can't, Sonny," he said. "My wife's expecting me home."

Komanski looked personally offended.

"It's the Governor, Maurice. It will only take a few minutes. I'm sure your wife will understand. You can call her from the car."

Komanski held up a phone that was in the backseat. There was something about Sonny Komanski that Maurice didn't trust. It was magnified by the fact Komanski was smiling at him.

Maurice knew exactly why Durkin wanted to talk with him. From the moment he decided he was going to make a direct approach to Tina Manning, he knew he would have to answer for his actions. He knew Frank Durkin would not be happy about the fact he had not given him a heads-up about Tina Manning, but Bass had decided he had no other choice. He couldn't risk his potential star witness getting ring-fenced behind a team of Ray Manning's lawyers before he had a chance to speak with her directly.

Komanski stepped out of the car and looked across the roof.

"It won't take long," Komanski said. "Frank's up the street at the Westin. He's waiting for you."

Maurice thought quickly about the files that were in his briefcase before saying, "Okay."

"Better to just get the inevitable out of the way," he decided, before climbing into the backseat of the Lincoln.

"Drop us at the rear entrance," Komanski instructed the driver.

Neither man spoke as they drove up International Boulevard to the loading dock underneath the Westin Peachtree Plaza hotel. When they got out, Maurice followed Sonny through a pair of swinging doors and onto a service elevator that took them up to the 8th floor, where they switched elevators for the ride up to 70.

On the 12th floor, a busboy pushing a food cart started to walk on until Sonny stepped forward. "Next one is yours," he said, as his six four frame blocked the way. The busboy didn't argue. The elevator stopped at 70, and Sonny waited as Maurice walked out first.

"Follow me," he said, and headed down the hall, where a uniformed State Trooper was sitting on a banquet chair outside the door to the two story Presidential Suite. The trooper nodded in acknowledgment to Komanski, who used a keycard to open the door.

Sonny led Maurice past a small kitchen into a large living room, where Frank Durkin was sitting in a cloth-back chair. He looked freshly dressed, in a crisp black tuxedo, as he drank from a full flute of champagne.

Durkin didn't get up.

"Have a seat, Maurice," he said. "Would you care for something to drink?"

"Please," Bass said.

"Bring him a water, Sonny."

Bass stayed silent as he took a mental survey of the scene. He and Lisa had stayed in the suite to celebrate their wedding night, and he noticed it had been nicely renovated since that time.

Durkin's hair looked damp. There was a silver platter with some leftover chocolate covered strawberries and an open bottle of Moet on the marble credenza behind him. The door to the suite's bedroom was closed.

Komanski walked up to Maurice from behind and tapped him on the shoulder with an unopened water bottle.

"Ray Manning called me yesterday afternoon, Maurice," Durkin said. "He was very upset. More upset than I've ever heard him. He told me you found out his wife was in the car with Remo Centrella, and he wanted to know what it was going to take to bury the information. I was embarrassed to have to tell him I had no idea what he was talking about."

"I just found out about it a couple of days ago, Governor," Maurice said. "I thought about coming directly to you, but I knew there was nothing you could do. I figured it was better to keep you out of what is obviously an extremely sensitive situation."

"That's not your decision to make," Durkin said. "That's mine. You would be surprised what I can do when necessary."

"The FBI is involved," Maurice said.

Durkin looked at Komanski for a moment and then back to Maurice.

"The Feds?"

Maurice reached into his briefcase and pulled out a copy of the document Jamie Alexander had given to him. He handed the report to Durkin. "This is what the FBI sent to my office early in the week."

Durkin studied the document, which had the FBI's insignia prominently displayed on the front page.

"Page three."

Durkin flipped to the page where Tina Manning's married name was circled in red.

"The same list has been sent to APD," Bass said, strategically omitting that he was the one who sent it to them. "Once I saw the FBI was involved, I knew there was nothing I could do. Their involvement is a game changer."

Komanski gave Durkin a look that said Maurice was right.

"So you contacted Tina Manning directly?" Durkin said.

"I had to. I found out that Ray Manning was out of the country. I wanted to convince her to turn herself in to try and minimize the embarrassment."

"Because the police are going to arrest her?"

"Because the world was going to find out Ray Manning's wife was having an affair with Remo Centrella," Bass said. His face had a pained look on it. "There were no good choices, Governor. *No way to keep this under wraps.* I was looking at major downside no matter what course of action I chose."

Durkin looked down and studied the list of names for several seconds before nodding his head.

"What a fucking mess. I told him not to divorce Monica," Durkin said, shaking his head. "She's a good gal. But when it comes to women, he won't listen to reason."

Komanski's cellphone rang and he answered it. "The First Lady has arrived, Sir," he said.

"Already?" Durkin said, and stood up. He looked at his wristwatch, guzzled the last of his champagne, and smoothed out the sleeves of his tuxedo. He looked at Sonny and nodded towards the bedroom.

Sonny nodded back in acknowledgment.

"I appreciate you coming to see me on such short notice, Maurice. I apologize I gotta cut out of here so quick, but I'm giving the keynote address to the Farm Bureau's annual convention."

Maurice nodded. "I understand," he said.

"You'd be surprised how much money those boys have," Durkin said, and began to head towards the door.

"I'll call Ray later and explain the situation to him," he said. "The last thing we need is for the Feds to start poking their nose around in Georgia."

Maurice nodded in agreement.

"Let Sonny know if you need anything, Maurice,"

Durkin said, before exiting the suite.

By 7 p.m. that evening, every major news outlet in the country was reporting on Tina Manning's arrest and the fact she had been the woman in the car with Remo. The AP's Atlanta bureau put together a seventeen-paragraph story for their subscribers, which included a statement that Linda Slotnick's office had faxed to them. The fax was signed by Tina Manning and stated:

Earlier today, I turned myself in to the Atlanta police department pursuant to the warrant that was out for my arrest. I am the previously unidentified woman who was with Remo Centrella on the evening he was killed.

I am deeply regretful of my actions and would like to sincerely apologize to my husband for the pain and embarrassment I have caused him. I would also like to apologize to the Atlanta Police Department. I did not previously come forward because I was scared and embarrassed about my actions. I chose to protect my family and myself. I was wrong.

While married to Ray Manning, I had an inappropriate relationship with Remo Centrella. For this, I would also like to sincerely apologize to Tiffany Hill.

From this point forward, I plan to cooperate fully with the authorities in order to ensure they will have full knowledge surrounding all the facts that took place on the evening Remo was killed.

I know this process is going to be an extremely painful one for everybody involved. Therefore, I would ask the media, and all of Remo's fans, to please respect my and my husband's privacy, as well as Ms. Hill's, as we pass through this very difficult time. Thank you.

On Saturday morning, Whitney Taylor sat with his wife in the breakfast nook of their house.

"This isn't good," he said, as he took a bite of his English muffin and stared down at the morning edition of the paper. There was a picture of Tina Manning on the cover, underneath a 48-point headline. The accompanying story described her arrest and plans to cooperate with the prosecution. "He beat me to the punch."

Three months away from turning 60 years old, and nearing the twilight of a legal career in which he had minted enough money to ensure his grandchildren would never want for anything, Whitney Taylor had forgotten what it was like to feel like a sucker.

But that's exactly how he felt as he read the story. He fully understood the implication of Tina Manning's decision to cooperate. It meant everything he had assumed about the upcoming trial was no longer valid, and that Dave might have been better off to have chosen Barry Reed as his lawyer.

Whitney couldn't believe how quickly the ground had shifted underneath his feet. Less than two months earlier, he had been a guy expecting an uneventful run towards retirement. Then, out of nowhere, a cop he hadn't remembered called and asked him to take on the highest profile case of his career. A case Whitney knew would likely define it.

At the time, Whitney felt like the call from Dave was a form of divine intervention. Confirmation of his life-long belief that God wanted good things to happen to him. It was a case that offered him the opportunity to validate his opinion that he was the best defense attorney in the Southeastern United States.

But now, all those thoughts, which had seemed so justified, felt embarrassingly grandiose and self-indulgent. Whitney was no longer feeling singled out for greatness by destiny. He was feeling like a chump who had been knocked down by a punch he had never even seen coming.

As Whitney re-read Tina Manning's statement for the third time, he realized what he would have to do. Even though it was a Saturday, he would need to summon Dave to a meeting in which he would be obligated to tell him, for the first time since he agreed to the representation, that Dave better begin to prepare himself mentally, and Darlene emotionally, for the very real likelihood he might be going to prison.

12

___

THREE NIGHTS after Christmas, Maurice Bass' father-in-law, Charlie Simmons, was admitted to Atlanta Medical Center after suffering a stroke.

Lisa and Maurice found out the news when they were awoken by a call from Lisa's mother, Helen, who told her Charlie collapsed while getting up for a glass of water. She told Lisa her father had not been responsive when the EMTs arrived.

Maurice and Lisa jumped out of bed and gathered up their 7-year-old twins for the trip to the hospital. When they arrived at AMC, Maurice dropped Lisa at the entrance to the ER, while he drove with the girls to the parking deck adjacent to it.

As soon as Maurice found Lisa, he could see from the looks on her and Helen's face that things were as grim as he expected. Helen looked dazed as she gave her sleepy granddaughters a hug.

Within a few minutes, a Doctor came to the waiting room where they were sitting. "Your husband's a fighter, Mrs. Simmons," he said, "but it was a major stroke. It will take some time to determine how much damage he suffered. You can go in and see him now, if you wish, but he's heavily sedated."

"Thank you," Lisa said.

She and her mother went in to see Charlie, while Maurice waited with the girls, who had fallen asleep on the sofas. Twenty minutes later, they came out and

Maurice went in. The room was quiet and softly lit by a nightlight in the ceiling. Charlie, who was hooked up to several tubes and machines, looked like he was sleeping peacefully.

"Charlie," Maurice whispered. "It's me, Maurice."

Maurice sat down in a chair next to the bed and took hold of Charlie's hand. There were tears in his eyes.

"How you doing, Man?" he said, while looking around the room. "We need to get you up on out of here."

Charlie had no response.

It was hard for Maurice to believe it had been less than 72 hours since they were at Christmas dinner at Charlie's house. At the time, Charlie had looked like a man near the peak of his powers. Maurice would have never guessed he was close to having a stroke because Charlie had projected the same level of strength and high spirits that he always had. He was so full of energy during the Christmas dinner that Maurice had said to Lisa, "Your father's a force of nature. He's going to outlive all of us."

Now, looking at Charlie, Maurice knew that wasn't true.

It felt impossible to believe. How could the life of such a big man, a guy with such a strong life force, be extinguished so suddenly? Maurice asked himself. How could a stroke fell somebody as tough as Charlie?

Maurice first met Charlie during his freshman year at Morehouse, at a time when his relationship with his parents was near an all-time low. A time when Maurice was struggling with his racial identity and still trying to figure out what it meant to be authentically black.

Almost nobody who knew Maurice Bass would have ever guessed he once struggled with his racial identity. He was, as *Atlanta Weekly* liked to call him, "the legal lion of black Atlanta." But racial identity had been a struggle for him because of his family background. Because Maurice had been adopted into a white family.

It was the greatest regret of his life. *Not the act of being adopted itself*, but the fact he had been adopted by white parents who tried to pretend society was colorblind. It wasn't, which was one of the reasons

Maurice and his parents had spent so much time arguing about his accusations that they had tried to force him to "grow up white."

That charge caused a lot of pain for his parents, but nothing ever hurt them more than the period during college when he referred to them as his "foster parents."

The idea came to him during his freshman year at Morehouse. It was freshman orientation week, and he and some of the guys on his floor were hanging out, indulging in the narcissistic conversation that's a staple of the freshman experience. The guys were enjoying the freedom of being on their own, talking about their backgrounds, families, and the societal challenges they faced growing up as black men in America.

Maurice had managed to avoid talking about his background as long as he could, but he knew the conversation was heading squarely in his direction.

"What's your story, Maurice?" one of his hall mates said, after everyone else had shared their background.

Maurice was just about to cop to being the adopted child of a couple of white hippies, when he heard himself say, "I was raised by some whites in a foster home up north Atlanta."

The statement surprised everyone in the room.

"Word? That's some heavy shit," one of the guys, a freshman from Teaneck, New Jersey said.

Maurice saw the surprise, and more unexpectedly, the respect, in the other guys' eyes when he said it. He wasn't completely sure where the answer had come from, but through it he found an identity he could embrace.

Maurice never forgot the feeling he had that night while sitting on the floor of his dorm room, the pleasantly bitter taste of beer in his mouth and the scent of marijuana lingering in the air. It was as if all the fragmented pieces of his background clicked together into an integrated image of himself: *Maurice Bass, a poor black kid from Atlanta, abandoned by his mother and forced to grow up in a white foster family.*

Before matriculating at Morehouse, Maurice had attended Dumont High School, an elite day school in

Northwest Atlanta, where his older brother and sister had attended. It was at Dumont, during his sophomore year, when Maurice found out the world wasn't color blind. He found it out the first time he got his heart broken.

The girl's name was Erin. She was a senior co-captain on the cheerleading team and the most beautiful girl Maurice had ever seen. She called Maurice "baby bear," and he had fallen in love with her. On the Friday night before Thanksgiving, Erin was at his house for a sleepover with his sister, Rachel, and some of her other friends. Maurice's parents were upstairs in their room reading, trying to give the girls some space in which they could feel independent. Maurice was supposed to be in his room, as well, but he had slipped downstairs and walked up quietly behind Erin.

Earlier in the week, he had taken the bus to Rich's department store and used most of his savings to buy Erin a 14 carat gold necklace as a present. He couldn't wait to see her reaction.

Right before Maurice reached her, Erin turned around and saw him. He stammered something about a gift, and nervously put the square white box in her hands. Erin looked thrilled. She smiled at him and said, "Awww, bay-bee bear," before moving in close to give him a hug.

It was too much for Maurice's 15 year old body to take. He leaned in and kissed her on the lips. It was the first kiss of his life, and Erin's lips were softer than he had imagined. He could feel the endorphins explode in his head, but as he waited for her to kiss him back, he felt her body stiffen and saw her face start to crumble. Erin started to shake before she started to cry.

Maurice felt scared as he saw the girl he loved looking so upset. He gently clasped her shoulder to try and comfort her, but she became more upset. He pulled his hand away from her as Rachel and her friends ran into the kitchen. They came around the corner and saw Maurice standing across from her.

The mini-pack of girls ignored Maurice and huddled around Erin. Nobody asked him what happened before they escorted her back into the family room. But Rachel stared hard and pointed at Maurice. She shook her head with contempt, before she shut the door and set the lock. Maurice got scared. He went up to his room, afraid Erin would call her parents and that he would be in trouble.

But Erin's parents never showed up, and Rachel didn't get their parents involved. By the time Maurice woke up the next morning, Rachel and her friends had left for the homecoming game. He was supposed to go and meet his own friends there, but he didn't. Instead, he stayed in his room for most of the day, looking at himself in the mirror, and fully recognizing his blackness for the first time.

As Maurice stared at himself in the mirror, he knew Erin had rejected him simply because of the color of his skin. Simply because he was black.

After that, it didn't take long before Maurice's parents started to notice changes in him. Their sweet, sometimes silly, but always happy and talkative son, steadily became a more serious and withdrawn kid. The gregarious boy, who had been born with a naturally outgoing personality, became more scarce at home, as he pursued a path that he was determined would lead him away from the white culture in which he had been raised.

As his sophomore year progressed, Maurice found the first true love of his life: music. He replaced his Peter Frampton and Simon & Garfunkel albums with ones by funk groups, soul musicians and jazz artists. He began to read books about the civil rights struggle and slavery, and, for the first time, he started to identify with black culture and its thought leaders.

Maurice's teachers at Dumont had no clue how to handle the changes in him. As an elite private school in Atlanta, it was set up to deal with the problems of privileged white kids, not black kids who were starting to question the foundational structures of society. The administration became concerned with what they described as his "militant" voice.

"This isn't San Francisco, Mr. and Mrs. Bass," Dumont's principal said. "This is Atlanta. Everybody here's supposed to go along to get along."

No one on the faculty spent time wondering if schools like Dumont "perpetuated institutionalized racism," much less had any experience dealing with a student who wanted to confront it. *They were perfectly content with the status quo.* Issues of racial equality and the amelioration of social injustice simply were not part of the school's fabric. They were already too busy planning pep rallies, homecoming weekend, and Sadie Hawkins' dances.

Being called in to discuss what the Dean of Students called Maurice's "anti-social tendencies" was a first for his parents. With their oldest two children already proud alumni of Dumont, their initial instinct was to be supportive of the faculty. But when Maurice claimed they were treating him like a token, they changed their minds and told the administration they supported their son.

After some serious soul-searching, Maurice's parents promised to make amends for not having done more to expose him to black culture. His mother started to drive him down to the King Recreation Center, which was south of downtown and comprised of primarily black members. And one night, during his junior year, Maurice's father stayed parked outside West Side High for three hours while Maurice attended a dance with the daughter of one of his father's few black friends.

When Maurice turned 17, his parents bought him a used Ford Pinto. Without asking permission, he sold it and bought a new hi-fi system, motorcycle and color television.

His mother was furious with him, he already had a perfectly good stereo system, but his father said they needed to respect Maurice's decisions even if they didn't agree with them. Which his mother certainly did not.

From the moment Anne Bass first laid eyes on Maurice, she considered him her bonus gift from God. Before the adoption, she had braced herself for the chance Maurice might be more difficult and challenging than her two natural born children. But her worries had been a waste of time. Maurice had been much easier than his older brother and sister. He had been the textbook "angel" baby, blessed with a naturally happy disposition.

Even as a baby, it was obvious that Maurice was scary smart. His mother had been the first one in the family to recognize it, and she never had a problem telling people he was the smartest of her three children.

At one point in time, Anne Bass might have been the proudest mother in Atlanta as she envisioned the day when Maurice would grow up and use his gifts to become a transformative figure. One night, when Maurice was in grade school and his parents were discussing the fact he might need to skip a grade, Anne told her husband that God had given her a vision that Maurice would help bring racial healing to America. And even though the adoption agency told her Maurice's birth father was from Chicago, a part of her secretly believed it was possible he could be the progeny of Dr. King.

Anne Bass would have never dreamt the child she had often referred to as the "chosen one" would one day grow up to be a divisive civil rights lawyer, openly despised by much of white Atlanta. Or that he would casually announce, over a holiday dinner, that he had come to think of himself as being raised in a foster family.

It was Thanksgiving night of Maurice's freshman year, and he made the comment, seemingly off the cuff, near the end of the meal. Throughout the dinner, Maurice had been masterful in steering the conversation towards life at Morehouse, and how exhilarating it was to finally be immersed in the culture of his own people. The "my own people" comment had been heard enough times that his parents had become immune to it. But Maurice was just warming up.

Almost 19 years old, Maurice now looked like a hard-core intellectual. He had finally been able to grow a full goatee, and he wore the brow-line style glasses favored by Malcolm X. No one at the table had any doubt how seriously Maurice took himself. His mother was simply praying that dinner would end without any major upsets.

Externally, Maurice maintained an almost detached visage, as he lectured about how imperative it was to be vigilant in the fight against racial stereotypes. Internally, he felt almost giddy as he wound the clock towards a confrontation.

One of the things Maurice loved about addressing racial injustice with his family was the way he could completely marginalize his brother and sister. What could they know about the authentic experience of being a black man in America? Rachel was a junior at Duke, and Harold was in a fraternity at LSU, where Maurice found out they still dressed up as Confederate Generals to celebrate Jefferson Davis' birthday.

As Thanksgiving dinner neared an end, Maurice began discussing the high caliber students at Morehouse, and how they were completely at odds with the media's stereotypes of black people. It was a safe topic, one to which his parents could voice their full support. His mother had actually started to relax. But just as she did, Maurice made his move. Without skipping a beat, or changing his expression, Maurice explained how he was one of the few students at Morehouse who had been raised in a foster home and how excited he was that his academic advisor had tapped him to help write a paper on the negative aspects of inter-racial adoption.

The words "foster parents" stunned his family. It was more than his mother could take. She began to cry, and in one of the few times Maurice could recall, his father lost his temper. He stood up and knocked over the gravy boat as he ordered Maurice to take his "ungrateful ass" away from the table and not come back until he apologized to the entire family.

"I won't tolerate that kind of disrespect towards your mother or yourself," he said.

"Fine," Maurice said, as sullenly as possible. "I was done eating anyway."

He got up from the table and walked away. At 18 years old, he wasn't concerned about hurting his mother's feelings. He was completely stoked by the turmoil he created. He went to his room, grabbed his duffel bag, and left for Morehouse without even a good-bye.

Maurice felt completely liberated as he walked out of the house. Heading back to campus before the end of break made him feel like a genuine hardship case.

When Maurice got back to his dorm, he ran into a couple of the guys who hadn't been able to afford to go home for Thanksgiving. They were surprised to see him back and asked him what was going on.

"Too much drama with my foster family," Maurice said cryptically, and the other guys had nodded knowingly in response.

On Saturday, his roommate invited Maurice to an off-campus dinner at the home of a wealthy Morehouse alum named Charlie Simmons.

Charlie was a big-time donor to the University, who had one daughter at Spelman and another on the way. He took an instant liking to Maurice, and they ended up talking after dinner for over an hour. Maurice explained the challenges of his background, and Charlie empathized with his plight.

During the conversation, he confided to Maurice what he said was the greatest truth he knew. "Never fully trust any white person, Maurice. I don't care who they are or what they promise. When it gets down to it, they'll always try to cheat you out of what is rightfully yours.

"They can't help it," he said, "that's just the way they're made."

It was a lesson Charlie said he had been forced to learn the hard way, and it was the reason he had started his own insurance agency.

"No way I was going to let any white person control my destiny," he said. "Not after they kept me out of the Major Leagues."

"How did they do that?" Maurice said.

"By labeling me a trouble maker," Charlie said.

He led Maurice out to his basement level patio, where he lit an after-dinner cigar. It was an Oliva.

"I was better than 90% of the whites they had playing," Charlie said, as if simply stating a fact. "But when they started to integrate the Leagues, I never got my shot."

Charlie tapped his index finger to his chest.

"Even though I had served during the war; even though I was one of the guys that helped liberate some of

Hitler's camps."

"You helped liberate concentration camps?" Bass said.

"Don't look so surprised, Maurice," Charlie said, with the cigar in his mouth. "Just because the history books don't teach it, doesn't mean it didn't happen."

"I never even heard about anything like that," Maurice said.

"There's a whole lot of stuff you've never heard about," Charlie said. "Remember who's writing the books."

"True," Maurice said. He recalled saying the almost exact same words to a history teacher at Dumont.

"When the war ended, I came back to Georgia and started playing ball again for one of the teams down in Columbus. In the next couple of years, baseball started to integrate, and I saw it as my opportunity. I was in my mid-twenties. Still in my prime, and most people knew I was as good as anybody in the state."

Charlie shook his head.

"Problem was, they never gave me my opportunity."

"Why not?"

"Because I stood up for myself," Charlie said. "Because I had to take a piss."

Charlie added a couple of logs to his fire pit before sitting down in one of his Adirondack chairs.

"We were down in Bradenton," Charlie said, as he let out a big puff from his cigar. "We were on a road trip to play three games against the Nine Devils. It was the middle of July and hot as Hell. We had a night game scheduled, so I grabbed a couple of my guys, and we took a trolley over to the Ringling museum. It was full of the art he picked up from all over the world, and we ended up staying there until closing time. We were about to leave, when I realized I had to piss like a racehorse. So I walked up to one of the guards they had dressed up like a ringmaster and asked him where the john was located. He told me the white restrooms were inside, but that the colored ones were outside, behind the building.

"That wasn't a surprise. You gotta remember, it was still the 1940s, and it was the Deep South. Segregation was just part of life, *like going to church*, so I didn't think anything about it at the time. He walked back towards the exhibits and we started walking towards the front door.

"By this time, I really gotta go. Right as we're about to leave, I see a perfectly good restroom next to the exit with a sign that said "men" on it. So I stopped. I looked around and the place is empty. I say to my guys, 'I can't wait. I'm going to use the white lavatory."

A smile of remembrance came to Charlie's face.

"Eustis, who was one of the older guys on the team, he tells me I'm crazy and that I better get my ass outside before I get us in trouble. But I could see he didn't fully mean what he was saying," Charlie said. "I could see a part of him wanted to see if I actually had the guts to use the whites' bathroom. The other guy, a younger kid we used to call Woody, didn't say anything. He was from Alabama. He was just stunned I would even think about the idea."

Charlie laughed.

"'*Relax*,' I said to Eustis. 'Nobody will even notice. Just wait here and I'll be right back out.' I figured it didn't really matter to the urinal if I was black or white, if you know what I mean.

"What I didn't know was that the security guard, who I thought walked away, was watching us."

Charlie brought the cigar to his mouth, struck another match, and said, before re-lighting his cigar, "Back then they used to teach the little bastards to be vigilant about threats to their way of life."

Maurice nodded his head as Charlie let out a few quick puffs of his cigar.

"So I'm in the john, about halfway done taking a leak, when the little man comes charging in and starts accusing me of breaking the law. Now, you got to remember, Maurice, I was twenty four years old at the time and built like a South Georgia brick house. I finish up my business and tell him it won't be a problem because I'm already done. But the security guard, who must have been a foot shorter than me, wasn't just going to let me walk after breaking the law. Didn't matter to him how big I was because I wasn't a threat. I was just supposed to be a docile Negro who knew my place.

"The problem for him was that I wasn't intimidated by white people. I'd been around them during the war, and I had figured out they weren't anything special. I wasn't about to feel guilty about taking a piss in the their bathroom."

Maurice was smiling as Charlie told his story.

"I'm about to walk out the door when the little sonuvabitch decides to step in front of me."

"Blocking it?" Maurice said.

"Trying to....but that wasn't going to happen. I told him it would be highly advisable for him to get out of my way."

"Did he?"

"No," Charlie said. "Little man stepped towards me. 'B-b--boy,' he says to me, 'you don't go nowhere until I get the police.'"

Charlie clasped his hands together.

"Well, when he called me that, I stepped right into his face,"

"'Now you listen to me,' I whispered. 'I'm gonna let that comment slide because I've had a real pleasant day here at your museum, and I need to get to a ball game. But I'm finished with this lavatory, and I'm fixing to leave. I can either walk by you or through you. The choice is yours, *Boy.*"

Charlie's eyes danced. *"He didn't like that."*

"What happened?"

"He stepped aside, and we left the museum. We went back to the hotel, got our gear, and went to the game."

Charlie stood up and led Maurice back to the bar area, where he refreshed their drinks and sat down on one of the bar stools.

"We crushed the Nine Devils that night," Charlie said. "I think I went 3 for 4, with a triple. After the game, everybody was in a good mood. We were packing up, bullshitting back and forth, when a couple of police sedans came driving into the parking lot. They stopped next to the field, and four cops started walking towards us."

Charlie shook his head. "The little SOB was trailing right behind them," he said. "One of the cops came up to me and said I was under arrest for using the whites' bathroom and threatening to assault the guard.

"'I didn't threaten to assault anybody,' I said, but he didn't care. 'Tell it to the judge,' he says.

"I didn't resist, of course. I was angry, but I knew better than to give a white cop an excuse to crack open my head. It wasn't like today. There wasn't anybody around back then to protect your rights. They took me to their little one-story cement police station near the river and threw me into their drunk cell for the night. The next morning, they brought me in front of the local judge, and I thought I was in big trouble. He was an old white man with a face as red as a watermelon. One look at him and you knew he must have spent most of the day pickled.

"He starts up the trial, they didn't even give me a defense attorney, and after about ten minutes, says he's heard enough. That he's ready to rule, but do I want to say anything for myself. Just as I'm about to say something, my manager stood up and told the judge I had a wife back in Georgia and that I was a veteran.

"'You served in the war?" the Judge said, addressing me directly for the first time.

"'Yes sir,' I said. "761st Battalion, the Black Panthers. Nazi killers, through and through."

Charlie was beaming.

"Then the Judge looks at the guard and says 'How about you?

"'Me?' the little man says.

"'Yeah, you. You a veteran?' the Judge asked him.

"'Uh, no," the dude says, and starts saying he's got a bad back or some bullshit excuse like that. I don't remember what exactly, but the Judge didn't care. He cut him off and said it's time to make his ruling."

Charlie paused for a moment and looked directly into Maurice's eyes.

"Not guilty. Case dismissed," Charlie said, and clapped his hands together.

"Dang," Maurice said.

"Turns out, the judge's son had been killed at Normandy," Charlie said, and pursed his lips. "The judge respected me for my service and kept me out of jail. But the security guard still kept me out of the big leagues."

"How'd he do that?" Bass said.

"Baseball's a small world, Maurice. When we got back to Georgia, word got around to the scouts that I had been arrested for breaking segregation laws. They started saying I was a troublemaker who didn't want to follow the rules. *That I was too proud. That I wasn't the kind of guy who would be good for integration.*

"I didn't know it at the time, but after the arrest down in Bradenton, I never even had a chance. I played another couple of years for Columbus until I blew out my knee trying to turn a double play. When that happened, it was lights out."

Charlie snapped his fingers.

"My baseball career was over. Helen and I moved up to Atlanta so I could attend Morehouse on the GI Bill. After graduation, I started selling life insurance. Within 18 months, I went out on my own and never looked back.

"I've had my insurance agency for over thirty years, Maurice, and now I'm a multi-millionaire. Look around this house, Son. Everything you see I earned by working for myself."

Maurice saw the pride burning in Charlie's eyes.

"If I've learned one thing in life Maurice, it's this—If you work hard, the world will give you what you earn. *Especially if you got your education.* That's how they kept us down in the past. Keeping us in third-rate schools to keep us ignorant. Refusing to educate us and then saying we can't learn. But Thurgood changed that for us, didn't he?"

Maurice nodded. "Yes, sir," he said.

"Now young brothers like you, cats willing to stand up and fight for what you deserve, *willing to demand equal opportunities*, you're the ones that are going to help undo the centuries of damage they put on us."

Charlie paused and pointed directly at Maurice.

"But let me warn you, Maurice, it's going to have to be

done through the courts. It'll never happen by legislation, and it'll never happen voluntarily. They won't let it. There's too many of them and not enough of us. We're going to have to force them to do it by changing the laws. Don't ever forget that. If you're serious about wanting to help your people, you need to become a lawyer. That's how change will happen. By brothers like you fighting for it."

The conversation changed Maurice's life and set him on a path towards law school. He had never been around anyone like Charlie Simmons, a self-made black man with a confidence and character that seemed like it was poured out of a concrete truck. He was the polar opposite of who Maurice was at the time.

When Charlie's younger daughter, Lisa, started at Spelman the next year, she and Maurice began dating. As good-looking as she was, part of the reason Maurice wanted to date her was the opportunity to spend some more time around her father.

Charlie had been as good a father-in-law as Maurice could have imagined. Over the years, they had forged a tight bond, even while Maurice had repaired the relationship with his own parents. It was the reason that saying good-bye to Charlie was going to be so hard.

"Charlie, can you hear me?" Maurice said.

There was still no response.

"I want to thank you for everything. All you've done for me. I'm going to try and take everything I learned from you and pass it on. I'll do my best to make you proud, Charlie."

Maurice squeezed Charlie's hand and was convinced he heard him say, in a voice that was barely audible, "I already am."

Charlie didn't make it through the next night. His vitals turned for the worse and he died with Maurice, Lisa, her sister who had flown in from Texas, and Helen praying by his side.

Four days later, after a wake at which almost every prominent African American in Atlanta stopped by to pay their last respects, Charlie Simmons was buried in

Oakland cemetery.

13

DAVE'S TRIAL for manslaughter began the third week of February inside Judge Margaret Friedman's courtroom.

Friedman had been a judge in Atlanta for over twenty years. Raised down in Thomasville, Georgia, she was handpicked for the trial by Robinson Everett, Chief Judge of the Circuit, whose main goal was to try and keep the trial from turning into an "Ito-esque" circus that would embarrass the city.

Other judges had lobbied hard for the case, but Everett knew Friedman would be the least likely candidate to go shopping for a book deal after the trial.

Judge Friedman had short black hair and wore coke bottle glasses on a five foot one, no frills frame. She was the polar opposite of a stereotypical Southern belle, but whatever she lacked in physical gifts, she more than made up for with mental ones. Smart and efficient, it took her four days to seat the jury. Two days less than most legal pundits predicted.

Whitney had filed a pre-trial motion to get the trial moved out of Atlanta. He argued Dave wouldn't be able to get a fair trial in a city where Remo had been so revered, but Judge Friedman denied it. She told Whitney she was confident in her ability to find a pool of 12 objective jurors within a city of four million people.

Whitney had not expected to win the motion, *trials were rarely moved out of a city the size of Atlanta,* but it had been an easy shot across Bass' bow, and it sent the message he wasn't going to concede anything.

Under the Rules of Criminal Procedure, the prosecution begins a trial by delivering the first opening statement. So, once the jury was seated, Judge Friedman gaveled her courtroom into session and asked Maurice if the State of Georgia was ready to proceed.

"We are, Your Honor," Bass said, and stepped forward to address the jury. "Ladies and Gentlemen, we begin this trial with a very simple premise. It is this: The concept of self-defense, *while firmly established in the law*, is not applicable in all situations. As a matter of fact, it's only justified in very limited situations. Situations in which very specific criteria must be met.

"And," Bass said, "that's not just me saying it. That's the law. Those are the instructions which the Judge will give to you. *Self-Defense can only be used as an affirmative defense when specific conditions are met.*

"Here, Ladies and Gentlemen, is the bottom line truth of this case: this defendant's actions do not meet the criteria where he will be entitled to an acquittal. Put simply, as you learn the true facts of this case, you will realize that the killing of Remo Centrella was not a matter of self-defense."

"Now, let's be honest with ourselves, the defense is going to tell you something different. They're going to try and get you to acquit the defendant based upon a self-defense argument.

"That, Ladies and Gentlemen, would be incorrect under the law. It would be incorrect for several reasons. First, the doctrine of self-defense does not allow a person to be the aggressor. Second, the doctrine of self-defense does not allow a person the right to commit a felony. And thirdly, the doctrine of self-defense does not relieve a police officer, *or anybody else*, from the requirement they act in the way that a reasonable man would.

"Unfortunately for this defendant," Bass said, "he did not meet those requirements. Quite the opposite. As this trial will show, prior to shooting Remo Centrella, the defendant did a surprisingly high number of things wrong. He acted in a way that one of our expert witnesses will tell you was 'incompetent.' He was the aggressor in the situation, he used excessive force, and, perhaps most egregiously, he failed to call for backup.

"To put it simply, Ladies and Gentlemen, this defendant's actions failed to meet the legal standard required for you to acquit him.

"This defendant," Bass said and pointed directly at Dave, "did not act in a reasonable manner. He acted in a manner that was reckless. It was his provocation, *his negligence in rapidly escalating the situation*, that made it necessary to use excessive force. And it is for that reason, the law will require you to vote him guilty.

"*But for* the accused's mistakes, miscalculations, and recklessness," Bass said and once again jabbed his finger towards Dave, "Remo Centrella would be alive today, getting ready to play another season of baseball for the Atlanta Barons."

Behind a look that conveyed an image of complete serenity, Whitney was studying the jury intently. He saw they were open to accepting Bass' argument. A dozen years after their first confrontation, Bass had become even better than Whitney had expected. There were no longer any rough edges to him. He looked and sounded as confident as if the jury had already delivered a guilty verdict. He wasn't even *asking* the jury to convict Dave, he was instructing them to do it.

But it was more than just Bass' style that impressed Whitney. He thought the content and focus of his opening statement was almost pitch perfect. Bass had found the exact seam Whitney would have tried to exploit if he was prosecuting the case: the rapid escalation of the situation, Dave's failure to diffuse it by calling for back-up, and his initiation of the physical confrontation. They were all points Whitney knew would resonate with the jury, and they were all points Bass was clearly going to try and hammer into the jurors' minds.

"Now, let me take a moment to talk about this process, if I can," Bass said. "I've been through enough jury cases in my career to know how stressful it is to serve on one.

There's nothing fun about serving on a jury. That's why, when most people get a jury summons, the first thing they do is try and think of a way to get out of it. Am I right?"

There were some heads nodding and even a couple of soft "uh-hmms" from the jurors.

"But that's not what y'all did. No. Fortunately for us, y'all did the right thing. You stepped up to do your civic duty. You stepped up to make sure our justice system works. To make sure that this defendant gets his Constitutional right to a fair trial.

"Let me just say, I commend you for that because without citizens like you willing to serve on juries, that fundamental right, *the right to a fair trial*, would be nothing more than an empty promise."

Bass pointed at the jury box.

"Each one of you should feel extremely proud of yourselves for ensuring that this defendant's constitutional rights are protected."

"That's damn good," Whitney thought to himself. He knew Bass wasn't just bonding with the jury by complimenting them and addressing them as "y'all," he was also sending them the message that he was also concerned about Dave getting a fair trial.

Whitney knew some jurors would interpret Bass' statement to mean he had no personal vendetta against Dave. That he must have only brought the charges against Dave because he was convinced of his guilt. It was the kind of thinking that, if left unchecked, could end up being dangerous to Dave.

"And I understand," Bass said, "that with this process comes nerves because you want to get it right. As a matter of fact, if there's one truth on which everyone in this courtroom can agree, it's that none of us would ever want to convict an innocent man. Am I right?"

Once again, Whitney saw that all the jurors nodded their heads. Like any good trial attorney, Bass was doing his best to get the jurors in the habit of agreeing with him.

"If that's a fear you have," Bass said, "let me assure

you, it is not an irrational one. As a matter of fact, it's perfectly normal. What it simply means is you want to get the verdict right.

"The good news is," he said and took a step backwards, "I'm confident you will. As I stand before you today, I have no doubt that by the time this trial is over, by the time you have seen all the evidence, and heard all the testimony, you will be firmly convinced of this defendant's guilt. That is a promise I make to you, Ladies and Gentlemen, and let me assure you, it is not one I make lightly. When I make a promise, I keep it.

"I thank you for your service on this jury, and I look forward to the opportunity to present evidence to you on behalf of the great state of Georgia."

Bass turned towards Judge Friedman. "Thank you, Your Honor," he said. He gave the slightest of bows to the jury box and returned to his seat at the prosecution table.

It was then Whitney's turn to make his opening statement, in which he planned to try and undermine everything Bass had just told the jury.

"Ladies and Gentlemen," Whitney began, "I want to start this process by making one thing perfectly clear. The only reason my client, Detective David Mackno, is sitting in this courtroom today is because he has been unjustly and unfairly accused by this prosecutor."

Whitney turned and pointed accusingly at Bass, *just as Bass had done to Dave.* It was an aggressive move, designed to let the jury know how strongly he felt about his case, and to plant the seed in their minds that Bass' motives deserved some scrutiny.

"Now, just like this prosecutor, I have had the opportunity to try many cases in my legal career. And if there's one thing I've learned during that time, *if there's one thing that makes total sense,* it's that when the state of Georgia brings a man into a courtroom, sits him down in front of a jury, and tells the jury he's guilty, there's a natural inclination for you, as jurors, to probably believe the Defendant is, in fact, guilty.

"It's human nature, is it not? Common sense to think, no, *scratch that*, to trust, that the State of Georgia would not spend all of this time, effort and resources to put a man on trial unless they were convinced of his guilt."

Whitney paused for several seconds.

"You want to know the truth?" he said. "Most of the time that assumption is correct. Most of the time, when a jury is empaneled in a criminal matter, it's because the defendant is, in fact, guilty. I'll be the first one in this courtroom to admit that the State of Georgia is not in the business of putting innocent people on trial. I agree one hundred percent that their overriding goal is in putting guilty people on trial.

But, *and this is what you need to remember*, that's not always the case. The criminal system is far from perfect, and sometimes a person is brought to trial for reasons that don't have anything to do with guilt and innocence. Sometimes a defendant is put on trial due to political pressure, public outcry, or even the desire to make an example of somebody.

"I know that might sound a little controversial, but I'm sure that everybody in this courtroom knows it's true."

Whitney pointed into the air.

"That's *exactly* what has happened in this case, Ladies and Gentlemen. My client, *a good man*, a veteran detective, is on trial for one simple reason: Remo Centrella was a famous athlete who didn't think that the normal rules of life applied to him.

"Remo Centrella was a star, Ladies and Gentlemen. No one could ever deny that. To be completely candid, when it came to hitting a baseball, I don't think anyone has ever been better. He was the *home run king*. A hero to most of us in Atlanta. And because of that, the prosecution has decided that a different set of rules should apply to him.

"They seem to think Remo Centrella is entitled to a different standard than you or I would be. That he was above the law."

Whitney shook his head remorsefully. "That's not right, is it? *That's wrong*. Thankfully, that's not how our legal system works. We don't have different standards for different people. *Or at least we're not supposed to.* Justice is *supposed to be* blind.

"Every person who comes into this courtroom is supposed to have a Constitutional guarantee of equal protection under the law. Each one of us is supposed to be treated the same. That's not a goal, Ladies and Gentlemen. That's not an ideal. That's the law.

"Now, you heard Mr. Bass make reference in his opening statement to protecting the Defendant's rights. If you're like me, you might have been a little bit moved when you heard him say it. Perhaps you thought this isn't personal for Mr. Bass, that he's just as concerned about protecting Mr. Mackno's rights as you and I are."

Whitney pointed at the jury.

"Don't believe it," he said. "Not even for a second. Mr. Bass is interested in one thing and one thing only, trying to convict my client.

"Doesn't make him a bad person. That's his job. The fact is, if Mr. Bass were not the District Attorney, if he were still in private practice, Mr. Mackno might have hired him to be his defense counsel. Mr. Bass might be the one standing in front of you right now, making just as passionate an argument in favor of Detective Mackno's innocence, as I will. He would be the one explaining to you all the reasons why Mr. Mackno isn't guilty. That's just the way our adversarial system is set up to work."

Whitney paused for a few seconds to make sure the jury was focused.

"You want to know who is here to protect Mr. Mackno's rights?" Whitney said. "You are. You're the ones who will stand up and say that the truth matters. You're the ones who will make it clear to everybody watching this trial that there are not two separate standards of justice under the law.

"*And for that*, Ladies and Gentlemen, I'm extremely grateful. I'm grateful because I'm very confident you twelve jurors will be able see the truth of this case for what it is. As you watch this trial unfold, Ladies and Gentlemen, I hope you ask yourself this question—'If an average citizen went into an alcohol-fueled steroid rage, in which that citizen tried to kick a police officer to death, and that police officer was forced to discharge his weapon to defend his own life, do you think you would be sitting in court today in judgment of that officer?

"No, of course you wouldn't," Whitney said, "because it would be an obvious case of self-defense. The DA's office would close it as a matter of common sense, and each of us in here would know that the person who had been killed was the person at fault. That the police officer, just like any other citizen in this city, had the legal right to defend himself.

"It's one of the simplest and most well established concepts in the law. If a person is about to be killed, they have the absolute right to defend themselves. That fundamental truth applies whether that violent attacker happens to be a rapist, a home invader, a terrorist, or a home run king trying to kick a cop to death. The right of self-defense *always* remains, even if the person acting in self-defense is acting against a famous athlete.

"Ladies and Gentlemen, there's only one person who should be blamed for Remo Centrella's death and that's him. He's the one who resisted a lawful arrest, he's the one who tried to run over my client, and he's the one who tried to kill Mr. Mackno."

Whitney lowered his voice and slowed down his speech.

"Now, you might be asking yourself 'why did Remo do it?' Why did Remo act the way he did. I'll tell you why. It was because he was about to be exposed as a complete fraud, whose true character was the exact opposite of the image he sold to us."

Whitney paused, pursed his lips, and nodded his head several times.

"That's a harsh statement, I know. I understand that. As people of good will, we want to think the best of our athletic heroes. We don't want to believe that somebody would intentionally mislead us or willfully prey upon our trust. But that, unfortunately, is what Mr. Centrella did.

"Facts are stubborn things, Ladies and Gentlemen, and we now know more facts about Mr. Centrella than we ever wanted. We now know that Remo Centrella, a man who publicly denied using steroids, had two different kinds of illegal steroids in his system when he died. And we now know that Remo Centrella, the man who claimed God and family were the two most important things in his life, was in a car at three in the morning with a woman who was not his wife."

Whitney looked down towards the floor and raised his index finger into the air. "But it wasn't just some random woman, Ladies and Gentleman. Not at all. It was the wife of Ray Manning, owner of the Atlanta Barons. A man who considered Remo a close friend. A man who trusted Remo Centrella. A man who even asked him to be the best man in their wedding. Stunning when you think about it, but that's the kind of guy Remo Centrella truly was.

"Here's the truth, Ladies and Gentlemen: Remo Salvatori Centrella was the opposite of a hero. He wasn't a moral person. He was an immoral one. *That's an indisputable fact*, and you need to remember it."

Whitney moved closer towards the jury box.

"Let me conclude my opening statement by making one final point," he said. *"This is extremely important.* You're going to hear a lot of different witnesses say a lot of contradictory things during this trial. And as jurors, you're going to need to use your best judgment to make a determination of what the truth is. Who is telling it, and who isn't. Who's testifying, and who is, as they like to say, *testi-lying.*

"But the one thing I want you to remember, the one thing that will never be in dispute in this case, is that at the exact moment Mr. Mackno fired his weapon, he was almost dead. He was at a point where he could no longer protect himself from the violence Remo Centrella was inflicting upon him.

"Remo Centrella was kicking Mr. Mackno to death," Whitney grunted, and began to imitate kicking an invisible man. "He was just giving it to Detective Mackno. *Kicking, kicking, kicking!* Unleashing a steroid laced anger to try and kill him.

"You can imagine the horror that Detective Mackno must have felt. Remo Centrella, a six foot six, 250 pound athlete, full of demons, full of uncontrolled rage, and unleashing a relentless barrage of attacks delivered with the sole and specific intent of trying...to...kill...him.

"Don't ever lose track of that fact, Ladies and Gentlemen. *Remo Centrella was trying to kill Mr. Mackno.* Thankfully, Detective Mackno was able to locate his weapon, and use it in a way that the law allows. *He was able to use it in self-defense.*"

Whitney stopped, and his eyes went back and forth across the jury box. He slowed his speech and lowered his voice to a stage whisper: "When he had no other choice."

"Remember that, Ladies and Gentlemen," Whitney said. "Remo Centrella left Mr. Mackno *no other choice.*

"I thank you for your service," he said, before nodding to Judge Friedman and returning to his seat.

With both opening statements finished, Judge Friedman declared a recess for lunch. Court went out of session until shortly after one o'clock, when the prosecution called its first witness to the stand.

14

———

MAURICE BASS had always been an aggressive litigator and his plan was to inflict as much damage to Dave's reputation as he could. "If you destroy the reputation, you kill the credibility," was the trial maxim Bass lived by in court. He wanted the jury to form a visceral dislike of Dave that they would bring with them into deliberations. To accomplish that, he wanted to get the jury to think of Dave as a cop with a propensity towards violence.

In the months leading up to the trial, Jamie Alexander had been able to locate five witnesses who swore out affidavits that Dave used excessive force while arresting them.

Dave wasn't surprised. He knew Bass' office would have been able to find five witnesses that claimed Mother Theresa roughed them up, if she had spent twenty years working in Zone 3.

Whitney argued to try and keep the witnesses out. He said that testimony about previous actions by Dave was irrelevant to what took place on the night Remo was killed, and that the prejudicial value of the testimony far outweighed its probative value.

But Judge Friedman ruled the prosecution had the right to argue "pattern." She said Bass could call the witnesses, but that she was going to limit him to two.

"You don't need five people to make your point," she said. "You can put two of your five on the stand."

The first witness Bass called to the stand was Cary

Limerick, a small-time hood from South Boston, who had jumped bail on a "Breaking and Entering" charge and fled to Atlanta with a couple thousand bucks and some fake I.D.s.

Limerick tried to go straight for a couple of months by bartending at the Foxxy Lady, a third rate strip club on Roswell Road, but he was fired after he punched another bartender who thought he might be gay and grabbed his ass.

With almost no legitimate skills, and unable to find another job, he started stealing cars from the long-term lots at Hartsfield International Airport. It turned out to be a pretty easy and lucrative gig for almost a year.

As part of what Cary called his "Cars4Cash" system, he would check into a room at the Sheraton Gateway hotel that overlooked the extended stay lots and use binoculars to identify a family that was traveling with a large amount of luggage.

The next morning, when the airport started to get active, he would ride one of the parking shuttles into the lot and boost the car he had targeted. He would then drive it up I-85 to Charlotte and hand it off to a guy who worked for his uncle.

Flush with fresh cash, Limerick would hop an Amtrak back to Atlanta and act like a big shot until his stack ran out. It was a system as simple as rinse, wash, and repeat until the 11th car was stolen and the Inquirer ran a front-page article titled **"Stolen Car Epidemic takes hold at Hartsfield."**

After the article ran, APD put together a task force to start staking out the lots. Dave was one of the cops assigned on the morning Limerick tried to steal a Q45. He was in the process of popping the driver's side lock, when two unmarked police cars turned on their grill lights and drove up behind him.

The cops jumped out of their cars, and Limerick made a break for it. Dave, who was stationed behind a Hertz bus in the rental car lot, gunned his police motorcycle and raced through a back entrance, where he saw Limerick running towards a fence that would give him access to Airport Boulevard and I-75.

As Limerick jumped onto the fence, Dave grabbed him from behind and pulled him back to the ground.

"He horse-collared me down onto the pavement is what he did," Limerick said, in his South Boston accent.

"Were you resisting arrest, Mr. Limerick?" Bass asked.

"By no means. I was running, but I wasn't resisting. He never yelled stop or nothing. He just grabbed me from behind and slammed me down *WWE style* without any warning."

"You subsequently filed a lawsuit against the City, isn't that correct, Mr. Limerick?" Bass said.

"Yes, sir, I did. I filed a case against the Atlanta Police Department for police brutality, and my attorney sued them for damages."

"What happened with your lawsuit, Mr. Limerick?"

"They settled before we went to trial. They agreed to pay for my medical bills and have an expert treat my shoulder."

Bass moved to admit Limerick's medical records into evidence.

"How is your shoulder now, Mr. Limerick?"

"Not good," he said. "It's never worked good since the attack. The thing hurts all the time."

Bass nodded in sympathy for Limerick's plight.

"I thank you for your willingness to testify about your experience at the hands of this defendant," Bass said. "No further questions, Your Honor."

Whitney rose to begin his cross-examination of Limerick.

"Mr. Limerick, you were attempting to flee when the police approached you, isn't that correct?"

"I guess," Limerick said.

"And you were about to hop over a fence when Detective Mackno was able to reach you, is that correct?"

"Yeah."

"But your testimony is that Mr. Mackno used too much force to get you off the fence?"

"Like I said, he horse-collared me. *Like he had the right.*"

"I gather, based upon your testimony, you would have liked him to say something along the lines of "freeze." Is that correct, Mr. Limerick?"

"Woulda been nice. My shoulder might not have been destroyed."

"Because you would have stopped. Is that your testimony?"

"Exactly," Limerick said. He was only in his 30s, but his wiseguy style of speaking, thin frame, and bald head made him seem a lot older. "This whole thing could have been avoided if your client wasn't such a violent individual. If he just simply told me to stop, instead of flinging me on the ground. I mean look at me. I'm a hundred and fifty four pounds for crying out loud."

"But you didn't stop when two police cars approached you with their sirens flashing, did you, Mr. Limerick? You fled, isn't that correct?"

"I did," he said.

"Thank you. Now with regards to the lawsuit you filed against the city, that was done after you were arrested for stealing over a dozen cars, was it not?"

"I don't recall the exact number, but yeah, sounds about right."

"And when you say the city 'settled,' do you recall that the settlement stipulated, and you averred, that Mr. Mackno did not use excessive force against you during the arrest?"

"That was just language the lawyers put in there to cover themselves," Limerick said.

"How do you know that, Mr. Limerick? You're not a lawyer, are you?" Whitney said. "According to your prison records, you were kicked out of high school in the eleventh-grade."

"I don't need a degree to know common sense. I got a Master's Degree in the school of hard knocks, if you know what I'm saying."

Limerick smiled at the jury.

"I know what you're saying, Mr. Limerick," Whitney said. "But your comment about the settlement is just your opinion, is it not?"

"Just because it's my opinion doesn't mean it isn't true, right?"

"The opinion of a man serving ten years in prison, correct? The opinion of a man who moved to Atlanta as a fugitive and tried to start a new life using somebody else's stolen identity, am I right?"

Limerick smirked, as if insulted.

"This isn't about my crimes," he said. "I'm *doing* my time. This is about what that man over there did to my shoulder by using excessive force."

"No," Whitney said, "this is one hundred percent about your credibility, Mr. Limerick. The credibility of a man who was sent to prison after victimizing over 12 different Georgia families."

"I didn't victimize anybody. I never hurt nobody in my life."

"Tell that to the families whose cars were stolen."

Limerick rolled his eyes.

"It says here you've filed six different appeals of your sentence since you've been incarcerated, is that number accurate, Mr. Limerick?"

"Probably. I don't keep a detailed list of everything that happens in my life. I didn't realize you wanted to do a documentary on me. I'm kinda flattered."

"Any of those appeals been successful?"

"I'm still sitting in prison, aren't I?"

"Yes, you are," Whitney said. "And I think that answer tells this court all we need to know with respect to any other questions I might have. Thank you for your time, Mr. Limerick. Enjoy the ride back to prison."

Judge Friedman admonished Whitney for the comment with her eyes, but didn't say anything on the record.

Limerick stepped down, Whitney returned to his seat, and Bass stood up to call his second witness, *a man he knew the jury was going to believe.*

From the first moment they met, Maurice Bass knew that the credibility of Curtis Pressley, a black MBA from Georgia Tech, would be nearly unassailable.

Originally from Silver Springs, Maryland, Pressley

traveled south to attend Clark Atlanta University on a full academic scholarship. He graduated *magna cum laude* and joined Coca-Cola's fast track management program, through which he was able to earn his MBA at Tech.

Aside from one speeding ticket in South Carolina, Pressley had never had even a brush with the law. He was handsome and carried himself like a CPA. As he walked across the courtroom, his perfectly tailored look left no doubt he was on his way to becoming a full-fledged member of Atlanta's monied class.

Bass began by asking Pressley about a protest march he helped organize during the Rodney King riots. "Why were you out on the street marching when the Mayor had instituted a curfew?"

"We did it in response to what we were seeing on television," Pressley said. "As you may remember, the riots in Atlanta started when another protest march, *two nights earlier,* turned violent."

Pressley shook his head.

"That's what CNN and the other channels kept talking about. How a group of black college students from the Atlanta University Center triggered the riots. As if we were just a bunch of thugs who had been biding our time, waiting for our chance to cause mayhem on the streets of Atlanta. It was a completely false portrayal of who we were and what we were all about. So a group of us decided to go back out. We wanted to have a peaceful march in order to try and change the narrative they were pushing.

"We *specifically* organized it to be a peaceful protest," Pressley said. "Before marching, we all got together and agreed that doing anything violent would be self-defeating. That it wouldn't do anything but lower us down to the level of the cops we were protesting."

"So you decided to disobey the curfew?"

"We didn't think we had any other choice. We were outraged at how the media was portraying African Americans. They were depicting it like the entire black community was out *wilding* in the streets. We were determined to show there was a large group of young, educated black men in Atlanta who knew how to protest peacefully. Which we did, by the way, until the cops got violent with us."

"What do you mean the cops got violent with you?" Bass said.

"What I mean," Pressley said, and looked towards the jury box, "is they didn't care about the fact we were marching peacefully. They just saw a bunch of African Americans, and they were determined to shut us down by any means necessary."

"You were a victim of excessive force that evening, were you not, Mr. Pressley?"

"I was," he said. "I got hit so hard with a nightstick that it broke my clavicle and tore my rotator cuff."

Based on the statement, Bass submitted Curtis Pressley's medical records into evidence.

"Do you know the name of the cop who hit you, Mr. Pressley?"

"I do," he said.

"And is that police officer in this courtroom today?"

"He is."

"Can you please identify that person for the jury?

"I can," Pressley said. He stood up and pointed at Dave.

"Let the record reflect that Mr. Pressley pointed at the defendant," Bass said.

Dave stared back placidly as Pressley pointed at him. He didn't look the least bit fazed by the allegations.

"How do you know that it was the defendant who hit you?" Bass said.

"Because I wrote his name down after he did it."

Pressley held up a piece of yellowed notebook paper that had already been admitted into evidence. The word "Makno" was scrawled on it.

"I'm right handed," Pressley said. "But I was in so much pain that I had to write it with my left hand when I got back to my dorm."

"Why did you do that, Mr. Pressley? Why did you write the down the name Mackno?"

"Because I assumed the police department would hold

him accountable for what he did to me. *I was obviously wrong.* I went to the Atlanta public affairs officer, but he stonewalled me. He took my information down and said he would look into it, but I don't think he ever did. He called me a couple of weeks later and said there wasn't enough evidence to begin a formal process."

Pressley turned to look more squarely at Dave.

"Nobody wanted to investigate how the police had acted in putting down the riots," Pressley said. "In fact, if you do some research, I don't think any cops, black or white, were ever charged for their actions during the riots."

"Did you consider initiating a lawsuit?" Bass asked.

"I went to a guy at Palmer & Marks, but he said it would be hard to sue because I was in violation of the curfew. Looking back, he would have probably preferred if I was the victim of a car accident."

"Why did you come forward now, Mr. Pressley? After all these years, what is it you're trying to accomplish?"

"I just want the truth to be known. That's my only agenda," Pressley said. "I want people to know how the cops treated us when we were being nothing but peaceful."

Bass nodded his approval.

"Mr. Pressley," he said, "would you please lift your arm up for the jury."

Pressley lifted his arm halfway above his shoulder.

"All the way please."

"That's the farthest I can lift it," he said.

Bass turned and looked at the jury to make sure they remembered seeing that Pressley's arm was permanently damaged. He wanted them to remember what Dave had done.

The atmosphere in the courtroom, which had been buzzing with energy in the morning, felt almost funereal as Whitney rose to begin his cross-examination. It was almost like there was a sense of shame that what Pressley described could have happened in Atlanta, a city whose identity was largely predicated on positive race relations.

"That's all I have for my witness, Your Honor," Bass

said.

"Thank you, Mr. Bass," Judge Friedman said. "Mr. Taylor, your witness."

Whitney rose from the defense table.

Dave had remained stone faced during Pressley's testimony. There were many moments from the Atlanta riots that he would never forget, but he had no recollection of Pressley. As he watched Whitney step up to begin the cross-examination, he remembered one of the warnings Whitney had given him before the trial.

"Parts of this trial will get very ugly. They always do for defendants. The only way you're going to stay sane is to ignore what is said about you and stay focused on the outcome."

Glancing over at the jury, none of whom were looking in his direction, Dave understood that Pressley's testimony sounded barbaric when viewed through the prism of an Atlanta courthouse on a sunny day, when there was order on the streets. But at the time of the riots, when a violent anarchy had taken hold, normal police procedures were not going to get the job done.

While Dave felt bad about the fact Pressley had an injured arm, he didn't feel guilty about it. Good intentions or not, Pressley and his fraternity brothers deliberately broke curfew during the riots. How did they expect the police to react to them?

Whitney tried to minimize Pressley's testimony by pointing out he had never filed a formal complaint, but he understood he was fighting a losing battle. No matter how tough he got with Pressley, no matter how much he tried to impeach his motivation, Whitney knew the jury would believe him.

For that reason, Whitney kept his cross-examination short. No point in prolonging the pain. The sooner he got Pressley off the stand, the better it would be for Dave.

When Whitney was finished, he returned to his seat. Day one of the trial was over.

15

——

DAY TWO began when Bass called Sean Fencil, a national expert on police procedure to the stand. A former Chicago cop who favored boxy suits and loud ties, Fencil had carved out a lucrative second career as an expert witness on police procedures.

After some initial questions to establish his credentials, Maurice asked Fencil to give his opinion on Dave's performance the night Remo was killed.

"One of the worst implementations of standard police procedure and protocols I have ever reviewed," Fencil said. "Detective Mackno did so many things wrong, from the initial approach in an un-marked car to his failure to call for backup, that the best way to describe his actions that night is to say they were tantamount to a non-stop sequence of clear and escalating mistakes. It was incompetence personified."

Whitney slipped a note in front of Dave that said, "Ignore him. Hired gun."

Dave gave Whitney a slight nod in acknowledgment, even though there was no way he could ignore him. Dave had never been more harshly criticized in his life, and it was taking a conscious effort not to show how he felt about what Fencil was saying. He felt angry and embarrassed, as if he were being humiliated by a bully while the rest of the schoolyard watched.

"Did his mistakes constitute negligence?" Bass said.

"They absolutely did."

"In what way?"

"In the purest sense of the word. Mackno's actions, and more importantly his decision-making, failed to meet the standard of competence required of a police officer. Because of those failings, he created an extremely dangerous and volatile situation that no law abiding citizen should ever have to find themselves subject to."

Dave could feel his blood pressure rising. Fencil was the kind of self-important, holier-than-thou type of cop that Dave had always disliked. The kind of guy who thought that graduating from the Police Academy gave him the right to tell everybody else how to live.

The insults were compounded by Fencil's arrogance of refusing to even look in Dave's direction. He was talking about Dave as if he wasn't even in the courtroom.

"Replay the exact same scenario with a hundred other cops," Fencil continued, "and Remo Centrella lives every single time. It should have been a routine stop that ended with either a warning or peaceful arrest of Mr. Centrella."

"Is there any scenario you can imagine where it would have been justified for Detective Mackno to act as he did?" Bass said.

"No," Fencil said, in a stentorian tone. "You had an unarmed citizen whose car was parked in such a way that prevented him from going anywhere, and Mackno approached in an un-marked vehicle. Based upon those facts alone, proper procedure would have dictated he call in an official police vehicle as backup in order to clearly establish policing authority."

Fencil, who was built like an offensive lineman for the Bears, raised his hands and shrugged the huge shoulders of his suit in an exaggerated manner to emphasize just how much of a stooge he considered Dave to be. "The bottom line," he said, "and where everything began to spin out of control, was when Mackno decided he wasn't going to call for any backup."

"So, in your expert opinion, Mr. Fencil, Detective Mackno's actions were clearly negligent?"

"Yes," Fencil said.

"Were they reckless?"

"His actions demonstrated a reckless disregard for proper police procedures."

"The defense claims Mr. Mackno shot Remo Centrella in self-defense," Bass said. "What is your opinion as it pertains to that claim?"

"It's invalid. For a self-defense claim to be valid, you need to analyze the situation in its entirety, not just the final moments. Under the legal doctrine of self-defense, a person is not allowed to instigate a situation to the point where deadly force is required, and then simply claim 'self-defense' in an attempt to exonerate themselves for their action. Certain criteria have to be met for that defense, *including not being the aggressor*.

"An assailant can't attack a victim, *provoke the victim to fight back to defend himself*, and then kill the victim in self-defense. That's not how self-defense works. It wouldn't be logical."

"What about a duty to retreat?" Bass said. "Did Mr. Mackno have a duty to retreat?"

"No, not under Georgia law. But what Mackno did have was the absolute duty to act with reasonableness."

"That being defined as what under the law?" Bass said.

"It's a legal fiction, *a term of art, so to speak*," Fencil said, "that attempts to determine how a reasonable person would have acted in the situation."

"Fucking guy thinks he's a lawyer," Dave thought to himself.

"And that's a determination for the jury, is it not?" Bass said.

"It is. It's an objective standard, but the jury is the one who applies it to each case."

"In your opinion, Mr. Fencil, did the defendant act reasonably under the circumstances?" Bass said.

"By any objective standard, I do not believe that he did. I do not believe he acted in accordance with the expectations for a reasonable person."

"Why do you say that?" Bass said.

"Because a reasonable man who found himself alone with an unarmed driver in the middle of the night, having made sure the driver could not go anywhere by virtue of

175

shooting out his tire, would not have attempted a physical take-down of Mr. Centrella, when he could have simply made a radio call for backup."

"What would backup have done?" Bass asked.

"It would have saved Mr. Centrella's life."

"Thank you for your expertise, Mr. Fencil," Bass said. "No more questions, Your Honor."

On Judge Friedman's signal, Whitney stood up and walked over towards the witness box.

"Mr. Fencil, just to make sure I'm one hundred percent clear," he said, "you're here to provide your expert testimony about the way my client handled himself on the night Remo Centrella was killed, is that correct?"

"That is."

"So, if I were to ask you some specific questions about the night in question, would you be able to tell us, in your expert opinion, what it is you think my client did right and did wrong?

"That's why I'm here."

"Okay, good," Whitney said. "I'd like to start with some basic questions."

"Sure."

"Have you ever worked with Mr. Mackno?"

"Have I ever *worked* with Mackno?"

"Yes," Whitney said. "You know, have you ever spent any time working together?"

"No," Fencil said. "I spent my career as a cop in Chicago. How could I have worked with him?"

"Did you know, Mr. Centrella?"

"No."

"Ever meet him?" Whitney said.

Fencil sighed.

"No," he said.

"Were you aware Remo Centrella was a steroid user?"

"I read about it in the paper."

Whitney smiled at Fencil. "I'll state my question more precisely. Before his death, were you aware that Mr. Centrella was a steroid user."

"No."

"Were you in Atlanta on the night of the shooting?"

Whitney said.

"I was not."

"In the state of Georgia?"

"No."

Whitney shook his head.

"Where were you, Mr. Fencil?"

"Objection, Your Honor," Bass said. "Relevance."

"Your Honor," Whitney said, "Mr. Bass put Mr. Fencil on the stand in order to provide us with his expert opinion about what took place the night Mr. Centrella was shot. This witness has been very outspoken, in a way that makes it almost seem as if he was there when the shooting happened. I'm simply trying to establish for the record just where exactly Mr. Fencil was when the events, upon which he's basing his expert opinion, took place."

"I'll permit the question," Judge Friedman said, "but I will also remind the jury that Mr. Fencil need not have been at the scene in order to give an expert opinion about the defendant's actions on the night in question."

"Your answer Mr. Fencil?" Whitney said.

"I was in California."

"California?" Whitney said and let out a very short whistle. "We do certainly appreciate your candor."

"Mr. Taylor," Judge Friedman said and knocked her gavel.

Whitney nodded in acknowledgment of the warning.

"Let me ask you, Mr. Fencil, do you have any relevant information on how Mr. Centrella conducted himself on the night my client tried to arrest him?"

"It looks, based upon the evidence, that Mackno—"

"No, no, Mr. Fencil. Stop," Whitney said, cutting him off sharply. "Not Detective Mackno. *Remo Centrella*. What I would like to know is if you could describe for the jury how Mr. Centrella conducted himself. What he did, what he said, how he acted? For example, would you be able to tell this jury how Mr. Centrella responded when Detective Mackno approached him?"

"I know what's in the record," Fencil said.

"So do I. But I'm not asking you about the record. I'm asking if you have any actual firsthand knowledge about

Mr. Centrella's behavior?"

"That's not my job," Fencil said. "I'm not an eyewitness. I'm an expert witness. I assume you know the difference."

"Because you weren't there, correct?" Whitney said and put his palms up. He wasn't going to let Fencil bait him into getting side-tracked. "Because you were in California, right? Thus, you have no actual way of knowing how Mr. Centrella acted that evening, other than how you *speculate* he might have acted. Isn't that the bottom line truth about your testimony, Mr. Fencil?"

"That's the role of an expert witness, sir, to look at facts and make judgments."

"Isn't that the jury's job?" Whitney said.

"They are the trier of fact, sure, but they're not expected to develop an expertise on the standards of policing."

"But you are?"

"I have testified in over 30 trials, and in each and every one of them the court has, in fact, designated me an expert."

"So you think the jury should adhere to your opinion. Is that your position?"

"I think they should give it some strong weight."

"Even though you weren't at the scene?"

"I know what proper police procedure is and what it is not, Mr. Taylor. You might not want to hear it, but, the fact of the matter is, your client failed to follow it."

"Based upon what criteria, Mr. Fencil?"

"Based upon established standards, and based upon the standards required of a reasonable person."

"But there is no perfectly fixed standard, Mr. Fencil," Whitney said, pounding the lectern a couple of times. "Even you, the quote unquote expert has to admit—"

"Objection, Your Honor," Bass said. "Mr. Fencil isn't a quote unquote expert, he's a court recognized expert."

"Sustained."

"I'll re-phrase. Even you, a court recognized expert, has to admit the reasonable person standard must be adjusted based upon the facts as they happen. As an *expert* on police procedure, wouldn't you agree that what is reasonable in one situation might be unreasonable in another. And vice versa."

"I would agree with that statement."

"Okay, good. Let's step back a moment and look at what happened, shall we?" Whitney said. "We've got two people involved in an altercation, right? Two people whose actions are what this trial is ultimately about, and you have already conceded, on the record, that you have zero way of knowing how one of the two people acted. Isn't that correct, Mr. Fencil?"

Fencil didn't respond.

"That has to be a 'yes' if you want to be consistent with your previous testimony, sir."

"It's too complicated a question to just give you a 'yes or no' answer," Fencil said.

"What's so complicated?" Whitney said. "You were either at the scene and saw how Mr. Centrella acted, or you were not. With all due respect, Mr. Fencil, that's one of the simpler questions I've asked during this trial."

"You already know my answer," Fencil said. "I wasn't there, but I have seen enough of the evidence to render an expert opinion."

"And at the end of the day, that's exactly what it is, isn't it Mr. Fencil, your opinion?"

"Yes."

"And thus, not a fact," Whitney said, once again looking frustrated with Fencil. "You're just sitting up there, making all these tremendously pontificated pronouncements about the actions of Mr. Mackno, in a situation where you *literally* have zero information to provide this jury about the way Mr. Centrella acted. That's the true bottom line of your testimony, is it not?"

"I would strongly disagree with that characterization, sir," Fencil said.

"I'm sure that you would, Mr. Fencil. I'm sure you would have no problem with this jury substituting your opinion in place of the facts, but thankfully that's not how our jury system works, is it? Facts trump opinions, even when those opinions happen to come from a court-recognized expert.

"No further questions, Your Honor," Whitney said, with a small shake of his head. He turned his back to the witness stand as he said, "Thank you for your time, Mr. Fencil."

Fencil stepped down from the seat and made his departure from the courtroom. Whitney sat down next to Dave.

"Nice work," Dave whispered.

With Fencil's appearance complete, Bass stood up to begin what would be the most mundane stage of the trial, a series of witnesses for the prosecution whose testimony was mostly limited to the physical evidence in the case. It was testimony that was almost all foundational: Where Remo had been shot, where the shell casings were found, the position of his body, the trajectory of the bullets, what items had been found in his car, what items were found at the scene.

It was testimony that would not ultimately matter to the jury during deliberations, but facts Maurice had to make sure were formally established in the record in order to meet his burden.

No sparks flew between Maurice and Whitney over any of the testimony, as most of it involved black and white physical aspects of the case.

They both knew where the real battle lines were drawn: in the grey areas of the case, where testimony was in direct dispute. Those were the places in which the jury would have to decide who was telling the truth. They were the battlegrounds that were going to determine Dave's fate.

When it came to those areas, nobody's testimony, other than Dave's, would be more important than Tina Manning's.

16

———

THE PROSECUTION began the fourth day of the trial by calling Tina Manning to the stand. She was escorted into court by Linda Slotnick, who took a seat in the second row behind Maurice Bass.

Tina Manning's appearance in court was one of the few times she had been seen in public in almost three months. During that time, she had been living as a virtual shut-in, having become, as one columnist for the Inquirer called her, the "Hester Prynne of the New South."

Ray had refused any of her attempts to meet with him. The only thing he had to offer her was an extra one hundred thousand dollars, on top of the three hundred thousand she was entitled to receive under their pre-nuptial agreement, in exchange for her willingness to expedite the divorce.

Johnny Wiemer made the offer through Linda Slotnick. He explained Ray was willing to pay a premium if their divorce was completed before the start of the trial. Tina accepted the deal, and the divorce decree was signed a month before the trial began.

When Tina walked across the courtroom, she looked very different from the last time Dave had seen her. She was about 15 pounds heavier and wearing a conservative beige skirt-suit over a button-down royal blue shirt. Her hair was coiffed and brownish blonde instead of long and platinum. She now looked more like a lawyer than a trophy wife.

Bass started her testimony with some basic informational questions to try and reduce any nerves she might be feeling. Name, age, a little bit of her work history. *Just enough to get her relaxed and into a rhythm.*

Once he could see she felt comfortable, he began asking her some pre-emptive questions in order to diffuse the impact of some of the questions he knew Whitney would ask her.

He decided to start with the biggest elephant in the room.

"Why did you wait three months after Mr. Centrella was killed to turn yourself into the police, Mrs. Manning?"

" Because I was scared," she said.

Dave had never before heard Tina's voice, and it sounded much more pure and confident than he expected.

"I was embarrassed and ashamed of what I had done," she said.

"Did you think your husband would be angry when he found out?"

"Yes, angry and hurt. Ray was already devastated about Remo's death, and I wasn't sure how much more he could take. I thought I was actually being protective by not telling him." Tina wiped a tear from her eye. "I didn't want to cause him any more pain."

"Was it also because you didn't want to get divorced?"

"That was part of it, too."

"And that's what happened, is it not? Your husband divorced you when he found out about your affair, did he not?"

"He did."

"You are currently divorced from your husband?"

"I am."

Bass flipped over a page in his legal pad.

"I'd like to take a step back in time a bit, Mrs. Manning. Can you please tell this court when your affair with Mr. Centrella began?

"It began last March," she said, "while we were down in Florida for Spring Training."

"Was it something you planned?"

"Not at all," Tina said, with a look of pain on her face. "I never had any intention of having an affair with Remo Centrella or anybody else. I was looking forward to the chance to spend a month with my husband at the Don. I saw it as a chance for us to reconnect as a couple."

"The Don is a hotel?"

"Yes, the Don CeSar in St. Pete. We were supposed to stay there for the month of March, but a few days after we arrived, Ray got a call there were more problems in Alberta."

"What was going on up there?"

"Donergy, Ray's oil exploration company, was working on an oil sands project," Tina explained. "It's the biggest project in their history, and it was taking up almost all of his time. That's one of the reasons I was so excited about the chance to spend a month with him."

"What happened when your husband found out they needed him in Canada?"

"He was really disappointed," she said. "But he was hoping it would only take a few days and that he could get back to Florida. That's why he had me stay down there instead of flying home. Unfortunately, it took almost ten days for him to get back. It was during that time my affair with Remo began."

"I see," Bass said. "Tell me, Mrs. Manning, did you love Remo Centrella?"

"No, I don't believe that I did."

"Then why did you have the affair?"

"I can't explain it," she said. "Remo was staying next door in the Presidential Suite, and I was alone in the Penthouse. I was a young wife, feeling a little bit neglected, when Remo started to pay a lot of attention to me."

"And you enjoyed that, Mrs. Manning?"

"I did. I was flattered by it. Remo was, obviously, a very attractive and charismatic man. *He was beautiful.*"

"So you were physically attracted to him?"

"I was," she said, "but I would have never acted upon it if Remo hadn't pursued me so aggressively."

"What do you mean by that statement, Mrs. Manning?"

"My birthday is March 11th, and somehow Remo found out about it. He showed up at my door with a bottle of champagne. *He was already a little tipsy*, and he said it was his chivalrous duty not to let me spend my birthday alone. I told him I would be fine. I was planning to have a quiet night, but he wouldn't take no for an answer. He said it would be rude to make him drink the champagne all by himself.

"He eventually wore me down, and I agreed to let him in for just one drink. Twenty minutes later, a woman from room service knocked on the door. Remo let her in, and she set up dinner for two of lobster and stone crabs on the terrace that overlooks the Gulf."

"And was that the night you began the affair?"

"It was," Tina said, with a distant look in her eyes. "Halfway through dinner, while re-filling my glass of champagne, Remo bent down and kissed me."

"You testified in your deposition it was more than just a one night stand, that it continued for five months, until the night Remo was killed. You must have wanted the affair to continue, Mrs. Manning."

"I was very torn," she said. "I loved my husband, but Remo was so aggressive in his pursuit of me that I was overwhelmed. I got caught up in a dynamic and started acting impulsively."

"Didn't it matter to you that Remo and your husband were such close friends?" Bass said.

"It did," she said. "It definitely did. I felt very guilty about it. I still do. I tried to end it so many times, but every time I did, Remo convinced me to keep seeing him."

Tina looked disappointed in herself.

"I should have found the courage to stop the affair," she said, as her voice trailed off a bit. "Maybe Remo would be alive if I had."

Maurice circled back towards his lectern and looked down at his notes for a moment.

"You were married once before, Mrs. Manning, is that correct?"

"I was."

"Can you tell the court what happened to your first marriage?"

"I divorced my first husband, Kenny, after he was arrested for dealing cocaine."

"You were arrested along with him, were you not, Mrs. Manning?"

"Yes. When the Las Vegas police department raided our apartment to arrest Kenny, they arrested me, too."

"And you were charged with dealing drugs, were you not?" Bass said, as a soft buzz of murmurs moved through the courtroom.

"Arrested, but never charged," she said, matter of factly. "I had no knowledge Kenny was hiding drugs in our apartment."

"You didn't know your husband used drugs?" Bass said.

"I knew he occasionally used drugs. I didn't know he dealt them."

"Understood. What happened after you were arrested, Mrs. Manning?"

"As soon as the police realized I had no idea what Kenny was doing, they dropped all the charges against me."

"So you weren't charged with any crime at all, is that correct?"

"That is correct."

"Have you ever been arrested for any other crime, Mrs. Manning?"

"No, sir," she said. "That was the only time."

Bass began to move away from his lectern and over towards the jury box. The most important part of Tina's testimony was coming up. He wanted her to be looking in the jury's direction when she testified about what happened during the confrontation with Dave.

"Mrs. Manning," Bass said, "would you please tell this

jury exactly what happened on the night Mr. Centrella was killed?"

"Yes," Tina said and inhaled a deep breath. "It was late, about 3 a.m. in the morning, when Remo drove me back to get my car. We had just pulled up to the parking lots and were kissing when we heard another car drive up behind us. I had no idea who it was, but my fear was it might be another player on the team, and that they would see me with Remo."

"Did Mr. Centrella say anything when he saw the car?" Bass asked.

"He told me to lock the door. I wasn't really sure what was going on, but I could see he was getting nervous. He didn't like the fact that he couldn't see into the other car."

"Why couldn't Mr. Centrella see into the other car?"

"Its high beams were on."

"I see."

"Remo thought there might be more than one person in the car. That it might be one of the local gangs."

"Did you feel threatened as the car approached?"

"I did. Remo said he was going to get the gun in his trunk, but then Mr. Mackno bumped into the back of our car."

"You didn't know it was Detective Mackno's car at the time, did you Mrs. Manning?"

"No, sir. I didn't know who it was, and it never crossed my mind that it could be a cop."

"Why not?"

"Because I didn't think a police officer would intentionally drive into the back of somebody's car."

"What happened when Mr. Mackno's car bumped into the back of yours?"

"It made me nervous. He was obviously trying to intimidate us."

Bass introduced two photographs confirming the fact that Dave's Sebring had bumped into the rear bumper of the Porsche.

"What did Mr. Centrella do after Detective Mackno bumped into your car?"

"He got concerned. He said 'we need to get out of here.'

I thought he was going to try and drive away, but then Mr. Mackno got out of his car."

"Did you think he was a cop at that point?"

"No. I thought we were getting car-jacked."

"Did the defendant display a badge or anything that identified him as a police officer?"

"Not right away. There was no siren or anything. It was just him walking towards the car with a gun aimed at us."

"At that point, did Mr. Centrella also think you were getting carjacked?"

"Yes, but then Mr. Mackno held up his badge and it was a huge relief. 'It's a cop,' I said to Remo, but he said the badge could be fake. That the Barons' security people had warned the players about carjackers using fake badges."

"So at this point, Mrs. Manning, is it fair to say you still weren't one hundred percent sure that you were dealing with a police officer? You were still feeling scared?"

"Completely."

"What happened next?"

"Mr. Mackno started to get real aggressive. His gun was drawn, and he started yelling at us. He kept yelling, *and excuse my language*, 'Get the fuck out of the car. Get the fuck out the car....Get the fuck out of the car. He kept repeating it, over and over, again."

"Did you get out?"

"No, sir," Tina said. "We were by ourselves, and it was the middle of the night. Remo told me to stay in the car until an official police car arrived."

"But no police cars showed up, correct? The defendant never called for backup, did he?"

"He never did," she said. "And that was the problem. The longer it went without a police car showing up, the more Remo became convinced he wasn't really a cop. It didn't help he was unshaven and wearing dark jeans with a black Polo shirt. I think that was part of the reason Remo tried to get away from him."

"How did Mr. Centrella try to do that?" Bass said.

"It happened really fast," she said. "Somehow, Remo was able to spin the car around backwards. When he did that, we were then facing Mr. Mackno head-on, and we could see exactly what he was doing. At that point, I thought Mr. Mackno would get out of the way and let us leave. But instead, he stepped directly in front of the car and aimed his gun at us."

Tina raised her hands in front of her face, as if she were holding an imaginary gun.

"He was waving his gun from side to side"—she imitated Dave's movement with her hands—"like he was letting us know he could shoot both of us if he wanted.

"That's when I completely panicked," she said, "and that's when Remo told me to run for it. I didn't listen at first, but then he said it again. *'Run for it!'* Like it was an order. 'I'll distract him,' Remo said. "You get out of here.'"

Tears were now streaming down Tina's cheeks.

"I know it was wrong to abandon him, but at the time I was so scared. I opened the door and I ran away."

Tina's voice cracked as she said, "I've never been so scared in my life."

"Where did you go when you ran, Mrs. Manning?"

"I headed back down Webster towards the highway. Halfway down, I cut through an alley between two houses. When I got to the other side, I looked around and I could see the light from the highway. But there was a concrete wall, so I couldn't get up to it. I turned north, towards downtown, and sprinted a few more blocks until I saw the MARTA station.

"I hopped the turnstile, and ran down the stairs. After a couple of minutes, I heard a train coming. It stopped and I got on. The train was completely empty, and I rode it up to the Perimeter. As soon as I got off, I looked for a payphone and called 911."

Maurice introduced a phone record into evidence that documented a 911 call was made from Perimeter Station at 4:17 a.m., reporting a carjacking at Wilson Field.

"What did you do after you called 911?"

"I broke down," she said. "I started bawling. I was by myself in the middle of the night, and I had no idea what might have happened to Remo. My shoes had come off when I was running. My feet were cut up, but I was so numb I didn't even feel any pain. I just wanted to sit down and cry, but I knew I had to get back to my house, so I started walking home."

"What time did you get back home, Mrs. Manning?"

"I'm not sure. Sometime between 5 and 5:30 a.m."

"Did you call Remo when you got home?"

"No, sir."

"Why not?"

"That was one thing we never did, call each other on our cellphones. It was one of his rules. Remo told me he gave his wife full access to his cellphone so she knew she could trust him. That meant I had to call a separate landline number she didn't know about."

"Did you call that number?"

"No," she said. "I collapsed onto my bed as soon as I got home and woke up around 10:30. I was still disoriented and wearing my clothes from the night before. I went into the master bathroom and took a hot shower. When I got done, I went downstairs, made a cup of coffee, and turned on the TV. News about Remo was on every channel. When I heard he had been killed, I fell on the floor."

"What did your husband say, Mrs. Manning? Was he worried that you had been out all night?"

"He wasn't home."

"Where was he?"

"In Europe."

"So you were alone?"

"Yes."

"Once you saw Mr. Centrella had been killed, why didn't you call the police then?"

"I almost did, but at that point, I didn't know *what* to do. A part of me wanted to call the police and tell them exactly what had happened, but at the same time, I realized there was nothing I could do. Remo was already dead."

"So you didn't say anything to anybody?" Bass said.

"No, sir. Only God. I made my confession to him and swore I would never be unfaithful to my husband again. I decided to put it in his hands and prayed that his will be done."

"What do you mean by that, Mrs. Manning?"

"It means I found a way to make peace with myself, Mr. Bass. I decided that if the police approached me, I would admit to everything, but if they didn't, then it was God's will that I get a second chance."

"What about Mr. Centrella? Didn't he enter into your calculation?"

"He did," Tina said, as tears began to flow down both her cheeks again. "Of course, he did. If there had been anything I could have done to help him I would have, but he was already dead. Mr. Mackno had already killed him. There was nothing I could do. The only thing I could do was wait and see if the police showed up at my house."

"But the cops never came, did they?" Bass said.

"No, sir."

"You did eventually turn yourself in, though."

"I did. I met with my attorney, Ms. Slotnick" Tina said, and pointed to where Linda was sitting. "After discussing my situation with her, we decided I should turn myself in."

"What made you decide that?" Whitney said.

"I decided to do it after Mr. Mackno was indicted. I was tired of having to constantly worry that the next knock on the door would be the police, and I also realized it was the right thing to do. That I owed it to Remo."

Maurice nodded at the answer, which he knew was technically true. *Tina Manning did decide to turn herself in after Dave was indicted. She was worried about the police knocking on her door, and she did realize it was the right thing to do.* Even if in her mind "right" meant doing what she needed to stay out of jail.

As for the fact Bass approached her and persuaded her to turn herself in, that was not something she, as a witness, or Maurice Bass, as a prosecutor, had an obligation to disclose in court. As far as Maurice was concerned, the strategy he had come up with to persuade Tina to cooperate fell within the category of "work-product privilege," which meant it was something he didn't have to volunteer.

That didn't mean Tina could lie if asked about it. Linda and Maurice made that explicitly clear to her. They told Tina that if Whitney Taylor asked any questions about meeting with Maurice prior to the arrest, then she was obligated to provide a truthful answer. But they also made it clear that if Whitney didn't ask it, she was under no type of affirmative duty to offer it.

By directly questioning Tina about her decision to turn herself in, Bass was gambling that Whitney would not. He walked back to the lectern and flipped over a page on his pad.

"I'd like to turn, if I could, Mrs. Manning, to ask you some more questions about your relationship with Remo Centrella."

Tina nodded her head.

"At any time during your relationship did Remo Centrella ever hit you?"

"No," she said. "Never."

"What about the bruise you had underneath your eye on the night Mr. Centrella was killed?"

"I didn't have a bruise."

"You didn't have a black eye?" Bass said.

"No, sir."

"Mrs. Manning, are you aware that in the official police report, Detective Mackno stated that he believed Mr. Centrella needed to be arrested because he suspected you had been the victim of physical abuse? Specifically, according to the police report, Mr. Mackno said quote 'she had a large, fresh, welt underneath her left eye."

"Yes, I'm aware of that," she said.

"Are you now saying that what Detective Mackno put into his official police report was incorrect?"

"Yes. Detective Mackno could not have seen a bruise under my eye because I didn't have one."

17

———

"YOU DIDN'T have any injury at or near your eye?"

"I've never had a black eye in my life."

Bass paused to let Tina's statement settle into the jury's minds.

"Let me ask you another question from the police report, Mrs. Manning. Detective Mackno stated you were struggling to get away from Remo when he approached your car. Is that an accurate statement?"

"No, it's not. As I believe I testified earlier, Remo and I were sitting in his car when he drove up from behind."

"So you were not struggling to get out of the car?"

"No. To be completely candid, we were kissing," Tina said, as her neck became flushed. "We were about to have sex."

"You were going to have sex outside the parking lots of Wilson Field at three in the morning?" Bass said, sounding surprised.

"We had done it two other times."

"But you didn't because the defendant arrived, is that correct?"

"We were still just kissing when we heard his car."

"I see," Bass said. "Tell me, have you had a chance to read the actual police report that Detective Mackno filed?"

"I did," Tina said. "My attorney gave it to me to read."

"And what did you think of it?"

"I was surprised by it. It wasn't what I expected."

"It wasn't?"

"No, sir. What Detective Mackno said happened and what actually happened are two completely different things."

"Two different things?"

"Yes, sir."

"How do you reconcile that, Mrs. Manning?"

"Detective Mackno didn't tell the truth," she said.

"You think he lied?"

"I know he lied," she said.

For a moment, Whitney considered objecting on the grounds of "speculation," but he knew Judge Friedman would overrule him on the basis that Tina Manning was entitled to offer her opinion on the content found in the police report.

"Why do you think he would do that?"

"I think he lied in order to cover-up his mistakes," she said. "I think he lied because he didn't want to take responsibility for his actions."

Maurice then did something that Whitney thought was brilliant. He had an "a-ha" moment while standing directly in front of the jury box. It was subtle, Bass didn't say a word or make a sound. It was simply a facial expression, a slight opening of his mouth, and a slow, half nod of his head. But the look on his face said it all.

Bass had been confused, but now Tina Manning had explained it to him. Dave had lied to avoid taking responsibility for his actions. *Finally, everything now made sense to Maurice.*

Whitney was actually impressed with how well Bass could fake sincerity.

"He missed his true calling," Whitney thought to himself as Bass ended his direct examination of Tina Manning.

Maurice looked triumphant as he took his seat. Tina Manning's direct testimony had been nearly flawless. She had come across as perfectly reasonable and believable.

She was just the kind of witness a jury would want to believe, which was why Dave felt so uneasy.

He had been dumbfounded as Tina Manning spun a version of the facts he knew was untrue. He couldn't believe how brazenly she had lied, or how credible she sounded while doing it.

Tina Manning was as good a liar as Dave had ever seen. So good, in fact, that if Dave hadn't seen her struggling to get out of Remo's car, and if he had not seen her bruised eye, he would have believed her testimony.

As Dave thought about Tina Manning's performance, Judge Friedman called Maurice and Whitney to the bench for a sidebar conference. It was early Friday afternoon, and she was trying to determine the schedule for Whitney's cross-examination.

She offered Whitney two options. He could immediately start his cross-examination of Tina, knowing it would need to be continued on Monday, or she could put the court into early recess for the weekend, and everyone could start fresh on Monday morning.

Whitney glanced over at the jurors. It was a no brainer. They were worn out after a long week of jury duty, but still alert enough to figure out what Friedman was asking him. There was no way he was going to be dumb enough to be the guy who held them late on a Friday.

"Let's come back and start again on Monday morning, Your Honor," Whitney said.

"Smart answer," Judge Friedman said.

She instructed Tina that she could step down from the stand and informed her courtroom the trial would be in recess until Monday morning. Friedman admonished the jurors not to watch media coverage of the trial, and she reminded them not to discuss it either among themselves, or with anybody else with whom they might interact.

The jurors nodded their agreement.

Judge Friedman gave her gavel a cursory tap, and the respective participants in the trial of <u>State of Georgia v. David Mackno</u> made their way to the exits.

———————

That evening, shortly after midnight, Ray Manning's driver delivered him back home after a six day trip to Canada. It had been a long, but productive week, that ended with a five-hour flight. Ray felt worn down, but between some booze on his plane and the time zone difference, he was too wired to sleep.

His house was empty, and the lights were off when he walked in the door. Tina had moved out three months earlier, and Ray was still trying to adjust to living by himself for the first time in almost thirty years. He felt out of sorts, as his thoughts continued to yo-yo between cautious optimism and despair.

From a business perspective, things were finally looking up. After months of contending with the threat of possible bankruptcy, Ray had engineered a solution to his financial problems.

But from a personal perspective, he was at his lowest point since his senior year of college. Tina's affair with Remo had been psychologically crushing. It wasn't just the personal humiliation of being cheated on by his wife, it was the fact Remo had blindsided him in such malicious fashion.

The truth was, Remo's betrayal hurt more than hers. A third wife with tan legs and a nice rack was easily replaceable when you were worth a billion dollars. But the memories from 17 years of friendship, including three World Series titles, were not.

Remo's actions had destroyed a huge part of Ray's history, and he knew there was no way to ever get it back. Even if he might one day find a way to forgive Remo, Ray knew he would never get back to the point where he would be able to find joy, or take pride, in what the Barons had accomplished with Remo on the team. The betrayal had been too big and too personal.

Ray had not watched the trial, including Tina's testimony. He had never been a voyeur and wasn't interested in the details of her and Remo's relationship.

He had no desire to wallow in the public humiliation that went with being the first owner in sports whose wife had screwed his star player.

Now that they were divorced, Ray didn't really care about Tina or what her future plans happened to be. That chapter in his life was over, and Ray had come to realize that whatever he might have once felt for Tina, it had never actually been love.

Like any victim of a traumatic event, Ray had played the "what if" and "if only" game a thousand times in his head. More often than not, "If I had just stayed married to Monica" was the answer that solved most of his problems.

Ray knew he had screwed up a good thing with her. Monica had been a good wife. Monogamous by nature, she had gone *all in* on their marriage and been committed to making it work. He could still remember how furious she looked when she and Chandler came home early from a trip to St. Simon's and saw Ray in the hot tub with Tina. It didn't help that she was drinking champagne out of one of the Waterford flutes Monica had bought for their tenth wedding anniversary.

Chandler looked like he was in a state of shock as Monica ran towards the hot tub with a meat hammer. Tina jumped out of the hot tub and ran topless into the pool house. She was trapped inside for almost 20 minutes, until Monica calmed down long enough that she could make it safely back to her car.

"What an idiot," Ray thought to himself as he remembered the incident which led to his second divorce and rebound marriage.

Looking back, it was obvious he had sabotaged his marriage to Monica because he had fallen in love with an idealized version of Tina. What should have been a simple fling turned into much more because Tina looked so much like Ray's first love, a girl from Oklahoma named Virginia Wallace.

Ray fell in love with Virginia the first time they met, at a sorority mixer during his sophomore year at Tulane. She and Ray went steady for almost two years. They would have almost certainly been married, if Ray's ego and libido had not ruined their relationship.

Three months after Virginia lost her virginity to Ray, he paid her back by giving her a case of the clap he picked up during a drunken visit to a brothel in the French Quarter. Horrified when the doctor gave her the diagnosis, *Virginia made the mistake of detailing some of her symptoms to a couple of her sisters in Tri-Delt,* she panicked and fled back home on a Greyhound bus to Tulsa.

Ray couldn't believe his bad luck. He called her house multiple times a day, but Virginia refused to speak with him. He felt so bad about giving her VD that he wrote her a letter of apology and swore he would never drink again if she gave him a second chance.

But Virginia never did. The only other contact he had with her family was on a sunny spring afternoon, a few weeks after she went home, when he got jumped off-campus by her father and uncle. In less than three minutes, *the time it took for five of Ray's fraternity brothers to come running out of their house,* Ray got the living shit kicked out of him. Virginia's old man and uncle knocked out three of Ray's teeth and broke his nose with a kick from one of their steel-toed work boots.

Ray's brothers in Kappa Alpha were able to pull him to safety, but none of them were dumb enough to try and confront two men who had spent their lives working in Oklahoma oil fields.

"You try to contact my daughter again and I'll kill you," Virginia's father said, as he spit in Ray's direction. "Not even once you little turd. Understand me?"

"Yes, sir," Ray said, in what might have been the most deferential statement of his life. He had no doubt Virginia's father was serious, so he forgot about her and ended up engaged to his first wife, Gail, the mother of Mitchell and Emily, eighteen months later. That marriage lasted fourteen years until Ray met Monica, a former University of Florida cheerleader, and aspiring television reporter, who had moved to Atlanta from Gainesville. Ray had first seen her when she was doing some on-air work for the Barons' public relations department.

"You think those are real?" he said to Wiemer, the first time they previewed one of her segments.

"Tough to tell," Johnny said. "They look almost too perfect."

"Then I better find out," Ray said.

They were, and six months later Monica was pregnant with Chandler. She and Ray eventually married, a month after Chandler's second birthday.

Looking back, Ray knew he would still be married to Monica if Tina had not reminded him so much of Virginia. From her first time working on one of his flights, he became obsessed. He went so far as having Wiemer arrange with LuxJets for Tina to be the flight attendant on a four-day trip to Monaco. Ray told Monica he had to fly to Monte Carlo in order to meet with potential investors from the Middle East. But the real purpose of the trip was his pursuit of Tina, whom he booked into a room next to his on the top floor of the Hotel de Paris.

Ray rented a Ferrari convertible on the second day of the trip to take Tina sightseeing in the areas outside of Monte Carlo. That night, he bought her an emerald necklace from *Cartier's* and took her to the Casino de Monte-Carlo, where she watched him play baccarat at a table while seated between Kevin Costner and Lee Majors.

It was a heady night that ended in Ray's suite, where he surprised them both by telling Tina he had fallen in love with her. After seeing the kind of lifestyle Ray lived, Tina agreed to do the same.

"Schmuck," Ray said to himself, as he thought back to his "OCD-like" pursuit of her. His stupidity was obvious in retrospect, but at the time, he had been completely irrational, *manic, really*, in his lust.

Ray lit another cigarette, peeled off his shirt, and picked up a bottle of Jack Daniels from the bar. He walked into the main foyer of his house and opened up a FedEx package that arrived while he was away. It was a letter from Malcolm Gaffney that Ray had been expecting. Inside the envelope was a loan extension in the form of an Addendum to the original loan documents.

By counter-signing the letter, Ray would formalize a 180-day forbearance and extension of the three loan payments he missed, while also eliminating the need to pledge alternative collateral to Cohen, Wolfe. They were major financial concessions the Wolfe was offering in exchange for an exclusive "12-month Right of First Refusal" on any equity Ray sold in the Barons.

Ray had a look of contempt on his face as he read the letter. He knew the only reason Cohen, Wolfe was offering the extension and forbearance was because they were convinced he would need to sell off a piece of the Barons, in order to remain solvent. Ray knew the Wolfe was convinced of it because he had been the one who convinced them.

Sixty days earlier, he sent Johnny Wiemer to New York for high-level meetings with the heads of Morgan Stanley, Goldman Sachs, and Bank of America's investment banking divisions. During the meetings, Wiemer told the banks that Ray needed to find a way to borrow 100 million dollars in order to keep his Alberta operation viable.

"The situation is getting desperate," Wiemer confided. "If Ray can't borrow the money he needs from y'all, he's going to have to either shut down Alberta or sell off a piece of the team. He doesn't have any other options."

As Ray expected, it didn't take long for Malcolm Gaffney to find out Wiemer was making the rounds in Manhattan and shaking his tin cup. Gaffney called Ray the day after Wiemer returned to Atlanta, proving once again that nobody on Wall Street could smell blood better than the Wolfe.

Gaffney played dumb about Wiemer's trip to New York. He simply told Ray he had gone directly to Lloyd Molendyke to get a loan extension approved in exchange for the Right of First Refusal that Ray had previously suggested.

As Ray thought about his call with Gaffney, he smiled for one of the few times all week. Ray Manning, a "C student" at Tulane, who had purchased most of his term papers from a head shop in New Orleans, had outsmarted a building full of Ivy League MBAs, and secured the financial breathing room he needed in exchange for a "Rofer" that wasn't worth the paper it was printed on.

The "Rofer" was worthless because Ray had figured out a way to raise 50 million dollars. And that was an amount, based upon the most recent geologicals he had seen, which would be at least 10 million more than Donergy needed to finally start producing oil in Alberta.

Once that happened, *once oil actually started flowing*, Ray would have more than enough cash flow to stay current on his loan to CW, and the threat of bankruptcy would be lifted.

Ray had never actually needed to raise anywhere close to 100 million dollars, as long as he could prevent CW from declaring him "in breach" and calling the entire loan due. The only reason he told Wiemer to use that number was to make him look so desperate that Malcolm Gaffney wouldn't be able to resist the opportunity to try and take advantage of him.

"Wolfe bait," as he explained it to Wiemer.

"Cohen, Wolfe won't be able to resist trying to screw me out of a piece of the Barons in exchange for an extension of my loan terms," Ray had predicted. "They'll be so blinded by the shiny object I dangle in front of them, *a piece of the team,* they won't even realize they're giving me the time I need to survive."

And now they had.

Thirty of the 50 million dollars Ray needed was going to come from the All-Life Insurance policy on Remo. Now that Dave had been indicted on the manslaughter charge, William Cutter's attorneys in the U.S. had advised him they could no longer cite, *in good faith*, the felony clause as a reason to deny the Barons' claim. That meant Ray would be getting the full 45 million from Remo's life insurance policy. From that amount, he was going to be able to allocate 30 million dollars to his Alberta project. He could now do that because he had been able to re-structure Remo's contract.

Instead of paying Tiffany Hill 45 million dollars right away, Ray agreed to pay her 65 million dollars over ten years. Under the restructured deal, the Barons would need to pay her 15 million up-front, with an additional 50 million dollars payable in ten annual installments. Even better for Ray, the first installment on the 50 million dollar tranche would not be due for 12 months.

It would be relatively easy for the Barons to pay Tiffany Hill 5 million dollars a year out of cash flow. *Infinitely easier than having to come up with 50 million in fresh capital at a time when Ray was teetering on the financial edge.*

The restructured deal had been an easy sell to Remo's agent, Shane Straka, who would collect his 4% off the top. They had negotiated it over lunch at Chop's Lobster Bar in Buckhead.

"Extend Pedro Trujillo for three years at two million per," Straka said, after listening to Ray's offer, "and I'll recommend she take the deal."

"Trujillo hit .227 last year," Ray said.

"Tiffany Hill likes to play the diva. It'll take more than just a phone call to get her to agree."

"Three years at one point six," Ray said.

"Done your way," Straka said, and they shook hands on the restructured deal that freed up the 30 million dollars in cash.

The other 20 million Ray needed to raise was going to come from the Builders' Trust Life Insurance Company, courtesy of a 10-year naming rights deal for the Keith.

Ray knew he would take some heat from fans and the media for getting rid of such an iconic name. Not least because he once proclaimed, "any owner who would name his stadium after a supermarket chain should be shot."

"That's life," Ray reminded himself. He never had any problem accepting the fact success in life often required large doses of hypocrisy. Thus, beginning on Opening Day, Keith Wilson Field would be officially re-christened Builders Trust Life Insurance Stadium.

Ray was trying his best to stay positive by thinking

about the financial alchemy he had been able to perform, but his positive thoughts kept getting pushed aside by negative ones about what Remo had done to him.

"Fucking Judas," he said as he walked up the stairs to the second story, where the bedrooms of his three children stood empty.

Ray felt bittersweet as he looked into the still largely intact rooms of Mitchell and Emily. He would have killed to go back to the days when they were bouncing around the house, little balls of energy that required constant vigilance.

Ray had been an enthusiastic father when Mitchell and Emily were young. It was a time before he had taken ownership of the Barons, when he technically worked for his father, but hadn't been trusted with the kind of responsibility that required him to put in long hours. A time in his life when he could collect a quarter million dollar paycheck just for being Chet Manning's son.

Looking through Mitchell and Emily's rooms, he remembered the good times he had with them. *The racecars, the tea parties, the toys scattered everywhere.* Ray remembered all the time he spent crawling around the floor, determined to be the father Chet never was. He almost gave in to a drunken sob as he looked at a picture of him, Mitchell and Emily. They were smiling and eating cotton candy together at a Fireman's fair.

"There was a time I had it all," he said to the picture. "You were my Camelot."

He felt even worse when he walked into Chandler's room. Ray had been a decade older and sole owner of the Barons by the time he divorced Gail and married Monica. He didn't remember spending any time crawling around the floor with Chandler. By the time he and Monica got married, Ray had already been seduced by the glamour of owning a baseball team. He was spending most of his time being Ray Manning, the public figure, instead of being Ray Manning, the dad.

He walked towards the desk in Chandler's room and looked at the model rocket ships on the shelf. He had no memories of Chandler even building them.

"I've completely fucked it up with Chandler," Ray said as he picked up a Saturn V rocket and rotated it in his hands. It said **USA** down the side and reminded him of a similar one he built, a few years before Neil Armstrong walked on the moon.

Ray took a large hit of Jack as he walked out of Chandler's room and back towards the stairs that led to the third floor. He stopped just before he reached the stairs and looked at himself in the large mirror that hung next to an oil painting of his father.

Ray shook his head in disappointment. "You were right, Dad," he said.

It had been almost twenty years since Chet died, but Ray could still hear his father's Cajun accent, usually soaked in Old Charter whiskey, as he condemned something Ray had done, or failed to do, as another "typical *fuck-up*."

Ray took off the World Series ring he was wearing and let it fall to the floor.

"Were they worth it?" he said to the mirror. "Three ex-wives and a kid who will be ruined before he turns 18?"

Ray took a defiant pull from his bottle. The Jack Daniels was beginning to make him feel dizzy and tired.

"What's Chandler got to do, flip a car? Get arrested for assaulting a cop? Is that what it's going to take? Cause that's what's fixing to happen."

Ray shook his head and took another long drink of whiskey. His thoughts were becoming unfocused, and he was beginning to feel like he might pass out.

"What?" he said, remembering what he had been thinking about.

Ray smirked at his image in the mirror.

"He's got your DNA. He's not going to accept being ignored any more than you did. He's gonna keep fucking up until he gets your full attention. Just remember, there won't be enough whiskey in the world if he ends up dead of an overdose or crashes into a telephone pole."

As Ray looked at his image in the mirror, he saw he had started to cry. He then laughed loudly.

"Now you're crying?" he said. "That's some funny shit.

Big Ray Manning, alone in his mansion, crying into the mirror. That says it all, Hoss....that says it all."

Ray lay down on the floor in order to rest. He tried to take another drink from the bottle, but most of the whiskey slipped down his cheek, and onto the floor as he passed out.

18

WHEN COURT resumed on Monday morning, Tina returned to the witness stand for her cross-examination.

"Good morning, Mrs. Manning," Whitney said, solicitously, after she had been sworn in. "I appreciate you being here today."

"Thank you," Tina said and smiled at him.

"Now as you know, and as I'm sure Mr. Bass and Ms. Slotnick explained to you, I'm here to ask you some additional questions about your testimony on Friday. Some questions about the night Mr. Centrella was killed. I hope you'll be willing to answer them. Can you agree to do that for me, Mrs. Manning?"

Tina nodded. "Of course," she said.

"Thank you," Whitney said.

As Maurice Bass sat at the prosecution table, he hoped Tina would remember the multiple warnings he had given her about not falling for the genteel Southern lawyer routine.

"Don't be lulled into a false sense of security by the deferential treatment he gave you during the deposition," Bass had told her. "That was just posturing. You're going to see a very different Whitney Taylor during your cross-examination. You're going to see the Whitney Taylor that knows how to bite."

"Let me begin by asking what I hope will be a simple question, Mrs. Manning," Whitney said.

Tina nodded.

"Do you consider yourself to be an honest woman?"

Tina paused for a moment, as if pondering all the hidden implications contained in the term "honest woman," before answering "yes."

"And do you consider yourself to be truthful?"

"I do," she said.

"In all matters or just in most matters?"

It was a standard question Whitney liked to use, knowing it created a dilemma for a witness.

"Most matters," Tina said, "but always when I'm testifying under oath."

Whitney smiled and gave her the subtlest of winks. It was the perfect answer, and he suspected Bass had given it to her. "He probably went back and pulled some of my transcripts," Whitney thought to himself.

"When you say you're especially truthful when testifying under oath, I presume you're referring to the testimony you gave on Friday, as well as the sworn statements made in your depositions. Is that presumption correct, Mrs. Manning?"

"It is."

"But you haven't always been a very truthful person, Mrs. Manning, have you? A large part of your adult life has been spent lying, has it not?"

"Objection, Your Honor, argumentative," Bass said, standing up.

"Overruled."

"As a matter of fact, a large part of your adult life has been spent being deceitful, has it not?"

"No, not at all."

"Are you claiming you're not a liar?"

"I'm insulted by your question, Mr. Taylor."

"I'm sorry you feel that way, but it's a yes or no question, Mrs. Manning."

"Please answer the question," Judge Friedman said.

Tina Manning shifted in her seat. "The answer is no, Your Honor, I am not a liar."

"But you lied on your pre-nuptial agreement, didn't you?" Whitney said.

"Excuse me?"

"Your pre-nuptial contract? You lied on that, didn't you?"

Tina looked confused.

"No," she said, and looked over at Judge Friedman for help that wasn't there.

"You didn't lie?" Whitney said, before going to the defense table and offering a copy of the Mannings' pre-nuptial agreement into evidence. He handed a copy to the bailiff, who handed it to Tina.

"Please allow me to direct your attention to Page 4, Paragraph 17, Mrs. Manning. It states that you had never been previously married. That was a lie wasn't it?"

"No" Tina said. "I didn't—"

"That wasn't a lie?" Whitney said. "I thought you testified on Friday that you had been married to a convicted drug dealer by the name of Kenny Valescu."

The first hint of a hard edge was now in Whitney's voice.

"Objection, Your Honor," Bass said. "Prejudicial."

"It's in the record," Whitney said.

"No," Bass said. "What's in the record, Your Honor, is that Mrs. Manning expressed shock at the fact her ex-husband was dealing drugs."

"Overruled."

"Thank you, Your Honor," Whitney said. "Mrs. Manning, you stated on Friday that you had previously been married to a convicted cocaine dealer, isn't that correct?"

"Kenny pleaded to—"

Whitney cut her off. "Under the law, a plea deal is the same as a conviction, Mrs. Manning," he said. "Please just answer the questions as they are asked. We have a lot of ground we need to cover today."

"I did, but—," Tina said.

"I'm not interested in 'buts,' Mrs. Manning. All I'm interested in is a simple yes or no answer to my questions."

Whitney raised his voice a notch.

"When you claimed in your pre-nuptial agreement that you had never been married, that was a lie, was it not?"

Tina took a moment to read paragraph 17 of the pre-nuptial agreement.

"It's a very simple question, Mrs. Manning."

"Give her a moment to read the document, Mr. Taylor," Judge Friedman said.

Tina squinted as she read the document.

"I honestly had no idea that language was in there," Tina said, when she looked back up. "To be completely honest, I never even read the agreement."

"You never read your pre-nuptial contract?"

"No, sir. I wasn't worried about it. My husband told me his lawyers needed us to sign it because of the trusts that were set up. He couldn't legally get married if we didn't sign one."

"And you believed that?" Whitney said.

"Believed what?"

"That your husband couldn't legally get married unless you signed a pre-nuptial agreement?"

"Of course I believed him," she said. "It was the truth. He has three children from previous marriages, and a lot of different trusts are set up. But the truth is, I didn't really care. I was only thinking about getting married to him. I wasn't thinking about getting divorced."

"What did *your* attorney say about it, Mrs. Manning?"

"I didn't use one."

"You didn't use an attorney?" Whitney said. "Are you sure about that, Mrs. Manning? Because that's not what the agreement says. The agreement says something quite different."

"It does?"

"Yes. Turn to the last page of the contract, where you signed your name."

Tina flipped to the last page of the agreement.

"Your Honor," Whitney said, "I would request to have the witness please read aloud for the jury the last paragraph above her signature. The words that are capitalized and in bold."

"I'll permit that," Judge Friedman said. "When you're ready, Mrs. Manning."

"Yes, ma'am," she said.

Tina put her finger to the document and began reading aloud.

"It says 'Both parties fully acknowledge he or she has been afforded an adequate opportunity and time to review and understand this agreement. In addition, each party acknowledges they have retained the service of an attorney with said attorney individually and independently selected by each party, without any kind of pressure, coercion, or duress. Moreover, each signee acknowledges he or she has thoroughly reviewed and examined the Agreement in its entirety before signing it, and has been fully advised by their independent legal counsel concerning the rights, liabilities and implications attendant to and incorporated within this agreement."

When Tina Manning looked back up at Whitney, her neck was flushed.

"Is that your signature underneath that paragraph, Mrs. Manning?"

"Yes."

"But now you're saying you never consulted an attorney, is that correct?"

"I never read the document," she said.

"But you signed it, correct? You signed your name to it."

"I did."

"So basically when you signed it, you lied. You signed it, affirming that you read it and that you had an attorney review it, but now, under oath, you're saying that didn't happen. Thus, by signing the document you lied, did you not?"

"I don't see it that way," Tina said. "I didn't know what I was signing. All I knew was it entitled me to a set amount of money in the event Ray initiated divorce proceedings."

Whitney shook his head, as if he was beginning to get frustrated with her.

"How many times have you been arrested, Mrs. Manning?"

"Once."

"Only once?"

209

"Yes, sir" Tina said.

"In Las Vegas?"

"Correct."

"With your drug dealing husband, correct?"

"Objection, Your Honor. Inflammatory."

"Sustained. That was gratuitous, Mr. Taylor."

"Yes, Your Honor," Whitney said. He walked back to the defense table and picked up a manila folder, which he handed to the clerk of court. The clerk marked the envelope for identification purposes and handed it to Judge Friedman. Inside the folder was a document that had been hand delivered to Whitney from the University of Kentucky.

"Your Honor, I would like to submit a copy of a second arrest report into the record," Whitney said.

"Objection, Your Honor," Bass said. "Lack of notice. The prosecution hasn't been furnished with the document that Mr. Taylor is purporting to put into evidence. We've had no notice, nor was the document disclosed to us in discovery."

"Your Honor," Whitney said, "the defense is submitting this evidence for impeachment purposes. Mrs. Manning just gave sworn testimony she has only been arrested once. We're allowed to offer documented proof she was being untruthful. I'm sure Mr. Bass understands we don't have to give him notice on evidence used for impeachment purposes."

"Let me see the evidence," Judge Friedman said, before looking at the report Whitney wanted to submit. "Your objection is overruled. I'll admit the document into evidence for impeachment purposes."

"Thank you, Your Honor," Whitney said, and handed the document to the bailiff. He marked it for the record and handed a copy of it to Tina.

"Do you recognize that document, Mrs. Manning?" Whitney said.

She looked down at the report for several seconds before looking back at him. Her body language was now looking a lot less confident than it had when she was sworn in.

"I do," she said.

"Would you please tell this court what it is?"

"It's an arrest report from my freshman year of college."

"At the University of Kentucky, correct?"

"That's correct."

"Your Honor, with your permission, the defense would like to display this document for the jury."

"I'll permit it."

"Thank you," Whitney said. He walked over and placed a slide onto the courtroom's overhead projector. A black and white mug shot of Tina Manning appeared on the screen. In the photograph, she was holding up a black square felt board. It said *U.K.P.D, Valentine, Christine C.* in white plastic letters.

"Mrs. Manning, would you please tell this jury the reason for your arrest at the University of Kentucky, or would you prefer I do it?"

"It was for underage drinking," she said.

"And also for using a fake ID, correct? According to the arrest report, you were in possession of forged identification at the time of your arrest were you not, Mrs. Manning?"

"I guess I was," she said.

"Using false or forged identification is dishonest in and of itself, is it not?"

"Most people I knew at Kentucky had a fake ID."

"Be that as it may, Mrs. Manning, it's still dishonest. And you still lied about the number of times you were arrested, did you not?"

Dave glanced over at Maurice to see how he was taking the news about Tina's arrest at the University of Kentucky. He had been waiting all trial for this moment, and was expecting him to look upset. Instead, Maurice looked completely calm, as if he wasn't the least bit concerned about a previously undisclosed arrest back in college that his star witness had just lied about.

Maurice may have looked completely tranquil on the outside, but on the inside he was fuming. He had no idea how his office could have missed something as obvious as an arrest in Tina's background, or why she would have been so stupid as to not to disclose it to him. Whitney Taylor now had a sledgehammer he could use to bang away at her credibility.

"Un-fucking believable," he thought to himself.

It was only after he scrutinized the front page of the arrest report that he figured out why nobody in his office had found it. Tina Manning had not been arrested by a municipality. She had been arrested by the University's police department, which, like most campus police departments in the United States, did not report misdemeanors to the national database.

That meant the only way to have found the information would have been for Tina to confess it, or someone to have gone to Lexington and speak with the campus police. But Bass saw the arrest was made in Tina's maiden name, *Valentine.*

"How the hell would Whitney Taylor have known to go looking for an arrest report at the University of Kentucky that was issued in her maiden name?" Bass asked himself.

Bobby had been the one who found out about the arrest. He had traveled to the University of Kentucky in early January, a day after spending an afternoon with Tina Manning's mother in Darien, Ohio.

To successfully defend Dave, Whitney knew he needed to find out more about Tina Manning's past. He already knew about the arrest out in Vegas, *Bass had been required to disclose it under the Rules of Criminal Procedure,* but he didn't know much about her life before that. He planned to engage Victor Bolch to dig around, until Bobby volunteered for the job.

"I got seven weeks vacation saved up," he said. "I can find out just as much as your investigator. And with all due respect, I don't charge 200 bucks an hour. I'll do it for free."

That sounded like a better idea to Dave, so, on January 3rd, Bobby caught a late morning flight from Atlanta to

Columbus, Ohio. It was a Saturday. Bobby expected the plane to be empty, but it wasn't. It was packed with rowdy Ohio State fans traveling through Atlanta on their way home from the Orange Bowl, where the Buckeyes had beaten Alabama in overtime.

The OSU fans were still feeling good about the victory, *a few of them looked like they were still drunk*, and the flight had a celebratory quality to it. Adding to the fans' excitement was the fact Mary McNeill, Ohio's Governor, and a former astronaut on the Space Shuttle, was traveling with them. Near the end of the flight, she stood up and led the plane in an O-H-I-O cheer to loud applause.

When they landed, Bobby picked up a rental car from the National counter in Columbus and drove an hour and a half south to Darien, a small farming community near the Kentucky state line. Darien's economy had always relied on agriculture, not factories, which meant it had been spared much of the economic and social upheaval that had taken place, as the Rust Belt's manufacturing base had been degraded into a fast food and discount store based economy.

It was almost dark when Bobby rolled into town. He grabbed a quick dinner at Bob Evans before checking into the Comfort Inn. The next morning he found three "Valentines" listed in the phone book. The first number was disconnected, but at the second one a woman answered and acknowledged she was Tina Valentine's mother. Bobby said he was a police officer from Atlanta, who had traveled to Darien as part of the investigation into the Remo Centrella shooting. The woman said her name was Rose and that Bobby could stop by after two o'clock.

Her house was on the edge of the small town, a ten-minute drive from Bobby's hotel. A long, well-worn dirt driveway led the way to a classic white, A-frame, farmhouse. He went up to the door and a woman, who looked like she was in her early 50s, answered. Bobby flashed his badge and she invited him inside.

Rose Valentine was slightly plump and walked as if she

might have a bad hip. She led Bobby onto an enclosed back porch, where she sat down and took a healthy gulp from her coffee mug, before lighting up a long, thin cigarette.

There was an empty bottle of Zinfandel on the side-table next to her, and at least a dozen family photographs hung on the wall. Bobby's attention was held by one that had been taken in front of Cinderella's castle. There were four people in what looked to be the picture of a quintessentially Midwestern family.

The man in the picture had a huge smile on his face. He was square jawed and broad shouldered. He smiled like a guy who wanted the world to think his life was perfect. A pretty blonde teenager, with a self-conscious smile, was tucked into his left shoulder. She didn't look like a girl who would grow up to become somebody's third wife. The older woman in the picture was sporting aggressively blonde hair and breasts that looked like they were trying to break out of her pink tennis shirt. She looked a lot different than the drab-looking woman sitting across from Bobby in a loose-fitting Cincinnati Bengals' jersey.

Rounding out the photograph was a squinting boy with shaggy hair and a mouth full of metal. He looked like he was about six or seven years younger than Tina, which meant, Bobby figured, he was now probably around college age.

"Is your son around, Mrs. Valentine?"

"No," Rose said, with a cigarette dangling out of her mouth. "He's up North."

"Ohio State?" Bobby asked. "I was on a flight with a bunch of their fans yesterday."

She let out a short laugh.

"No. Luke's not exactly college material at the moment. His daddy went to Wesleyan, but he's at a place where they're trying to teach him some better manners."

Bobby was about to ask her what she meant when he figured it out.

"How about Mr. Valentine? Is your husband around?"

"No, he's gone," she said.

"Passed on?"

She gave out another short, disappointed laugh.

"Not that lucky. The Reverend Valentine's very much alive. Living in Northern California, the last I heard."

"What's he doing out there?"

"That's where he went to live when they ran him out of town."

"Who?"

"The church elders," Rose said, nonchalantly, as she stubbed out her cigarette and lit a new one. "They didn't appreciate what he did to our church. I was mostly upset about what he did to our family."

"What was that?" Bobby said.

"He broke us."

19

——

"WHAT HAPPENED?" Bobby said.

Rose Valentine paused as she exhaled the long pull she had taken from her Virginia Slim.

"The internet. Ruined our life the day Michael brought it home."

Rose stood up.

"I need some more Zinfandel," she said.

Bobby followed her into her kitchen.

"Can you open this?" she said, and handed him a bottle of White Zinfandel that had a small red Mobil sticker on it. She took out two wine glasses from her kitchen cabinet. Bobby poured some wine into each glass, and Rose lifted her glass in toast.

"I had no clue about computers," Rose said, as they walked back out to the heated porch. "I thought only scientists used them. But one night, Michael brought one home and said it would help the kids with their homework. He said it would give them an educational advantage.

"I didn't know. I dropped out of college during my sophomore year, but it sounded good to me. The only problem was the kids got tired of it pretty quick, and Michael was the one who ended up using it. He became obsessed. That's all he started to talk about. *Internet, list servers, the web.* He said he was going to use the Internet to bring the Word of God to every corner of the world. He started creating on-line men's groups. Prayer rooms he called them."

Rose shook her head and Bobby thought he might have detected a tear in her eye.

"An internet prayer warrior," she said. "That's how Michael started to talk about himself. He was going to change the world, one dial-up connection at a time."

She let out another of her small laughs.

"He had half the damn town convinced. We even had a couple boys from Merrill Lynch come over from Cincinnati and tell us about how rich we could be if Michael went onto the stock exchange. We were going to own the 'religion vertical' they said. They couldn't have been more than 25 or 30 years old, but they were so confident about all the millions we were going to make that I actually began to think maybe God had anointed my husband. That me, a girl who was knocked up when I met Michael, was married to the man who was going to change the world."

Bobby realized he must have had a look of disbelief on his face because Rose said, "I know, *it sounds ridiculous*, but that's how I felt. And you couldn't have told me any different until the day Chrissie found the emails."

"What emails?"

"Emails to just about every hooker within a 90 mile radius of Darien," Rose said. "Turns out, half the time Michael was supposedly working on his prayer rooms, he was actually going into sex rooms. And all the daytrips he took to meet up with his followers were actually trips he took to meet up with women he met online."

"Wow," Bobby said.

"Pathetic, huh?"

"That's beyond pathetic."

"You can imagine how Chrissie felt when she found out her father, the man who had given her a purity ring, was a perv."

Dave saw that tears had formed in Rose's eyes. She picked up the bottle of wine and re-filled her glass. She went to pour some for Bobby, but he put his hand over his glass. One glass of wine bought from a gas station was more than enough.

"What did she do when she found them?" Bobby asked.

"She went to one of the Deacons who convinced her to tell me. A few days later, me, Larry Biederman and Bill Waters confronted Michael. He denied it, of course. Said he was doing research for an anti-pornography ministry, but they showed him the chats they printed out. Some of them were pretty graphic."

"What did he say then?"

Rose chuckled. "Being the master manipulator he was, Michael got on his knees and started to beg for forgiveness. He claimed he had an addiction and that he needed help. He begged them not to tell anybody. He said he would give them twenty percent of the shares when we went public. But Bill and Larry are men of principle. They weren't going to budge. They told Michael they had an obligation to inform the rest of the church."

Rose frowned.

"Darien's a small town, and it didn't take long for word to spread that Michael had been caught soliciting prostitutes. Once that news got out, all the people he had lined up as investors wanted their money back. The only problem was, most of it had been spent on hookers and hotel rooms."

Rose Valentine started to rub her forehead.

"It was terrible. A few of them threatened to go to the police and have us charged with embezzlement. I was scared to death, but Bill convinced them to back off. Him and Larry offered Michael a deal: Leave Darien, sign the house over to me, and the church would find a way to pay back the debt.

"But, they warned him, if he ever came back to Darien they would have him arrested."

"That had to be tough on you," Bobby said.

"It was worse for the kids. I had no clue how to handle Luke. It got so bad with him, I had to send him up to live with my cousin's family in Maumee. They kicked him out when he started selling their jewelry to pawn shops. He had no place else to go, so I let him move back in here."

Rose gave Bobby a pleading look.

"I'm his mother, what could I do? Eventually they picked him up for selling OxyContin. He's been in and out of the jails ever since.

"Chrissie ended up at Kentucky, instead of Ohio Wesleyan. But she was never the same. She started going with fraternity boys who got her into drugs."

Rose now had tears in her eyes.

"Can you imagine?" she said, as she picked up a Kleenex and blew her nose. "A straight A student at Harding High ends up flunking out of the University of Kentucky. That's why she ended up moving out to Vegas. She moved there with a guy who thought he was going to be a professional poker player."

Rose took a drag from her cigarette.

"That didn't last very long, of course, and the next thing I knew, she called to say she was married to a card dealer. I didn't hear too much from her after that. It wasn't until I saw her picture on television that I even knew she was living in Atlanta. I practically puked up my coffee when I read she told her husband that her father and me were dead."

"Have you spoken with your daughter since she's been arrested?"

"Once. I called and left a message with her attorney."

She leaned in a bit towards Bobby.

"She's a Jew, you know," Rose said in a whisper and nodded her head as if to say, "*it's true.*"

Bobby didn't know how to respond to the comment, so he just nodded his head noncommittally.

"It took her about a week to call back, but she finally did. We talked for a little bit, but she didn't sound like the Chrissie I knew. Actually asked me to address her as 'Tina.'"

Rose shook her head.

"Don't get me wrong, Mr. Morello. I offered to go down to Atlanta to support her, but she said it wasn't a good time."

"What about her father?" Bobby said. "Where's he in all this?"

"No clue. The sad thing is he isn't even her biological father."

"He's not?" Bobby said.

"We always acted like he was, but he wasn't. Her biological father was a boy I met when I was a sophomore at Youngstown State. His name was Danny Ryan. Very handsome boy, but not the most reliable guy I ever met. He quit school after I told him I was pregnant. Claimed his father had a heart attack, and he had to go back to Baltimore to help run the family bar."

Rose stubbed out her cigarette.

"I couldn't have a baby in the dormitory, obviously, so I moved back home to Toledo. That's where I met Michael, who was doing an apprenticeship at my parents' church. I was three months pregnant and feeling ashamed, but Michael went out of his way to be kind to me. *There are parts of him that were really good.* We got married a month before Chrissie was born.

"Danny called a couple of times until I told him I was engaged and that my fiancée wanted to adopt the baby. When Chrissie was born, we put Michael down as the father. It was a lot less complicated and expensive than having to go through a formal adoption."

"That was smart," Bobby said.

Rose drank down the rest of her Zinfandel.

"And that was that," she said. "Three years later, when Michael got his job with the church down here, I was already pregnant with Luke. Everybody just assumed I was pregnant with our second child. We never even considered telling Chrissie."

Rose paused to unwrap the cellophane from a new pack of Virginia Slims. She took out a new cigarette and lit it. "You smoke?" she said.

"Not anymore."

"To each his own," she said, after letting out a long exhale. "Who knows? Maybe I should have told her."

"Don't beat yourself up," Bobby said. "My shrink once told me life only makes sense when you're looking backwards. The problem is you have to live it going forward.'"

"Thank you," Rose said and seemed to mean it. She patted the top of Bobby's hand.

"You're welcome," Bobby said.

They talked for a little while longer, and it was almost 5 p.m. by the time he left her house. Bobby headed west on I-64 towards Lexington, Kentucky where he checked into a Red Roof Inn near the University. The next morning, he woke up and introduced himself to the head of the University of Kentucky's campus police, who was more than happy to cooperate with a detective from Atlanta.

Bobby shared a little inside information on Dave's case with him, and the Chief had one of his assistants run Tina's maiden name through their records. Nobody in the UK police department had even realized Tina Manning attended UK, but by the time Bobby left the campus he had documented proof she had, in the form of the arrest report and mug shot that was being displayed for the jury.

"You seem to have a serious predilection towards dishonesty, don't you Mrs. Manning?" Whitney said, continuing to go after her aggressively.

"No, sir."

"In fact, you even went so far as telling your ex-husband that your parents were dead, isn't that correct?"

"I never said that."

"You didn't? That's what he told Sports Illustrated."

"I don't know why he said that," she said.

"Are you saying your ex-husband is a liar?"

"We were in the process of getting a divorce."

"Because you broke your wedding vows, correct?"

"Objection," Bass said, and stood up. "This trial is not about Mrs. Manning's personal life."

"Overruled."

"Because your husband found out you had a sexual relationship with one of his closest friends, isn't that right? An affair he was not aware of because you were dishonest about it. Because you deceived him, isn't that correct?"

Whitney was doubling down on his pace of questions.

"The fact of the matter is Mrs. Manning, you've proven yourself to be a very dishonest person, haven't you? You've told lie after lie after lie. Almost everything you said about the night Mr. Centrella was killed is a lie, isn't it?"

Tina shook her head and said, "No."

"You did have a black eye, didn't you? You had a black eye from where Remo hit you."

"No, sir," Tina said, "I never—"

"And the only reason you're testifying you didn't have one is because you're getting a deal for immunity from Mr. Bass in exchange for your false testimony, isn't that correct?"

"No, it's not," Tina said.

"In fact, you agreed to come into this courtroom and give false testimony in order to stay out of jail, didn't you?"

"Objection, Your Honor. Speculation."

"Overruled."

"Why would you expect this jury to believe anything you say after all the lies you've told? You're a natural born liar, aren't you, Mrs. Manning?"

"Objection," Bass said louder and now stood up. "This is no longer a cross examination, Your Honor, it's an attack on the witness."

"Sustained."

"Very well, Your Honor," Whitney said. "I'm finished, anyways. No further questions for the witness."

Tina Manning, who had radiated confidence when she stepped down from the stand on Friday afternoon, looked shaken up as she and Linda Slotnick left the courtroom. As she was escorted out, Dave caught Darlene's eye and gave her a slight nod of encouragement.

With Tina Manning off the stand, Judge Friedman asked Maurice if he planned to call any additional witnesses.

"No, Your Honor," he said. "We have no further witnesses. The State of Georgia rests its case."

"Thank you, Mr. Bass," Judge Friedman said. "Bailiff, please escort the jury from the courtroom."

Once the jurors were gone, Judge Friedman asked if either party had any motions they would like to make.

"I do, Your Honor," Whitney said and stood up. "The defense would like to move respectfully for a dismissal of the charges."

20

———

"YOU MAY proceed with your motion, Mr. Taylor."

"Thank you, Your Honor," Whitney said. He was still feeling the positive effects of the adrenaline that had been flowing during his cross-examination of Tina.

"In the name of justice, Your Honor, the defendant respectfully moves the court to dismiss this case, whereupon the State of Georgia has failed to meet its burden. I submit, Your Honor, there is no possible way, based upon the evidence and testimony put forward during the prosecution's phase of the case, that any reasonable jury could find Mr. Mackno guilty."

Whitney's Motion to Dismiss was *de rigueur,* a standard motion made by almost all defense attorneys at the completion of the prosecution's case. It was a formal request that was almost never granted.

Whitney knew there was an almost zero percent chance Judge Friedman would grant a dismissal in such a high profile case, but that was not going to prevent him from arguing it will full enthusiasm. With the television cameras rolling, he was making his argument more to the court of public opinion than he was to Judge Friedman. He wanted to do his best to convince those watching the trial that Dave wasn't just *not guilty,* but that he was, in fact, *innocent* of the charges. He wanted to convince the public of Dave's innocence because he knew Dave wanted to return to the police department.

Whitney knew that forcefully arguing the Motion for Dismissal was one of the best opportunities he would have to undo some of the reputational damage wrought by the indictment, even though he thought it would be a mistake for Dave to try and resume his career in Atlanta.

In Whitney's opinion, which he had kept to himself, the best thing for Dave to do after the trial would be to move to a different part of the country and seek a fresh start. He was convinced Dave had attained too much notoriety to ever blend back into APD, and that even with an acquittal, he would always be damaged goods in Atlanta.

"Justice *demands* a dismissal, Your Honor," Whitney stated. "Even if, Your Honor, all the evidence presented by the prosecution is viewed in the light most favorable to the State, they have absolutely failed to meet their burden.

"It is time to end this farce," he said, as all eyes in the courtroom focused on him. "Your Honor, justice demands that you, the objective referee within this adversarial process, dismiss an indictment that should have never been filed in the first place. Now that the State of Georgia has been granted its full and open opportunity to be heard, it's time for this court to acknowledge the truth. Now is the time to let this good man, a man who has devoted his life to protecting the people of this great city, go free and once again serve the city he loves.

"I appeal to your good senses, Your Honor. You have seen the same things I have. You have borne witness to the fact the prosecution has been unable to meet their statutorily required burden. I beseech you, Your Honor, exercise the power that the State of Georgia, *that its people,* has entrusted in you. Dismiss these charges in the name of justice and bring this proceeding to an end.

"Thank you," Whitney said and bowed his head slightly towards Judge Friedman.

"Thank you, Mr. Taylor," Judge Friedman said and clicked her gavel. "Your motion is denied. Court will be in recess until the morning, at which time the defense may present its case."

Bass caught Whitney's eye and couldn't resist a wink.

During the prosecution's phase of a trial, the defense is entitled to cross-examine any witness called by the state. During the cross, they can ask questions of, and submit materials into evidence, to try and directly refute the testimony given by the prosecution witness. They can also do their best to try and impeach the witness' credibility.

But they are not allowed to call anyone to the stand in order to contradict the testimony of the witness. That's because the defense is not allowed to call any of their own witnesses during the prosecution's phase of the trial. They have to wait until the prosecution rests their case and it becomes their turn to present their defense. *The same rules apply to the prosecution once the defense begins to present their side of the case.*

As a result, even if the defense has what they believe to be a "lockdown" rebuttal witness, they have to wait until the prosecution rests before they can get that witness in front of the jury. The forced delay can be a serious problem for the defense in situations where they have been unable to undermine the credibility of a prosecution witness during cross-examination. That's because it allows an opportunity for the prosecution witness' testimony to shape the jury's view of the case. It's even worse for the defense when the prosecution puts on a strong, persuasive witness like Curtis Pressley.

Whitney knew Curtis Pressley's testimony had negatively impacted the way the jury viewed Dave. He knew he needed to try and undo some of that damage, which was the reason he slotted Bobby as his first witness.

Bobby looked sharp as he stepped up to the stand. He'd always had a muscular build, and it was accentuated by his blue blazer and gray flannels. He wasn't wearing a necktie, but Dave still thought Bobby looked like he might be a mid-level corporate executive.

"Detective Morello, can you please tell this court how long you have known Detective Mackno?" Whitney said, after Bobby had been sworn in.

"Over twenty years," Bobby said.

"Would it be fair to say that during that time you've formed an opinion about the kind of police officer Mr. Mackno has been?"

"Dave's a very good cop," Bobby said, matter of factly. "Ask anybody who worked with him. They'll tell you the same thing."

"How would you describe his approach to police work?"

"Professional and dedicated."

"During the time you have known Mr. Mackno, have you ever seen him get violent with anyone?"

"No, sir."

"How about rough?"

Bobby paused.

"Yes," he said. "I've seen Dave get rough with some suspects."

Whitney made a note on his pad.

"Approximately how many times?"

"I've probably seen him get rough with suspects about 15 to 20 times."

Whitney made another note.

"So a little bit less than once per year?" he said.

"Sounds about right, but again, it's a rough guess."

Bobby glanced over at the jury. "No pun intended," he said.

Several of the jurors, and even Judge Friedman, smiled at Bobby's attempted humor.

Whitney paused as if he were thinking of his next question, even though it was written on his legal pad.

"Detective Morello, could you explain for this jury how you are able to reconcile your statement that you have seen Mr. Mackno get rough with people almost 20 times, while also claiming you have never seen him get violent?"

"Sure" Bobby said. "As I think has already been discussed by some of the other witnesses, Dave and I have spent most of our careers patrolling in Zone 3. By almost any standard, it's the roughest zone in the city. We're not spending a lot of time interfacing with choirboys, so to speak. We're usually dealing with the tougher elements of society.

"A lot of the time, being a cop is pretty uneventful. We're driving around, trying to be a visible presence, doing as much as we can to act as a deterrent. But a lot of times when we do get a call, it's not about a 13-year-old kid shoplifting at Wal-Mart. It's usually more serious, and it can often involve somebody acting violent.

"When that happens," Bobby said, still directing his comments directly towards the jury box, "if we're trying to arrest a guy, *and nine times out of ten it is a male*, he's not always putting his hands up and saying 'Okay, Officer, you got me.' Sometimes, the men we're trying to arrest might be high or they might have been previously incarcerated. They don't want to go back to prison, so they don't always give us their full cooperation. In those instances, if a guy is trying to resist being cuffed, it can require some force in order to facilitate the arrest. You may need to apply a little physicality in a way that might seem a little rough to the average guy on the street."

"Could you give us a couple of examples of what you mean by that, Detective?"

"Sure," Bobby said. "If a guy's resisting arrest, it might mean twisting his arm around a little to make him cooperate, or maybe you knock him off balance, give his leg a little sweep. You usually want to try and find a way to take him to the ground in order to get some leverage over him."

"You've seen Detective Mackno do that?"

"I have."

"What did you think when you saw Detective Mackno getting rough with a suspect?"

"I thought he was doing his job, that the use of force was required under the circumstances."

"It almost seems as if violence is part of the job of being an Atlanta police officer," Whitney said. "Would you agree with that statement, Detective?"

"Not at all," Bobby said. "I would actually disagree

with it."

"Perfect," Whitney thought to himself. Part of his strategy to maximize Bobby's credibility with the jury was to try and position him as his own man, not a rubber stamp for whatever Whitney said. In Whitney's experience, getting a witness to directly disagree with an assertion was one of the best techniques to accomplish that.

"But you just said you saw Detective Mackno get rough with suspects and that it was part of the job."

"I did."

"What's the difference?"

"It's a big one," Bobby said. "By getting rough, I mean using the physical force required to subdue someone who is trying to resist being lawfully arrested. It's simply doing what's required to complete an arrest. But violence? That's a completely different story. That's intentionally trying to hurt someone. That's using force when it's not necessary, or using excessive force when a lesser amount is required. In my experience, the line between the two is very clear."

"What makes it so clear?"

"Intent," Bobby said. "Is the intent to arrest the suspect or is the intent to hurt the suspect? That's the difference between necessary force and violence."

"Have you ever seen Detective Mackno *intend* to hurt anyone?"

"Never."

"Have you ever seen him act violent?"

"No. Dave is not a violent person."

"What about excessive force? Have you ever seen Detective Mackno use excessive force?"

"Excessive force doesn't happen as much as the media would make you think," Bobby said. "And it has definitely never happened with Dave."

"Do you recall Curtis Pressley's testimony, Detective Morello?"

"I do."

"In fact, you were sitting in court last week when he testified, were you not?"

"Yes, I was."

"Do you recall his testimony as to Detective Mackno's actions during the Rodney King riots."

"I do."

"What did you think when you heard it?"

"I knew his recollection was incorrect," Bobby said.

"Did you think he was lying?"

"Not necessarily," Bobby said. "I think Mr. Pressley did probably get hit by a cop during the riots. *I could see his arm was injured,* but I know Dave wasn't the cop who injured it."

"How do you know that, Detective?"

"Because Dave and I were assigned to the same bus on the night Mr. Pressley was talking about, and we didn't confront any line of college kids marching up Trinity from Vine City.

"There *had been* a march two nights earlier, the first night of the unrest," Bobby said. "It was that march, with the students from Atlanta University Center that actually started the riots in Atlanta. But two nights later, we didn't come across anything like the scene Mr. Pressley described."

"So what Mr. Pressley alleged happened never did?"

"I'm not saying it didn't happen. It could have. I'm just saying it would have been impossible for Dave to have been involved because he and I never confronted any kind of a march like the one he described."

"Are you sure about that, Detective? How confident are you in your recollection?"

"One hundred percent. I couldn't forget the riots if I tried."

"Was there any time on that third night when Detective Mackno might have confronted a line of marchers without you knowing about it?"

"No. Every stop Dave made, I made, too," Bobby said. "It would have been impossible for him to have confronted marchers by himself that night. Mr. Pressley's story might be one hundred percent true, but I can guarantee you he was hit by a different cop."

"Thank you, Detective Morello," Whitney said and

looked up at Judge Friedman. "I have no further questions, Your Honor."

"Your witness, Mr. Bass."

"Thank you, Your Honor," Bass said as he walked towards the lectern. "Detective Morello, you testified that you've known the defendant for over twenty years, is that correct?"

"It is," Bobby said.

"And you're close friends with the defendant?"

"I am."

"Best friends?"

"Yes."

Maurice glanced down for a moment at his legal pad before saying, "Mr. Morello, are you familiar with what is commonly referred to as the "Blue Code of Silence?"

"Objection, Your Honor," Whitney said, standing back up. "Foundation. Detective Morello is not a subject matter expert on policing."

"Overruled. Mr. Bass can ask what the witness has personal knowledge of."

"Thank you," Bass said. "Your answer, Detective Morello?"

"Yes," Bobby said. "I've heard the term."

"Would you describe for the court what that term 'Blue Code of Silence,' means?"

"Objection, Your Honor. Same grounds. The question goes beyond the witness' personal knowledge."

"Sustained," Judge Friedman said.

"May I approach, Your Honor?" Bass said. He looked surprised.

"You may."

Maurice and Whitney approached Judge Friedman's bench for a sidebar discussion that would be transcribed for the official record by the court stenographer, but would be held outside the earshot of the jury.

"Your Honor," Bass said, "you overruled Mr. Taylor's initial objection, I don't understand why you sustained his second one."

"The difference between the questions is that the first one asks the witness about his personal knowledge, while your second one asks him for his knowledge about a larger conspiracy theory, of which the witness lacks the expertise to testify. If you wanted to argue a Code of Silence conspiracy, Counselor, you should have done it during your phase of the case. *That door is now closed.* You're not entitled to bring up any new theories at this point of the trial, unless Mr. Taylor brings it up during his defense."

"But, Your Honor," Bass said, "with all due respect to this court, I'm not arguing a theory. I'm simply asking—"

"You are," Judge Friedman said. "I co-authored a treatise on criminal law, Mr. Bass. Code of Silence is merely a legal theory, which needs to be established by expert testimony if you want to try and argue it exists."

"You don't believe it does?"

"My personal views have no relevance to this proceeding. If you want to ask Detective Morello if he had motivations to keep quiet, I'll permit that. But I'm not going to permit you to engage in a discussion of a systemic conspiracy by police officers. You didn't establish it during the prosecution, and nothing in Mr. Morello's testimony, or Mr. Taylor's questions, has opened the door for you to bring it in at this juncture."

"Very well, Your Honor," Bass said. "But I would like the record to reflect I respectfully disagree with your decision to curtail what I believe to be a valid line of questioning."

"Your objection has been noted for the record."

Whitney returned to his seat, and Maurice returned to his lectern.

"Detective Morello, have you ever lied to protect Mr. Mackno?" Bass said.

"No."

"Never once in twenty years?"

"Never had to," Bobby said.

"What if you had needed to?"

"Objection," Whitney said. "Speculation."

"Sustained."

For the first time in the case Maurice Bass looked visibly annoyed. He disagreed with Friedman's interpretation of his code of silence questions, and had not appreciated her snarky comment about co-authoring a legal treatise. She had now, effectively, narrowed his planned cross-examination of Bobby, which meant he was going to have to re-work his questions on the fly.

"Detective Morello," Bass said, "you testified you've worked with the defendant for over 20 years, is that correct?"

"It is."

"During that time, the two of you have worked almost exclusively in Zone 3, correct?"

"Yes."

Bass looked down at his legal pad.

"An area of the city that you said, and I quote, 'by almost any standard, is the roughest zone in the city.' Do you remember saying those words, Detective?"

"I do."

"But your testimony is that the defendant never did anything, not even one act, that might constitute excessive force?"

"That's correct."

"You never saw Detective Mackno cross the line one time in twenty plus years?" Bass said, looking incredulous.

"I never did."

"That's quite amazing, Detective Morello, wouldn't you agree? Twenty plus years of being a cop in the roughest zone in Atlanta, dealing with some of the toughest elements in society, yet having an absolutely spotless record of never even once getting violent?"

The look of disbelief on Bass' face was now even more pronounced.

"Dave's a great cop," Bobby said.

"Sounds like you want this jury to think he's a perfect one," Bass said, while shaking his head. "No further questions, Your Honor."

"Thank you for your testimony, Detective. You may step down," Judge Friedman said.

"Thank you," Bobby said, and nodded to the jury as he returned to his seat in the gallery.

After Bobby's testimony, Whitney called a member of the Police Department's human resources division to the stand and walked her through Dave's official work history. It was monotonous testimony that made most of the jurors eyes glaze over, but Whitney had to do it in order to document that Dave had never been formally disciplined during his career.

It took over an hour to go through his personnel file, and it was after 5 p.m. before Judge Friedman put the court into recess for the evening.

Darlene had already left court to attend her monthly book club meeting. Both she and Dave thought she should make it a priority because her book club was one of the few places where Darlene could get a temporary respite from the pressures of the indictment and trial.

Because Darlene had taken the car, Bobby gave Dave a ride home. It had been an emotionally draining day, and neither man spoke much on the ride up to Alpharetta. They had been friends long enough that there was no need to verbalize what Bobby had done for Dave. It was tacitly understood.

"Thanks, Bobby," Dave said, when they pulled into his driveway. He clasped Bobby on the arm before opening the door.

"You know," Bobby said as Dave was getting out, "I still think about it sometimes....what I did to that kid."

"You gotta let it go," Dave said. "There's a reason nothing ever came of it. It was a crazy time, Bobby. We were playing under a different set of rules."

"I know," Bobby said, while looking straight ahead through his windshield. "You're right. I just need to get it locked back in its box."

"You want to come in for a beer?" Dave said. "We could listen to some Bruce, and I could fire up some steaks on the grill. *Try and forget about all this bullshit for a couple of hours.*"

"I can't," Bobby said. "I told Sheri I'd make it home for

dinner. I want to see Eric before he goes to bed."

"You're a good man, Bobby," Dave said, while pointing at him. "Don't ever lose sight."

"Yeah, sure," Bobby thought as he backed out of Dave's driveway. "I'm a good man, alright."

He hit the gas hard as he drove away. After spending the bulk of the afternoon perjuring himself, Bobby was ready to get home and take a shower.

21

DESPITE HIS testimony, Bobby had been one of the cops who confronted the marchers from Clark Atlanta on the third night of the riots. It was a confrontation that could still shake his soul when he thought back to it.

The riots in Atlanta over the Rodney King verdict had taken the city by surprise. Nobody had anticipated a jury verdict in Los Angeles would lead to mob violence in Atlanta. But it did. A protest march by students from the University Center turned violent and triggered the riots.

Because they started with no advance warning, the cops on duty were initially overwhelmed, which allowed the lawbreakers to gain the upper hand. APD was forced into pullback mode, and it wasn't long before CNN began broadcasting videos of smashed windows, looted stores, and torched vehicles.

Quicker than anybody could react, downtown Atlanta went from orderly to dangerous.

At one point, a rookie cop was trapped inside a Hardee's restroom, and it took eleven cops to extract him to safety. Bobby had been one of the cops sent to rescue him, although at one point during the mission it appeared they might have been too late.

While Bobby and the other cops were being driven to the scene, a report came across the radio that the rookie had been killed and was being dragged through the streets. It was a false report that was quickly corrected, but just the fact that such a scenario, *a police officer being dragged through the streets of Atlanta*, seemed plausible, was an indication to Bobby of just how fast anarchy could spread.

Conditions worsened throughout the night, and on day two of the riots, Frank Durkin's predecessor, Brian Sayers, told Atlanta's Mayor he had 24 hours to take back control of the streets. Otherwise, he said, he would call in the Georgia National Guard.

"We just got awarded the Olympics," Sayers said. "The last thing we need is CNN broadcasting images that make Atlanta look like Beirut."

The Mayor agreed and, in coordination with Ronnie Berzanski, the message went out that, short of killing somebody, APD could do what was necessary to restore order.

By the time the order filtered down to Dave and Bobby's Sergeant, it had been reduced to two words: *swing away.*

As part of the plan to end the riots, the lieutenant in charge of the downtown division was given authority to "strip the other police zones" of all personnel and bring every available cop into Zone 3.

Prisoner transport buses were delivered to a staging area at Wilson Field and then used to scramble teams of cops around the city to wherever there were reports of roving gangs. Bobby could still remember the look on many of the looters' faces when they saw a Bluebird bus come barreling around a corner, before screeching to a halt and releasing a couple of dozen cops decked out in riot gear. He remembered how animalistic it felt running off the bus, blackjacks raised to the sky, and war cries filling the air.

The bus on which Dave and Bobby were riding had made a half dozen stops before they got a call about marchers heading into downtown. It was after dark when their driver, a Vietnam vet, who seemed to be having the time of his life racing a bus around the city streets, received an urgent call. After listening to the dispatcher, he announced that a large group of men were marching into downtown with plans to storm the Capital building.

"They want to burn down the Statehouse," he yelled to the cops on his bus. "Orders are to protect it at all costs!"

When they reached the capital area, the driver skidded to a stop and let the cops out at the intersection of Trinity and Central. One of the guys got on a bullhorn and ordered the marchers to turn around and retreat, while the other cops formed a human barricade across Trinity.

But the gang of college kids, who had no clue about the mental state of the cops they were about to face, kept on coming. They were motivated by a combination of pride, testosterone, and images of their forefathers, who had marched during the Civil Rights movement. They kept marching forward, chanting, "No justice! No peace!"

When the marchers got within reach of the cops, they were pushed back a few times, but kept trying to proceed forward. Without any warning, one of the cops near the middle of the line let out a yell and took a swing at one of the kids with his billy club. Once that happened, it was game on.

Bobby remembered letting out a demonic yell as he charged into the scrum. He was in a blind rage. Not just about what was happening in Atlanta, but what was taking place in cities across the United States. He had seen the video of Reginald Denny getting pulled out of his truck and smashed in the head with a cinder block by a group of blacks. That footage made him think everything he took for granted as an American citizen was under attack, and that he was now, literally, on the front lines of a battle for the preservation of society.

Full of anger, and with his mind addled from a combination of caffeine, adrenaline, and lack of sleep, Bobby moved towards four of the kids who had broken off from the larger group.

"Get the fuck off my street," he ordered.

It felt good just to unleash those words and to have the freedom to put some punks in their place.

Three of the kids got the message and started to retreat towards safety, but a fourth one was taking his time.

Showing Bobby some attitude, and making it clear he wasn't about to scamper away just because some white cop ordered him to. It was the same "fuck you" attitude and swagger Bobby had to deal with everyday in exchange for his paycheck. But this time, he didn't have to take it. This time, Bobby could teach Homeboy a lesson and get away with it.

Bobby approached the kid from behind and threw a hard forearm into the back of his head. The kid lost his balance, stumbled forward, and fell to the ground. Bobby went after the kid and put a foot onto his back.

"You don't wanna listen to me?" he said, as he jabbed his blackjack hard into the kid's right side. The kid grabbed his hip and tried to cover up. "You gonna slow walk me when I tell you to move, motherfucker?"

Bobby bent over and put his face close to the kid's. "Were you trying to front on me, Cuz?"

The kid's three friends stopped and turned when they saw their friend getting assaulted, but two other cops stepped aggressively towards them.

"Get out of here," one of them said and made a threatening gesture with his billy club.

Bobby dropped his knee into the kid's back. The kid grunted, and Bobby spit on the ground.

"What you got?" he said, and smacked the kid in the side of the head. "Huh? Who's the Mack now, bitch?"

The kid didn't move as Bobby pressed his knee into his back.

"What's the matter, Homey? I thought you was a fucking 'G.'"

The kid stayed completely still until Bobby calmed down enough to get off him.

"That's what I thought," he said, and spit on the ground. "Get up."

Bobby yanked the kid off the ground.

"APD owns these streets," Bobby said, with his face pressed close against the kid's. "You understand me, Bro? You feeling me?"

The kid looked straight ahead, refusing to make eye contact. *It was the exact kind of disrespect that infuriated Bobby.*

"Yoa, Bobby Mo, let's go," someone yelled. "We gotta roll."

Bobby looked over at Kevin Conti, who had a crazed smile on his face.

"They're back at the Underground," Conti said.

Bobby saw most of the other cops, including Dave, were already back on the bus.

"I'm coming," Bobby yelled, before turning back to the kid. "Here's a little something to remember me by, Sambo."

Bobby cocked his blackjack back and brought it down hard towards the kid's lower back. But the kid saw Bobby start to swing and ducked reflexively, *directly into the path of his club.* Instead of hitting the kid in the side of the back, where it would hurt, but not do any lasting damage, Bobby's nightstick connected square into the kid's forehead.

It made a hollow, cracking, sound when it connected with the kid's head. It was such a sickening sound that a wave of nausea came over Bobby as he watched the kid crumple to the ground.

The kid wasn't knocked out, although he was writhing so slowly Bobby knew he had done some serious damage. The kid's eyes looked up into Bobby's, but he didn't see hatred or anger in them. He saw a look of despair. Bigger than he had ever seen, as if Bobby had taken something from the kid that could never be replaced.

"Come on, Morello," the driver yelled. "Leave him alone and get your ass back on the bus."

Bobby was paralyzed for a moment as he stared down at the kid lying broken in the middle of Trinity Avenue. Under any sort of remotely normal circumstances, the other cops on the bus would have stopped to ask what the hell had happened. But on that night, a mob mentality had taken over, and there was a savagery in Bobby's fellow cops he had never seen before or since.

The driver started honking loudly. "Let's go!"

For a moment, Bobby thought about staying behind and trying to get some help for the kid. Instead, he turned and walked back on the bus.

"What the hell were you doing?" Conti said, as Bobby walked toward the rear of the bus. "Admiring your handiwork?"

Conti laughed, while Bobby took a seat. The bus pulled away, while the kid remained in the middle of the street. Bobby was stunned by what he had done and the fact nobody cared.

When the bus arrived at the Underground, he was the last one to get off. He hung back for the rest of the night, avoiding altercations, and becoming increasingly haunted by the sound his nightstick had made when it connected with the kid's head.

By the end of the night, as the sun began to rise and darkness lift, APD had restored order to the city. The riots were over, and the madness of both the cops and the looters had come to an end. But for Bobby, the mental repercussions of his actions were just beginning. He had trouble sleeping for months afterwards, as the transition space between awake and sleep was invariably filled with the image of the damaged kid lying on the street.

It was the kind of incident that would have ended Bobby's career on any other night. But because it happened on the night when cops were given permission to swing away, the hit was forgotten.

Bobby never faced any official consequences for his actions, but he faced psychological ones. Bad enough that they led him into therapy to try and get some answers to who he was.

It was almost 7:30 by the time he made it home from Dave's. When he reached the front door, his son, Eric, ran to him with the enthusiasm four year old boys have for their fathers. Bobby swung Eric into his arms, gave him a big hug, and planted a kiss on his cheek.

Fatherhood had come late to Bobby, and like many parents who had children later in life, he was determined not to take a single moment for granted.

"You looked very handsome up there today, Bobby," his wife, Sheri, said as she followed Eric to him. She snuck her head past Eric's and gave Bobby a promising kiss on the lips. "I'm very proud of you, being such a good friend to Dave."

Bobby gave her a weak smile.

"Everything okay?" she asked.

"Yeah, I'm fine. Just tired. It was a long day," Bobby said. "This whole damn thing's been a drain. This trial's bringing up a lot of bad memories. I'm going to take a hot shower."

"Maybe I'll join you," Sheri whispered in his ear.

Bobby pulled Sheri's hand up towards his mouth and kissed it.

As Sheri stood next to Bobby, he looked at her for an extra moment. They had been married six years, but Bobby could still be taken aback by her beauty. It was a beauty he noticed the first time he saw her in a Criminal Justice class at Georgia State. Their Professor assigned them to the same study group, and within a month, Bobby, who was recently divorced, had fallen in love. He asked Sheri out for coffee one night, and they had been a couple ever since.

As Bobby carried Eric into the family room, his thoughts turned back to the eyes of the black kid he had left lying in the middle of the street. The kid's skin had been a little bit darker than Sheri's, but not much.

"Daddy look," Eric said, and climbed down. "It's my police station."

Bobby watched his son crawl under a blanket propped up by kitchen chairs. He popped out a second later, wearing Bobby's dark blue patrol hat.

"He's going to be a policeman, just like his daddy," Sheri said, as she hugged Bobby from behind. "My two protectors."

Bobby smiled, but didn't say anything. He just gave her hand a squeeze as he watched his most valued treasure, in the form of a mixed race son, buzz innocently around the living room.

"God forbid," he later told himself, while saying a silent prayer that his little boy would never have to pay the price for his father's sins.

22

—

ONE OF the central organizing principles of Dave's defense was that Remo Centrella carried a deep-seated anger within him that was explosive when triggered. It was a rage that had been caught on television three times.

The first time was when an umpire nullified a walk-off home run after ruling Remo's foot missed third while rounding the bases. Remo charged out of the dugout and had to be restrained by a half a dozen teammates. The second time was when Remo went after a pitcher he thought had intentionally thrown at his head. And the third time was when TV cameras caught Remo getting into a fight with a teammate that he didn't think had hustled.

Whitney wanted to play videotape from all three incidents for the jury, but Judge Friedman ruled the defense would only be allowed to play one of them.

"You can reference the other two as part of your theory," she instructed, "but I'm not going to take up a half a day of court time watching baseball fights. One video will make your point."

Bass objected to the admission of any of the fights. He claimed they should be excluded because they would have too prejudicial of an effect on the jury, but Friedman overruled him. She said the footage was close enough to the crux of Dave's defense that the probative value of showing the tape outweighed its prejudicial effect.

She gave Whitney the choice of which incident to use.

He chose the fight with Remo's teammate because it lasted twice as long as the other two confrontations and because he thought it showed Remo at his worst.

"That's how Centrella looked when I was on the ground," Dave said, when he and Whitney screened the fight together.

Remo's fight with Richie Decker was a national story when it happened. It was during Remo's fourth year with the Barons, and it started because he didn't think Richie hustled after a fly ball.

The Barons were playing Detroit at the Keith on a blistering Sunday afternoon in July. There were two outs in the top of the 8th, and Atlanta was getting shellacked, 9-3. The vast majority of fans, everybody but the die-hards, had left the stadium by the time Detroit's catcher, Lee Plasencia, connected with a hanging curve into left-center field that scored two more Detroit runners. It was a good hit, but one Decker would have caught if he ran hard after it.

On paper, Richie Decker was a player with all the gifts needed to be an All-Star. A nine-year veteran, he had the kind of natural ability that made General Managers drool, which was why there always seemed to be another team willing to take a chance on a player who had never lived up to his hype.

Before the season began, Ray Manning had been the latest guy to fall in love with Decker's upside. He talked himself into signing him as a free agent, rationalizing that all Richie needed was the chance to join a playoff contender.

Things hadn't worked out the way Ray hoped. Decker had shown some definite flashes of brilliance in Atlanta, but most of them had taken place on dance floors in Buckhead.

In a move the Barons didn't anticipate, Richie's wife divorced him before the start of the season. She stayed back in Seattle with their kids, while Atlanta's newest multi-millionaire rolled into town a free man.

Richie set the tone at his initial press conference, when one of the local beat writers asked what he was most looking forward to about playing for the Barons.

"Them "Dirty South" girls," Richie said, with a huge, gap-toothed, smile. "They're gonna love Richie Decker."

Ray fined him five grand for the answer, but Richie was just being honest. During the first two months of the season, he gave away tickets faster than the Barons' PR department.

The problem was, Richie's tickets were in the same section where the Barons' wives sat, and Richie's guests tended to look more like biker chicks from Daytona Beach than former sorority girls from the University of Georgia. Nobody in the Barons organization could figure out where Richie found such a steady supply of trashy women.

Several of the players' wives complained about the outfits that were showing up in the family section. At one point, after one of Richie's "dates" showed up wearing Daisy Dukes and a tight red, white and blue bikini top for a game on Independence Day, Barons catcher Greg Weatherford asked Richie to tone it down.

"My wife said the young lady spent half the game sticking her pierced tongue out while flashing devil horns up to the sky," Weatherford said. "My daughters were literally afraid of her."

Weatherford was the Barons' captain, but Richie didn't defer to him.

"I'm a popular guy, Greg. What can I say?" Richie said. "Matter of fact, you and me should hang out sometime. One of my lady friends said she wants to try and corrupt you."

"You're sick," Weatherford said and turned his back on Richie.

"Man can't live on bread alone, Greg," Richie said, with a loud laugh. "Man *cannot live* on bread alone."

By the time of the Detroit game, the tension between Richie and his teammates had been building for almost a month. Half the Barons weren't speaking to him, but Richie didn't care. He had been traded enough times to know baseball was a business and that teammates were temporary.

Remo had seen Richie come dragging into the locker room the morning of the Detroit game. The Barons had won the night before, and Richie looked like he had never made it home. At one point, during the top of the 6th inning, Remo looked over at Richie, who was in the middle of a full yawn. Richie didn't even bother trying to conceal it when he saw Remo looking at him. He just laughed, like the whole thing was a big goof.

So by the time Richie didn't hustle after the ball hit by Plasencia, Remo had seen enough. He sprinted back to the dugout when the inning ended and waited for Richie on the top step.

"Hit the showers. You're done for the day."

"What'd you say, C?" Richie said, waking up for the first time all game.

"I said get out of my dug-out, Richie. Hit the showers, and we can try it again tomorrow."

Richie smiled.

"Oh, so you the manager now, Remo? Give me a fucking break, Bro. That ball was hit harder than it looked. Now, let me get by....Richie needs some Gatorade."

By this time, most of the team, including their manager, Eddie Danko, saw Remo and Richie starting to square up. Danko was happy to see it; he had been waiting for Remo to assert himself as the Barons' leader.

"You're not getting any Gatorade, Richie. You haven't earned it. Now get into the tunnel before I kick your ass down there."

"Yoa, C, you better save the Rambo act for the rookies. You know you don't want a piece of me."

Richie tried to move forward.

"Don't do it, Richie," Remo said and blocked his path.

Richie Decker knew Remo was the Barons' franchise player, but he had too much ego to back down, especially now that all eyes in the dugout were on them.

Orlando Kure, the Barons' second baseman, was due up to bat, but he stayed in the dugout to watch the confrontation. Because Kure wasn't at the plate, the home plate umpire walked over to the dugout to give the Barons a delay of game warning. The TV cameras followed him, and when they did, they picked up on Remo and Richie jawing at each other.

"Pardon me," Richie said, and put his hand on Remo's chest.

Remo responded with a roundhouse to Richie's head, but Richie put his left hand up reflexively and blocked most of the punch.

"Now you done it," Richie said, and punched Remo in the mouth. The punch knocked Remo down onto the grass behind the first base line, but he didn't stay down. He jumped up and launched himself into Richie's mid-section. Richie stumbled backwards, but stayed on his feet by hanging on to Remo's shirt. Remo wrapped his arms around Richie's waist and began to drive him backwards, like a blocking sled.

Richie was backpedaling and punching Remo in the back of his head, but his punches didn't have any power because he was off-balance. They were glancing off Remo and just making him angrier.

By the time they reached home plate, Remo's momentum overwhelmed Richie, who fell backwards onto the ground. Remo stood halfway up and unloaded a punch down into Richie's face that fractured his cheekbone.

Richie turned over and covered up as Remo towered over him. By that point, Remo's teammates were pulling him off Richie, while the TV cameras zoomed in. Remo's facial features were contorted, and he was spitting blood, as he yelled at Richie that he would "fucking kill him."

Or at least that's what Whitney's lip reading expert claimed Remo was saying on the tape. There was no audio available, so there was no proof of what exactly Remo said. Just the expert's opinion. Although on cross-examination, Bass got her to concede it was possible Remo could have been saying, "I've had my fucking fill of you." Either way, the video was undeniable proof Remo could snap when angry.

Richie Decker ended up on the disabled list for almost a month and Dale Agee gave Remo a ten game suspension. Publicly, Ray and the Barons condemned the fight, but privately, they were happy Remo finally stepped up and demanded accountability from his teammates.

Remo and Richie never discussed the fight, but on the night Richie returned to the Barons' line-up, Remo gave him a public embrace. And instead of ripping the team apart, the fight seemed to bring it closer together. That October, with Richie Decker hustling on every play, the Barons won their first World Series title.

After the fight video was shown to the jury, Whitney wanted to follow-up with another witness who would reinforce that Remo had a violent streak. Originally, he had planned to call Mark Clemens to the stand after the Richie Decker fight tape. He thought Clemens' story that Remo beat him up in a Chicago hotel room would resonate with the jury. Unfortunately for Dave's defense, between the meeting in Whitney's office and the beginning of the trial, Clemens got arrested in Jacksonville, Florida for possession of three and a half pounds of marijuana that he was trying to mule from Miami.

Between the drug bust and a previous arrest for assault, Whitney decided Clemens was too toxic to associate with Dave. So he was forced to scratch him off the witness list.

Instead of calling Clemens to the stand, the next witness called by Whitney was Dr. Stuart W. Seewald, the endocrinologist from Emory, who had been quoted in the Inquirer about the impact steroids could have had on Remo's behavior.

After some preliminary questions about Seewald's education and experience, Whitney asked him what he considered to be one of the most important questions of the trial.

"Dr. Seewald, in your expert opinion, could double-stacking steroids trigger the type of uncontrollable anger commonly referred to as roid rage?'"

"It absolutely could have," Seewald said. "The amount of steroids found in Mr. Centrella's system would have been more than enough to trigger a psychotic episode in which his ability to control his impulses would have been significantly diminished to the point of inefficacy."

"What's the medical rationale behind that statement, Doctor?"

"The link between increased levels of testosterone and aggression is firmly established in the science," Seewald said. "Testosterone is known to attach itself to nerve cells, thus affecting moods. In Mr. Centrella's case, his use of steroids would have had the effect of raising his testosterone to a level that was both physically and psychologically dangerous."

Whitney nodded as Seewald continued.

"It's a virtual certainty that his use of steroids, combined with the fact he had been consuming alcohol on the evening he was killed, would create feelings of aggression and anger that he would have had difficulty controlling."

"You saw the video in which Mr. Centrella attacked his teammate during a game, did you not, Dr. Seewald?"

"I did."

"Were you aware that Mr. Centrella later admitted he attacked him because he wanted a cup of Gatorade?"

"I am, yes."

"In reviewing the video of that fight, and knowing it was over something so trivial as a cup of juice, is it fair to say Mr. Centrella demonstrated symptoms of a person who had difficulties with impulse control?"

"Yes, classic ones."

"And is it your opinion, Doctor, that a person with such demonstrated impulse control issues might exhibit even more problems if they had been taking two different kinds of steroids for almost 8 weeks?"

"I would say it would be extremely likely," Seewald said. "I would analogize it to throwing accelerant on a fire, in that it would create an extremely dangerous, and potentially deadly combination."

"Deadly for whom, Doctor?" Whitney said.

"For whomever made him angry."

"Thank you, Doctor Seewald," Whitney said. "No further questions, Your Honor."

"Mr. Bass?" Judge Friedman said and pointed towards him.

"Thank you, Your Honor," Maurice said as he stood up to begin his cross-examination.

"Dr. Seewald," he began, "based upon the biography you shared with this court, is it fair to say you consider yourself to be an expert on the use of steroids in professional sports?"

"Professional and collegiate," Seewald said.

"I had the chance to read one of the articles you penned on the proliferation of steroids in sports for the *Atlantic* magazine," Bass said. "I found it extremely thought provoking."

"Thank you. That was my intention."

"I'd like to ask you a few questions about it if I may."

"Certainly."

Maurice picked up a copy of the article from the defense table. It had already been admitted into evidence, and both Whitney and Judge Friedman had copies of it.

"In your article for the Atlantic, you wrote 'Steroids aren't just baseball's dirty little secret. They're the five thousand pound elephant in the room.' What did you mean by that statement, Doctor?"

"I think it's obvious," Seewald said. "The use of steroids and other performance enhancing drugs is not some small element within professional baseball. Their use has become pervasive. Almost commonplace, according to my research."

"Why do you think that is?"

"It's simple. We live in an extremely commercial era, Mr. Bass, in which Mr. Agee and the owners have made the financial calculation they want players who can hit baseballs over the fence. At its most fundamental level, baseball is a business, and they know that home runs sell tickets."

"Do you think that baseball is complicit in the use of steroids?"

"I think that word is appropriate."

"You realize some people may consider that to be a controversial statement?"

"I don't shy from controversy, Mr. Bass. Especially when it's backed up by my research. The fact is, it's likely that every team in the league has players using steroids."

"Every team in the league?" Maurice said.

"Yes."

Bass looked impressed by Seewald's statement.

"Sounds like baseball has an epidemic on its hands?" he said.

"I think my work makes the case that it does," Seewald said.

"But we don't have an epidemic of violence taking place, do we?"

"I'm not sure what you mean."

"This isn't the early 1980s where we've got Sports Illustrated putting out cover stories about professional athletes shooting themselves in the rear end with cow testosterone before tearing apart some Honky Tonk down in Texas, do we? I haven't read about any professional baseball players getting busted for trashing their hotel room, have you?"

"Trashing hotel rooms?"

"Yes. When is the last time you heard of any professional baseball player trashing a hotel room? Or even getting into a serious bar fight for that matter?"

"That's not something I keep tabs on," Seewald said.

"Is that the same as saying you haven't heard of it happening, Doctor?"

"My area of expertise is on the use of steroids in sports."

"Understood, but you've also presented yourself to this jury as an expert on steroid induced rage. Because of that, I would ask you to please provide this court another example of a baseball player, *other than Mr. Centrella,* who has attacked somebody because of a steroid induced rage?"

Seewald rubbed his beard for several seconds. He looked stumped by Bass' question. "Off the top of my head, I can't think of an answer," he said.

"Is that perhaps because this whole concept of roid rage is actually a myth, Doctor? A condition that sounds plausible in theory, but doesn't actually occur in reality?"

"No," Seewald said. "It's very real."

"Then where are the arrests, Doctor?" Bass said, in an accusatory tone. "Where are all the incidents of roid rage that your theory would predict?"

"I'm not an expert on criminal statistics," Seewald said.

"*Please, Doctor*, you just agreed you're one of the nation's foremost experts on steroids in professional sports. You've just spent an hour testifying that the use of steroids is at an epidemic level in baseball, yet you can't point to one incident, other than your speculation about Mr. Centrella, to back up your claims."

"I'm not sure you understand how the scientific method works," Seewald said.

"I understand how reality works, Doctor," Bass said. "I understand how evidence works, and I'm confident that if steroids really did cause people to have the impulse control issues you claim, then half the baseball players in America would have been in trouble with the law, wouldn't they?"

"You're obviously engaging in a gross exaggeration," Seewald said.

"Am I? Let me ask you this, Doctor. Your theory, the reason Mr. Taylor called you as a witness, is because you believe that Mr. Centrella's actions were consistent with roid rage, isn't that correct?"

"That is."

"But weren't his actions also consistent with an unarmed person who was trying to defend himself against a person with a gun?"

"I'm not sure I follow."

"Allow me to rephrase the question, Doctor. You claim Mr. Centrella acted out of roid rage, but isn't it more likely he acted out of common sense? That it was actually Mr. Centrella who was the one acting in self-defense?"

"I don't think so."

"Are you on steroids, Doctor?"

"Objection, relevancy," Whitney said.

"Overruled."

"No," Seewald said. "I'm not."

"So if, hypothetically, you were to attack somebody, I couldn't then attribute your actions to roid rage, isn't that correct? I would have to allege another reason for your actions. Do you agree with my premise?"

"I can't agree with your premise because I would not attack another person," Seewald said.

"Never?" Bass said. "What if you were parked quietly in one of the lots at Emory in the middle of the night? What if you were sitting there with your wife, minding your own business, and a non-police vehicle showed up out of nowhere? And what if a man wearing plainclothes approached your car, drew his gun, and eventually, when you tried to drive away, shot at your car? What if that same man then physically assaulted you, broke your wrist, and slammed your head into the pavement?

"Furthermore, what if that man had a gun and you did not? Would you simply let yourself be beaten or would you decide to try and fight for your life?"

Seewald did not answer for several seconds. He brought his hand to his mouth in order to think.

"There's no right or wrong answer, Doctor."

"Under those circumstances," Seewald said. "I guess I would probably try to defend myself."

"Even though you're not on steroids," Maurice said, with his finger in the air to emphasize the point. "Thank you, Doctor. No further questions, Your Honor."

"You may step down, Dr. Seewald," Judge Friedman said.

Following Dr. Seewald's testimony, Whitney spent the next day and a half calling medical experts to the stand in order to detail the severity of the injuries to Dave. It was a workmanlike process that focused on mostly incontrovertible minutiae.

The most compelling pieces of evidence offered during this stage of the trial were the photos of Dave's injuries that Whitney projected onto the overhead screen. A couple of them were so gruesome that a few of the jurors averted their eyes.

By the time the last medical expert stepped down, Whitney was feeling very good about his defense of Dave. He was confident he had created some serious doubts in the minds of the jurors.

"Now," Whitney thought to himself the night before Dave was scheduled to take the stand, "it's up to Dave to close the deal."

23

FROM THE moment Judge Friedman first banged her gavel to begin his trial, there was never really any doubt Dave would take the stand. Because of that, Dave knew that everything leading up to his testimony had been a series of undercards in preparation for the main event.

He could feel the adrenaline in his system as he walked across the courtroom for the chance to finally tell the world what happened on the night he shot Remo.

He took the stand wearing a new suit he bought for the occasion from Nordstrom's. It was nicely tailored, but no suit would ever be able to make Dave look like anything other than what he was, a cop.

Whitney began his direct of Dave by walking him through the events that led up to the shooting. Dave testified he had been near the end of a five-hour stakeout when Remo had come flying by, at a speed Dave estimated to have been close to 80 miles an hour.

"Why did you decide to leave the stakeout and follow the car?" Whitney said.

"Reckless driving is against the law," Dave said. "I was simply meeting my obligation as a police officer. We chase down speeding cars everyday."

Dave winced a touch inside. He still wasn't in love with the answer Whitney had helped him craft, but he hoped it sounded convincing.

"Were you worried about leaving the stakeout?" Whitney said.

"No," Dave said. "It was 3 a.m. All the lights in the target house were off, and I hadn't seen movement from inside the residence since before one o'clock. It was my third night on the stakeout, and I was confident the subject was in bed for the night."

Whitney nodded his head in affirmation.

"What type of situation did you think you might encounter when you pursued the Porsche?"

"Based upon the way it had been weaving as it sped past me on Haywood, I figured I was probably looking at an impaired driving situation. And because I knew Webster dead-ended at the stadium, I thought I was probably dealing with a driver who was not familiar with the area."

"What did you see when you made the turn onto Webster Drive?"

"I saw the car parked close to the fence that surrounds the Wilson Field parking lots. The passenger door was open and a young woman, who looked to be in her mid twenties, was struggling to get out. As I pulled closer, I saw the driver had a hold of her by the left wrist."

"What did that make you think?"

"That she was in trouble. That she was trying to get away from the driver, but he was refusing to let her go."

"Did you notice anything else?"

"I did," Dave said and turned slightly to face the jury. "I saw that the woman, who I now know to be Mrs. Manning, had a pretty decent sized bruise underneath her left eye."

"Could you describe what that bruise looked like, Detective?"

"It looked puffy, like it was new."

"What did that make you think?"

"That the person driving the car had probably given it to her."

"Why did you think that?"

"Context clues," Dave said. "Within the context of what I was seeing, *her struggling, him holding onto her,* that was the logical conclusion."

"Did the bruise under Mrs. Manning's eye change what

you were thinking?"

"It made me think I was likely dealing with a domestic violence situation, and that I would need to help the woman make a transition to a safe location."

"You were in court last week, Detective, when Mrs. Manning stated she didn't have a contusion under her eye. What do you say with regard to that testimony?"

"She wasn't being truthful," Dave said. "Mrs. Manning had definitely been hit. I can't say with one hundred percent certainty Remo Centrella hit her because I wasn't there to see it, but I can say without a doubt she was struggling to get away from him, and that she did, in fact, have a fresh bruise underneath her left eye."

"Thank you, Detective. Let's step back for a moment, if we can."

Dave nodded.

"Are you a fan of the Atlanta Barons?"

"Yes, I am," Dave said.

"So you were aware of who Remo Centrella was?"

"Yes, I was."

"What was your opinion of him?"

"I thought he was a great baseball player. In my opinion, he's the best player to ever wear a Barons' uniform."

"So you didn't have any type of animosity or anger towards Remo Centrella?"

"Quite the opposite. I had always been a fan of his."

Whitney nodded his head at Dave's answer.

"At what point did you realize it was him in the car?"

"When I saw his license plate. It said big stick."

"Did that in any way change the way you approached the situation, Mr. Mackno?"

"Somewhat," Dave said. "I was still very concerned about the fact the woman had been hit and was being held against her will, but I also relaxed a little bit knowing it was Remo Centrella in the car."

"Did Mr. Centrella get out of the car?"

"No," Dave said. "When I got out of my vehicle and started to approach his car, he pulled Mrs. Manning back inside, and they just sat there. Their car lights were on, the engine was idling, and they were looking straight ahead. I think they thought I might go away if they simply sat quietly in the car."

"Why didn't you, Mr. Mackno? Once they were back in the car, minding their own business, why didn't you just leave them alone?"

"Because I'm an Atlanta police officer. I have a job to do."

"So you felt it was your duty to find out what happened?"

"I knew it was my duty."

"Was your gun drawn when you approached the car?"

"Not initially," Dave said. "Because I realized it was Remo Centrella, I simply held my badge up to identify myself. I wanted to let him know I was an Atlanta Police Officer and that I needed him to exit his vehicle."

"Did Mr. Centrella see your badge?"

"He did."

"Are you sure?"

"One hundred percent."

"How are you so sure?"

"Because when Mr. Centrella saw the badge, he looked at me and mouthed, 'fuck you.'"

Whitney feigned some mild surprise. "Remo Centrella mouthed 'fuck you?'"

"Yes, he did."

"What did you think when he did that?'"

"It was confirmation to me that he was impaired."

"Why do you say that?"

"Because that's not something a sober person would do. That's something a drunk would do."

"I see. What happened after he said fuck you?"

"He started gunning his engine to try and get me to back off."

"Did you back off?"

"No," Dave said. "I stayed in the same place and continued to instruct him to exit his vehicle."

"Did he?"

"No, he started blasting his speaker system. He started playing a Guns N Roses' song very loudly, as if he could drown me out with noise. That was the point at which I realized Mr. Centrella was not going to exit his vehicle voluntarily."

"What did you do when you came to that realization, Detective?"

"I went to call for backup. I started walking back to my car to retrieve my radio so that I could make the call."

Whitney paused for a moment in order to emphasize Dave's answer.

"Would you please repeat that for the jury, Detective? You said that once you realized Mr. Centrella was not going to exit his vehicle voluntarily, you made the decision to go back to your car and call for back-up, is that correct?"

"It is."

"That's a very important point for the jury to remember."

"Objection," Bass said. "Testifying."

"Sustained," Judge Friedman said. "Please refrain from commentary about the witness' testimony, Mr. Taylor."

"Yes, Your Honor," Whitney said and turned back towards Dave. "What happened when you went to call for backup?"

"When I headed back to my car, Mr. Centrella attempted to drive his vehicle through the chain-link fence."

Whitney paused Dave's testimony to introduce photos of the damaged fence and dented hood of Remo's car into evidence.

"Is that a picture of the fence he tried to drive through?" Whitney said, while pointing to a picture, which had the damaged part of the fence blown-up and circled in red.

"It is."

"But he didn't make it through the fence did he?"

"No, the fence was too strong," Dave said. "Instead, he put his car in reverse and spun it around backwards so that he was now facing me."

"Where were you positioned when this happened?"

"I was between his Porsche and my car."

"Trapped between the two?"

"That's what it felt like."

"What was going through your mind at the time?" Whitney said.

"That I was in trouble. That Remo Centrella had escalated what should have been a routine stop into a very dangerous situation."

"What did you do when you realized that?"

"I tried to make eye contact with him."

"Were you able to?"

"No. I couldn't see past his high beams."

"Approximately how much distance was between you and Mr. Centrella's car at this time?"

"Fifteen to twenty feet. It was close enough that I wasn't sure if I could get out of the way if he tried to run me over."

"Did you think he might actually do that?"

"No."

"But Mr. Centrella did try to run you over, didn't he, Detective?"

"Yes, he did," Dave said. "Remo Centrella tried to drive over me."

"Could you describe for us what happened?"

"It happened without any warning. I was looking in Mr. Centrella's direction, trying to figure out what his next move was going to be. I was yelling for him to exit his vehicle when his car accelerated towards me. I dove to my right and shot at his tires. The first shot hit a tire and the second one missed."

"Why did you fire your weapon, Detective?"

"Because he was trying to run me over," Dave said.

"Why didn't you try to shoot him through his windshield? Your life was in danger, why didn't you go for a kill shot?"

Dave didn't speak for several seconds. He nodded his head. It was clear that describing Remo's attempt to run him over was unsettling.

"Two reasons," he said. "First, as police officers, we're trained to never use deadly force unless it's an absolute necessity to protect your life or the life of an innocent party. *A kill shot should always be the very last resort.* More importantly, Mr. Centrella had a passenger in his vehicle. I couldn't get a clear shot at him because I couldn't see past the headlights. There was no way I was going to risk shooting Mrs. Manning."

"How were you able to make that decision so quickly, Detective?"

"It was instinct," Dave said. "When I dove to my right and fired my weapon, I was thinking one thing: *Don't shoot inside the car.*"

"What happened after you shot out the tire?"

"The front left tire pulled away from the axel and the front corner of his car started scraping into the pavement. Mr. Centrella kept trying to drive forward, but the car was digging into the parking lot. It was un-driveable."

"What did you do when you saw the car was stuck?"

"I jumped up from the ground. When I did, I saw Mrs. Manning was once again trying to get out of the car, but Centrella had her by the dress."

"Let's talk about that for a moment, Detective Mackno," Whitney said. "During her testimony, Mrs. Manning stated she got out of the car and ran from the scene before you shot out the tire. Do you recall that testimony?"

"I do."

"How do you respond to that?"

"It's not true. Mrs. Manning was in the car when I shot the tire out."

"How can you be sure of that, Detective?" Whitney said.

"Because her presence in the car was one of the reasons I aimed for the tire instead of the windshield."

"What happened after you got up from the ground?"

"I still had my gun drawn. I moved towards the passenger side to try and help her, but she broke free from his grasp before I got there. She ran off, and Centrella got out of the car."

"Did you see where she went?"

"She ran back up Webster."

"What did Mr. Centrella do?"

"He started yelling after her."

"What was he yelling?"

"I don't remember the exact words, but they were to the effect of *'get back here, what are you doing, where you going?'* He was just yelling after her, although I think he realized pretty quick she wasn't coming back. That's when he started yelling some vulgarities."

"Could you give the court an example?"

"He called her a 'stupid bitch' and said 'get your ass back here you little whore.'"

Whitney paused a few beats before his next question in order to maximize the impact of Remo's words.

"What did Mr. Centrella do when he figured out Mrs. Manning wasn't coming back?"

"He took out his wallet and asked me how much it would take to let him go."

"Remo Centrella tried to bribe you, Detective Mackno?" Whitney said.

"Yes," Dave said. "He said his agent would give me as much money as I wanted if we could find a way to get everything worked out."

"What do you think he said that?"

"I thought he was delusional. That he wasn't living in the same reality I was."

"Why do you say that?"

"Because how could he think he was going to walk after everything that had taken place? The front tire of his car was shot out, he had hit a woman, and tried to run over an Atlanta police officer. There was no way his agent, or anybody in the world, was going to be able to fix those problems for him."

"But Remo thought he could buy his way out of the situation?"

"He seemed to. He started to pull some money out of his wallet until I knocked it out of his hand."

"Why did you do that?"

"Partly out of anger at the fact he tried to run me over, and partly because it was a way of asserting some authority over him. A way to show him exactly what I thought about his attempt to bribe me. To make it clear I was the one in charge of the situation."

Whitney walked over to the easel and pointed to a blown-up photograph of Remo's wallet lying on the ground. His cash and credit cards were spread out nearby.

"I told Mr. Centrella to turn around and put his hands behind his back. That he was under arrest."

"Did he cooperate?"

"No."

"Did you have your gun drawn and leveled at Mr. Centrella during this time?"

"I did."

"Why?"

"For my protection."

"Why didn't you call for backup at this point, Detective Mackno? Now that it was just you and Mr. Centrella alone, now that he's out of his vehicle, why didn't you try and get some other police assets to the scene?"

"You know," Dave said, in a voice that was low, as if he and Whitney were the only two people in the courtroom, "looking back on what happened, I wish I had called for backup at that point. I wish Remo Centrella had stayed calm and allowed me to get back to my car and make the call. Unfortunately, the dynamics of the situation didn't allow it."

"The *dynamics of the* situation?" Whitney said. "Can you explain what you mean by that, Detective?"

"Sure," Dave said. "As I mentioned in my earlier testimony, at one point during the stop I returned to my vehicle to call for backup. That was when Mr. Centrella tried to make his escape by running me over."

Dave shifted in his seat.

"By the time he got out of the car, my adrenaline was pumping at full capacity. I had almost been run over, and I had been forced to discharge my weapon. I didn't know if Centrella had a gun or if he would try and attack me physically. It was just him and I alone in the middle of the night. All I wanted to do was to try and get the situation under control. In my experience, that meant finding a way to get Mr. Centrella into handcuffs and placing him under arrest."

"And is that what you tried to do?"

"It is," Dave said.

"But it required force because Mr. Centrella refused to cooperate, isn't that correct, Detective?"

"It is."

"What kind of force did you bring to bear upon Mr. Centrella?"

"Non-deadly," Dave said and made sure to make full eye contact with the jurors. "I tried to get Mr. Centrella into handcuffs using just my physical strength. By this point, he seemed to be calming down. He understood he couldn't bribe his way out of the situation and that he would have to face the consequences for his actions. At one point, he stopped looking directly at me and instead was looking up into the sky. I saw it as an opening to make the arrest.

"I re-holstered my gun, and used a leg whip to take him to the ground. We struggled for a bit, but I had him face-down and was using my knee to pin him. I thought I was in control of the situation because I almost had him in handcuffs. One wrist was cuffed, and I was just about to cuff the second one when he twisted around and flipped me off his back.

"When I fell to the ground, I went for my gun, but it was gone. It had flown out when he flipped me off his back. Centrella was back on his feet, and he assumed a martial arts' style attack position."

Dave put his hands in front of him to demonstrate how Remo had his hands positioned.

"He started to hiss at me and that's when I knew he was going to attack. My back was against the fence when he charged into me. I slid to the side and he missed me, but he grabbed hold of my shirt. I tried to pull away, but he reeled me back in and threw a punch down on my head. It didn't hurt me, and I hit him back. I punched him twice with my fists, and once with my elbow, but my hits didn't have any effect on him. I then pushed him in the chest to try and get some separation between us.

That's when he hit me with a roundhouse kick to the head."

Dave took a breath.

"It was the hardest hit of my life, and it almost knocked me out. My head went fuzzy. I tried to slide backwards, but I couldn't move my feet. I had lost control of my fine motor skills. I was like a puppet on strings that had gone slack.

"Remo grabbed me by the front collar of my shirt and yanked me hard towards him. As he pulled me to him, he slammed the heel of his hand into the bottom of my chin. It snapped my head backwards, and that was it. I was done.

"Remo let go of me and I fell backwards to the fence. Everything was wobbly. I looked up at Remo and saw him make a gang gesture, like he was slashing his throat with a knife. Everything was swaying back and forth, and I had lost the ability to differentiate between sounds. The only thing I could hear was the noise buzzing inside my head. My back was propped up against the fence, but I felt like I was falling backwards, down into a huge hole.

"Remo was probably only about five or ten feet away from me, but he looked much further. He was yelling something, but I couldn't understand it. I tried to curl forward into a ball to protect myself, but couldn't. My shirt was caught on the fence, and I didn't have enough strength to pull free.

"Remo started kicking me and I was about to fall unconscious. At that point, I thought I was going to die."

"But you survived."

"Yes. One of Remo's kicks knocked me off the fence, and I fell over. My head was sideways on the pavement as I looked up at him. I didn't have any conscious thoughts; it was like I was a detached observer watching what was happening to me. Remo was still yelling, but I couldn't decipher any individual sounds. I saw him raise his foot back into the air and knew he was about to bring it down on me again."

Dave paused to swallow.

"That's when I felt metal against my hand. It was the

barrel of my gun. I felt for the grip and found it. I turned it over into my palm and laced my finger into the trigger. I tried to get it aimed in Remo's direction. I closed my eyes to concentrate and pulled the trigger four times.

"When I was done, I opened my eyes and watched Remo fall backwards. It looked like it was in slow motion and that he was stunned.

"That's the last memory I have at Wilson Field. The next thing I can remember is waking up at Grady Memorial Hospital. I was in a body cast, connected to a bunch of machines. I looked over and I saw my wife, Darlene, sleeping in a chair next to my bed. That's when I realized I wasn't dead."

Dave's voice cracked when he mentioned Darlene's name. He stopped talking, and the entire courtroom remained silent for several seconds until Whitney spoke.

"Thank you Detective Mackno," he said. "I have no further questions for my client, Your Honor."

It took Judge Friedman a moment to acknowledge Whitney's remarks. She had been as caught up in Dave's testimony as everyone else in court.

When she did acknowledge Whitney, she looked at her watch and announced that court would be placed into recess for lunch.

When court returned to session in the afternoon, Judge Friedman signaled for Maurice to begin his cross-examination of Dave.

"Thank you, Your Honor," Bass said. He stood up, buttoned his suit jacket, and walked to the center of the courtroom. Dave noticed Bass was walking with a little bit of swagger, like he was looking forward to the chance to cross-examine him.

"Detective Mackno," he began, "I'd like to begin our cross examination by asking you a simple 'yes or no' question. Would that be okay with you?"

"That would be fine," Dave said.

"Do you consider yourself to be a good cop, Mr. Mackno?"

"I do."

"Do you think you did a good job the night you killed Remo Centrella?"

"Based upon the circumstances, I do. I was doing my job, and Mr. Centrella gave me no other choice."

Bass had a look of disbelief on his face.

"No other choice?" he said. "Remo Centrella *had* to die that night? Is that what you honestly believe?"

Dave didn't answer.

"I asked you a question, Mr. Mackno."

"Mr. Centrella was trying to kill me," Dave said, remaining calm. "As I testified, I shot him in self-defense, as he was attempting to kill me."

"So you claim, but you do understand that this jury, not you, will be the one to decide that question, Mr. Mackno."

"I do."

"Let me ask you, Sir, would you please tell this court what you were doing before you attempted to arrest Mr. Centrella. We know you were on a stakeout; I'm not interested in the details of that. What I want to know is what your *mental* state was at the time? How were you feeling when you pulled up behind Mr. Centrella's Porsche?"

"I felt like I did anytime I made a stop," Dave said. "I wanted to be alert and cautious. The fact it was taking place at three in the morning probably made me a little more aware of my surroundings and the situation."

"Would you say you were thinking clearly at the time you approached Mr. Centrella's vehicle?"

"Yes."

"Was your mind impaired in any way?"

Dave felt his stomach tighten up. A sense of apprehension entered his mind as he thought about the beer he had been drinking on the stakeout.

"No," Dave said, trying not to show his discomfort at the question.

Settle down, he told himself. *It's a standard question.*

"So you were one hundred percent fine? Is that your testimony?" Bass said, in a way that indicated he was implying something sinister.

"That's correct."

"Mr. Mackno," Bass said, picking up a piece of photo paper from his lectern and shifting into a more authoritative tone. "You own a blue and white Playmate brand cooler, do you not? One that looks like this one?"

Bass displayed a photograph of a cooler that looked identical to the one Dave had taken on the stakeout.

The question was out of left field, but Bass had asked it in such a matter of fact way that it sounded like the most logical question in the world. It caught Dave off-guard and, for a split second, his face showed it. He looked over at Whitney to see if he was going to object, but Whitney looked as if he hadn't even heard the question.

Whitney had seen the momentary look of panic on Dave's face, but was hoping the jurors did not. He couldn't object to the photograph of the cooler on *notice* grounds because Bass wasn't trying to introduce a cooler into evidence. He was simply asking Dave if he owned a cooler that looked like the one in the photograph.

"How bad is this about to get?" Whitney wondered.

Dave had never been questioned about the cooler at any point in the pre-trial process. Bass hadn't asked about it during the pre-trial deposition, and Dave knew there had not been any mention of a cooler in any of the police or media reports that appeared after the shooting.

The subject had been broached only once after the shooting and that had been in the privacy of his hospital room by Jimmy Coyle, a cop Dave trusted completely.

Coyle had stopped by Grady unannounced a couple of weeks after the shooting. Bobby was there and Jimmy asked if he could speak with Dave alone for a few minutes.

"Maybe you could run my Vette thru the wash while I'm talking to Dave," he said to Bobby.

"You know what they say about guys with Corvettes, Jimmy?" Bobby said.

"The same thing your ex-girlfriend says about you?"

"Hey—how *is* your mother doing these days?" Bobby said.

Coyle chuckled and gave Bobby the middle finger as he walked into the room.

"I heard you met with the crew from Internal Affairs the other day?" Coyle said to Dave, when they were alone.

"Routine," Dave said. "They know it was self-defense."

"One would hope," Jimmy said. "But with those guys, you never know. All the fucking head cases they attract."

"True," Dave said, and winced.

"But that's not the reason I'm here, Pal," Coyle said, his Rhode Island accent still thick even after fifteen years of living in Georgia. "I stopped by your house on the way over here."

"You what?"

"And whaddya know? Your garage door was open."

Coyle reached his hand into the pocket of his pants and pulled out a garage door opener. It was from Darlene's Sebring. Coyle opened the drawer in the nightstand next to Dave's hospital bed and put it underneath the phone book.

"For safekeeping," he said. "By the way, I was happy to see your cooler was still on the shelf where it's obviously been gathering dust all summer, right Mack?"

"I can explain," Dave said.

Coyle shook his head and patted Dave's hand.

"You got nothing to explain. We known each other what, fifteen years?"

Dave nodded.

"Two beers? Gimme a break." Jimmy made a dismissive gesture with his hand. "That wouldn't affect my grandmother. Bobby might get shitfaced from it, but not you and me."

Dave tried not to laugh. "Please, Jimmy, don't," he said. "Laughing hurts."

Coyle winked and gave Dave a big smile.

"But serious," he said, "you and I know Internal Affairs would try and turn it into a federal case."

He pointed at Dave.

"Be smart, don't give them the chance to twist around something that was no big deal."

"Thanks, Jimmy," Dave said. He knew Coyle was right

and that he would have done the same thing for him.

"Don't mention it, Pal," Coyle said, and stood up. "I'll send your loser partner back in here."

Coyle opened the door to Dave's room.

"Hey asshole," Coyle said, loud enough for the nurses down the hall to hear him. "Get back in here. Mack needs his bedpan changed."

Bobby was smiling as he walked back into the room.

"No burgundy leather jacket today?" he said.

"You only wish you had a jacket that looked that good on you," Coyle said.

"I just want to make sure the last member on the planet hasn't resigned."

"I see somebody's been watching Comedy Central," Coyle said.

"Hey, do me a favor, Jimmy," Bobby said. "Tell your wife to stop calling. I got a kid now. I'm off the market."

Dave laughed.

"Keep trying, Bobby. You might finally say something somebody other than Dave and your mother finds funny."

Bobby shook his head as Jimmy winked at Dave and walked out of the room.

"What was that all about?" Bobby said when Coyle was gone.

"Jimmy just came by to say hi."

"Yeah, sure, Dave. I guess they got Jimmy back working the Welcome Wagon again, huh?'

Dave shut his eyes to let Bobby know there wasn't going to be a discussion. He wasn't going to burden Bobby, or anybody else, with his stupidity.

Dave never said a word to anyone, including Darlene, about the fact he had brought a six-pack with him on the stakeout. And he knew there was no way Coyle had either. If Coyle said the cooler had never been there, it meant, for all practical purposes, the beer cans had never existed.

"They'd have had to cut Jimmy's tongue out," Dave reminded himself, which was why he had been so stunned by the question.

"It's a simple question, Mr. Mackno," Bass said. "Do you need me to repeat it?" Bass had his hands open, emphasizing the delay in Dave's answering the question.

"No," Dave said. "You don't need to repeat it."

He wasn't worried about admitting that he owned the cooler. He knew that could be proven without much effort and that to lie about it would just be stupid. Dave's concern was with what the next question was going to be.

"Yes," Dave said. "I own a similar cooler."

"And you had it with you that night on the stakeout, didn't you, Mr. Mackno?"

"No. I did not."

Bass stepped forward towards Dave.

"Because you were drinking beer on the night you shot Remo Centrella, weren't you?"

"No," Dave said, hoping he sounded indignant. "I was on a stakeout."

"We know you were on a stakeout, Detective," Bass said. "That wasn't my question. My question is, why were you drinking beer on the stakeout?"

"I wasn't drinking beer on the stakeout," Dave said. "I have way too much integrity to ever do something like that."

"Fuck," his internal voice said. He regretted the extra words before they got halfway out of his mouth. Dave knew he had just protested a little too much, which put him in the category of every stupid perp he ever interrogated.

"*Stupid.*" He knew he should have simply said, "I wasn't drinking," instead of adding the extra phase that made him sound defensive.

"Are you denying under oath that you bought a six pack of beer on the way to your stakeout that evening?"

Dave felt the back of his neck getting moist. He wondered how much Bass knew, *how he knew it,* and if he was about to blow his entire defense out of the water. If bringing a six-pack with him on a stakeout was going to end up costing him his freedom.

24

———

DAVE KNEW his only viable option was to double down and deny Bass' question.

"That's correct," Dave said.

Bass brought a finger to his lips, and there it was: a momentary look of self-doubt, a touch of regret in Bass' eyes. *A tell.*

Dave didn't know how he knew it was a tell, except he had been a cop long enough that picking up on tells had become second nature. It told him Bass was bluffing, just like he had bluffed a hundred times during his career.

Dave felt the fear leave his body, as he realized Bass must not have anything concrete to use against him. The logic made sense to Dave. If Bass had something concrete, he would have introduced it early in the case, probably during the opening statement, in order to try and bury Dave from day one.

"No way he would wait until now to bring it up if he had proof," Dave told himself. "He would have already used it against me."

"Are you claiming you didn't buy a six pack of beer before the stakeout?" Bass said.

"Objection, Your Honor," Whitney said, standing up. "Asked and answered. When did Mr. Bass even attempt to lay the foundation for this question? This is nothing more than false innuendo, disguised as a cross examination, to try and smear Detective Mackno in a patently obvious false light."

Whitney looked angrier than he had at any point during the trial. "This is completely out of line, Your Honor."

"Mr. Bass," Judge Friedman said, "do you have any evidentiary basis or foundation for your question?"

"I do, Your Honor," he said. "We've already laid the evidentiary foundation in the form of a sales receipt."

"A sales receipt, Your Honor?" Whitney said. "Mr. Bass hasn't disclosed a sales receipt. He can't spring a purported receipt into court without giving us proper notice."

"It's already in evidence, Counselor," Bass said, turning towards Whitney. "*Exhibit E-3*. Instead of lecturing me about the Rules of Criminal Procedure, Mr. Taylor, perhaps you might want to pay closer attention to the evidence in this case."

He turned his back to Whitney and towards Judge Friedman.

"I'll be happy to furnish defense counsel a copy of the receipt if he's been unable to keep track of it, Your Honor," he said.

Whitney looked caught off guard as he raised a finger. "Would Your Honor grant me a moment to review this information, please?" he said.

"Granted," Judge Friedman said to Whitney. She looked annoyed.

Bass stood with his arms folded, and even dared Judge Friedman's wrath with a couple of foot taps, as Whitney opened a large binder.

Whitney leafed through it and went to a tab marked E-3, *"Physical contents of Defendant's Vehicle."* He flipped through a couple of pages and saw a copy of a generic receipt from a store named "A & G." The receipt was from an older cash register that only included the prices, not the names of any of the items. That was a vital piece of information Whitney needed to communicate to Dave.

"I see it, Your Honor," he said, "but it's nothing more than a generic receipt with a set of numbers on it. Those numbers could represent absolutely anything."

"Your Honor," Bass said, "I have a sworn affidavit from the current owner of the store, Mr. Dee Rajnaratnam, which asserts that the item rung up at $5.75 was for a six pack of beer."

Bass handed the affidavit to a bailiff who handed it to Judge Friedman.

"I'll admit the affidavit into evidence," Judge Friedman said after giving it a quick scan. "You may proceed."

"Thank you, Your Honor."

Bass waited for Whitney to sit back down.

"Do you recognize this receipt, Mr. Mackno?" he said.

Dave looked at the receipt quizzically.

"No. I recognize the name of the store, but I don't recognize the receipt."

"Do you recall stopping there on the night of the stakeout?"

"Yes, now that you showed me the receipt, I do."

"Do you remember what you bought?"

"Not specifically. Probably a couple of hot dogs and a soda. I remember getting some food before going on the stakeout, but I can't tell you exactly what it was."

"Did you eat the food in your car?"

"I don't remember," Dave said.

"You don't remember?"

"That's correct."

"Do you consider the A&G convenience store to be a nice facility, Mr. Mackno?"

"It's nothing special."

"The store has metal bars on the windows, does it not?"

"Most of the stores in Zone 3 do."

"Would it surprise you to know, Detective, that A&G was cited three times in the past fifteen months for having unsanitary conditions?"

Dave shrugged his shoulders.

"It wouldn't surprise me one way or the other," he said. "It was just a convenient place to get a hot dog and soda once in a while."

"You live in Alpharetta, is that correct, Mr. Mackno?"

"I do."

"And that's what, about thirty to forty minutes north of Wilson Field, depending on traffic?"

"That's about right," Dave said. "Depending on the time of day."

"Alpharetta's a pretty upscale area, is it not? You'd agree there are a lot of nice take-out and fast food places by your house, wouldn't you, Detective?"

"I would."

"But yet, instead of going to one of these nice places by your home in Alpharetta, you want this jury to believe you ended up going to an inner-city convenience store and buying a couple of those hot dogs that spin around for hours at a time?"

"I don't recall the specifics about it."

"What would you say, Mr. Mackno, if the store owner took the stand and testified that he specifically recalled selling you a six-pack of beer on the night you killed Remo Centrella?"

Dave paused for a moment. He didn't remember who sold him the beer, and he doubted if there was any way the storeowner could have remembered him. He decided to trust his instinct that Bass was attempting to bluff him.

"I'd say he was mistaken," Dave said.

"Would you say he was lying?"

"I don't know what would motivate him to lie, so I'd say he's mistaken. I've never purchased any beer from the A&G."

"So Mr. Rajnaratnam was mistaken? Is that your answer?"

"Yes," Dave said.

"Okay," Bass said. He headed back towards the lectern before suddenly turning back around towards Dave. "One more question before we move on, Detective. What happened to the wrappers from the food you bought?"

"The wrappers?"

"Yes. When the investigators took an inventory of your wife's car, there were no food wrappers in it."

"I don't know," Dave said.

"Did you leave your stakeout to throw them away?"

"I don't recall."

"Did they just magically disappear?" Bass said.

"Objection, Your Honor. Asked and answered. The defendant said he does not recall," Whitney said.

"Sustained."

"Very well, Your Honor," Bass said. "Let's move on, Detective, shall we?"

Bass went back to the lectern and took a drink of bottled water as he looked down at his notepad. After a few moments, he looked back up towards Dave.

"Mr. Mackno, you testified earlier this afternoon that you thought you had done a pretty good job on the night Mr. Centrella was killed. Do you recall that testimony?"

"Yes," Dave said.

"What did you think when you heard a certified police expert, Sean Fencil, say it was the one of the worst jobs of policing he had ever reviewed?"

"Not much," Dave said, remembering how powerless he felt as Fencil excoriated him from the witness stand. "I knew he was a hired gun who was getting paid to say what you wanted him to."

Bass looked startled. "You think my office told a court approved expert what to say?" he said.

"I've attended a lot of trials, Mr. Bass. I've never seen one yet where an expert getting paid by the prosecution doesn't say what they want."

"That's a very interesting comment, Mr. Mackno. Are you claiming to be an expert on the criminal justice system?"

Dave heard a few muffled laughs.

"I'm just passing along my observations."

"Let's discuss some of those observations for a moment. Is it your opinion, *observation as you call it,* that the testimony given for the prosecution by its experts is based on the fact they're getting compensated for their testimony, instead of being based on their actual opinions?"

"Honestly?" Dave said, and paused for several beats, while he stared at Bass. "It is. Especially because your experts never asked *me* about what happened."

"Let me make sure I understand what you're saying, Mr. Mackno. You're testifying you think you did a good job on the night you killed Mr. Centrella and that the experts who said you did an incompetent job are wrong in their analysis. Is that correct?"

"That is."

"What about Tina Manning, Detective? You testified you were concerned when you saw she had a black eye, but Mrs. Manning testified under oath she didn't have one. She said Mr. Centrella never hit her. Was she telling the truth, Detective?"

"No," Dave said.

"She was lying?"

"I think that my attorney showed —"

"No, no, no," Bass said, and pointed at Dave. "I'm not asking you what Mr. Taylor may or may not have shown. I'm asking for your opinion as to whether or not Mrs. Manning lied on the stand?"

As Dave paused, the look on his face made it clear just how much contempt he had for Maurice Bass. Despite being coached by Whitney not to display any negative feelings towards him, Dave was not doing a good job masking his thoughts. He had grown to hate Maurice Bass and it was obvious.

"Yes," Dave said, calmly. "I know, for a fact, she was lying."

"What about Curtis Pressley? He testified you beat him during the '92 King riots. Was he lying too?"

Bass had picked up the pace of his questions, and they sounded more like indictments than inquiries. Dave was trying, as Whitney had coached, to slow him down by pausing between answers, but Bass was pressing him hard.

"I asked you a question, Detective Mackno. Was Curtis Pressley lying when he said you broke his shoulder? It's a simple question, sir."

"He might have been hit by a cop that night, but he wasn't hit by me."

"How do you know that, Detective? How do you know you didn't hit Curtis Pressley? You were working during the riots that night, were you not?"

"I was, but I never came into contact with a group of marchers. As Detective Morello testified, we were primarily going after small groups of looters."

"How do you explain the fact Curtis Pressley wrote *your* name down?"

"I have no idea."

"Out of all the police officers on the Atlanta force, Mr. Pressley just happened to write down your name. A coincidence?"

"Maybe he wrote it down after I was indicted."

"Really? That's your explanation, Detective? Curtis Pressley, as upstanding a citizen as I have ever met, came into court and perjured himself? Is that what you really expect this jury to believe?"

"I don't know why he did it, but I do know I didn't hit him."

"Who *did* you hit that night, Detective?"

"I didn't hit Mr. Pressley, and I don't recall hitting anyone that night. I would have remembered it if I had."

Bass came to a complete stop.

"You just lied, didn't you, Mr. Mackno?" he said.

"Excuse me?" Dave said.

"About not hitting anybody during the riots. You just lied, didn't you? You hit people during the riots and you, I, and everybody in this courtroom knows it."

"Objection."

"Sustained."

"You hit people during the riots didn't you, Mr. Mackno?"

"No, I didn't," Dave said, trying to stay calm.

"Don't you think it's about time you start being honest with this jury? Just admit it: you hit Mr. Pressley. You broke his shoulder. You're the reason he can't lift up his arm. That's the truth, isn't it?"

"No, it's not."

"And Tina Manning didn't have a black eye, did she? That's just another lie you told to cover up for your mistakes, isn't it? You made that up to try and justify your actions, didn't you, Mr. Mackno?"

"No, I did not."

"In fact, Mr. Mackno, you've told lie after lie after lie, haven't you? Both to the investigators with Internal Affairs and now here, *under oath*, to try and cover up for the fact your recklessness and incompetence are the reasons Remo Centrella is dead. Isn't that the bottom-line truth, Detective?"

Dave could feel himself getting angry as Bass kept attacking him in open court.

"Not true," he said.

"Not true? You really expect this jury to believe that, Mr. Mackno?" Bass said, with his arms stretched out to his side. "That all these people, who have come into court to testify against you, are lying and misrepresenting the truth? That's there's some kind of conspiracy against you, but that you're the one telling the truth?"

Bass had begun to raise his voice.

"That you, the person with the most to lose in this proceeding, the person whose freedom is on the line, you're the one who is being honest?"

Dave felt as if the courtroom was crowding in on him. "It's the truth," he said.

Dave knew that being forced to remain seated, while Bass had free range to move around and raise his voice, made his answers sound weak in contrast to Bass' questions.

"You did everything wrong that night, didn't you Mr. Mackno?" Bass said, now with open contempt in his voice. "You acted recklessly. You left your stakeout and acted like the normal rules of being a police officer didn't apply to you. And for what reason? We'll never truly know your true motivations, will we? But we do know one thing: *Remo Centrella, a man who had never even been arrested, ended up dead at your hands.*

"He ended up dead in a parking lot, lying in a pool of his own blood because of the negligent and incompetent way you performed your duties that evening. Isn't that the truth of this entire case, Detective?"

"No," Dave said, but his answer was drowned out by Bass.

"It was your negligence that created a situation where you had to shoot Mr. Centrella. Your failure to call for backup, your failure to diffuse the situation, and your failure to discharge your duties to a standard that the law requires. That's why Remo Centrella is dead."

"No, it's not."

"Remo Centrella wasn't attacking you because he wanted to hurt you, he was attacking you in order to try and defend himself. He was scared of you, Mr. Mackno, wasn't he? He was the one acting in self-defense."

"No, he wasn't."

"He was scared because you had already shot at him once and because you had broken his wrist."

Bass raised his voice.

"Your attorney didn't bring that up during your testimony, did he, Mr. Mackno? But the medical records show it. They show you used such excessive force in trying to handcuff Mr. Centrella that you actually broke his wrist.

"But now you want to come into this courtroom and pretend that you were not the aggressor in the situation. You want to claim self-defense when the person who would actually be entitled to that defense, *the person in the confrontation who didn't have a gun*, is the one who is dead."

Bass looked like a man full of righteous anger.

"Is it any surprise that Tina Manning became so scared that she had to run into the middle of one of the most crime ridden neighborhoods in Atlanta. She did it because she realized her life was in danger."

Dave pointed at Bass. "You're taking things completely out of context," he said.

"Taking things out of context?"

Bass bent halfway over and stretched his hands wide to the side in mock shock.

"Out of what context, Detective? Your context? Your version of the truth? Your version of the facts, in which you refuse to take even one ounce of responsibility for the killing of Remo Centrella? Your version of the facts where you refuse to admit your actions make you criminally liable for his murder?"

"Objection, Your Honor. *Inflammatory*. These are no longer questions, this has devolved into a verbal attack on my client."

Bass took a step closer to Dave and pulled an Atlanta Police Department badge out of the inner pocket of his suit coat.

"Sustained," Judge Friedman said.

"You've disgraced this badge, haven't you?" Bass said, as he showed the badge to Dave, before raising it above his shoulder. "You failed to live up to the standards required of an Atlanta police officer."

Judge Friedman banged her gavel as Bass held the badge high in the air.

"Enough!" she said.

"You deserve to be held accountable don't you, Mr. Mackno?" he said, openly ignoring Judge Friedman for the first time during the trial. He was now standing directly in front of Dave, showing him the badge. "You're trying to hide behind a shield that you have disgraced."

Judge Friedman stood up and banged her gavel even louder. "Mr. Bass, I will hold you in contempt!"

Bass stepped back. His shirt was half un-tucked and his face was glistening with sweat. He looked angry as he stared at Dave for several seconds.

"I apologize for letting my passion get the best of me, Your Honor, but I'm not the person in this courtroom who needs to be held in contempt.

"No further questions," he said, and walked back to his seat.

25

"I AGREE with a lot of what you're saying, I'm just afraid if we let Detective Mackno walk, we're going to make it more likely another unarmed individual gets killed by a cop," Dixon Garcia, Juror number 9 said. "Or maybe he breaks somebody else's arm. *That's my biggest concern.* What kind of message do we send with an acquittal."

"I hear you what you're saying, Dixon," juror number 4, a bank manager from Decatur named Kathi said. "I respect that, and I agree there's a lot of things about this defendant that I don't like. But I also agree with what Kirstie said. There's been a lot of dishonesty on both sides of this case."

"Uh-hmm," Kirstie said. "Neither side's hands are clean."

"But I think, as a jury, we should try and limit it to the facts we think we can trust. As the judge said, we should use our judgment to try to come as close to the truth as we can and then apply the law."

Dixon nodded, as Kathi spoke.

"Is it possible Mrs. Manning didn't have a bruise?" she said. "Yes. The problem I have is the defense showed she lied about an arrest. Set aside the fact she was cheating on her husband. That doesn't bother me. Even the fact she was arrested for a fake ID. *I had one myself in college.* But the fact she lied about it? That makes me question her honesty. I don't know about anybody else, but if I was ever arrested, I'm pretty sure that wouldn't slip my mind. In my opinion, she tried to cover up the truth, and that means we need to give more scrutiny to her testimony. Not to even mention the fact it took her three months to turn herself in."

"What about the cooler?" Dixon said. "I saw Detective Mackno's face when attorney Bass asked him if he'd been drinking. He looked stunned by the question, like a guy who got blindsided."

"I saw his face, too," Kathi said, "but I'm going to have to agree with Witt on that one. The prosecution never fully proved it. I don't doubt that there's a very good chance Mr. Mackno was drinking on the stakeout. If that had been proven, he would deserve to be convicted. But on the other hand, it was a convenience store so there's a chance it was actually food. As long as there's that chance, and as long as we're talking about a man's freedom, I keep going back to the presumption of innocence and the fact the burden of proof is on the prosecution. Is he innocent? Not completely. But should we find him not guilty under the rules of the jury system? I have to say yes because of the presumption of innocence and the fact we're required to convict beyond a reasonable doubt. If the opposite presumption was true, I'd be sitting on your side of the table. Even if the burden was just fifty-fifty, I would vote to convict."

"So in your mind," Dixon said, "this is more about reasonable doubt that actual guilt or innocence?"

"It's what the legal system requires of us," she said.

"Do you think that's right?"

"Tough question. I don't think there's a black and white answer."

Cheryl, the jury's forewoman stood halfway up in her chair.

"Hold on guys," she said. "Let's not get sidetracked into a debate on legal theory. Let's stay focused on the specific case. We've worked too hard to let this process end up being a waste of time. Let's try to finish strong and get a verdict across the finish line. As Judge Friedman said this morning, nobody will be able to do a better job than the twelve of us."

"She's the one person in this trial who has been honest," Dixon said.

"I'll tell you what," Gus, an assistant hotel manager, said, "if Dixon goes for acquittal, so will I."

"You serious, Gus? You're going to put it all on me?" Dixon said, with half a crooked smile. "No pressure, right?"

"I got your back either way," Gus said.

It was almost lunchtime on Saturday, the fifth day of deliberations, and everyone in the room was worn down. They were tired of deliberating Dave's fate and ready to go home. Even Dixon, who had been the strongest proponent for conviction, seemed like he was coming around towards an acquittal.

"Can you read those instructions one more time, Cheryl?" he said.

"Sure," she said and picked up a copy of the "Allen Charge" that Judge Friedman had read to the jurors earlier that morning in court.

The Allen Charge, sometimes referred to as a "Dynamite Charge," was originally derived from an 1896 U.S. Supreme Court case involving a murder. Since that time, the instructions, which the Supreme Court ruled constitutional, had been reduced to boilerplate language that judges can use in situations of jury deadlock.

The version that Judge Friedman provided to the jury, and the one Cheryl began to read, were from the *5th Circuit Pattern Criminal Jury Instructions* manual. They stated:

"Jurors, I'm going to ask that you continue your deliberations in an effort to reach agreement upon a verdict and dispose of this case; and I have a few additional comments I would like for you to consider as you do so. This is an important case. The trial has been expensive in time, effort, money and emotional strain to both the defense and the prosecution. If you should fail to agree upon a verdict, the case will be left open and may have to be tried again. Obviously, another trial would only serve to increase the cost to both sides, and there is no reason to believe that the case can be tried again by either side any better or more exhaustively than it has been tried before you.

Any future jury must be selected in the same manner and from the same source as you were chosen, and there is no reason to believe that the case could ever be submitted to twelve men and women more conscientious, more impartial, or more competent to decide it, or that more or clearer evidence could be produced.

If a substantial majority of your number are in favor of a conviction, those of you who disagree should reconsider whether your doubt is a reasonable one since it appears to make no effective impression upon the minds of the others. On the other hand, if a majority or even a lesser number of you are in favor of an acquittal, the rest of you should ask yourselves again, and most thoughtfully, whether you should accept the weight and sufficiency of evidence which fails to convince your fellow jurors beyond a reasonable doubt.

Remember at all times that no juror is expected to give up an honest belief he or she may have as to the weight or effect of the evidence; but, after full deliberation and consideration of the evidence in the case, it is your duty to agree upon a verdict if you can do so.

You must also remember that if the evidence in the case fails to establish guilt beyond a reasonable doubt the Defendant should have your unanimous verdict of Not Guilty.

You may be as leisurely in your deliberations as the occasion may require and should take all the time which you may feel is necessary.

I will ask now that you retire once again and continue your deliberations with these additional comments in mind to be applied, of course, in conjunction with all of the other instructions I have previously given to you."

———

Dixon stood up and let out a loud breath. "I'm feeling torn over this, but I truly don't want anyone else to have to go through the same ordeal. Part of me wants to go for conviction, but I won't stand in the way of a unanimous verdict."

"Gus, does that mean you'll go for acquittal, too?" Cheryl said.

"I will," he said.

"Okay," Cheryl said. "Let's take one last formal vote, and if we can get it unanimous, I'll send it out to the Judge."

Nobody was smiling as the voice vote was taken, but everyone looked a lot happier than they had an hour earlier.

When the vote was tallied, Cheryl notified the bailiff, who informed Judge Friedman that the jury had reached a verdict.

"Notify all parties to be back in my courtroom in thirty minutes," she said before turning around and heading back into her chambers.

As Judge Friedman went back to her chambers to prepare for the announcement of the verdict, Dave sat alone in the basement of the courthouse. He took a sip from the cup of grape soda he had purchased from one of the archaic vending machines in the building's canteen.

Dave was one of the few people inside the courthouse on a Saturday. He had seen at least a dozen news trucks parked outside when he arrived, and he knew that the crowd of people would grow throughout the day. It had been widely reported that the jury was stuck, and everyone sensed that either a verdict or declaration of a mistrial could come down at any moment.

Conventional wisdom from the television punditry was that this would likely be the final day of deliberations.

Dave was trying to avoid thinking about a mistrial or

guilty verdict as he drank his soda. With a guilty verdict, life, as he knew it, would be over. And a mistrial wouldn't be much better. Dave didn't think he and Darlene could handle a second trial. Their resources, *financial, physical, and emotional,* were already too depleted.

As Dave drank his soda, he tried to enjoy a few minutes of peace by thinking about what he would do if, as he expected, the jury acquitted him.

Fishing. Down in the Florida Keys. That was the image, *that was the dream,* that kept coming into Dave's mind. He and Darlene spending a couple months in a small house that overlooked mangroves and turquoise water. No television, no telephones, and no attorneys. Just cold beer, good fishing, and fat red sunsets every night.

Dave could practically feel some of the pressure drain from his body as he thought about driving down to Islamorada after the trial.

He lingered with his thoughts for almost fifteen minutes before getting back on the elevator to go back to the fifth floor break-out room that he had come to think of as his own personal holding tank.

As the elevator rose, a bell rang and it stopped on the first floor. The doors opened and he found himself looking directly at Maurice Bass.

26

BASS PAUSED for a moment, as if he might wait for the next elevator, before stepping inside.

Dave and Maurice had been together in the same room countless times during the trial, but they had never been alone. There had always been a layer of lawyers and court personnel between them. They had not spoken directly, apart from the question and answer format of the pre-trial deposition and the cross-examination.

Dave felt himself get tense. The anger he felt towards Bass rose up inside him, making it feel like the temperature inside his head had spiked.

The doors closed, and Maurice pushed the button for the fourth floor. He nodded in acknowledgment to Dave.

"Detective," he said, in a voice too loud for the small space.

Dave didn't say anything as he tried to ignore the small current of electricity he now sensed in the air. It was the same uneasiness he often felt before a calm situation turned violent.

As Maurice stared up at the numbers above the doors, Dave gave him a discreet look up and down. He noticed his gold Rolex, expensive suit, and the black tasseled loafers that were so polished they glowed silver. Looking at Maurice Bass reminded Dave how little money he and Darlene would have left after paying their legal bills. Dave knew he would never own a Rolex.

He cleared his throat.

"I've disgraced the badge, is that right, Mr. Bass?"

Maurice didn't answer.

The number 2 lit up and another bell rang, as the elevator moved towards 3.

"What's the matter, Bass? You don't feel like talking? I guess you don't have such a big mouth when nobody's around to protect you."

Bass stayed silent, and Dave took a step towards him. He was now inside Bass' personal space as he reached across him and pulled the elevator's "STOP" button.

"You think you can ignore me?" Dave said. The elevator came to a halt.

Bass squared around slowly to look at Dave.

"What do you think you're doing, Detective? Are you really going to start a problem now that the jury has come back with a verdict? That wouldn't be very smart."

Dave was surprised by the news about the verdict, but didn't show it.

"I don't need advice from you," he said. "I should have never been put on trial in the first place, and you know it. If you had a shred of integrity, you would have done the right thing and followed the recommendation of Internal Affairs."

"And let you get away with shooting an unarmed man after you had been drinking on the job?"

"I already told you," Dave said, staring hard at Maurice. "That didn't happen."

"You can dispense with the denials, Detective. The trial's over. This is just you and me, and we both know the truth."

"I'm innocent," Dave said. "The jury's gonna let me walk and you know it."

"You're probably right," Bass said. "But it's not because you're innocent....it's because I let you."

"Because you let me?" Dave said. "How do you figure that, Bass?"

"Because it's the truth. The only reason you might walk out of here a free man is because I made that choice. Because I was paying back a debt."

"Paying back a debt?" Dave said. "To who?"

"To you, Mr. Mackno."

"What the fuck are you talking about, Bass?"

"This trial isn't the first time we met, Detective. You and I met many years ago, in one of the stripped out hallways of Father Paneck Village. You and your partner, *Detective Morello*, chased me in there one summer night after you ran me over with your car."

Dave's eyes showed a flash of recognition.

"You remember it, don't you?" Bass said.

Dave nodded as his mouth went completely dry. "I do," he said.

"I realized who you were when I took his deposition. As soon as Morello walked in the room, I knew he was the cop who called me a nigger when I was 17 years old. That's not the type of thing you forget.

"But you were okay," Bass said as a more distant look came into his eyes. "He wanted to arrest me, but you somehow over-ruled him. You took my word over a white woman who thought I wanted to rob her just because I was black."

Dave nodded in remembrance.

"That's why I decided to cut you a break, Detective. That's why I decided to put my thumb on the scale of justice and tip it in your favor. To give you a legitimate shot at your freedom," Bass said, as if fully articulating his thoughts for the first time.

"I couldn't just drop the charges, of course. That would have been too much of a break. *Disproportionate*, I told myself. No way I was going to give you, or any other cop, a free pass after shooting an unarmed man. That would have gone against everything I believe.

"No, you had to be held accountable for the shooting. You had to be put on trial, and a jury had to be the one to decide your fate. *That was non-negotiable.* But I also knew that if I wanted to live with myself, I had to find a way to square the books on the break you cut me down at Father Paneck. That's why I kept out the testimony about the Bud Light cans you had in your car, Detective. The ones that Sergeant Coyle removed from the scene."

Dave took a step back. He looked as stunned as he felt.

"I know the truth, Detective," Bass said. "One of the cops on the scene, *doesn't matter who,* contacted my office and told me what happened. He told me exactly what he saw, that Jimmy Coyle drove away from the scene with evidence in his car. He didn't say anything at the time, but he's an honest cop and decided you shouldn't get away with killing Centrella. He said he would be willing to take the stand and testify to what he witnessed."

"But nobody testified," Dave said. "All you showed was the receipt. I thought you were bluffing."

"That's because I never took his affidavit," Bass said. "I told him I had what I needed to bring my case, and that I wouldn't let him throw away his career. I know what the repercussions would be for a cop with the integrity to break the code of silence."

"But you asked me about it? You came after me hard about buying the beer."

"That's because I was willing to give you a break, not a pass, Detective. Once I cut you the break, I was going to do everything in my power to get a conviction. I meant every word I said during the trial. Your negligence killed Remo Centrella. He was unarmed and didn't have to die. No matter what this jury says, you and I know that's the truth."

Neither man spoke for several seconds.

"So that's how you do it?" Dave said, breaking the silence and still staring at Bass.

"Do what?"

"Live with yourself. Convince yourself that somehow what you've done to me is acceptable because you sat on a piece of evidence."

"A devastating piece of evidence," Bass said.

"It had nothing to do with what happened between me and Centrella."

"Don't be naïve, Detective. If the jury had proof you were drinking they would have felt morally obligated to convict you. There's no way they would have let you walk. You know it's true. But I chose to keep the evidence out. I chose to do what was noble."

"Noble?" Dave said. "Do you have any idea the price I've paid because of this trial?"

Maurice didn't answer.

"I've been a cop a long time, Bass, a lot longer than you've been a lawyer, and in that time, I've busted a lot of lowlifes. Pimps, pushers, whores, you name it, I've taken them down. And you want to know something? They were all scum. The kind of people who make you lose faith in humanity. But they were also people who had one thing in common. You know what that is, Bass?"

Maurice didn't answer.

"Each one of them had more integrity than you because they were honest about who they were. They didn't pretend to be something they weren't."

Dave took a step closer to Bass. Their faces were almost touching.

"There's nothing noble about who you are or what you do," Dave said. "You're just a lawyer who's smart enough to know how to play the system to get what you want. You may have done what you did to try and absolve your conscience, but it doesn't make you noble. *It doesn't change who you are*: an opportunist who exploited the death of Remo Centrella, just like you exploited the death of those two little girls. You want to talk about the truth, Bass, there it is."

Dave pushed the stop button again, and the elevator began moving. He pushed the button for 3, and the doors opened.

Dave hitched his shoulder and neck. "I would advise you to step off this elevator," he said, "because I'm done being polite."

Bass stepped off, and Dave let out a huge exhale after the doors closed. The elevator rose to 5, where Dave exited and headed to the conference room. When he opened the door, he saw Whitney pacing while Joan was holding a cigarette in one hand and rosary beads in the other.

"Where have you been?" Whitney said. "The jury reached a verdict."

"I know."

Thirty minutes later, Judge Friedman called her courtroom to order for the reading of the verdict in <u>State of Georgia vs. David Mackno</u>. Once the jurors took their seats, she asked them if they had reached a verdict.

"We have, Your Honor," Cheryl said. She folded the verdict form in two and handed it to a Deputy, who gave it to Judge Friedman. She unfolded the sheet and read their decision without any change of expression on her face.

"Please publish the verdict," Judge Friedman said and handed the sheet of paper to the court reporter.

Dave, Whitney and Maurice stood up.

The court reporter read the verdict form. "We the jury find the defendant, David Mackno, not guilty," she said.

"Thank you," Judge Friedman said as a low rustle moved through the courtroom.

Dave had a minimal reaction, other than a small, quick smile when the verdict was read. No matter what the verdict, Remo Centrella was still dead and his reputation was still ruined. As far as Dave was concerned, there was nothing to be happy about. The only strong feeling he had was one of relief. He wasn't going to prison.

Judge Friedman thanked the jurors for their service and told them they were now free to leave. In her parting instructions, she informed them of their Constitutional right to speak, or not, with the media, now that the case was over.

"You are now released from your service to this court," she said. "The state of Georgia thanks you. From this point forward, you're free to do as you choose."

Judge Friedman then turned to Dave.

"Mr. Mackno," she said, "this proceeding is now concluded. You are hereby free to leave."

No words had ever sounded better to Dave. He and Whitney hugged. "This jury did the right thing," Whitney said in his ear. "Maurice Bass dragged you into Hell, but you made it out the other side. He can never take you back."

"Thank you," Dave said. "I'll always be grateful."

Darlene was the next person to reach Dave and gave him the tightest hug of their marriage. "Thank God," she said, with tears streaming onto his cheek. "We get our lives back."

"We do," Dave said and kissed the side of her head. "I love you."

"I love you, too."

It was as Dave hugged Darlene, that he admitted to himself a truth he might have always known: He was never going back to APD.

From his first days after waking up at Grady, through rehabilitation, the indictment, and the trial, Dave always told himself he would one day return to the force.

"I won't let anybody take away my identity," had been the mantra Dave relied upon to make it through the toughest times. That determination, his eventual return to the department, had been the goal that sustained him.

But now that he had been acquitted, he could admit to himself that he wanted to get away from Atlanta. He didn't want to re-join APD and have to forever live with the stigma of being the cop who shot Remo Centrella.

EPILOGUE

A MONTH after Dave submitted his resignation to the Department, Buddy McCray announced he would not be seeking re-election to his Senate seat. The decision stunned most politicos in Georgia, *McCray was looking at an almost guaranteed re-election*, until the Inquirer ran a front-page story in its Sunday edition, in which it revealed McCray, a grandfather, who had been married for 34 years, had fathered a daughter, who was almost two years old, out of wedlock.

According to the Inquirer's investigative report, the child was the result of an affair with a lobbyist for the soft drink industry. Even worse, it alleged the Senator had been paying her three thousand dollars a month in child support with funds diverted from his Political Action Committee "Restoring Virtue in Government."

McCray issued a public apology to both his wife and the lobbyist. He also indicated he planned to be involved in all aspects of his daughter's life while remaining married to his wife.

"It will be a difficult challenge for all of us and one best undertaken outside the public eye," he stated in his press release.

Three weeks later, with Frank Durkin standing next to him, Brian Pike announced he was running for the office.

With Pike running for the Senate, the seat in District 4 opened up and, much to the surprise of many in the local media, there appeared to be a groundswell of support for

Maurice Bass to fill it.

A PAC was set up and funded by some anonymous donors to encourage Maurice to run. It wasn't long before it became conventional wisdom that Maurice possessed the talent, name recognition and oratorical skills that would make him a formidable candidate.

When asked his opinion about Bass running for Congress, Frank Durkin said it would be a no brainer for the voters of 4 to elect such a "stalwart champion of the people.

"His track record of success, combined with his passion to help people, make him an ideal candidate," Durkin said.

In early May, Bass called a press conference at the Westin Peachtree, where he announced, "after extensive meditation on my future, I have reached the conclusion that I must put aside my own self-interest and accede to the will of the voters.

"If my experience as District Attorney has taught me anything," he said, "it's that I have a heart for public service. If elected to this great office, the people of District 4 can be assured I will strive everyday to continue Congressman Pike's legacy of leadership, honesty, and integrity."

On the Friday afternoon of Memorial Day Weekend, Ray Manning delivered his annual "State of the Barons" press conference.

It was Ray's first public appearance since the verdict, and nearly 20 reporters surrounded him as he sat in the Barons' dugout.

He began by reading a prepared statement:

"On behalf of the entire Barons' organization, I want to thank our wonderful fans for your continued dedication and support. You are a major part of this team's success and legacy.

The past ten months have been an extraordinarily difficult time for our team, our organization, and our city. I know there will be a lot of questions and interest regarding the events of the past year, but the truth is, I've never found much benefit in focusing on the past, when there's a lot of work that needs to be done for the future.

The Atlanta Barons have a bright future ahead of us, and I look forward to bringing more championships to this great city."

"Thank you," Ray said and lit a cigarette. "I'll now be happy to answer some questions."

"No. I have no plans to sell the Barons.

"I laughed when I saw the reports we had retained an investment bank to try and find a buyer for the team. That won't happen. I'm not selling the team, and when I die my kids are not selling the team, either. If they even think about it, I'll rise from my grave and scare them out of it. My estate has already been structured to ensure ownership of the Barons will be passed down to my grandchildren.

"Johnny Wiemer has conversations with Wall Street all the time. I'm not going to address rumors, but I can assure you, I never had any need to raise one hundred million dollars in order to avoid bankruptcy. As a matter of fact, thanks to our recently completed extension of our cable television contract, cash flow this season should be as strong as it has been in almost five years.

"Not only is it a frivolous lawsuit, which, I might add, any decent lawyer would have been embarrassed to file, but I find it ironic that Cohen, Wolfe, of all companies, is claiming I somehow took advantage of their innocence. I don't think I'd be breaking any news here if I said I know plenty of people who think the Wolfe's entire business model is predicated upon taking advantage of their clients' naiveté.

"Donergy is doing extremely well. S&P just raised our credit rating and, as a matter of fact, we're projecting record revenues over the next decade to be generated from our Canadian operations.

"Obviously it was painful to learn about what

happened, however, I learned a long time ago you can't get where you're trying to go if you're looking backwards.

"I'm probably not the best person to be commenting on the institution of marriage.

"The honest answer is I don't know. Due to the circumstances, she and I have not spoken directly since the dissolution of our marriage. I don't have any information to share other than to say I wish her nothing but the best.

"Most likely. From what I've been told by Monsignor, the short duration of our marriage, and the fact we did not have children together makes the granting of one much more likely.

"No, I don't hold any anger towards Remo. We had a great run together.

"It isn't tarnished in the least.

"It wasn't my decision to get rid of his mural. That decision was made by our marketing department out of respect for our fans. They didn't think people would want to be reminded of a senseless tragedy every time they come to a game at Builders Life.

"I wasn't surprised, were you? I didn't watch the trial, so I can't speak to exactly what did or didn't happen inside the courtroom, but I do think the prosecution was facing an uphill battle because the defendant was a cop.

"Again, I didn't watch it, but to me, it was a pretty simple calculation. Remo Centrella was unarmed. He was parked outside my stadium, minding his own business, and he ended up dead at the hands of a cop. That seems like a pretty straightforward scenario as far as I'm concerned."

Ray stubbed out his Marlboro Light and paused to light another one.

"We've already turned the page as an organization. My job as leader is to make sure everyone stays one hundred percent focused on the future success of the team.

"They mean as much to me as they always have because they were won by a team, not by an individual.

"I expect us to be playing plenty of baseball come October.

"That's an accurate story. We do have a son together, so obviously there's a history there.

"I think it's only natural to re-assess what's important in life when you go through a difficult time.

"No. As long as we're offering players millions of dollars per year based upon their on-field performance, there will be players who are going to seek an edge.

"I have great respect for P.J. Foley, both as a person and a writer, but the idea of an asterisk is a ridiculous one.

"I would like to see them legalized and regulated. But then I'm a libertarian, not a "puritarian."

"Part of me admires the players willing to do whatever it takes to win. Isn't that the reason we play baseball? I've never understood why baseball writers were so against a medical product that enhances performance. You think we should start testing our players for Viagra? Better yet, you want us to start testing you guys for Viagra?"

The assembled reporters laughed, and an executive with the Barons signaled to Ray that time was up.

"Okay, guys, I need to run. Thank you," he said and stood up. "Have a great holiday weekend. This was enjoyable, as always."

******

By late October, Dave and Darlene were living in a small house in Santa Rosa Beach, Florida, that had an unobstructed view of Choctawhatchee Bay. The house was single-story and had an attached dock where Dave kept a beat up fishing boat he had inherited from his father.

He and Darlene had made the move down to Florida's "Emerald Coast" largely because one of his former supervisors, Joe Forness, offered him a job as a security guard at the local college in Niceville.

"It's a world away from Zone 3," Forness told Dave when he offered him the job. "But the water's blue, the beer is cold, and the fishing doesn't get much better."

The security guard position paid a lot less than Dave earned as a cop, but the benefits were good, and Darlene was able to find a bookkeeping job with a condo developer in the area.

"After a lifetime spent chasing bad guys in Atlanta, this place is Shangri-La," Forness told Dave one night over a fish dinner at Pompano Joe's. "You'll never want to go back."

"You're probably right," Dave said. "I loved Atlanta once, but not anymore."

On the first Tuesday in November, Darlene had gone to bed and Dave was sitting in their living room watching the local news. It was election night, and the anchors were reporting results from around the region.

Most of the reports were about local races, *town council and county commission seats*, but halfway through the telecast, the lead anchor perked up as she reported, "Away from the Panhandle, one of the more interesting stories of the night is taking place up in Atlanta. Viewers will remember Atlanta District Attorney, Maurice Bass, as the prosecutor in the case involving the death of baseball star Remo Centrella."

A headshot of Bass appeared over the anchor's right shoulder.

"Maurice Bass might not have won that case," she said, 'but tonight, he has won a seat in Congress. Our affiliate in Atlanta has the story."

The local channel cut into the feed of an Atlanta-based reporter doing a live shot from inside Maurice Bass' campaign headquarters. The camera panned to the stage, where Maurice and Lisa were holding hands and smiling as confetti fell and balloons were batted through the air.

Dave could feel himself begin to get angry. The last thing he wanted to see was Maurice Bass celebrating a victory that had been built on the fame he had garnered from the Centrella trial.

Dave turned off the television and picked up his bottle of Budweiser. He took a pull, but it was empty. For a moment he thought about getting a fresh one, but decided it was already too late.

Instead of getting up right away, Dave leaned back in his chair and allowed his thoughts go back to the night he shot Remo. He thought about his decision to leave the stakeout and pursue a speeding car. How that one impulsive choice started a chain of events that led to him and Darlene living in a rental house in Northwest Florida, while Maurice Bass was elected to Congress.

"I was just a pawn that got played," he said to himself as he pondered the divergent paths he and Bass were now traveling, as a result of Remo Centrella's death.

Election to Congress would be just the beginning of Maurice Bass' political career in Washington. He would arrive in the nation's capital with name recognition and a skill set tailor-made for success. So much so, that by the end of his second term, he would become a favorite of both the media and the power brokers who ran the Capital.

Within a decade, Bass would make a big enough mark in national politics that his prosecution of Dave would end up being a footnote in a career that would eventually take him to the top job in the United States Department of Justice.

The same kind of good fortune would not shine on Dave. Repercussions from the shooting would define the next decade of his life. It would be a decade in which his life would stagnate, and his marriage to Darlene would reach the breaking point.

But Dave would refuse to quit. As much as Atlanta had taken from him, he still believed the world would eventually yield to his will, as long as he never gave up.

By the end of the decade, it did. Ten years after shooting Remo Centrella in a parking lot outside of Wilson Field in Atlanta, Dave's life would be back on track. His marriage to Darlene would survive, and he would eventually find work as a small town cop in Florida.

Dave would once again get to a place where life was good, and where Atlanta felt as distant as a past life. He would find peace living on the Florida Panhandle, enjoying a slow-paced, but happy and contented life.

His life would be just about ideal, until a brilliant fall day when a local widow named Barbara Spencer would be reported missing, and Dave would need to choose between doing his job or getting even with Maurice Bass.

THE END

AUTHOR'S NOTE

Now that you've reached the end of Hallways in the Night, I would like to take a moment to say thank you for reading and let you know how much I appreciate the time you've invested in this book. I truly enjoyed the process of writing Hallways in the Night and tried my best to write a book that would maintain a strong pace from start to finish, hold readers' attention, and offer a mix of engaging characters, as well as some surprises along the way.

Since publication, I have had the chance to interact with and receive feedback from readers. That has turned out to be one of the most enjoyable parts of writing a book. Along those lines, I would love to hear your thoughts and feedback, so please feel free to email me anytime at rcowriting@gmail.com.

Regarding the story itself, I began writing Hallways in the Night several years ago, usually between 10 p.m. and midnight when my wife and kids were asleep. It actually began as a backstory to the book I planned to write before becoming its own stand-alone story.

As the book indicates on the last page, I plan to write a sequel to the story. In the sequel, which will begin ten years after Dave's trial, he will once again find himself up against some of the same characters who impacted his life in HITN. Without giving too much away, Dave will find the body of a local widow within two weeks of a Presidential election. Her death will not have been random, and it will have the potential to impact the election. Which will, in turn, impact the lives of Maurice Bass, Frank Durkin and others, including Mary McNeill. You may remember McNeill as a very minor character, *Governor of Ohio and former NASA astronaut,* who made a brief appearance on Bobby's flight up to Ohio. In book two, she'll be on the verge of winning election to the White House.

I'm excited to write the sequel.

Having read Hallways in the Night (and hopefully enjoyed it), there are two small things you could do that would be a major help to the book. The first would be to please consider recommending *Hallways in the Night* to other readers. Not only would that be the highest compliment I could receive, I also believe that book recommendations to friends, co-workers and family are the most effective way to build an audience for the book: one reader at a time.

The second thing that would be a huge help would be if you could take a few minutes and review the book on Amazon. Since publishing this book, I've come to understand just how important reviews are to both Amazon and prospective readers.

Amazon will, I believe, eventually help this book get more exposure, but from what I have been told by other writers, the key is to get enough reviews that it "gets their attention."

Reader reviews seem to be one of the bigger metrics that Amazon uses in order to determine a book's relevance. So, if you have the time to write a quick review, whatever you feel the book rates, I would be very grateful and it would be very helpful to the book's long-term success. Thank you in advance for anything you may do.

Sincerely yours,

R.C. O'Leary

P.S.

One final note to the book. As a work of fiction, I took substantial liberties with the rules of criminal procedure, often ignoring them completely, to try and make the trial and the events leading up to it more dramatic.

Dedication

This book is dedicated to Jennifer--thank you for being a wonderful wife, friend, and mother. For all you are and all you will be during our journey.

For my children, thank you for all the joy and goodness you bring to our lives. Your stories will always be the ones I enjoy the most.

ACKNOWLEDGMENTS

My mother, Joanne Bradshaw, and sister, Katie O'Leary, were always there with words of support and positive feedback when needed.

This book would not have been completed without the consistent encouragement and support of Dave Manning. He was steadfast in his belief in this story from day one and helped me to believe I could reach the finish line. In addition, Jerry Berzanski gave me positive encouragement and feedback on this book, as he has on many other aspects of my life. I appreciate them both for their friendship and for always having my best interests in heart.

My father-in-law, Tom Umphress, a former lieutenant with the Atlanta Police Department, provided me with some technical expertise and anecdotes that he likely won't recognize because they were fictionalized for the purpose of the story.

My mother-in-law, Pat Windham, is one of the more courageous people I know and has been extremely positive in her support.

Chris Bass read an earlier version of the MS and provided some very valuable feedback.

Finally, my father, Robert J. O'Leary. He loved books and reading more than anyone I ever met. I recall many visits to Fairfield, Connecticut's great libraries with him. He is not here to see the final product, but I had the opportunity to read some pages to him while he was in hospice care. It is a memory for which I will always be grateful.

31325422R00176

Made in the USA
Lexington, KY
12 April 2014